'Looking for breakneck pace and a relentless hero?
Alex Shaw has you covered'

James Swallow

'Alex Shaw is one of the best thriller writers around.
Fast paced, *Total Blackout* gripped from page one and
didn't let go ... as fast as a Hollywood movie'
Stephen Leather

'Compelling and authentic. An explosive new series
with an uncompromising hero'
Tom Wood

'A perfect mix of hi-tech, high-concept modern action
thriller and old school, Cold War espionage where evil
Russians are still plotting the downfall of the West
and only one man can stop them'
Simon Toyne

'Jack Tate is a powerful character, a true Brit hero.
A cracking start to a new series!'
Alan McDermott

'Alex Shaw is a master of the action thriller. Grabbed
me from the first page and never let go'
Michael Ridpath

'Riveting thriller with an original plot and surprising
twists. Tate is totally convincing as a classic Brit operative.
Great drama and characterisation'
Duncan Falconer

Also by Alex Shaw

TRAITORS

ALEX SHAW

ONE PLACE. MANY STORIES

HQ
An imprint of HarperCollins*Publishers* Ltd
1 London Bridge Street
London SE1 9GF

www.harpercollins.co.uk

HarperCollins*Publishers* Ltd
1st Floor, Watermarque Building, Ringsend Road
Dublin 4, Ireland

This paperback edition 2021

1
First published in Great Britain by
HQ, an imprint of HarperCollins*Publishers* Ltd 2021

Copyright © Alex Shaw 2021

Alex Shaw asserts the moral right to be
identified as the author of this work.
A catalogue record for this book is
available from the British Library.

ISBN: 9780008441746

MIX
Paper from
responsible sources
FSC™ C007454

For my wife Galia, my sons Alexander and Jonathan, and our family in England and Ukraine.

PROLOGUE

Central Tunis, Tunisia

Racine confirmed the man entering the hotel was her target. She knew his face and his gait. The French national wore a navy-blue business suit and carried a briefcase. He looked unremarkable. He was anything but. Unseen, as she hung back across the avenue, in the shadow of a large tree, Racine continued to sip from her bottle of Orangina and scroll her smartphone.

The hotel was the tallest building in this part of the capital. Its glass-sided tower looked out of place but afforded panoramic views of the city.

Racine waited for five minutes, to give her target time to get settled into his room. Her encrypted iPhone vibrated in her hand. A message. A random word that had been chosen as her 'go' command. She crossed the busy Avenue Habib Bourguiba and entered the hotel lobby. Bright lights reflected against the white marble flooring. Cognac-coloured marble panelling covered the walls and matched the hue of leather armchairs, dotted beside curtained windows. Off to her right was a bar area and to her left the front desk, manned by three suited men, each sporting a short haircut and moustache. They were busy with guests. She strode directly past them to the lifts. The flooring now changed

1

to a brown and white marble chequerboard.

In her peripheral vision, a figure rose from a chair and followed her. Before she could press the call button, the lift doors opened and three men exited. One was dressed in a grey business suit, with a pair of bronze-lensed sunglasses obscuring his face; the others wore matching black Adidas tracksuits and carried large, heavy-looking, identical sports bags. Racine entered the lift and so did the man who had followed her. His clothes marked him out as a businessman but his hair, cut extremely close to his scalp, did not. He made no eye contact and said not one word as he pressed the button for the fourteenth floor and then stood with his back to her. They rode the lift up in silence, the overhead light glinting on his stubbly scalp. The man exited the lift first and immediately turned left into the hallway. Racine followed a couple of paces behind. The man passed three doors before slowing to touch a key card against a lock on the fourth door. It opened with an electronic tone. He carried on walking and vanished from view through the door at the end of the hallway.

Racine entered the room he had unlocked. She kept low, darted towards the bathroom on her immediate right. It was empty. She knew it would be, but a failure to confirm this could be fatal. Moving back out into the sleeping area she noted a shoebox on the bed next to a pair of surgical rubber gloves. Inside the box lay a subcompact Glock 26 pistol, a magazine, a custom suppressor and a dull, metal key. Racine pulled on the gloves, slotted the full magazine into the body of the Glock and then screwed on the suppressor. The Austrian handgun felt unbalanced with the added weight and length of the sound-deadening device, but it was a trade-off she was willing to make, and the combination was effective for close-quarter work.

At the foot of the bed and next to the bulky, outdated television set was a door in the party wall. Behind it was a second door that opened into the adjoining room. Two doors were all that

2

separated Racine from her target – former paratrooper Jean Yotte.

On leaving the paras, Yotte had become a private military contractor. For three years he had undertaken overseas security and bodyguard positions, but what had pinged him on the threat radar of France's foreign intelligence agency, the DGSE, were the highly lucrative yet highly illegal contracts he had been taking for the last eighteen months. Intelligence confirmed that the private military contractor had become an assassin. What was more worrying for the French was that his new paymasters had direct links to known terrorist organisations. With the flick of a pen in Paris, Yotte's fate was determined and without any trace of irony, Racine of the DGSE's *Division Action* was ordered to assassinate the assassin.

Racine had no qualms about what she was going to do, of the life she was on the cusp of ending. Her target was a threat to the security of the French Republic. He was a traitor, and there was nothing Racine detested more.

Her phone vibrated. It displayed a new message. It confirmed the water in her target's room had been running for five minutes. She pushed the phone back into her pocket. She was exactly on schedule. Four days of surveillance had shown Yotte to be a creature of habit. Each time he returned to his room the man took a ten-minute shower. But habits were bad, and her target would find out why in less than five minutes.

Racine silently moved forward. The lock on her side was not engaged. Placing her left ear flat against the door, she listened. A low-level burble emanated from the other side. Racine drew the handle down, millimetre by millimetre, the mechanism pre-oiled to make no sound. She then pulled the door open on silent hinges. Racine stepped back quickly, half expecting the second door to disintegrate as rounds ripped towards her. But nothing happened. Music, the CNN intro theme, and then an excited female voice speaking in American-accented English. On her haunches, Racine peered through the lock. She could make out the foot of the bed, and a sports bag lying on it, nothing more. She could now hear the water running in the bathroom. Rising to her feet, she kept her hand steady and inserted the key into the lock. As she started to turn the key, there was a knocking sound, coming from the other side of the target's room, followed by an electronic beep.

The shower abruptly stopped. Her hand froze, the key half-turned. She sensed movement and felt footfall. On the other side of the target's room, the main door opened and a voice called out, 'Housekeeping.' The phone in Racine's pocket vibrated. A warning, she knew, a message that a third party was entering the target's room, an innocent. It was an order to abort. She didn't look at it. Racine closed her eyes, swore under her breath in French and quickly turned the key, knowing she had only a matter of seconds. Then she heard him – Jean Yotte – asking angry questions. Racine swung out with the open door into the room. Going low she raised the Glock and acquired her target.

The scene that greeted her made her pause, made her slow, for fear of hitting the wrong person. The housekeeper stood at the door as Yotte, dripping wet and wearing just a towel around his waist, berated her. His right hand, held behind his back, clasped a sub-compact handgun. The maid's face contorted as she saw Racine and Yotte spun, his towel falling to the floor and the gun rising fast.

Racine was faster. She fired. A double tap. Her suppressed rounds sounded like large books dropping on a tiled floor. The first round shattered Yotte's forehead and the second shredded his heart. Neither low-velocity slug exited his body.

Racine stood. The smell of gunpowder filled the room. The maid was immobile. Her eyes wide and her jaw slack. Racine pointed the Glock at her and beckoned her to enter Yotte's room. The maid's head twitched, and she jerked to the right and ran screaming, away from the door along the hallway.

'*Merde!*' Racine swore.

Things had turned noisy but, she reasoned, she had got the

job done.

She shut the door, then stepped back into the room, negotiated Yotte's corpse and collected her two spent shells. She had to exfil the hotel. Her phone was vibrating in her pocket, but she ignored it again. Racine was in the room and her controller was not. As her eyes took in the scene, she paused . . . the sports bag on the bed. She had seen the exact same bag before. It was identical to the bags carried by the two men who had exited her lift. She bounded to the bed and opened the zip. Inside were three brick-sized blocks wrapped in a waxy paper. The markings confirmed that she was looking at several kilos of military-grade plastic explosive. It was more than enough to flatten the hotel and most of the surrounding city block.

She took a long calming breath, her heart thumping in her chest as she checked for any wiring or a detonator. There was neither. Moving to the window she looked out at the street far below. She had a view half a mile up the Avenue Habib Bourguiba in either direction. Tunis city centre was a target-rich environment with a myriad of shops, cafés, local attractions, government offices and embassies.

A sudden, shrill sound attacked her ears. Yotte's mobile phone was ringing. It was on the pillow of the bed he would never sleep in again. She picked it up and inspected the display. Her eyes flicked back to the bag. Had she missed the detonator? Had she missed the wires? Was this the end of it all? The phone stopped ringing and then started again. She pressed the 'answer' icon. There was no explosion. She was still alive, and Yotte was still dead.

A Tunisian voice spoke in rapid French. 'We are at the cathedral and in place.'

Racine had never wanted to be a man, until that moment. She had no alternative, she had to risk a reply. She placed her hand over the phone and tried to disguise her voice. 'Await my command.'

'*D'accord.*' The caller hung up.

Racine checked the phone's saved contacts. Three numbers

only, and one of these she'd just been connected to. She knew she couldn't call either number if what she suspected was true. She retrieved her own iPhone and with no time to fully explain her suspicions tapped out a text to secure the room. *Explosives found. Send cleaner.*

Pushing her Glock into the waistband of her trousers, Racine left the room and took the fire escape down. The stairwell walls were unpainted concrete and each footstep kicked up dust, which worked its way into her eyes and nose. As she reached the lobby level, she heard sirens on the avenue outside, not unusual for a capital city but she had no illusions that they were heading her way. She continued down another floor and exited into the underground parking level. Fastening her denim jacket, she sprinted up the ramp. She burst out onto the pavement and into the sunlight, directly to the left of the entrance lobby. At that moment two police cars squealed to a halt in front of the hotel's revolving doors. She froze on the pavement, but the uniformed men spilt out of their vehicles and pushed past her into the building.

Racine ran.

There was no time for pleasantries or stealth as she barged her tall frame past and between pedestrians on the pavement. Under her jacket, the Glock painfully dug into her stomach with each stride and the warm suppressor scalded her skin. She could already see the Cathedral of St Vincent de Paul. It was at the Place de l'Indépendence, at the end of Avenue Habib Bourguiba and directly opposite the French embassy. She slowed her pace to a brisk walk, attempted to steady her breathing and entered the square.

A group of European tourists stood at the foot of the cathedral steps, listening to a guide holding a red parasol. In between the group and a refreshment stall a man stood. She recognised him from the lift. He was dressed in a tracksuit and had a large sports bag at his feet.

Racine knew it was reckless, but she had no other option but to

6

act. She skirted the square and angled for the stall. As she reached it, the man paid her no attention; she was just another tourist. Turning sideways on to mask her actions, Racine slowly withdrew the Glock from her waistband. Shielding it with her jacket until the last possible moment, she fired twice, at close range, into the man's head. He dropped. Almost before he had stopped falling, she searched his torso for a trigger or a wire. Nothing.

She felt a wave of panic break around her, as first the tourists and then the locals comprehended what had happened. They scattered noisily, like startled pigeons. Racine felt a roaring in her ears and nausea build in her stomach. Where was the trigger? Had she been mistaken? Had she executed an innocent civilian? But she couldn't have. He was one of the men from the lift, wasn't he? But was he linked to her target at the hotel? He had to be otherwise . . . She reached for the sports bag . . .

An angry yell, and then a single shot rang out. Without thinking, Racine spun to her right. Above her now on the top step, another tracksuited man pointed a Kalashnikov at her. The second man from the hotel lift. She saw him flinch as he pulled the trigger again and a second single shot chipped the concrete of the pavement where, a moment ago, she had been. Racine kept moving, as confusion crossed his face, he glanced down at the Russian weapon. Adjusting his grip, he thumbed the selector switch up from "semiautomatic" to "automatic" fire.

Racine came up, firing. Her shots hit him in the chest. The gunman's finger tightened around the trigger and as he fell, he emptied the Kalashnikov's magazine into the stone steps and wooden doors of the cathedral, a line of strike marks tracing their way skywards.

Tourists continued to scream and run across the square. Sirens sounded in the distance, getting closer by the second; she didn't know if they were heading for her or the hotel but either way she wasn't going to hang around. Racine bounded up the steps and kicked the weapon away from the gunman's hand. He was still alive and bloody bubbles seeped from his mouth. He tried to speak; however, he didn't get the chance as Racine shot him in the right eye. She searched him and just like his comrade, found no trigger or wires. His Kalashnikov was the folding-stock version, compact enough to conceal within his bag. The bag . . .

Racine looked up and through the open door. Inside the cathedral, his sports bag lay open. She ran towards it, crouched down and without giving pause for her own safety, checked the contents – a stack of spare magazines for the Kalashnikov, but no explosives. She put away her Glock, hung his weapon from her shoulder, zipped up the bag and carried it towards the other one still lying on the pavement beside the first gunman. Her eyes scanned the immediate area, for any threats, before she opened the bag. No explosives. No detonator. It too contained spare magazines and also the Kalashnikov that the first gunman had not had the time to use. Were there to be two attacks: a shooting and then a bombing? Or had the two intended to take hostages into the cathedral?

Racine didn't have the answer but all she knew was that she had neutralised the immediate threat. Holding a bag in each hand, forearms and shoulders straining, Racine jogged as well as she was able back around the square, parting the increasing crowd of onlookers who didn't know whether to cheer or cower. Many gawped, and several – to her chagrin – held up smartphones. This included a man in a grey business suit, wearing a pair of bronze-lensed sunglasses. She glowered at him, trying to place him as she increased her pace and headed towards the French Embassy. All she had to do now was persuade them to let her back in before she was gunned down by overzealous local police.

ONE

Three Months Later

Centre Administratif des Tourelles (CAT),
DGSE headquarters, Paris, France

Jean Baptiste Moreau believed that in addition to hard work, much of any intelligence agency's success was down to luck and coincidence. As he entered the interview room, Baptiste hoped the luck and coincidence he was now experiencing could be verified with tangible results. His guest was sitting on the far side of a table. Their eyes immediately met, and the man stood. Roman Magidov was a 'walk-in', an unsolicited and unexpected visitor who had arrived at the front desk with information he wanted to personally deliver to the DGSE. Just over an hour later, after having his identity verified and giving a brief outline of what he knew to a receiving officer he had been asked to sit and wait for a more senior member of staff to continue his interview.

On reading the initial notes, both Baptiste's pulse and his interest had started to rise as he realised the significance of what Magidov had relayed. The man seemingly had fresh intelligence on a target Baptiste's department had been seeking for over a decade, and this had come less than twenty-four hours after a photograph of his target had surfaced on the internet. Luck and coincidence. The question was always the same – was it real?

'My name is Ozanne,' Baptiste said, using an alias. 'I understand you have information you'd like to share with us?'

'Do you work on the Ukrainian desk, Monsieur Ozanne?'

'I do,' Baptiste replied. He didn't and the use of the word 'desk' wasn't a French term, but then his guest wasn't French. Roman Magidov was a Ukrainian lawyer from the city of Donetsk. Baptiste imagined the man was used to the process and techniques of cross-examination, but today it was he who was the subject of Baptiste's line of inquiry. 'Let's sit and we can discuss what it is you would like to share with us, and why.'

As they sat down, Baptiste poured them both a glass of water from a bottle on the table then switched on the recording equipment. He sat upright in his chair and looked Magidov in the eye. 'Let me start by making you aware that anything you voluntarily offer the DGSE will be dealt with in the strictest confidence but that you may also be held criminally liable if it is proven what you tell me is an intentional fabrication.'

'I understand.' The Ukrainian's left eye twitched and, as it did so, the red birthmark above it seemed to dance. 'Do you think I fled Ukraine with the intent of sharing fairy tales, Monsieur Ozanne?'

'I hope that is not the case.'

'It is not.'

'I'd like you to explain to me how this all started. I'll interrupt you if I have any questions.'

'OK.' Magidov nodded and spoke slowly with the measured cadence of a non-native French speaker. 'When the Russian-backed DNR militants took over the city, we attempted to continue with our lives, but the rule of law was ignored. These men were not freedom fighters, rather members of criminal gangs. To prevent the Ukrainian army from retaking Donetsk they relied on Russia shelling the Ukrainian army positions. But the Ukrainian troops fired back. Tens of thousands fled Donetsk, including three-quarters of my community – the city's Jewish population. We who remained did so because we felt a duty, regardless of religion, language or nationality, to our hometown and to those who could not leave. As a lawyer, a defender of justice and truth, I tried to navigate the new laws and regulations the DNR introduced. So, life carried on in the new normal of the new republic, until suddenly it did not. I was abducted from my office and accused of conducting acts of espionage against the Donetsk People's Republic.'

'Where was your office located?' Magidov gave the address and Baptiste made a note of this. 'Who abducted you?'

'Thugs in mismatched army uniforms.'

So far Baptiste had learnt nothing new or anything of note. 'OK, go on.'

'Chronologically?'

Baptiste tried not to let his impatience show. 'Yes.'

'Very well. They marched me out the building, pushed me into a Lada and put a sack over my head. They spoke not a word. It was hard to keep track of time, but I'd estimate after about half an hour or so we stopped. I was taken into a building and placed on a chair. When they removed the sack, I saw that I was in an empty garage.'

'How did you know it was a garage?' Baptiste asked.

'It had a concrete floor covered in oil stains. It smelled of diesel.'

'Did you see the outside of the building at all?'

'No.'

'Continue, please,' Baptiste urged.

'They started to question me; actually, they interrogated me I . . . I . . .' Magidov's voice faltered. He closed his eyes and took a deep breath in and out before continuing. 'I was punched, kicked, and they even put a wet cloth on my face and poured water over it. I don't know the French term for it. In English they call it "waterboarding".'

'Waterboarding, I understand; they waterboarded you. And they interrogated you for two days?'

'Yes.' He took a gulp of water.

'What did they want to know?'

'They wanted to know who I really worked for. Who was paying me to spy for the Kyiv government. Who my contacts were.'

'What did you tell them?'

Anger flashed across Magidov's face. 'What could I tell them? I am not a spy. I was a lawyer serving the people of Donetsk.'

Baptiste noted the man's quick temper. 'I understand this is difficult for you, and I apologise, but I need to hear everything.'

Magidov took a deep breath and continued. 'On the third day they let me go.'

'Just like that?'

'Yes. Looking back now, I realise it was odd but at the time I was just relieved.'

'I understand.'

'They put the hood back on my head, drove me to a part of the city I didn't know well, and left me outside a church.'

'A church?'

'I think they were trying to be funny or make a point.'

'Make a point?'

Magidov's left eye twitched. 'Where are you from?'

Baptiste's brow furrowed. 'I was born in Paris.'

'Where were your parents born?'

The furrows deepened. 'Senegal. Why?'

'You are first-generation French, but you are undoubtedly French. Without question. Personally, I can trace my family back for generations and I am Ukrainian. Yet because I am also Jewish, the militants did not accept I could be Ukrainian. That is the difference between our two nations; that is the difference between East and West.'

'I understand.'

'I went home, had a few drinks. I went back to work the next day. At work my director told me I no longer worked there. So, I went home. An hour later my phone rang. It was my boss's wife screaming at me.'

'Screaming?'

'Her husband had been – because of me she insisted – taken by the militants. This was unthinkable as he was "connected" – if you understand what I mean – he had a "roof". If they could take him with impunity, they could take anyone.'

'Was he Jewish too?'

'No. He was an idiot. I decided that I had to get out of Donetsk. I had to report what had happened to me, but also what my interrogator had boasted about.'

'So you reported all this to the Ukrainian authorities?'

'I did not. What could they do? No. I wanted to come to Paris to escape Ukraine and to inform your authorities. It is your country that he said he was going to attack.'

Baptiste looked back at the notes. So far Magidov had been merely mentally clearing his throat and Baptiste had let him do so. The more he talked the more he'd relax. 'Let's circle back a bit. Tell me about the other man the militants were holding.'

Magidov sipped his water before he replied. 'He was a foreign student, British, but his family was originally from Pakistan.'

This tallied with what Baptiste knew. 'Tell me more about the man who interrogated you?'

'Men. At first it was the locals who asked me questions; although, they seemed more concerned with beating me.' Magidov closed his eyes again, this time screwing them shut momentarily. 'Then a new interrogator arrived. He used different methods, worse methods, psychological methods. He was not a local either. He was Russian Jew. He told me so.'

'What did he ask you?'

'He probed into my background. When he found out I'd studied French and law at university, not English, he became very interested indeed.'

13

'In what way?'

'He switched to French. He spoke French. Fluent French.' Magidov shook his head slowly. 'He became suddenly very aggressive. He asked me if I was a spy for the DGSE.'

'He specifically used the acronym DGSE?'

'Sorry you are not as famous as the CIA—' the Ukrainian shrugged '—so he angrily explained to me what each letter stood for.'

Baptiste battled his growing sense of excitement. 'And you told him what?'

'I told him the truth. I am not a spy.'

'Why did you learn French?'

'I love languages. During soviet times we were suppressed so much that I decided the more languages I spoke the more opportunities I would have. I watched American movies to improve my English, and I listened to anything I could in French. Then the realities of life got in the way. I graduated and found myself back in Donetsk, not even speaking my mother tongue but forced to use Russian.'

Baptiste needed to focus his guest. 'Did you learn the name of this interrogator?'

'We did not swap business cards, but I did hear one of the men call him "Raduga".'

'Raduga?'

'It was a nickname maybe.'

'Why do you think so?'

'Raduga is the Russian for "Rainbow".'

Baptiste made a mental note of the word and its usage. He'd add it to the 'keywords' their monitoring stations listened out for. 'You said he boasted about his plans. What did he say?'

'He said Donetsk was too small for him, that he had larger projects. He talked about a foiled attack in Tunis. He told me that he had learnt even from that mistake and adapted. He liked to talk a lot to me, perhaps because we were both Jewish and also because we could both speak French.'

Magidov was rambling again. For a lawyer he was not concise, which probably had worked in his own favour if he was paid by the hour, Baptiste surmised. 'You said he had plans. What were these?'

'He told me he was going to attack Paris.'

'When?'

'He said within the next two weeks.'

'How?'

'He didn't say. I am sorry that is all I have. Apart from his face. That I have in my mind. That I will never forget.'

'I'm going to show you a few photographs. I'd like you to tell me if you recognise any of the people in them.'

'Of course.'

Baptiste shuffled the papers he had brought into the room until what he wanted was on top. He fanned out several 10 X 8 photographic prints to face the lawyer.

Magidov's eyes showed instant recognition; his left eye twitching again and his index finger stabbed at one of the photos. 'That is the man who tortured me!'

'Are you certain?' Baptiste hoped his voice sounded calm.

Magidov nodded. 'Without a doubt. That is Raduga.'

Baptiste took a moment to compose himself. Luck and coincidence. 'This is extremely helpful.'

Magidov looked up, anger once again in his eyes. 'Who is he?'

'He is a traitor.'

Noisy-le-Sec, Paris

The fort at Noisy-le-Sec was one of sixteen forts that originally formed the enclosure of Thiers, the nineteenth-century fortified ring encircling the city of Paris. It was decommissioned in 1919 and now a hundred years later the fort housed the clandestine operations division of France's General Directorate for External Security, the DGSE.

Known as the *Division Action*, its mandate included the design and delivery of clandestine and covert operations. The DA specialised in the black arts of sabotage, assassination, detention and kidnapping, and the infiltration and exfiltration of agents into and out of hostile territory.

Its deputy director, Maurice Jacob, looked at his boss, Colonel Christophe Grillot. Jacob was a decade senior to Grillot but a grade lower within the DGSE. 'So?'

Grillot wet his lips. 'The minister is still pleased with you due to the result of the Tunis operation, even if he did have to smooth out a few ruffled Tunisian feathers.'

Maurice Jacob concurred. 'I'm sure the prevention of a mass shooting of tourists was greatly appreciated.'

'Did we know what Yotte had planned?'

'No. There was no intelligence to suggest it at all, which is a worry. It was a simple kill mission. Our operative used her initiative to achieve the best possible result.'

'That part the minister does not need to know.'

'Quite.' Jacob knew Grillot understood the real reason why he'd scheduled the meeting.

'You have finally found him?'

'Yes,' Maurice Jacob replied, 'we have.'

'Where?'

'Eastern Ukraine.'

'Where, exactly?'

'Donetsk.'

Grillot seemed surprised. 'In the territory controlled by terrorists?'

'Russian-backed insurgents.'

Grillot shuffled in his seat. 'Vasilev is now overtly working for the Russians?'

'In a covert capacity. If we believe the Russian foreign ministry, there are no Russians in Eastern Ukraine.'

'How did you find him?'

Jacob explained. The intelligence business had changed since he'd been a young man. New technology had made intelligence gathering quicker and easier than ever, but it had also made it harder to hide; and the fundamentals remained the same – greed, pride and opportunity were the downfall of most.

'And now you've found a link between him and the failed Tunis attack?' Grillot asked.

'I have.'

'So, you are seeking my authorisation to take action against him?'

'I am.'

'Then, Maurice, you had better present your plan.'

'Thank you.' Jacob lifted his attaché case from the floor, fished into it and retrieved an A4 manila envelope. He pushed it across the desk to Grillot. *'Voila.'*

'Merci.'

Jacob felt like a schoolboy desperately awaiting his master's assessment of his latest essay, but of course this was far more important than any previous operation he had undertaken.

Grillot took his wireframe reading glasses from their case and popped them on his nose. Jacob mused that the man was as physically fit as the young soldier he once was, but alas the one thing he could not exercise were his eyes.

Without looking up Grillot asked, 'Would you like a glass of water or anything, Maurice?'

'No. I'm fine.'

Grillot turned his attention to the intelligence report. Eight minutes later he looked up. 'My initial concern is that of verification. How do we know that this Magidov is telling the truth?'

'He picked our man from a pile of photographs. We know our target was in Donetsk at the time. I agree it is coincidental, but then you know the old saying about luck and coincidence.'

Grillot inclined his head slightly, his eyes flicking up and right. 'I think you need more time to gather verified intel before you attempt this mission.'

Jacob sighed. 'In an ideal world yes, but we do not live in one. Our target has appeared for the first time in eight years; he may very well disappear if we do not strike now. We cannot lose him like before.'

'Why has he appeared?'

'He believes he is entirely safe in the epicentre of a Russian-backed puppet state. It's the perfect base of operations for him.'

'You believe he intends to launch terror attacks on the Republic of France?'

'That is what our walk-in stated, but it could just be an idle threat? You and I both know our target is a very troubled and dangerous individual. Direct threat or not, we can't let him slip away again.'

Grillot removed his glasses. 'Do you think your choice of personnel is prudent?'

'I do.'

'In Tunis, she disobeyed a direct order to abort. Her actions could have so easily not gone in our favour. It could be argued she is a liability, a loose cannon rolling around on a sinking ship.'

'I'm sinking?'

Grillot waved his hand. 'You know what I mean.'

'I never took you for a poet.'

'The fact remains, she did not follow orders.'

'But she saved lives.'

'The ends justify the means? Is that the excuse?'

Jacob shook his head. 'No excuse. She was on the ground. She used her instincts. She was resourceful. She saved lives.'

Grillot sighed. 'I know. But she was hardly discreet.'

'Look, I made a promise to her. This target is after all the reason why she joined our service.'

'What if she fails?'

'Racine is the best I have ever seen. If I were to assign another operator and the mission failed, well, that would be unforgivable.'

Grillot wet his lips before he replied. 'The question I have is can she do it?'

'Yes, and she will, without hesitation.'

Grillot pushed himself away from his desk and steepled his fingers. 'In that case, Maurice, you have my full authority to liquidate the target.'

'Thank you, Colonel.' Jacob made no attempt to disguise his relief.

*

Jacob left his director's office invigorated. The veteran intelligence officer took the stairs down to the ground floor of the nineteenth-century fort and found his DGSE driver outside standing next to the large, dark blue Citroën. He had a phone to his ear, which he hurriedly pocketed as Jacob stepped out into the cold Parisian air. Jacob looked questioningly at the man.

'I apologise. It was my mother.' His driver was embarrassed. 'If I don't pick up she presumes I've been abducted or involved in an accident.'

Jacob waved away the excuse with a friendly flourish of his hand as the rear door was opened for him. 'And how is she?'

'Old.'

Jacob paused, holding on to the Citroën's roof. 'Old?'

'That is what she tells me. I ask her, "Mother, how are you?" and she always replies, "I am old."'

Jacob smiled. 'There are few worse things to be.'

Door shut, the driver got into his seat. 'Where to: home, the bistro or the other place?'

'The other place, please.'

'Right.' The engine started.

It had been twelve years, yet Jacob could not bring himself to think of the DGSE headquarters as his office rather than the Noisy-le-Sec facility. It was a constant reminder to him of the pariah he had become.

But now he could see an end to the indignity of his existence. With each successful operation his team undertook he felt as though he was regaining, bit by bit, the respect of those who mattered including the Director General of the DGSE, and of course the Minister of Defence, who had not even been a politician when the scandal had happened.

Without another word to his driver, Jacob pressed the button, raising the privacy panel between them. Once hidden, he retrieved his hip flask from his briefcase and took a long swig of cognac. Relishing the burn, he let himself relax into the soft, dark leather. He sincerely hoped he would soon be drinking to celebrate another positive result.

DGSE headquarters, Paris

Even though it wasn't an old building his part of it always smelled musty. Maurice Jacob wondered what the office cleaners did each evening when he was gone. Through his open blinds the weak Parisian sun illuminated the dust as it wafted across the utilitarian space. His desk was devoid of any sentimental items that would have hinted at his life outside of the French Directorate-General for External Security. Jacob popped a breath mint and then tapped his desk with his forefinger.

'I personally hold myself responsible for this man's actions, for the deaths he has caused. I who employed him, I who trained him and I who eventually lost him . . .'

Jacob's career in French intelligence had not been without distinction, but the repercussions from having one of his own prodigies, Sasha Vasilev, identified as a Russian sleeper, a sleeper who had then given up DGSE operatives, had turned Jacob into a pariah.

Following a full internal investigation, which had found him neither culpable nor guilty of any wrongdoing, it was agreed

Jacob was to be removed from the Noisy-le-Sec facility. He would continue his duties, with somewhat reduced resources and limited influence in a nondescript office in the DGSE's soulless headquarters. The main stipulation was Grillot would have the final say on all operations of Jacob's 'deniable department'. This mattered little to Jacob. He had never wanted to run the department; he was not a political beast. He was an intelligence officer.

Jacob wanted to savour this moment, his first step on the road to redemption. He kept Baptiste waiting whilst he crushed the remains of his mint in his mouth and slipped in another. He didn't offer Baptiste one. 'Colonel Grillot has given the mission the go-ahead. We have his full authority to liquidate Sasha Vasilev.'

Baptiste's relief was evident to Jacob. 'Thank you, sir.'

'Don't thank me, Baptiste. Taking a life must never be something we are thankful for.'

'Yes, sir.'

'I have made a few changes to your plan.'

'Oh?'

'We will use Racine.'

'Even after her actions during the Tunis operation?'

'Because of them.'

Baptiste's brow furrowed. 'And she operates alone.'

'I am aware of that.' Jacob hadn't expected this level of opposition from his junior. 'Is there a problem or something I should be aware of?'

'My plan called for a team. Surely that would be more prudent? Is sending a lone woman into a conflict zone really a wise decision?'

'I see.' Jacob's eyes glinted as he looked at the younger man. 'You think of her as a woman, whereas I think of her as a weapon.'

'That is not what I meant.'

'Is it not? You know as well as I do that the French Republic, as a NATO member, cannot been seen in any way shape or form to be assisting either side of the Ukrainian conflict. Especially not by assassinating a man who is the holder of a Russian passport personally presented to him – I have been told – by the Russian President. The larger the number of personnel we use the greater the risk we run of compromising the mission. No. We must use a sole operator. Racine is the best deniable asset we have. She goes in. Alone.'

'Yes, Director.'

'Is there something you wish to say, Baptiste?'

'No.'

'That is all.'

*

After Baptiste had left the room, Jacob closed his eyes and sighed deeply. So much death, so many lives destroyed by the traitor, and all because he had been taken in, all because he had felt a duty to the man's family and their shared religion.

The energy he had earlier was no more; it had been replaced by a creeping fear, the realisation about what a monumental mission lay ahead of them. Was sending in Racine really the best course of action? There was a high possibility that she could be killed, or worse captured – and then what would happen? Was it his own vanity that demanded she be the tool of his vengeance? He grimaced. No. The vengeance was theirs; they shared it, Racine and he. This was not the time to start questioning his decisions and his course of action, not now.

Jacob gingerly pushed himself up from the desk and shuffled wearily to the window. The DGSE headquarters, where he was forced to work, were located on the eastern edge of Paris in the 20th arrondissement and as such there was very little of note to see. The ornate architecture of central Paris was replaced here by mostly red-bricked, utilitarian, low-rise apartment buildings. There were plenty of trees, but it wasn't the picture-postcard Paris favoured by foreign tourists. And today the sky was grey.

But to Jacob the entire city was magnificent, and he loved her just as much as ever.

He was a patriot. He'd spent his entire life defending the country of his birth. He was born after the war, and his parents would tell him of the horrors they had endured in the concentration camps after being rounded up and sent there by the noxious Vichy government. Seventy-five per cent of the French Jewish population had survived the war and with the influx of Sephardi and Mizrahi North African Jews from former French colonies, France boasted the third largest Jewish population after Israel and the United States. And boast they should. Jacob was proud to be French, and he was proud to be Jewish. He had never blamed the French people for his parents' forced deportation, but he had blamed the French government and had vowed to do all in his power to ensure that nothing of the sort ever happened again. That no more citizens of France would be betrayed.

Sasha Vasilev was a Russian Jew whose scientist parents had fled Russia when he was a teenager and been granted asylum in Paris. The boy was a talented linguist and after graduating joined the DGSE, on Jacob's recommendation, and proceeded to work his way up through the ranks. It was only after his disappearance that his treachery and the body of his lover had been discovered. Sasha Vasilev had been a malevolent mole for Russian military intelligence. The operational details and names he had passed on to his true masters in the Kremlin had caused the deaths of officers and operatives and dealt the DGSE's *Division Action* a devastating blow.

Sasha Vasilev had betrayed him, betrayed France. The blood of French patriots was on Vasilev's hands. If Jacob had not admitted the man to the service, and had not taught him his trade, those victims would still be alive and serving their country.

Finding and finishing Vasilev would not bring any of those fine, noble people back, nor would it bring peace, but it would prevent the man from betraying France and its citizens any further. It would also be a stark warning to any pernicious foreign agencies: there is nowhere to hide.

Jacob's rage caused a tremor in his right hand as he thrust it into his trouser pocket to retrieve his hip flask. It was almost empty. He swigged the remains. The mints had ruined the taste of the cognac but he welcomed the fiery liquid as it burned his insides. He noticed he'd been drinking far more than usual recently. He thought about the personnel file he kept locked in his desk, and the legacy of its subject: Sophie Racine.

TWO

Eight Years Ago

Central Paris

With her small backpack weighed down by her legal textbooks, and left hand holding up a collapsible umbrella, Sophie headed home. It was a twenty-five-minute brisk walk from the lecture hall to the three-bedroom apartment she shared with two other students: Gaspard – another law student and Saskia, her crazy British best friend she'd met at sixth form in England who'd opted to join her in Paris to study French literature.

Sophie was an only child and sharing a flat for her was still a novelty. She got on well with her flatmates; that was, once both she and Saskia had explained to Gaspard nothing romantic was ever going to happen between them. Sophie had taken the opportunity to casually mention her training in self-defence. Gaspard had raised his eyebrows and said no more. After this he had brought back a procession of women, as if to subconsciously prove to them that he wasn't a gargoyle (a nickname Saskia had coined).

On nights when the two women were not studying or hitting

the town, they'd share bottles of red wine, with Saskia constantly exclaiming how cheap it was. Her father was 'something in city' – after knowing Saskia for almost three years, Sophie still had no idea what that meant. Sophie took every opportunity to perfect her already fluent English, even picking up 'posh slang'. Sophie smirked and wondered if she should stop by Monoprix to get some 'plonk'?

Looking left and right before stepping off the pavement she noticed a man at her shoulder. They crossed at the same time and he hurried ahead, carrying his briefcase over his head. Partly curious as to why someone would wear a raincoat but neglect to pack an umbrella, Sophie crossed the road, now several steps behind, and watched him turn right into an alleyway. Moments later two men, dressed in jeans with rain dripping from their leather jackets, followed him at an even faster pace. Sophie shrugged and carried on walking, still with thoughts of wine in her head, and then she drew level with the alley and glanced right.

The two men had slowed their pace; one held out an object in his right hand. Briefcase-man had his back to them and had paused to search for something.

She saw it start in slow motion and knew exactly what was about to happen. Two white thugs attacking an African immigrant. Sophie knew it was wrong, and knew she had to react.

Impulsively, with little thought for her own safety and without warning, she dropped her umbrella and slipped her pack from her back, took a deep breath and sprinted up the alley – the footfall of her trainers dampened by the sound of the rushing rain. She drew within ten feet of the second man, the one without the weapon, and swung her rucksack as hard as she could. It shot the short distance through the dank air and collided with the back of the man's head. He was already off balance, and the full weight of the law books caused him to crash sideways into the wall, his head hitting the wet brickwork, before he slid down to

26

the ground. Briefcase-man faced the remaining attacker but then a millisecond later his eyes widened as he spotted Sophie.

The man with the weapon, Sophie could now see it was some type of military baton, raised his arm. Briefcase-man, momentarily mesmerised by her presence, moved too late and it hit him on the shoulder. He dropped his briefcase and lurched forward. Sophie was three steps away, she took two then sprung from her left leg and struck a downward blow, an axe kick, to the back of the assailant's knee with the heel of her right foot. The man folded to the ground, grabbed his knee with both hands, and rolled to one side – his face contorted with pain. Sophie steadied herself. The first attacker was still dazed and the second wouldn't be jogging for a while. But then Briefcase-man aimed a fist at her. Instinctively Sophie blocked it with crossed arms, deflecting the blow to her right as she stepped left. Briefcase-man spun and a launched a kick at her. This she attempted to sidestep but it hit her in the thigh. Her eyes watered as a cold, dead pain engulfed her leg.

'Stop! I was trying to help you!' she shouted. But he sent a second fist and then a quick third towards her. Sophie realised that she was now cornered in the alley, with Briefcase-man blocking her exit one way and two dumpsters shoring up the other. She didn't understand what was happening but knew he was continuing the attack. She adopted a fighting stance, raised her fists and looked him in the eyes. 'Go now or I'll kill you.'

'And your colleagues will attack me later? I don't think so.' Briefcase-man spat, and then he lunged at her. Sophie noticed his stance, recognised his fighting style and knew how to counter it. She feigned a jab with her right, telegraphed a straight kick and as he reached for her leg, she delivered a sickening left elbow to the side of his head. His grip relaxed and he fell. Not waiting to understand what had happened she collected her rucksack and ran back the way she had come.

'ENDEX!' a man in a long, camel-coloured coat shouted as he

stepped between her and the safety of the street. Sophie skidded to a halt six feet in front of him. 'And who are you?' His wizened face was quizzical.

'I . . . they . . . I was attacked!' Sophie managed to say as her chest heaved.

'That is not what I asked you, young woman.'

She heard noises from behind and whirled round. The three men were now walking towards her, slowly. The first attacker had a large graze on his cheek and was helping the second, who was limping, and Briefcase-man was holding his head and seemed very unsteady on his feet. 'But they . . . I was trying to . . .'

The man blocking the exit switched to English. 'Don't you speak French? Is that your problem?'

She glared at him, and also switched languages. 'My name is Sophie Racine, and I demand to know who the hell you are.'

'You demand?' The man let a broad smile split his lined face, and continued in English. 'I am Deputy Director Jacob of the French Directorate-General for External Security, and you, Racine, have interrupted a training exercise!'

'Wait what? She wasn't part of this?' Briefcase-man asked.

'No, Baptiste, she was not. Which is all the worse for you as she handed you your backside on a silver platter.'

Sophie was indignant. 'Your men attacked me. I wish to press charges!'

'Oh, do grow up, you attacked them. And from what I can see it is they who should be charging you. In fact I should be charging you! But I won't.'

Sophie bristled.

'Tell me, who taught you to fight like that?'

'My father,' Sophie replied, hating the fact that it was he who again would define her. 'My father was a Legionnaire.'

'Was? What is he now?'

'A successful defence lawyer.'

The man raised his eyebrows, then spoke over her head. 'Noah,

Yann, Baptiste, go and get whatever medical treatment you need.'
His gaze moved back to her. His features seemed to have softened.
'Racine, you look familiar. Have we met before?'

'No.'

'Very well. I'd like to buy you a coffee. I think we should have
a chat.'

THREE

Present Day

Central Paris

Racine stared out of the apartment at the wet street below. It always rained at this time of year in Paris. Whilst unprepared tourists hid under boutique awnings, locals sported chic, black umbrellas and carried on as usual. She envied them, the people below with normal lives and everyday hopes and fears. The biggest decision most of them would have to make would be to decide what to have for dinner, what colour scarf to wear or whom to sleep with. They didn't make life-or-death decisions, well apart from the doctors, she conceded, but even they didn't get ordered to take lives. The people of Paris, like civilians everywhere, were civil. She was not. The life she had chosen was decidedly uncivilised and at the age of twenty-nine she had potentially many decades of incivility ahead of her. What had driven her to become so adept at hastening the death of enemies of the state, she did not know, but what had forced her to act in the first instance – to take her first step into the world she now lived in – was to right a wrong. She believed in justice and always had.

Racine turned away from the window of her DGSE Paris apartment. In her hand she held an envelope containing her briefing notes. She felt an odd sense of calm determination that she had finally arrived at this point in her journey. She would read and memorise its contents before returning it to her controller – the man who now looked at her from across her kitchen table.

'This is a high-risk mission, Racine.' They never used her first name and hadn't since she'd joined the service. To those who knew of her existence she was simply known by her surname. Baptiste in turn used his middle name. 'This is the first confirmed sighting of our target for eight years.'

Racine sat and emptied the envelope onto the table and arranged its contents into neat rows. Baptiste, never briefed her at the office. It was a place that she had rarely entered. The situation surrounding the operation of *The Department* called for complete deniability. To anyone who cared to ask, Racine was a human resources consultant specialising in employment law. An occupation vague enough to draw no further questions when paraded out at parties, not that she attended many anymore. Racine hated small talk. She equated it with small minds. She looked up from the papers and met Baptiste's eyes. 'So he's in Ukraine. He's materialised as a "military adviser" to the insurgents calling themselves the government of the Donetsk People's Republic?'

Baptiste nodded.

Racine looked back at the tabletop. Outwardly, her face was a mask of calm; inside was another matter. She studied the image of the man whom the DGSE was ordering her to terminate with extreme prejudice. She had been chosen to be his assassin, to be the one to end his life, the moment she joined the service. Her director had expressly stated why. It was a secret they shared, which even her controller and former boyfriend Baptiste did not know. Racine's revenge, as Jacob had called it, would not merely be served cold, it would be icy.

She studied the eyes of her target in the photograph before her, Vasilev the bogeyman. His actions had been the driving force in the creation of *The Department*. Without his pernicious, traitorous actions, the DGSE perhaps would never have sanctioned her director's quest. The Department's sole remit, after all, was to locate and liquidate targets that other DGSE teams could not. Racine was aware of the weight of expectation on her shoulders, but this was nothing compared to the duty she felt to the dead. 'How was he found?'

'Identified by a refugee and confirmed by social media,' Baptiste replied.

'Social media? Really?' Even if she had been permitted to do so, Racine had never understood the urge to discuss her breakfast or ailments with innumerable strangers. It was a concept alien to her. 'Which one?'

'*VKontakte.*'

This made sense, the Slavic copy of Facebook had a greater market share amongst Russian speakers. 'How?'

'The DNR has an official VKontakte page where they inform the "Russian world" of their latest proclamations and "successes". They posted several photographs boasting about having apprehended a foreign agent.' Baptiste pointed to an image from the envelope. 'Vasilev was in the background.'

Racine studied the second 10 X 8 print with incredulity. It showed a man seated on a bare concrete floor, cross-legged and with his hands on his head. Next to the man, a figure in military fatigues stood holding an AK-74 and beside him another figure smirked at the camera. The smirking man was Sasha Vasilev. She felt her stomach begin to knot. 'When was this posted?'

'Yesterday . . . hence this briefing today.'

'Yesterday? You mean this operation has been agreed and the intel verified in a day?'

'Yes.'

'Where was the photograph taken?'

'The image was geotagged. It was taken at a commercial garage in Donetsk. The DNR are either amateurs or believe themselves to be untouchable.'

'Maybe.' Racine's eyes narrowed. 'Either he's taunting us or his Russian masters are. Is Vasilev still there?'

'We believe so.'

'Hm.' Racine looked at another image of Vasilev. He stood with a man she recognised as Igor Strelkov. A GRU colonel infamous amongst the intelligence community as the man tasked to oversee Russia's seizure of Crimea and invasion of the Donbas. 'What about Strelkov?'

'You are not to harm him or ruffle as much as a single hair on his manicured moustache. The CIA has the first claim on him.'

Racine scowled. The Americans thought they were the world's policemen. 'Since when did we start taking orders from Langley?'

'This time we do, OK?' Baptiste seemed unusually tense. He took a breath and let it out slowly before he continued. 'There's a lot of pressure on me to ensure this mission is a success and . . .' He paused. 'Look, I'm not comfortable about sending you in.'

'Because you think I'll fail?'

'Because I think you won't come back.' Baptiste became solemn. 'You know it's too rushed. It's a fastball. The chance of success is small.'

'Thanks for the vote of confidence.' Racine understood exactly what he meant, and that he of all people would be reluctant to let her go, but she had never liked showing her emotions, and wasn't about to start today. What they'd once shared together had been a fun but immature mistake on her part. She knew he still felt the same way about her as he had done then, but she had ended it and moved on. Or so she told herself. No. She had. Racine crossed her arms. Her love life was irrelevant. All that mattered was revenge. It had taken the DGSE thirteen years. What would another one, two or three make? And yet she personally could not let Vasilev get away, even if eliminating him cost her life too. 'I'm a field agent, an operational asset, and I'm a damned good one.'

Baptiste sat back and rubbed the stubble on the back of his head. 'I know.'

The external discussion was over, but Racine's doubts still gnawed at her. 'Tell me, how do we know Vasilev is still there?'

'Our officer at the embassy in Moscow is in contact with a pro-Ukrainian partisan unit operating in the area. They call themselves "The Shadows".'

Racine sighed. She wasn't one for theatrical codenames. 'They have eyes on the target for us?'

'They've started monitoring his movements.'

'Am I expected just to creep into the middle of a conflict zone and assassinate a high-ranking member of the Donetsk People's Republic?'

'No. You need the right type of access in order to get anywhere near the target. Any new face will sound alarm bells in Donetsk. I've worked up a legend for you. You'll be posing as a junior reporter for a pro-Russian mouthpiece. Luckily for us the real woman's boss is a paid DGSE informer. He's arranged for you to travel with the next aid convoy into Donetsk to interview key people in the Donetsk People's Republic, including Strelkov himself. As de facto head of the DNR armed forces, Strelkov works hand in glove with Vasilev. Yes, I accept it's risky, but the Kremlin needs all the positive PR they can get for the DNR and it's so audacious they would not expect it. If they believe you're writing up a piece glorifying their humanitarian convoys and praising their fight against foreign terrorists, you'll be given full access. You'll be hiding in plain sight.'

'Until I shoot Vasilev.'

'When and how you do that is up to you. You know best.'

'I presume we're holding the real journalist?'

'We have her in a safe house outside of Moscow. As far as we know she hasn't met any of the people you will be seeing.'

'As far as we know?'

'As I said this mission is a fastball and this was the quickest, cleanest route into Donetsk. This is the least bad option.' Baptiste shook his head and looked away. 'I'm sorry.'

Racine said nothing whilst she read the rest of her briefing documents, which detailed her ingress into Russia, before butting them and the photographs into a neat pile. The meeting was over. She looked up at Baptiste and without emotion asked him, 'When do I leave?'

'Tonight.'

'Good.'

'Racine, I—'

'What?'

Baptiste blew out his cheeks. 'I'll see you when you get back.'

'You will.'

Baptiste collected the documents he had brought. He met her eyes and then saying nothing more left the flat. Racine made sure the heavy security door was closed behind him before she moved back to the window and waited for him to appear on the street below, climb into his car and drive off. She was still watching when a larger, dark executive saloon pulled into the kerb and a grey-haired figure climbed out. Racine frowned as her eyes followed him heading for her building.

Racine crossed to the bedroom and scooped up her personal iPhone. There was a WhatsApp message from Saskia with more photographs of her ex-pat life in Singapore, and a text message from her father. She quickly replied to both then powered off the phone and put it in a drawer, next to her work iPhone. Her life was now on hold. She'd not be using either again until she returned from her mission.

Racine heard a noise on the landing outside her flat. It was the creaking of the door that faced hers and belonged to her elderly and somewhat nosy neighbour, Madame Cadieux. Racine studied the video display screen, and saw her neighbour in conversation with her boss, Maurice Jacob. Racine rolled her eyes. Jacob turned and pressed the bell. Racine counted to ten and then opened the door at the same time as the one opposite shut.

'Hello, Racine, may I come in?' Maurice Jacob asked.

'Of course.' She took a step to one side, let him in and then locked the door again.

Jacob walked to the window and looked out. 'Are you ready?'

'Always.'

Jacob turned, his face now in shadow. He raised his arm and pointed at the kitchen area. 'Have you any wine in there?'

'I'll get you a glass.'

Racine moved to the kitchen, took a wineglass from the draining board then picked up a bottle of supermarket red next to the breadbin and poured the remains, filling the glass higher than any respectable Parisian would. She crossed the room and handed it to her director.

'*Merci.*' He took a sip, pulled a face. 'Still drinking your cheap plonk.'

Racine shrugged. 'It does the job.'

'Let's sit.' Jacob took a chair facing the kitchen. After a second's pause Racine sat opposite him. 'We are almost at the end. Now is when you will be tested like never before, emotionally and physically. A lesser person would crumble. I myself am in the process of doing so.' He waggled his wineglass before continuing. 'I can't pretend to fully understand what must be going through your mind at the moment.'

Racine folded her arms. Said nothing. She didn't know either. She waited for her boss to make his point.

'You and I, and now of course Director Grillot, are the only people who know of the historical connection you share with our target.' Jacob took a large swig of wine, before he placed the glass on the table. 'I am here to give you the opportunity to back out of this operation. Racine, neither Grillot nor I will say a word more if you decide to do so. You have my word on that.'

A voice in her head screamed at her to decline the mission, but other weaker voices called for revenge. When she spoke, Racine's tone was resolute. 'I am not going to back out.'

'I knew you would not.'

Undisclosed location, Donetsk, Ukraine

What air there was in the locked room was tainted by the heavy tang of motor oil, and the only light came from a high, frosted window. The space was not meant for human habitation, but for the past month that's exactly the use it had been put to. Mohammed Iqbal sat in the corner on the bare concrete floor, thankful for the fact he had been snatched in autumn after the oppressive heat of the Ukrainian summer had eased. He just hoped he'd be released before the winter snows started and temperatures plummeted.

Iqbal had become philosophical during his time in captivity. At any given moment his captors could kill him; on the other hand, they could just as easily set him free. He was no threat to them, the men of the DNR; what did he know about them? And what could he do? This wasn't his fight; he had no dog in the ring. He was a medical student, and not a spy, he told himself. Two days into his incarceration, a Chechen had come to see him. A fellow Muslim. They had prayed together. The man gave his name as Artur but he had heard the jailer refer to him as Boroda. Many of the DNR fighters used a nom de guerre, a nickname to fight under. Most were chosen to intimidate enemies such as 'Wolf' – or 'Diablo'; others were plain bizarre such as 'Marlboro' and 'Motorola'. Iqbal knew 'Boroda' was Russian for 'beard' – the Chechen had a black, bushy beard. They spoke in Arabic, their accents competing with each other, but understandable enough. Boroda, Iqbal believed, seemed satisfied that he was neither a spy nor indeed an Islamic State terrorist, even though he questioned how a student from Birmingham spoke Arabic. Yet he was not released.

Afterwards, he had been kept isolated for two weeks until another prisoner joined him. The new arrival wore a suit and at first Iqbal had believed he was there to arrange his release, a liaison from the British Embassy perhaps. But no, the man was a Jewish lawyer called Magidov, who had been targeted because of his work for the prosecutor's office. The lawyer was extremely anxious but talkative and spoke good English. Abruptly he was taken away and again Iqbal found himself alone with his thoughts.

So Iqbal continued to sit and wait. The thing he missed the most was not the fresh air, the daylight or, as he had discovered to his surprise, his girlfriend. What he missed the most was his wristwatch. He hated not knowing what the time was and having to guess. His watch had not been expensive or flashy; just a simple Casio G-Shock he'd bought on sale at ASDA back home. But it had been taken from him, along with his trainers. His footwear was returned when he was taken outside and made to work on the trench. At first, he thought they were ordering him to dig his own grave; however, as time progressed, it became clear the trench was for his jailers' amusement. The majority of the time, though, he was in his socks and had freezing feet.

Iqbal yawned. He was always tired. He was no longer hungry; time had shrunk his stomach and, with it, his appetite. Through the small, square, high window, the sky was still dark; it could be eleven p.m. or three a.m. – he didn't know. He yawned once more and closed his eyes, and relived once again the events that led up to his abduction . . .

*

Iqbal shut his apartment door, still smiling at the image of his girl-friend, Tanya, lying naked on his bed. He'd met her in his second year at the Donetsk National Medical University (DNMU) when she'd worked in the canteen. Her English was minimal but that had helped Iqbal improve his Russian. When the city around them started to fall apart, Iqbal's parents and family, from both the UK and Pakistan, had begged him to return to England. He nobly refused to leave Tanya behind as even his dad hadn't been able to get her a visa. DNMU had been relocated south to the Ukrainian port city of Mariupol, outside militant control. Those who could relocated; others stayed behind and continued to work and study. Iqbal chose to stay, along with the majority of students on his course. It wasn't his war and it had nothing to do with him.

The one-room apartment was in a grim 1980s Soviet block, far enough away from downtown Donetsk to keep the rent low. But it was next to a gastronom – a Soviet-era grocery store. Since the conflict started, many things had increased in price or become scarce, especially western brands. Yet, somehow, the gastronom managed to keep supplies at an adequate level, even if most products were now Russian imports of dubious quality and provenance.

Iqbal made for the alcohol counter. It was barely midday, yet a pair of drinkers were propping up the 'bar area', which consisted of a shelf against the window and another wrapped around one of the building's supporting columns. The two men were speaking animatedly to each other in Russian and eight or so empty plastic cups were strewn across the window shelf. It looked like they had been ordering cheap no-name vodka in fifty-gram shots. Although Muslim, Iqbal was not practising and drank alcohol, but the fact he point-blank refused to eat pork was harder for locals to swallow. Iqbal reached the counter and beamed at the woman behind it. She was young and always seemed pleased to see him, especially when he was on his own.

'Butylka kon'yaka, pozhaluysta.' A bottle of cognac, please, he asked in Russian.

'Yes,' the girl replied in English before turning and taking a bottle. She held it up for his perusal and he nodded.

'Come and drink with us, Blackie,' a voice from behind called, the language Russian, the words slurred.

Iqbal gritted his teeth. Old Soviet prejudices labelled anyone *whose skin was not white as 'black' regardless of race or nationality. Iqbal attempted to ignore the insult and continued with his transaction before thanking her and moving away.*

'I said drink with us, Blackie!'

Iqbal stared questioningly at the drunks.

The man spoke again. 'What, you too good to have a drink with us real working men?'

'Ya vas ne ponimayu.' I don't understand you, he replied in Russian.

'Look at the idiot; he can't even speak our language.'

'Ah, leave him.' The second drunk waved his hand.

'You.' The first drunk pointed at Iqbal. 'Drink.' He mimed drinking.

'Nyet, spasibo.' No, thanks. Iqbal wanted to get back to Tanya.

The drunk shook his head and pushed away from his perch. 'Buy me a bottle and we'll drink it together.'

Iqbal looked into the man's eyes. His tone had become aggressive. Iqbal held up his palms and repeated again in Russian. 'I don't understand.'

'Oh yes you do!' The drunk stepped forward and pushed him hard. Iqbal stumbled.

'Just piss off!' Iqbal snapped back in English, unable to control himself anymore. 'Who the bloody hell do you think you are? Leave me alone, man!'

The drunk looked confused. 'Piss?'

'Eeennngleesh?' the second drunk said, in thickly accented English. 'You American man?'

'No, I'm English.' Iqbal moved forwards with the intention of making for the door, but the first drunk shoved him again.

'Back off, yer twat!' Iqbal raised his voice, his Brummie accent becoming more pronounced.

Without warning, the drunk swung his fist. It connected with Iqbal's jaw, sending him sideways. Iqbal fell against the pillar, and the shelf splintered. The drunk threw another punch. This time

Iqbal blocked the haymaker with his left hand and lashed out with his foot. The drunk grunted as Iqbal's foot hit his shin. The second drunk now joined in. He grabbed Iqbal's left arm with one hand and punched him in the face with the other. Iqbal staggered, managed to raise his right arm, and brought down his bottle of cognac on the second drunk's head. The drunk let go, a cocktail of cognac, blood, and glass trickling down his face. He touched his head, lifted his hand away to look at it, and fell to his knees.

Iqbal realised he was breathing heavily; he was a lover, not a fighter and hadn't been involved in any fisticuffs since a schoolyard tussle when he was seven. The first drunk swayed unsteadily in front of him but didn't speak. Iqbal was about to leave when loud voices sounded in the doorway. Three men, dressed in camouflaged fatigues and holding Kalashnikovs, entered the shop. Before Iqbal had time to understand what was happening, one of the men produced a can of Mace and sprayed him in the face while another punched him hard in the gut.

Unable to see and barely able to breathe, Iqbal was lifted bodily out onto the street and bundled into the boot of a waiting car. Once inside, a hessian sack was placed over his head and unseen fists and feet pummelled him. Iqbal lost consciousness and when he awoke, found himself in the garage.

*

Iqbal opened his eyes. He heard a scraping outside, a sound he'd come to associate with one of two things – food or fists. The door opened and one of the DNR militants appeared. 'Get up.'

Iqbal slowly staggered to his feet.

'Raduga is ready for you.' The man jeered and despite himself Iqbal felt scared.

FOUR

DGSE Headquarters, Paris

The door was open, so Jacob didn't knock. Baptiste glanced up from his military-clean steel desk, registered his boss's appearance, and his eyebrows arched. Jacob, wearing his ancient camel-coloured overcoat, stepped inside the room. He shut the door on the blue-walled corridor behind and started to speak. 'I'm heading out to meet with the British.'

'I see.'

'Yes.' Jacob had made the decision that they would delay informing the British authorities of Mohammed Iqbal's location until the DGSE mission was underway.

'Do you have any updated intel on his location or condition?'

'None.'

'Our official belief is that Iqbal is being held at the place we pinpointed?'

'It is, sir.'

Jacob ran his tongue over his top lip. 'Remind me of the details of Racine's insertion?'

'Are you going to share that with the British?'

'Of course not. The British are our close colleagues, not our dear friends. I'll inform them that there are assets in the region but there is no need for us to tell them about our specific involvement.' Baptiste remained silent, but Jacob could see he was not happy. 'Go ahead; say what it is you want to say.'

'Do you not think it would be wise to say exactly what we have underway? That we have located a rogue agent.'

'In order to assassinate him?' Jacob asked.

'That is not what I meant. Surely they know of Vasilev's actions and our claim on him? Besides they will see it's him who has been interrogating their citizen.'

'Do you think the British would agree to me sending in Racine, or someone like her, if they had any say in the matter? Believe me, Baptiste, they would wave their arms around, huff and puff and demand that we make this an official joint operation.' Jacob noticed that his hand had gone into his pocket and was clutching his hip flask. He caught Baptiste watching him and looked away. 'Our objective is the elimination of Vasilev,' Jacob continued. 'Theirs would be the rescue of Iqbal. I'll admit, begrudgingly, that they are the best in the world at hostage rescue, but how would an SAS team be able to work around our sole, surgical operative?'

'The British have access to ECHELON, and that could be useful to us.' Once classified, the ECHELON surveillance programme was operated by the US and four other English-speaking, signatory states – Australia, Canada, New Zealand, and the United Kingdom – collectively known as 'the five eyes'. It originally monitored the diplomatic messages of the Soviet Union and the Warsaw Pact countries. Now it boasted intelligent keyword algorithms to monitor all private communication and was a key tool in identifying terrorists and their targets.

'Baptiste, I am sure they will alert us to anything relevant, without us having to go cap in hand and ask them. And let us not forget the time factor.'

Jacob left his junior to his paperwork and took the stairs two floors down to the side exit where his car was waiting for him. He greeted his driver, and once the security gates shut behind them, they sped through the suburbs. Although he had a liking for motor cars, Jacob wasn't fond of driving. This in part was due to his fondness of drinking. He raised the privacy screen and pulled his faithful hip flask from his pocket, now refilled from a bottle of Courvoisier he kept locked in his desk. Jacob allowed himself a sip, as outside Paris rushed past. His driver knew where they were going and how to get there, and this afforded Jacob a few minutes for reflective thought.

*

After taking a circuitous route, to avoid the worst of the lunch-time traffic and to check for any tails, Jacob stepped out of the cavernous Citroën saloon a block away from the bistro. He immediately walked to the railings that overlooked the dark river, rushing below. There was a slight chill in the air but his coat remained unbuttoned, making it all the easier to draw his personal sidearm if it was required. In all his years of service it had been required just twice: once to fend off overexuberant looters during a riot and the second time to stop a suspected Libyan operative from using his own 9mm on him. Jacob did not think of himself as a man of action, and never had, but now as he pushed pensionable age he knew that his physical powers were draining away. He took a nip from his flask, just to ward off the cold, and casually turned around.

The immediate area was not busy but there were a few people taking the air or posing for photographs. A couple stood with their backs to the river, the woman holding aloft a camera phone affixed to a metal pole. Jacob watched them and wondered where they were from. They could be Japanese, and some of the many tourists who for years had flocked to Paris like excited birds and chattered around its landmarks. And now they even tweeted too! He smirked at his own play on words. But became serious when they neared, phone still swinging on the pole.

He hated phones with cameras, the ability to send a high-quality digital photograph across the world in seconds was as problematic to the intelligence community as it was helpful. They stopped a few paces from him, so enamoured it seemed of each other and their surroundings that he had been rendered invisible. He hoped they would remain happy as they continued to explore France's capital city and not succumb to Paris syndrome. He'd scoffed at the idea but apparently *Pari sh k gun*, as it was known in Japanese, was a real thing. It was a severe form of culture shock or a transient mental disorder, depending who you believed, which affected a percentage of Japanese tourists who arrived in Paris and discovered that Paris was not what they had expected it to be.

He wondered if he'd go mad if he ever visited Tokyo? He walked away and then noticed a tall man standing looking in a shop window, his back turned towards him. It looked like an everyday scene except Jacob knew for a fact that the shop was a ballet boutique and boasted some of the best tutus in Paris. Men of course entered such establishments, but it was an unusual occurrence. He noted that the man's long, dark coat was also undone, and his hands were out of his pockets. Jacob had already started to walk towards him and would be visible as an approaching apparition reflected in the window glass, so he carried on his course towards him. The man turned to look back and for a moment made eye contact with Jacob. Jacob felt a simultaneous chill in his spine and a pulsating heat in his chest. He instinctively flexed his hands.

There was a sudden squeal of tyres and Jacob involuntarily flinched, then taking a sidestep faced the noise. It was a large, low-slung, BMW 7 series. The back door opened, Jacob's right hand started to move towards the pancake holster under his left arm . . . An even taller man in a suit stepped out . . . Jacob's hand continued to move . . . There was a flash of movement . . . Jacob's hand started to pull the pistol . . . and then a blonde-haired woman sprang out. The man at the ballet shop window loped towards her, his arms outstretched. Jacob took a deep breath and felt himself deflate.

He leant against the wall and noticed his hand was shaking. Calming his breathing, he took another sip from his hip flask and continued to walk, berating himself for getting worked up about nothing. He passed the happy duo several strides later. He continued to carry out his counter-surveillance measures by walking a meandering route before some twenty minutes later arriving at the meeting place. Hip flask empty, he was chilled and ready for a drink.

The bistro looked unremarkable from the outside, which was why the wrong sort of people paid it no attention. Perched on a steep slope and sandwiched between two similar, minimal establishments – one selling shoes and the other hats – it had an unrestricted view of the Seine. Inside the bistro seemed not to have been redecorated since the war. It was a welcoming cave of dark woods and burgundy upholstery. Jacob peered through the window. His guest was early and had taken a table at the back. Both a plate of cheese and a select bottle of red from the extensive wine list sat breathing. The man stifled a yawn as he checked his iPhone. The bistro owner was behind the bar polishing glasses, which seemed to Jacob like a never-ending task – almost like intelligence gathering.

Jacob entered and the bell above the door jingled. He made a beeline for his guest. 'My dear old friend. How nice to see you here, in Paris.'

'It's nice to be here, Maurice.' The man's French was good, but his accent was unmistakable.

Jacob shook hands with the senior SIS (MI6) officer. He marvelled at how the man, who was now in his mid-fifties, hadn't seemed to age. He subconsciously smoothed down his own coarse, grey locks, removed his coat and took a seat.

Before either man could say another word, the elderly bistro owner had appeared at the table to pour their wine. 'How are you today, Maurice?'

Jacob smiled the same as he always did. 'I am comfortable, Francois.'

Francois nodded at the Englishman. 'I told him he still looks like a young Robert Redford.'

'And I asked him what he was after,' the Englishman replied, with good humour.

Francois retreated, but ignored Jacob's coat, which lay on the empty chair to his left.

'Jack, you needn't have come all this way to see me.'

'I came for the cheese and wine; seeing you was an added extra,' Patchem said.

'To your good health!' Jacob raised his glass. The wine was exquisite, as it always was at the bistro. He never quite knew if it was because as a customer he chose well or because Francois only stocked the finest. He relaxed a fraction. He really was happy to see Jack Patchem, head of what the Secret Intelligence Service still referred to as 'The Russian Desk' and felt a pang of guilt at the words he had used in front of Baptiste.

'So why are we here?' Patchem asked, as he took a piece of brie.

'We have received intel that a British citizen is being held prisoner in Eastern Ukraine by the Russian-backed militia.'

'Do you have a name?'

'Mohammed Iqbal.'

Patchem seemed to be racking his brain. 'Doesn't ring a bell.'

Jacob ran his tongue along his top lip before he replied. 'He's just a student who was in the wrong place at the wrong time.'

'What type of intel?'

Jacob explained and then retrieved a folded A4 envelope from his coat. 'And as soon as we realised he was a British citizen, I contacted you.'

'Thank you, Maurice.' Patchem removed the papers from the envelope and glanced at them briefly before he slipped them into his briefcase.

'I of course will tell Baptiste to immediately send your people

47

all this in an electronic format. I imagine you will want to reach out to the relevant authorities to ensure his swift release?'

'As far as I am aware the OSCE has a mandate to facilitate prisoner swaps between all sides of the Minsk II agreement.'

'Ah, well that is the official line.' Jacob emptied his glass. 'Will you send in a team, perhaps "The Increment"?'

He saw Patchem feign surprise. 'The Increment' was a classified cell of the United Kingdom's Special Forces troops selected to carry out operations for the Secret Intelligence Service. For the past few years, however, it had been known as 'E Squadron'. Jacob knew this but wanted to play dumb.

'I see you have your sources.'

'I do,' Jacob replied.

'Given the tricky, diplomatic situation – an undeclared war in Ukraine – I will have to decide on the best course of action.' Patchem finished his own glass. 'And I have a man for such action.'

'You do?' Jacob was surprised.

'I do.' Patchem filled both glasses. 'He's somewhat of an expert on Ukraine.'

Roissy-Charles de Gaulle International Airport, Paris, France
The flight time from Paris to Vienna, the first leg of Racine's journey, took only two hours. For this reason and the fact she was playing the role of a single, Swiss tourist, she flew economy class, wore nondescript clothes and carried just hand luggage. She had the window seat and the two seats next to her were empty. The three across the aisle were occupied by a French family. The father – thin and angular – had the window seat; the mother – a large woman – was squashed in the middle; whilst her pre-teen daughter, who looked to have inherited her mother's girth, sat nearest the aisle. As the plane taxied towards the runway, the mother produced a packet of boiled sweets from the pocket of her cardigan and handed one to the little girl. She popped it

into her mouth obediently. The plane accelerated and they lost contact with the ground.

Racine took innumerable flights each year and understood the mechanics of flying, yet it still never ceased to amaze her – the moment of weightlessness in her stomach followed by the G-force pressing her back into her seat. Over the whine of the jet engines she heard the girl give a squeal of delight. Racine turned her head and saw a wide smile filling a chubby face. Then there was a crunch as the girl chewed on her boiled sweet. Her mother tutted and, unbid, popped a new one into her mouth.

Racine turned her head away and closed her eyes. She'd try to sleep for most of the flight as she didn't know when it would be safe enough to do so again. Another crunch and another tut reached Racine's ears as she drifted off.

FIVE

Fifteen Years Ago

Nice, France

The puddles formed by the overnight rain had not yet dried out and her feet had seemingly landed in every one of them as she ran. But her discomfort was cast aside as she focused on moving, hitting the pavement with one stride after another. Her daily run took her from their house on the hill down through the old town and along the promenade before turning and heading back, a circular route and quite pointless unless one counted exercise as the point. It was a little over two kilometres in length. 'A short, easy length' – said her father who ran with her when work allowed him to – yet it had taken her the best part of a month before she had managed to run it without stopping or feeling sick. The uphill part was the hardest, but she relished the extra challenge, the heightened effort to maintain her progress on the ever-increasing slope.

Her mother of course had been worried about her daughter being out on the streets alone before seven a.m. Sophie promised not to get into any strange men's cars, especially if they had a box of puppies with them. Her father had laughed at this but her mother had not understood the sarcasm and explained that 'one did not transport puppies in a cardboard box' and did she really believe that any man would entice a young lady with puppies?

Sophie's mother had become increasingly difficult over the past year, and the rows between her parents had become more frequent. What Sophie, as a kid, had put down to her mother and father just getting on each other's nerves, she realised now as a young woman was due rather to a fundamental incompatibility. Her mother and father were too much alike in their impenetrable belief that their view on raising their daughter was correct. Neither would bend nor compromise. Her mother had given up her career as a pastry chef to become a housewife and her father was a former Legionnaire turned defence lawyer. In short Madame Racine loved to cook, whilst Monsieur Racine lived to exercise. It should have worked. It didn't.

As her feet continued to splash along the wet cobbles Sophie concluded that it probably hadn't mattered before she'd been born. She'd seen photos of her mother and she'd never been model slim – her father had obviously enjoyed her curves. And then she'd been born and come between her parents. Her mother had passed on her eating habits to her daughter who had become fat. This had eaten away at her father especially when the puppy fat had still not shifted when she'd entered her mid-teens. So he had taken action. She'd overheard them arguing about her weight. Her mother said she was developing 'a natural womanly figure' but her father said she was starting to resemble a hippo. Sophie had cried herself to sleep that night.

The next morning Sophie took a good look at herself as she dressed in front of her mirror and then decided to side with her father. She wanted to change. She'd become the fat kid, and that had to stop. And so she ran. It made her father proud, but it worried her mother. She'd heard them argue again, but this time she was not upset by it at all.

Sophie's legs had started to feel tired as she hit the uphill part of her run. At this time of day, the narrow, cobbled streets of the old town were empty. The restaurants were closed, and the cafés had yet to open up for their breakfast customers. She turned a corner, took an alleyway between two old stone buildings and came to a halt. A boy was standing in her way, his arms folded and a sneer spread across his face.

Sixteen-year-old Louis Brissot lived two streets over from her in a flat above the family-run butcher's shop. No one liked him.

'Hello, Pie Face!'

'Move out of my way, Louis.'

'No. I won't. What are you going to do about it?'

'I'm going to ask you nicely.'

'I've seen you running in the mornings, wobbling along. Following your dad. But you're not with him today.'

'Wow, you have excellent eyesight.'

'Better than yours.'

'If you say so.'

'I do.'

'Move out of my way.'

'No. You're not better than me! You and your rich parents living in that big house. Who do you think you are?'

Sophie frowned. She didn't know what to do and she didn't know why he was angry. She certainly didn't view herself as being rich.

'Give me your money, then you can pass,' Louis demanded.

She crossed her arms. 'Who carries money when they go jogging, you imbecile?'

'You called me an imbecile? I'm going to tell my mum.'

'Why bother? She already knows you're an imbecile.'

Louis' nostrils flared. 'I'm going to punch you!'

'Is that what boys do – punch girls?'

'If the girls don't do what they are told to!' Louis took a step forward, his right hand clenched in a meaty fist. Sophie took a step backwards and then turned. 'Go on run away – Fat Pie Face!'

Sophie stopped. She faced him. She glared at him. She held her head high and jutted her chin at him. 'Move out of my way.'

Louis snorted; he took a large step forward and swung his right fist. Sophie didn't flinch, and the fist connected with her jaw. She stumbled sideways and thrust out her arm against the wall for support. It was the first time she had been punched in the face and it was a strange sensation. Her jaw itself did not hurt but she could feel the tendons that joined the bone to the rest of her skull. They ached, and then she realised she could taste blood, but it was the shock that was the worst part.

'Next time I ask you for money you'd better have it!' Louis said as he stood before her, triumphantly.

Sophie straightened herself up, worked her jaw and then said, 'Get out of my way, you imbecile.'

'What? Do you want another?' Emboldened with power and anger, Louis swung his fist again. But this time Sophie ducked and he hit the wall. He let out a yell as the rough stone skinned his knuckles and bruised his hand. Without thinking, Sophie kicked him as hard as she could between the legs. Her Nike trainers were soft, but her rage made the impact brutal. Louis fell to his knees and vomited. Sophie stepped over him and carried on with her run, hardly noticing that she was all but sprinting up the steepest part of the hill with ease.

That evening, over a huge, homemade meat pie, her mother told her father that the only way to stop Louis' mother from calling the police and creating a scandal was to agree to buy a month's worth of meat from the family's butcher's shop. Sophie had sat, hardly touching her food. Very worried, but she needn't have been because her father placed his hand gently on her bruised cheek and said that it was high time he trained her how to fight properly. No daughter of his was ever going to allow a boy to punch her again.

SIX

Present Day

Minsk National Airport, Belarus

Minsk National Airport was the name given to what was actually Belarus' international airport. It was from here that the elite of the former Soviet Republic escaped the stiflingly hot summers, and the bone-chilling winters, to holiday at their villas in Cyprus or alpine chalets in Klosters. The late Seventies Soviet terminal building looked old but was clean and sturdy; Racine much preferred its functional honesty to the glass greenhouses of Western Europe, which masqueraded as shopping malls. Avoiding the heightened security measures of the Moscow airports had been tedious yet necessary. Landing in the Austrian capital Vienna with a Swiss passport, she had quickly cleared customs. Once she had the run of the terminal, Racine collected her clothes from a locker, swapped passports – leaving the Swiss one – and continued her journey as Russian businesswoman, Victoria Petrovska.

As a business-class passenger, she was amongst the first off the Austrian Airlines flight and the third passenger to arrive at the immigration counter. She stood behind the thickly painted yellow line that separated returning travellers from the border guards who each sat at their computer terminals in individual glass-sided boxes. The nearest official, a woman in a dark green serge uniform, beckoned Racine forward and she presented her passport. The woman made no eye contact as she took the document and scanned it on her terminal. She had auburn hair, cut in a stylish bob. Her make-up, however, had been applied in a heavy layer, which would have drawn the wrong type of attention in Paris, and the top button of her uniform tunic was pushed open by her cleavage. Racine imagined many businessmen enjoyed returning home.

She looked up, matched Racine's face to her passport, stamped it and handed it back – all without uttering a single word. Racine strode through the customs hall. The empty luggage carousel turned noisily. She carried an oversized leather satchel and was dressed in an expensively tailored, charcoal grey, boot-cut trouser suit and wore a waist-length winter coat, popular in the Moscow fashion world. Her own make-up too was more elaborate than she would have liked, but she was currently Russian not French. A trio of border guards eyed her unashamedly as she passed. She was not stopped for any other type of inspection and less than a minute later stepped through double sliding doors and into the arrivals hall. Behind a metal barrier, no more than ten feet ahead, eager crowds pushed, attempting to catch a glimpse of their loved ones. Amongst the throng, large men in suits held up name cards. Racine scanned the crowd for any sign that she was under surveillance. With the exception of some men ogling her as usual, she detected nothing. Following the barrier, she pushed through the crowd, which was reluctant to let her pass.

Immediately out of the fray she was accosted by freelance taxi drivers, each seeking a juicy fare to the city centre. They were dressed in the former Soviet uniform of flat cap, heavy fur-collared leather jacket, and jeans. They looked vaguely Germanic.

Racine's contact was not meeting her at the airport for fear of being spotted. He was to collect her at a restaurant on the side of the Minsk highway, halfway to the capital. Racine continued to walk through the melee of drivers hawking their services until one got directly in her path. His leather jacket was open to reveal a large stomach straining against a blue woollen sweater.

'You want a taxi? I am the best.'

'How much to downtown?' Racine replied, in curt, Moscow-accented Russian.

'One hundred dollars,' the rotund driver offered; the US dollar was still preferred by most in the former Soviet republics over local currency.

'To go forty-two kilometres?' Racine raised her perfectly painted eyebrows, haughtily. 'I'll give you fifty.'

'Take a bus.' The driver folded his arms across his wide chest and started to turn his back, his key negotiation strategy.

Racine had no time for amateur dramatics and pointed to another driver. 'Seventy to take me to the city.'

'Done,' the new driver agreed, smiling.

'Hang on!' The first driver was outraged. 'She's my fare!'

'Your trouble, Sergey, is that you are too greedy!' The second driver tapped his belly playfully.

'Get off!' Sergey brushed his arm away and looked at Racine with a pained expression on his face. 'Sixty.'

'Agreed.'

Racine followed the portly driver out of the terminal building, down a ramp, and into the car park. Sergey withdrew his keys from his pocket and a set of lights flashed on a white Lada 110 saloon. 'Hand luggage only?'

'Yes.'

'You want to put it in the boot?'

'No, I shall hold it. I have bottles in there.'

'An important cargo,' Sergey conceded. 'Which hotel am I taking you to?'

'The Hotel Europe.'

'Hmm . . . classy. How many nights are you staying?'

'Just one.'

'A quick "in and out"?' He leered. 'That is always fun.'

'Yes.' Racine wanted to punch him in the head, take the wheel herself, and drive off. But she resisted the urge and climbed into the back, and the taxi pulled away.

Sergey stopped at the manual barrier to pay the attendant, handing him several crumpled notes before they left the airport slip road and joined the M1 highway heading west. His phone chirped, alerting him to an incoming text. The car swerved slightly as he checked it and replied. 'Sorry, it is my brother, Danik. You are from Moscow?'

'Yes.' Racine had no desire to talk.

'It is an amazing city, but I have only been once. I went to see Granddad Lenin. I waved at him in the mausoleum, but he ignored me!' He laughed at his own joke. Racine did not. 'So what is it you do? What type of business?'

'Human resources.'

'Ah, yes.' The driver clearly didn't understand her reply.

The traffic was brisk in both directions and the driver didn't speak for several minutes as he split his concentration between fiddling with his cell phone and driving. Racine took in the countryside. Flat fields mottled with clumps of dark trees flashed past on both sides. Twenty more minutes, she estimated, would see them in Minsk but her rendezvous point was only a matter of five up the road. Soon she would ask the driver to slow and explain her change of destination.

But then the car did slow. Sergey swore. A militia officer, part of the Belarusian traffic police, stood in the slow lane with a white flashing baton pointing at them; behind him, a patrol car sat facing the highway. It was the signal to stop and Racine knew it was usually the start of a well-rehearsed shakedown. The salary of a normal militia officer was below the cost of living, yet those in the militia who could paid their way into the traffic police to profit from the extraction of motoring bribes. Sergey muttered to himself some more and the car stopped at the side of the road. Outwardly, Racine looked like a confused passenger, but on the inside she started to consider all possible scenarios. Was it a normal 'stop', or had her cover been blown? Racine relaxed her body and prepared for action.

'Zdravstvuyte,' Sergey greeted the officer in Russian.

'Your documents, please.'

'Here.' Sergey passed his licence through his open window.

The militia officer glanced at the licence. 'You were recorded exceeding the speed limit; because of this, there will be a fine.'

Sergey didn't argue, even though the officer held no speed camera. 'How much?'

'Four hundred rubles.'

Sergey shook his head in a pantomime manner. 'Officer, please, that is a large sum. I am sure one hundred would cover my oversight, and pay for a good breakfast?'

'Three hundred.'

Racine looked right. A second militia officer now clambered out of his patrol car. Like her driver Sergey, he had a stomach that made his jacket strain. He approached the taxi with an assured, rolling gait, his right palm resting on his sidearm.

'Two hundred,' Sergey counter-offered.

The second officer reached the front of the car and stared at Racine through the windscreen before he joined his colleague.

'OK, I can accept two,' the first officer replied.

'One moment.' Sergey turned in his seat. 'I am sorry, and this is very embarrassing for me, but if I had not been driving you, I would not have been speeding. Can you give me the money for the fare now, so I can pay this officer?'

It wasn't an entirely unreasonable request, but something about Sergey's face looked different. 'OK.' She reached into her bag and withdrew a small purse and removed two notes.

Sergey leant backwards and grabbed her hand. 'Now give me the rest, like a nice lady.'

Racine handed him the purse. She couldn't jeopardise the mission. If losing a few hundred rubles meant it would continue then so be it. 'Please just pay the fine and take me to where I need to go.'

'No,' Sergey scoffed. 'That is not how this works.'

'I really haven't got the time for this,' Racine said.

'You haven't got the time? Do you think you are in control here?'

The second officer, the fat one, tapped on the window with his knuckles. 'Get out of the car, please.'

Fight or flight, the choice was hers, and she never ran away. Racine scooted swiftly across the back seat and exited the car on the driver's side, bag in hand. The bulk of the taxi was now between her and the fat officer.

Sergey climbed out. He stared at her. 'Give me your bag as well.'

'You don't want to do this,' Racine stated.

'Oh, but I do . . . and I will.'

'Raise your hands!' the fat officer ordered.

Sergey placed his hand on Racine's bag and heaved; her grip didn't break. 'Give me the bag!'

'I said, raise your hands!' The officer's voice was angry and his fingers started to undo the clip securing his pistol. 'I'm placing you under arrest!'

This wasn't normal. Something odd was happening and Racine was not going to hang around to find out what. As the officer removed his pistol from its holster, Racine took a step forward and delivered a straight-edge strike to Sergey's throat. He let go of her bag and grabbed at his neck. Racine now swung her bag and let it go. It sailed over the top of the car and hit the fat militia officer square in the face. At the same time he squeezed the trigger. A round arrowed into the air, hitting no one, but alerting all to the situation. Racine bounded around to the front of the car, switching her focus to the officer who had been extracting the speeding fine. She hit him with a rapid side kick, the sole of her ankle boot digging deep into his unprotected stomach. As the gaping officer folded, she delivered a left-handed palm strike to the side of his head. Without pausing, she took three quick steps to the fat officer, who was on his knees, and hit him square in the face with a powerful straight kick. He fell forward against the taxi and slid to the ground.

Sergey looked on, holding his throat. His eyes met Racine's and he shakily raised his hands. Racine grabbed the fat officer's service pistol – a Russian-made Makarov – as he lay on his face, wheezing and fighting for air. He gave no resistance as Racine took his cuffs and secured his hands.

'They are militia!' Sergey croaked. 'You will pay for what you have done.'

Racine pointed the Makarov at Sergey. 'Come over this side.'

The taxi driver trudged around the car and joined her. It was not beyond possibility that her cover had been blown and these two, however incompetent, had been ordered to bring her in. In that case why hadn't she simply been detained at the airport?

'Sergey,' the militia officer at Racine's feet uttered weakly, 'who is this madwoman?'

'You know him?' Racine's eyes narrowed and she stabbed Sergey in the chest with the Makarov. 'How?'

'He is my brother, Danik.'

It suddenly all became clear to Racine as her anger rose. 'So, you pair of cretins wanted to rob me? Was that it? Or was there more to this scam of yours?'

Sergey stammered, 'I . . . I . . . please . . . d . . . don't hurt me.'

On the highway, a large truck passed them, the wide-eyed driver rubbernecking at the scene. He brought the vehicle to a shuddering halt and raised a mobile phone to his ear. Racine swore under her breath and pointed the Makarov at the driver, who instantly got the message and pulled away. It wouldn't be long before someone else stopped or reported what they'd witnessed. She had to go . . . now. 'Lie down, next to your brother.'

Sergey hesitantly got on the ground. Racine pushed his face into the dirt with her boot before she checked the officer at the front of the car. He was out cold, but breathing normally. On the other side of the highway, a Lada Niva covered with militia decals screeched to a stop, creating a dust cloud. And then its sirens sounded. More sirens now as another militia vehicle, this one on her side of the road, swam into view.

'*Merde!*' This wasn't the time or the place for a firefight. Why couldn't they leave her alone?

'This is the militia. Put down your weapon!' Across the highway, a man with a bullhorn stood behind the Niva.

Racine scanned to her left. The second militia vehicle was almost upon her. If they had automatic weapons she was finished. Without warning, someone fired. A round pinged against the taxi; she scrambled to the wheel arch – the safest place. Another round; this one hitting the tyre and rendering it useless. They could shoot. Her situation was getting more complicated by the second, and she could feel her mission slipping away.

'This is your last warning!' the bullhorn boomed again.

Racine looked at Danik's patrol car. Surrender was not an option. Getting to her feet, she snapped off two quick rounds at the Niva before grabbing her bag and sprinting. Reaching the Lada, she mouthed a blasphemous prayer of thanks as she found the keys were in the ignition. She floored the accelerator pedal and screeched onto the highway. Checking the rear-view mirror, she saw a militia vehicle halt by the taxi and an officer spill out before it continued in pursuit. Racine put on the siren and lights and increased her speed; she had to reach the rendezvous and be away before the militia could catch her. She weaved in and out of traffic, her tactical driving skills being put to the test.

The car started to shudder as the needle moved past the one-hundred-kilometre mark. It wasn't a sports car, but neither was the Lada chasing her. In her rear-view mirror the pursuit car grew in size. She pushed her own car harder; the vibrations increased. Ahead, a large fuel tanker pulled in front to overtake a truck in the slow lane. There was nowhere to go. She had to slow. Racine sounded the horn but to no avail. The tanker did not move from her lane. Her rear-view mirror was now filled with the pursuit car. She tensed and hunkered down her shoulders to minimise the chance of whiplash . . . and then quickly stamped on the brake pedal and let the chasing car ram her.

Propelled forward by the impact, she swerved left as an opening appeared next to the tanker. Roaring into the slow lane, she was temporarily hidden from her pursuers. The tanker now came at her, wanting the same piece of tarmac. She dropped a gear and pushed her right foot, almost forcing it through the floor in an attempt to gain extra speed. The tanker struck a glancing blow to the back of her car. She was momentarily on two wheels and the car twisted sideways before it crashed back down. She fought for grip and managed to stay on the road and out of the crash barriers. Behind her, the tanker jack-knifed, and there was an almighty bang as the pursuit car collided with it. When she looked in her mirror, she saw the tanker driver fall out of his door just before his vehicle exploded. She couldn't see what had happened to the occupants of the militia vehicle.

Racine took deep breaths to regain her calm. What the hell had she just done? What the hell had just happened? Had she caused the death of law enforcement officers carrying out their duty? There was no time to second-guess, and definitely no time to grieve. The sign for the restaurant – a dark red wooden placard – appeared by the side of the road. Racine slowed the car, killing the carnival lights and sounds. Her contact was named "Noah", and she hoped that his ark hadn't sailed without her. She saw the entrance and bounced the battered militia cruiser off the smooth highway onto the uneven, gravel parking area. She didn't stop until she was at the rear of the car park, near some trees. It was the mid-afternoon lull between lunch and supper, and the parking area was mostly empty. She knew Noah's face, as he knew hers, but she had no idea what type of car he'd be driving. Giddy with adrenalin, and shaking, she grabbed her bag and hustled away.

'Either you've gotten rusty or I've got better,' a voice whispered behind her.

Racine spun and swung the Makarov pistol up in one fluid motion.

'It's me – Noah!' He grinned, an action barely visible under his full, dark beard. The last time they had worked together had been eighteen months earlier, a mission that also involved the assassination of a Russian. The beard was new, however. 'And it's nice to see you too.'

'We have to go; there was a problem with the militia.'

'That would explain the stolen car. C'mon, Rambo, this way.' Noah led her to an elderly panel van.

They got back on the M1 highway as the distant sound of rotor blades hit their ears. Racine frowned as Noah took the first turn he could across the central reservation to reverse direction. 'We're heading back past the airport and then to the "cold east".' It was standard operating procedure to double back and check for tails. On this occasion, however, the tail was on fire. 'There's a bag in the back with some more appropriate clothes for you, and in the glove box you'll find an envelope containing your new passports – internal and external and your press documentation.'

Victoria Petrovska was now a wanted woman. Racine exchanged the old document for the new ones to become a new person and untraceable. Racine relaxed, slightly. 'Any updates?'

'No. Our sources say that the target is still operating in the same location and from what they have seen he seems to be enjoying himself.'

'I bet he is.'

A minute later black smoke billowed towards them as they drew near the tanker; a large line of traffic had already concertinaed behind it. 'I take it that was your handiwork?' Noah chuckled mirthlessly.

'Yes,' Racine stated, flatly. 'I did warn them.'

They passed the militia Niva and saw how her rounds had holed its windscreen. Across the highway, a crowd of militia officers stood by the taxi.

'And that was you too?'

'Yes.'

'You don't change,' Noah stated. 'We can't take you anywhere except to apologise.'

'I'd forgotten you were a comedian. Now tell me exactly where you are taking me.'

'Gomel. You'll catch a train there across the border into Russia. Get off at Luzhki Orlovskie. There is a car ready for you; it's parked at this address.' Noah dictated the location to Racine and the vehicle details. 'There's a burner iPhone taped under the passenger seat; it's got the location of the safe house saved in a message,' he continued. 'It's a dacha in the middle of nowhere – it's stocked up for you. You'll be perfectly safe; at this time of year the neighbouring summer houses are empty and the nearest village is two kilometres away. Stay there overnight. In the morning, drive to the rendezvous with the Russian humanitarian convoy. The location is also in the phone. Got it?'

'Got it.'

'You're going to have to leave that Makarov with me.'

'Really? I was going to take it with me and pass it off to the border guards as a water pistol.'

Noah sighed. 'You'll be joining the convoy unarmed.'

'I told Baptiste I needed a suppressed Glock 26,' Racine said, flatly.

'And you shall get one once you reach your hotel in Donetsk.' He took his eyes off the road to face her. 'Strelkov is paranoid and The Shadows' guerrilla tactics aren't helping much. I've got word they're planning more imminent attacks. On top of that the Russians are going to search you.'

'Thanks.' Now it was Racine's turn to sigh. 'I'm just annoyed.'

'Annoyance is good.'

'A silenced 9mm handgun is better.' A pair of military helicopters screamed overhead towards, Racine imagined, the scene of her attack. 'And a gunship is better still.'

Undisclosed location, Russia

Racine killed the lights and stopped the car half a kilometre away from the target location. The chilly air drifted into the car through the open window of the old, midnight-blue Volkswagen Golf. The rural Russian night engulfed her. In the clear sky above innumerable stars twinkled as though bidding to outshine each other. She sat in silence and listened. She recognised the sound of the car ticking as the engine cooled and the local insects clicked. And then the loudest sound of all, the swish of the wind in the trees which hid the DGSE safe house from view.

Racine had left the undulating and cracked highway and taken the turning for the dacha. Rather than follow the tarmac as it arched through the trees towards the house, she'd angled off and driven into the shadows of the wood.

Racine got out of the car and started her tactical approach on foot. The gentle, precise steps meant that her rubber-soled boots made nothing more than a murmur on the worn asphalt. She stopped. Ahead, emerging from beyond the trees, she saw the safe house – a single-storey dacha, made ghostly in the moonlight, alone in an empty, flat landscape. Racine scanned the horizon in every direction and saw not a single light. She stepped off the road, moved down into the dip at edge of the field, and crouched.

After the incident with the Belarusian militia, Racine's insertion into Russia had been uneventful. As per the plan, Noah had driven her to Gomel railway station. At the border crossing point between Belarus and Russia, Racine hadn't warranted a second glance from the guard who had lazily inspected the train's passengers. Once in Russia, Racine had left the train and found the neglected-looking Golf parked in a residential street. Noah had assured her that the car was mechanically sound and drove much better than it looked.

She had met Noah the exact same time she'd met Baptiste, and she'd attacked them both. This time, however, he'd hugged her as she had left the van, and anyone who had bothered to watch them would have perhaps taken them for brother and sister. But Racine couldn't help but think there was something more to it. Noah had embraced her for too long, and when he had let her go there was a sadness in his eyes, as though he really was saying goodbye. Was there something he knew that she didn't? Should she be even more vigilant, or did Noah share Baptiste's belief that she wasn't coming back? She was tired and fatigue brought with it paranoia.

She snorted with derision. Men! Always so pessimistic, always thinking the worst, always believing they could do the job better. All except her boss. The head of *The Department*. Deputy Director Jacob believed in her. He had pushed her, adding her to previously male-only training exercises, and refusing to accept any excuses when initially she faltered and fell short. 'Warfare,' he had told her, 'is asymmetrical. You may be a woman, but the enemy may be a man and he will not make any allowances for your gender.'

And that was why she had chosen to accept this mission, a mission that was to be the first step in salvaging Jacob's legacy, but more importantly a mission that would bring closure for her. She knew it was an honour to be selected by Jacob and by extension her country; and she would do all she could to ensure that she succeeded, barring the odd run-in with corrupt law enforcement officers. She would make Jacob proud. Racine tutted. Pride was a very male emotion.

In the dark stillness, as she listened, her mind moved from thinking about her director to her father. Her father was fifty-four and still physically imposing even though now he only battled his enemies in court. She really should have called him before she left Paris, not texted. For the past eight years she'd lied to him, pretended that she was indeed just a law graduate who inhabited the thrilling world of international HR consulting and he was the one person in the world that she felt awful lying to.

Racine was overthinking again. Something her father had teased her about as a teenager, saying, 'Always so serious, so earnest – you look like a judge about to pass sentence.' All these years later here she was, handing out real death sentences. She frowned. There was no place for emotion or regret, not whilst she was working, but this assignment was different. What she had tried to push to the back of her mind and not acknowledge was threatening to destroy her, to eat her away. The mission was personal. It was her opportunity for revenge. For France, but most importantly for Celine.

A distant noise reached her ears, jarring her back to the present. She continued to remain motionless, eyes now fully accustomed to the night, scanning the surrounding countryside. She tilted her head, using the more sensitive rods in the corners of her eyes to pick out any detail she may have missed, any movement. Night-vision equipment would have been great right about now, she mused, but travelling light with nothing apart from herself to hide had been the best operational decision.

Eventually she became satisfied that there was nothing but the silent stars above and the sleeping fields below. She moved forward, like a scurrying nocturnal animal, knowing she was still visible to anyone with NVGs so moving as quickly as possible.

With two quick strides she bounded up the slight bank and sprinted across the small piece of hard standing in front of the building. Each time her foot hit the cracked tarmac she expected a round to hit her in return, but the night remained still. She came to a stop, crouched under the window, to the right of the front door.

Nothing. No sounds, no movements, no arrest team. She moved nearer the door, worked her key into the lock and pushed the door wide open. She counted sixty in her head before bursting into the interior, breaking left and low to avoid any potential shots. There were none. The dacha was unoccupied. She straightened up and looked around.

The front door led into a single large room. In the starlight she could make out the kitchen on the right, a fireplace directly in front of her and then a bedroom to her left. The dacha had only two windows, one either side of the door, which were shuttered against the wind and snow that would surely arrive within the next month and stay until April. She shut the door behind her, and the room fell into darkness again. She nodded and then flicked on a light switch. A single, naked bulb flickered then came to life, flooding the interior space with a yellow glow that reminded Racine of fairy-tale postcards.

She moved back to the front door. Switching the light off, she stood to one side of the door and waited. The wind had risen, and it whistled almost imperceptibly in through the crack between the door and its frame.

Once Racine had collected the car and parked it out of sight around the back of the dacha, she went into the kitchen area. If there was one fact she had learnt about residents of the former Soviet Union it was that they loved their white goods, and the owner of this dacha did not disappoint. A full-height, white fridge stood, like an alien visitor against the wall next to a Belfast sink. Inside, next to several bottles of water, was a litre of milk, six eggs and a packet of pre-cooked ham.

'How gourmet,' Racine muttered.

She took everything out, checked that it hadn't been tampered with and then found a frying pan. She used three of the six eggs, half of the ham and a dash of milk to make an omelette on the solitary gas ring. Without oil it stuck and became scrambled eggs, but she was too hungry to care. Her mother definitely would not have approved. She sat down to eat and checked her watch. She would allow herself five hours to sleep before she made the same meal again then started the long drive to reach the aid convoy . . .

SEVEN

Fifteen Years Ago

Nice, France

Sophie had continued to train, running most mornings and being taught how to fight Legion style by her father in the evenings. He was pleased with her progress and called her a natural, but she was just happy to be spending more time with him. Her mother's behaviour meanwhile had become erratic. She continued to cook, the food piling higher, almost – Sophie thought – in an attempt to justify her existence, her place in the house. She'd heard her mother sobbing when she thought she was alone in the house. The sound was not like a human sob, more like that of a cat keening. It was unnerving yet whenever Sophie tried to put her arms around her mother and hold her and tell her she loved her, her mother would pull away, her face rigid and hard. Sophie didn't understand. Was she reacting like this just because it was her father who was helping define her as his daughter? How had her mother become so cold? How had she become so distant? But then something happened to Sophie that pushed her mother away for good.

It had been several months since Louis had hit her and she had consigned the event to the past. She'd seen him lurking at school and on the street just like he always had. The weather had started to improve, and with warmer weather came high spirits and thoughts of beach days and swimming; and this year she would finally feel comfortable in her own skin. It was Friday afternoon and Sophie was looking forward to the weekend ahead. Even though she was wearing her favourite Dr Martens boots, she felt light-footed, all but jogging into the alley where Louis had attacked her. And then she saw that it was blocked. And then she saw who it was blocked by.

Two older girls, legally defined by their age as women, were leaning one against each wall and smoking. She vaguely recognised them from school the previous year; they had been four years above her and had gone off to college. And then there was sudden footfall and someone shoved her hard from behind.

'You're the bitch who attacked my brother!' The voice was loud, the tone low. 'We've been away, and now we're back.'

Sophie regained her footing, turned, and saw Louis' older sister – Marie. She was eighteen, sporty-looking in her Adidas tracksuit, and her angry pandalike eyes were framed by a dirty blonde bob. These were her friends, her gang, the gang of three who had – schoolyard rumours alleged – viciously beaten up several of their classmates on their last day of school.

'Yeah, it's you. Sophie, isn't it?' Marie continued.

Sophie felt her heart quicken and her mouth become dry. She swallowed and said nothing as her father's words sounded in her head. 'The best fight is the one you never have, the one you walk away from.' She couldn't walk away, could she?

'Me and the girls don't like people – especially ugly cows like you – who disrespect our families. Isn't that true, Pascal?'

'That's right,' said one of the two others, a giant woman with a round heavily made-up face, whose long, ginger hair was drawn back into a ponytail so tight it looked painful.

Sophie found her voice. 'Louis tried to rob me; he punched me.'

'And you kicked him in the balls!' Marie spat.

'Poor little love,' the third girl said. 'Poor little bits.'

'Sylvie?' Marie said. 'Really?'

Sylvie, who was smaller than the others and had wavy dark hair, shrugged and Pascal sniggered.

'Your brother punched me,' Sophie repeated, adamantly. 'What kind of boy does that to a girl? You should be apologising to me for him.'

Marie started to laugh. She opened her arms in a wide, exaggerated gesture. 'Are you stupid? You disrespected him. Now we should beat some respect into you, but we may not if you give us all your money. Look at it like a tax. Your dad knows all about taxes, being a rich lawyer.'

Sophie agreed, 'He does.'

'Yeah, hand it over,' Pascal said with a smirk.

Sophie's backpack was hanging on her right shoulder. She couldn't walk away. She couldn't let them have their victory. She slowly shrugged off her backpack and let it drop to the ground. As all three women looked at it, distracted, she swiftly swung her left arm out across her body, scything through the air. She delivered a heavy, backhand strike to Sylvie's face. Taken completely by surprise, the woman tumbled backwards and fell. Pascal was stunned but Marie was not and grabbed Sophie from behind and threw her against the wall. Sophie hit the brickwork hard and the air was forced out of her lungs.

For a moment she was beaten but then she heard her father's voice ringing in her ears, telling her that when she did fight, she must never stop until she was the last person standing. Sophie sprang forward, taking the smug-looking Pascal by surprise. Her right hand hit the older girl in the throat. A 'knife-edge strike' her father had called it. Pascal stumbled backwards over Sylvie's leg, landing with a heavy thud. Sophie turned, and took a quick two steps towards Marie. The woman was now open-mouthed until Sophie's right fist closed this for her. Marie's head jerked to the left as Sophie's jab hit her on the chin. '. . . and when you have to fight, don't stop until your opponent is on the floor . . .' her father's voice continued. Sophie now shot her left fist into Marie's stomach, doubling her up. And then she kicked her in the side of the head.

Sophie leant against the wall, panting and resting her hands on her knees. The women weren't speaking; they weren't moving. She looked down at Marie, and only then did Sophie realise that she hadn't been scared. She had felt no fear, rather a sense of indignation that they dared target her. She faced the other two. Sylvie was rubbing her cheek, as silent tears streamed from her eyes. Pascal was sitting on the ground, holding her throat, transfixed, frozen as though she didn't understand what was going on. Sophie took Pascal's ponytail and pulled her up to her knees and then took a step towards Sylvie. The woman jerked backwards, found her feet and ran away. Sophie locked eyes with Pascal. 'I don't think Marie is going to help you and Sylvie has run away. Now shall I hit you again, perhaps break your nose, or should I drag your pretty face against the wall?'

'N . . . no . . . please!' Pascal spluttered.

Sophie let go. 'Piss off.'

Pascal loped away after Sylvie.

Marie was now lying on her side, holding her head. Sophie crouched in front of her. 'Your brother is an imbecile, and you are an imbecile, which means your parents are probably imbeciles too. Unless you want me to slap your whole family around, you've got to promise me something.'

Marie didn't move. 'Wh . . . what?'

'You never, ever speak to me again. And if you see me on the street, you cross the road. The same goes for your brother. You got that?'

Marie opened her mouth to reply; however, Sophie didn't hear the words as a rough hand grabbed her left arm and dragged her upwards. Instinctively she used the motion to thrust her left elbow backwards, deep into the stomach of the attacker and then, pivoting, swung a powerful right hook into their face. And then Sophie became scared . . . very scared . . . as the grey-haired gendarme crashed to the ground.

EIGHT

Present Day

Izvarine border checkpoint, Russia–Ukraine border
Racine leant against the battered Golf as a seemingly unending line of white-painted Kamaz military trucks rumbled past in the watery light of dawn. Headed for the border with Ukraine, they were the latest convoy of Kremlin 'humanitarian aid' for the people of the Donbas region. Seen as a thinly veiled supply corridor for Russian-backed fighters, the first few convoys had attracted the world's attention and condemnation. Very few of the trucks, if any, carried food or medical supplies and those that did rarely reached the civilian population.

Several Russian army drivers waved at Racine as they went by, and she returned the gesture, smiling sweetly like the 'good, little journalist' she was pretending to be. Racine felt exposed as she stood at the side of the road next to her dilapidated-looking hatchback with the word 'PRESS' stencilled onto it using white tape. Noah had assured her that the cover story, her legend, would hold up to scrutiny. To anyone who asked – and they would – she was Olena Gaeva, the reporter. Her documents were in order and her internal passport was genuine. An internet search would further confirm her credentials with online versions of her previous articles emphatically promoting the Kremlin ideology. It also helped that Racine bore an uncanny resemblance to the journalist, which made Ms Gaeva pretty damn sexy, in her opinion.

The last truck in the convoy passed her position and as it did so, a black, long wheelbase Mercedes G Wagon came to a halt in front of her. A man dressed in immaculate Russian combat fatigues stepped out and approached. His unnaturally dark hair was parted to one side and he had a small, neat moustache. He looked like a villain from a 1950s B movie. She instantly recognised him.

'Good morning,' he said. 'Your press accreditation card and papers, please.'

Racine smiled – she knew her smile flustered most men. She replied in Moscow-accented Russian. 'Of course.' The man watched her with dark, alert eyes as she reached into her jacket pocket and produced her press card and internal Russian passport. 'Here.'

The Russian took the documents without a word and proceeded to study them. He checked her face against the passport then handed it and the press card back. 'I have read many of your articles, Ms Gaeva. You have undertaken valuable work, and I hope that you will continue to do so.'

'So do I.' Racine smiled again, and this time it was mimicked by the Russian. 'You have me at a disadvantage,' she lied. 'I don't know your name, but you look familiar?'

The Russian's smile widened, and his chest swelled with pride as he spoke. 'I am Igor Strelkov.'

Racine still wondered why the DGSE had not asked her to terminate him, but she raised her hand to her mouth for a moment as if to say sorry. 'Of course, how foolish I have been. Please forgive me. I had not expected to see you here.' In fact, the DGSE had pinpointed his location and that was the very reason she was there. Strelkov liked to meet all journalists who travelled into the Donbas, for fear that they may be foreign spies.

'That is quite all right, Ms Gaeva. I am not only a thinker; I also like to be out in the field with muddied hands.' Strelkov stood like a peacock attempting to impress a mate.

'Thank you for agreeing to be interviewed. I am sure it will make for a good article.'

'I am always happy to discuss our situation with the national press. We shall conduct our interview in the centre of Donetsk; this will enable you to appreciate further the vital work we are carrying out.'

Racine made her smile wide, to hide her frustration. She could have easily taken the Russian out now with her silenced 9mm or a stiletto blade to the neck. She was quick and Strelkov was at point-blank range.

She felt the hairs on the back of her neck stand up. Something in her peripheral vision made her turn her head, and ... a huge explosion tore through the convoy. The immense shock wave knocked both Racine and Strelkov from their feet. Dazed by the blast Racine looked up. Less than thirty feet along the road a gigantic fireball rose and tore into the clouds. The humanitarian convoy had been attacked. The illicit munitions inside were exploding with the force of a Bastille Day fireworks display. Strelkov pushed himself back up to his hands and knees as he watched the destruction.

Through the fog of hearing, dulled by the explosion, the voices of two Russian commandos shouted. Clad in black, they appeared like demons, grabbed Strelkov under the arms, lifted him to his feet, and hustled him back to the G Wagon. The Mercedes lurched forward. Tyres squealing, it performed a U-turn and reversed direction. Someone had messed up, and it wasn't her. Racine stumbled backwards away from the Golf, towards the ditch at the side of the road, and into cover. In her mind she ran through her options. Strelkov was her ticket into Donetsk; as the man who could introduce them, he was the door opener for Vasilev.

Racine looked down the road at the devastation. The Russians were firing in all directions; at ghosts and at shadows. She felt an icy finger caress her spine. She rolled over and looked behind her. A group of three figures were running at a crouch across the fields away from the road and the carnage they had created. Racine was impressed . . . She was also very annoyed.

'Hey, you!' an unseen voice called.

Racine gingerly got to her haunches. It was a Russian soldier. 'Does your car work?'

'I don't know.' She stood. 'I think so.'

He pointed. 'Drive back that way to the petrol station. All members of the press are to wait there for instructions.'

'OK.' Racine was compliant. In Russia, the media did what it was told or was shut down. She brushed herself off and got into the Golf. Turning it around, she headed back in the direction she had come from an hour before; this time, however, soldiers holding assault rifles stood on the road pointing her towards the entrance to the petrol station. She placed the car to one side of the large asphalt parking area, making sure that it was facing the road, before she took a burner phone from where it had been taped under the passenger seat and typed a text message to another untraceable phone. She had to let Noah know her mission was potentially blown before it had properly started; perhaps this had been one of the attacks he'd mentioned The Shadows had been planning? Once the message was sent, she removed the battery, took out the SIM card and broke it in half.

Her hearing had returned to near normal although her throat felt as though it had been cut. She retrieved a bottle of water from the glove box and drained it. She took another, wet her hands and wiped her face – luckily it was make-up free – flattened her hair and then got out of the Golf and looked around. There were now six cars, all like hers marked with the word 'PRESS', and several military trucks parked at the petrol station.

A man appeared from one of the vehicles and started to walk

towards her. He held his right hand above his eyes to block the glare of the sun. 'Excuse me, are you Olena Gaeva?' The words were Russian, but the accent was not.

'Yes.'

The man drew nearer. He was wearing a plain green field jacket that looked one size too big and dark blue jeans. What struck Racine the most, however, was his shiny, shoulder-length greasy hair, tied back in a ponytail. He spoke again, now switching to English with a distinct English accent. 'I'm Darren Weller with ON News. I heard you were joining us.'

Racine squinted, and delivered her English with a Russian accent, making her diction more staccato and less fluid. 'Yes, I have seen you on the television.'

'Fame eh?' Weller smiled. It was lopsided, and his eyes seemed to bulge.

'Yes, you are famous,' she replied noting that his face was as smooth as a young boy's.

'Ah, but it has its price. Can you believe I was arrested in Kyiv and banned from entering the territory of Ukraine for three years? Anyway, that doesn't matter because we're heading for the Donetsk People's Republic!'

Racine knew of Weller's exploits; he was infamous. He was a former British expat living in Kyiv who had taken it upon himself to become an investigative journalist. First freelancing from inside Ukraine, and now working for the Russian outlet *Our News* or 'ON' as the Kremlin-owned English language television news channel was known. He was ridiculous but could also be another way for her to get into Donetsk. She flashed him a smile. 'What are you doing here?'

Weller looked around dramatically before he spoke. 'I'm investigating claims that there is an anti-Russian Nazi group operating in the Donbas People's Republic. Have you heard about them?'

'No.'

'They call themselves The Shadows.'

'Wow.' Racine feigned surprise. 'That sounds very interesting.'

'It is.' Weller asked enthusiastically, 'What about you?'

Racine frowned, pretending that her English was worse than it was. 'Sorry?'

'Why are you here?'

'Sorry. I was to be riding with the convoy, and later interviewing Igor Strelkov in Donetsk.' She let out a sigh of resignation. 'Now I am not sure.'

'I interviewed him once. He's a genius. He won't let this attack stop him. Even if he's got to drive every single one of those trucks into Donetsk, he'll get them there.'

Racine was about to speak when she saw Strelkov's G Wagon pull up. It disgorged two commandos.

'*Zdravstvuyte*,' Weller greeted the men with the trademark 'eyes wide' smile she'd seen onscreen.

The nearest commando glared at them. 'We have come to inform you that no reports whatsoever are to mention today's attack on the convoy. As far as the media is concerned it did not happen. Understood?' Racine gave a nod while Weller seemed only to partially comprehend his quick-fire, Chechen-accented Russian. 'Once we have cleared the road, the convoy shall continue via Lugansk to Donetsk. We need to ensure that everyone is accounted for. Therefore, we will need to see your documentation again.'

Outwardly Racine remained calm; inside an alarm bell sounded.

British Embassy, Kyiv, Ukraine

Aidan Snow was no stranger to Ukraine and sitting once again in a commandeered office at the British Embassy in Kyiv, the intelligence operative felt oddly at home.

'Jacob gave me little in the way of new intel, rather what he did give me was by omission,' his boss Jack Patchem said from their London office.

Snow said, 'Meaning?'

'ECHELON had already sent us the exact same intel Jacob passed on to me regarding Iqbal.'

'So why arrange the meeting?'

'Apart from keeping in contact? The DGSE did not want us to learn about their mission. I believe Jacob was after a head start. This means only one thing in my mind. The DGSE are going after their French traitor in the photograph, Sasha Vasilev.'

'Vasilev, who just so happens to be holding Iqbal?'

'It would appear so.'

'That'll make it fun,' Snow said, deadpan.

'Look on the bright side, you're back in Ukraine.'

'Cheers, for that.' Unseen by his boss, Snow let himself smile. The former SAS man had lived in Kyiv as an ex-pat before reluctantly joining the Secret Intelligence Service. The network of contacts he had formed, including his close links with the local intelligence service, made him unofficially the SIS's go-to man for clandestine operations in the region. In reality Snow never needed much persuasion to return. There was something about the country that got under his skin even after all these years.

'You know how this has to go: don't get caught and bring Iqbal back. There's nothing more I can do at my end apart from wish you good luck.'

'Thanks.'

Call over, Snow sipped his embassy coffee and studied once more the photograph of Mohammed Iqbal. It was an image taken from the DNR's VKontakte page and showed the British student sitting in a stress position on a bare concrete floor. A caption accompanied it, penned by the Russian intelligence officer Igor Strelkov. It claimed Iqbal was a spy. Snow found it difficult to comprehend why any British national would remain within a foreign war zone when they didn't have to. War was not fair; it was violent, pernicious, and utterly unpredictable. Iqbal was lucky to be alive and even luckier to have a father who had the ear of the British Foreign Secretary.

Snow had been briefed by Patchem that it was a matter of national security that Iqbal be rescued, explaining that it had been an order from the very top. As such Snow felt the pressure on him to succeed more than ever. He didn't know why officially it was 'imperative that Iqbal be returned' but that made no difference to him. All that mattered was that Iqbal was a British citizen illegally held in Eastern Ukraine. Snow moved the photograph to one side and now focused again on the blueprints of the target building in Donetsk. It was a commercial garage with offices above and a large workshop bay at the back. From the intel garnered from the photographs, it appeared Iqbal was being held somewhere inside, probably on the ground floor.

Snow's mission was being conducted with a severe lack of time and intel. He would have help from the Ukrainian authorities to ingress into the Donetsk region, but they would not be able to assist him once he was there. He was to link up with a group known as The Shadows who would attack the target address with him, whilst he focused on locating and extracting Iqbal. Being ex-SAS, Snow was highly trained in hostage-rescue techniques but had no idea if The Shadows were too. As long as they shot the bad guys and neither him nor Iqbal that was really all that mattered.

He drained his coffee and left the small office. He moved along the hallway past framed ink illustrations depicting cricket matches in various grounds around England. This brought a smile to his face as he remembered the last time he'd been at the embassy when his Scottish associate Paddy Fox had complained that 'cricket' didn't represent the UK. Fox had been joking, on the surface at least.

Snow took a left and used a side door to exit the building. A VW Passat sat in the secure car park, a figure leaning against it, waiting for him. Vitaly Blazhevich was an agent of the Security Service of Ukraine – otherwise known as the SBU, the Ukrainian successor to the KGB. He would be assisting Snow on his mission to Donetsk. Snow flashed him a genuinely warm smile. 'Vitaly.'

'Aidan.' Blazhevich shook Snow's hand.

'Any intel updates?' Snow asked.

'None. Apart from being taken outside to dig trenches, the prisoners are still being kept in the same place.'

'Trenches?' Snow raised his eyebrows.

'The leader of the DNR is a WW1 enthusiast.'

The two intelligence operatives got into the Passat. Snow signalled to a security guard who released the blast-proof gates securing the car park. The VW pulled onto Desyatynna Street before turning right and negotiating the tourists on Mykhailivska Square. In less than forty minutes, an SBU passenger jet would be in the air en route to the small airfield at Mariupol, the closest they could safely get to Donetsk without risk of being shot out of sky.

'It's good to have you here again,' Blazhevich remarked as they reached Kyiv's central drag, Khreshatik Street.

'It's good to be back. I just wish it wasn't work-related.'

'The possibility of being shot does take the fun out of Donetsk sightseeing.'

Snow smirked. He and Blazhevich had been friends for years; since Snow's time as an ex-pat teacher in the Ukrainian capital.

'I know this man – Mohammed Iqbal – means a lot to the British,' Blazhevich said, 'but our drones have reported increased activity in the Donetsk area. There is what we believe to be a new Russian army FOB to the south of the city, and larger numbers of irregular forces to the north than we had previously estimated. You may not be able to evade them all.'

Snow agreed; it wasn't going to be a simple case of 'sightseeing'. 'What about The Shadows?'

Blazhevich sighed. 'We have no direct control over them; however, our field officer in Mariupol has been in contact with their leader - Victor Boyko. He has reiterated their promise to assist you.'

'I see.' The Shadows had been launching a classic counter-insurgency campaign across the Donbas against the DNR and the Russian army. They attacked fuel depots, cut supply lines, and took out key personnel. If Snow hadn't known better, he'd have sworn that his old regiment – the SAS – were operating in the area. 'So where have they been recently?'

'They claimed responsibility for attacking that Russian humanitarian convoy this morning. Apparently Russian bread and blankets are very explosive.'

Snow smirked. 'I bet the Russians loved that.'

'Officially it didn't happen – they initiated a media blackout.'

'I imagine that didn't stop locals from posting it on social media?'

'Exactly . . . and Darren Weller.'

'Darren Weller?' Snow knew Weller; they'd crossed paths several years before when Weller used to ogle women in Kyiv's ex-pat bars and pretend to be a photographer. 'He's an asset?'

Blazhevich sniggered. 'Of course not . . . he can barely tie his own shoelaces. We've been monitoring his phone and email. He really is a knob.'

Now it was Snow's turn to laugh. 'Vitaly, your mastery of English continues to improve.'

'He's also a dick. See? I speak American as well. He was texting a friend in Moscow about a journalist he's going to "bang". Apparently, Olena Gaeva is very hot.'

Snow pulled a face.

'They're both headed for Donetsk with the remainder of the humanitarian convoy. Strelkov is personally leading it to make a point.' Blazhevich paused before he spoke again. 'We believe this is why The Shadows attacked the convoy. Strelkov's movements are usually, well, "shadowy" but he made this trip public knowledge. If The Shadows took out Strelkov it would be a substantial blow to Russia and the DNR.'

'I can see that.'

'Look, Aidan, even with your abilities, this is still a very risky mission.'

'I know, and I do appreciate your concern.'

The VW slowed to feed into the traffic crossing the Dnipro River via the Paton Bridge. The SBU had moved their aircraft to Kyiv's international airport, Boryspil, which benefited from higher security measures than Zhuliany – the smaller national airport located in the southern city suburbs.

'I wouldn't put it past The Shadows to attack again,' Blazhevich stated, 'now that they know where Strelkov is.'

Blazhevich's mobile phone rang. He switched to Ukrainian. 'Hello? Now? OK, explain it to me . . . exactly what happened.' Blazhevich listened intently. 'Wait for us.' He snapped the phone closed. 'We have to make a detour.'

'Problem?'

'An operation has moved faster than expected. We have a suspected DNR agent under surveillance. She's at the war museum; we think she has a bomb.'

'So nothing major then?' Snow asked.

'Look, I'm sorry, this must come first.'

'Hey, don't apologise, just get us there.'

Blazhevich pressed a button, and a set of blue lights, hidden in the Passat's front grille, started to flash. He dropped a gear and powered the VW across the bridge before turning around and crossing back. In front of them sat the Pechersk district, dominated by the large Lavra Monastery and the vast World War II Museum complex.

'Tell me about the suspect,' Snow said.

'We've been monitoring a Russian agent, call-sign *Raduga* – "Rainbow". We don't know his real identity, but we believe he's in Donetsk. Last night he put a known associate, a woman named Irina Kovalenko, on a coach bound for Kyiv. The surveillance team saw her meet with a Russian businessman on arrival this morning; he gave her a bag. It's now been confirmed the man she met is a known Russian bomb maker.'

'Where's the bag?'

'It's a backpack and she's wearing it.'

'A suicide bomber?' Snow blinked. 'Why is she at the museum?'

'That we don't know.'

Blazhevich weaved the Passat through the mid-morning traffic, negotiating both trolleybuses and indignant motorists until they reached the top of the hill and stopped at the World War II memorial and museum car park. A pair of *politzia* officers let them through the entrance. Set on a hill overlooking the river, the Motherland Monument was a huge iron woman holding a sword in one hand and a shield in the other. Known colloquially as 'Brezhnev's Mother', as it had been a present from the Soviet leader to the people of Ukraine, it dominated the skyline. The museum was housed in its base and a memorial park stretched around it. Blazhevich and Snow pulled up in the car park and got out of the vehicle. They were greeted by another SBU agent.

'Where is she?' Blazhevich asked his colleague.

'Standing in front of the pink tanks, looking at the river.'

Two Soviet tanks, their turrets crossed, stood in front of the museum. Painted pink with brightly coloured flowers stencilled all over, they were a long-standing tourist attraction and meant to represent peace and love. Snow couldn't imagine them being driven by hippies.

'Is she on her own?' Blazhevich continued.

'Yes.'

'Have you evacuated the grounds yet?'

The agent shook his head. 'There is hardly anyone here, but we are stopping further visitors from entering. The bomb squad is on their way, ETA eight minutes.'

'Where's the bag?' Snow peered across the park.

'It's still on her back.'

'If it is a bomb and she detonates it, she's not going to injure anyone apart from herself.' Blazhevich frowned. 'We need "eyes on".'

Snow and Blazhevich exited the car park and met up with an SBU man who, supported by the perimeter wall, had a scoped rifle trained on the suspected bomber.

'Has she spoken to anyone?'

'No, sir.'

They stood in silence for a moment watching the woman who was clearly visible past the tanks. There was movement to the left, at the tunnel that joined this part of the war memorial park to the other. A group of people appeared, made minuscule in front of the ten-foot-tall granite tableaux depicting heroic Soviet soldiers.

'What's that?' Snow pointed. 'A television camera?'

'They must have been inside one of the buildings earlier,' Blazhevich stated.

'That's your reason,' Snow deduced. 'She wants to blow herself up in front of the cameras. It's political; the footage will go viral.'

'She's looking the other way; she hasn't seen them yet,' Blazhevich confirmed. 'Get to that crew and tell them to stop and turn around fast!'

The agent handed Blazhevich his rifle, broke cover, and loped towards the oncoming group.

'The bomb squad is still five minutes out.'

'That's five minutes too many,' Snow replied. 'Can you use that thing?'

Blazhevich squinted. 'We can't take her out, not until the threat is confirmed.'

'We're out of time. I'm going to skirt around that side.'

'Aidan, wait!'

Snow stepped onto the grass and jogged around the back of the giant monument as Blazhevich held the rifle down at his side and moved to the edge of the memorial concourse.

Facing the drop to the road and river below, the suspected bomber stepped up onto the low wall, which bordered the area and doubled as a bench seat for weary visitors. Her arms were by her sides. Then she abruptly turned and faced Snow.

Tears streamed down her face. 'Help me!' The language was Russian, the voice panicked.

Snow noted a wire leading from the bag into the collar of her coat and a trigger device dangling loose from her right sleeve. Had she lost her nerve, changed her mind, or been coerced into carrying the device in the first place? Whatever the reason, Snow had a chance of saving her. He asked, in Russian, 'What's your name?'

'Irina.'

'It's OK, Irina; you are going to be fine.'

'Please, I don't want to die!'

'You've chosen not to. That's good.'

Irina's words were fast and breathless. 'He told me there was no going back . . . that it would be symbolic. He assured me I'd be a martyr for the cause.'

'Who is "he"?'

'His call sign is Raduga. Please – you have to help me.'

'That's why I'm here.'

Her eyes darted to her sleeve. 'Please help me take this off.'

'The bomb squad will be here in a couple of minutes. They'll get you out of that.'

Eyes now wide, she started to pull at one of the shoulder straps. 'I need it off now. I'm scared!'

'No.' Snow fought to stay calm. An anti-tamper device may well have been fitted or even a timer set to detonate the device. 'We need to wait for the bomb squad; they're the experts.'

'I'm a bomb . . . a human bomb,' Irina wailed, her voice cracking.

Snow's gaze darted around. The TV crew was out of sight and he could see no other visitors. It was just the two of them who were within range of the device. 'Irina. I need you to look at my face. Look at me.' She met his gaze. 'You are going to live a long life. One day you will be able to look back on this and remember how brave you were, and that you made the right decision.'

Irina inclined her head slowly. 'I always wanted to come and see this place . . . see the Iron Woman and look at the river. My parents told me they would bring me some time, but they never did. Now they never will. My parents and my husband are dead because of the Ukrainian army. They shelled our village. Why would they do that, attack their own people?'

Snow had no idea where the woman came from but now knew it had to be somewhere within the Donbas. 'I'm very sorry to hear that, really I am.'

'They destroyed my home . . . They destroyed my life!' She glanced at the trigger.

Snow couldn't risk her changing her mind. 'This is your chance to do some good. Tell the SBU about the man who sent you here, about the other people involved. You can't bring back your family but you can save other innocent lives.'

*

Blazhevich blinked. Someone had entered the park from the southern entrance and managed to avoid being stopped. Blazhevich watched as he made his way up the steps towards the area housing the monument.

As the man's face came into focus via the scope, a panic gripped Blazhevich. He recognised the face. It was the same face he had seen on surveillance footage of a meeting that took place just hours before, and then the man had handed the woman he met what they now suspected to be a bomb.

Rapid thoughts ran through Blazhevich's mind; why was he here? Suddenly he knew. From this distance – using an unfamiliar rifle – he could hit him, but he couldn't guarantee a kill shot. 'Aidan!' he shouted. 'Get the bag off!'

Snow looked back, as if he'd heard Blazhevich, and then his head turned to face the man approaching them. Finger on trigger, Blazhevich flinched as he saw Snow throw himself at

Irina, knocking them both over the wall and down the steep grass bank leading to the treelined riverside road below. Now Blazhevich took the shot, but the man's hand had already been moving, reaching for his pocket. He fired once, and then again. The first shot missed but the second hit the man in the chest and punched him sideways. He staggered and fell backwards. Blazhevich dropped the rifle and pulled his SBU-issue sidearm from his holster, sprinting towards him. He skidded to a halt, Glock fixed on the man's head.

But Blazhevich was too late.

The man's right hand was gripping an elderly Nokia 8210 and his thumb depressed the call button. The full force of the explosion was funnelled by the hill up into the air and out towards the trees lining the riverfront road below the museum. Blazhevich stood, rendered mute – afraid to look over the edge. At his feet, the man had a smile on his face even as blood frothed at the corners of his mouth. Blazhevich's hand trembled, Glock still pointed at the man's face.

'Do it,' the man croaked as smoke rose from over the wall to his right.

Blazhevich didn't reply; his eyes now stared through the smoke as the river beyond continued to meander past regardless, as it had done for millennia.

'Hello? Can I have a hand please?'

Blazhevich shook his head. 'Aidan?'

Snow's head appeared above the wall; he had Irina Kovalenko by the arm. Two SBU officers now arrived and took the woman's hands, hauling her back up and over the wall.

'I'm glad it's not muddy,' Snow noted. 'I've got to get on a plane wearing these clothes.'

'Are you injured?' Blazhevich regarded his friend, with a concerned face.

'I'm fine,' Snow reassured them. 'But a couple of the trees down there aren't going to make it.'

NINE

Donetsk

Sasha Vasilev drew heavily on his cheap Russian cigarette; he loved the taste. He let the smoke escape leisurely from his nostrils as he examined the British student who sat across the table from him. Mohammed Iqbal intrigued him. He had something; a quality that had enabled him to endure isolation, beatings, hunger, and boredom without breaking, without complaint. It was a quality that had been sought by DGSE recruiters, and Vasilev knew all about the DGSE. After all, he had been one of their best, many believed *the* best, at the art of 'persuasive questioning'.

But that was irrelevant; a trained monkey was better than the men he now called 'comrades', those who had not been able to get anything from Iqbal with their fists and were too intellectually limited to be creative. Vasilev derived no pleasure from inflicting pain on others. What he enjoyed was the thrill of outsmarting and outwitting the subjects he interrogated and ultimately their masters. The very fact that he was alive now was proof that he had outwitted those who sought to destroy him. He drew on his cigarette again before stubbing it out and flicking it onto the floor where it joined his others to create a smoking man's Rorschach test pattern.

'How are you today, Mohammed?'

'Tired.'

'Apart from that?'

'Ready to go home.'

'As are we all. Where are you from?'

'You know. I already told you.'

Vasilev brushed errant cigarette ash from the sleeve of his brown pullover. 'This is a polite conversation – refresh my memory.'

'The UK.'

'Your accent is unusual.'

'Not for Birmingham.' Iqbal's eyes flicked to the discarded cigarettes. Vasilev knew he was no fan of smoking. 'Why are you holding me?'

'You know why. You attacked a man with a bottle; you hit him over the head.'

'It was self-defence!'

'A bottle, about the head?'

'So why was I not taken to a police station? You're not the official authorities.'

Vasilev leant in closer. 'Tell me about your parents.'

'Why?'

'That is a topic we have not discussed. They are British?'

'Yes.'

'First generation?'

'Yes.'

'What is your father's profession?'

'My father is a doctor.'

'Medicine is a family tradition?'

'It is.'

'Your father has a private practice?'

'He does.'

'And does your mother work?'

'My mother has always been a housewife.'

'Which is also work.'

'It is.'

'I'm glad we agree. So, to recap, your parents are wealthy, yet you chose to study medicine at a university where the cost is many times less than in the UK? Correct? This does not make any sense to me.'

'Two of my uncles studied in Donetsk.'

'Uncles from England?'

'From Pakistan, on my mother's side.'

Vasilev nodded. Tens of thousands of foreign students from developing nations had studied each year in the Soviet Union in the Seventies, Eighties and early Nineties. 'They are in Pakistan now?'

Iqbal nodded.

'Working as doctors?'

'As doctors.'

'That is excellent. Where would you work, if you had the choice?'

Iqbal made no reply, so Vasilev continued. 'Boroda told me you speak Arabic. How is that?'

'I learnt it at school.'

'In Birmingham?'

'In Doha.'

'You went to school in Qatar?'

Iqbal nodded, but remained silent.

Vasilev noticed a reticence to reply had now appeared. 'Why were you in Qatar?'

Iqbal didn't reply.

Vasilev pressed on. 'I know your father was working there as a doctor, for the Hamad General Hospital. Which school did you go to?'

'Why do you want to know that?'

'We are just chatting, you and I; I am just curious.'

'Doha English Speaking School.'

'Impressive, DESS was opened by Queen Elizabeth and the Emir of Qatar, was it not?'

'If you've already checked up on me, why are you asking me the same questions?'

'What about your brothers and sisters?'

'You know I'm an only child.'

'Is that not highly unusual for you people?'

Iqbal's nostrils flared. 'British people?'

'No. Pakistani.'

The room became quiet as both men stared at each other. Vasilev was glad he was starting to annoy the foreigner. 'So, your family has money. That is good.'

'Is it? Are you going to ask for a ransom? I'm a hostage now? Is that it?'

'No, we are not terrorists.' Vasilev's brow furrowed; Iqbal was not intimidated by him. This would have to change. 'Before I arrived you were treated badly.'

'I agree.'

'My job, as I am sure you understand, is to ensure that you tell me the truth. Can you do that?'

'Try to stop me.'

'Now, that is the spirit!' Vasilev exclaimed. 'So tell me, just to refresh my memory, what were you doing in Donetsk?'

Iqbal let out a long breath. 'I was, I still am, a medical student.'

'Why did you stay when so many other foreign students left the city?'

Iqbal opened his mouth to speak but then didn't.

Vasilev thought it was as if he didn't know quite what to say. 'If I had asked you this a month before I think you would have answered automatically? Isn't that right? You would have informed me that you were here, in Donetsk because you love Tanya.' Vasilev paused and studied the young Briton's face. 'Now I think you are not so sure.'

'That's not true.'

'Really? There is nothing to be gained by lying to me. The days of isolation have sharpened the doubts at the back of your mind. Those which told you the relationship with Tanya would never last, that she was only with you because you were a foreigner and her ticket out of the country. Isn't that so?'

'It's not.'

Vasilev smiled thinly; he could see he was making progress. He had not planted a seed, rather the green shoots of paranoia had already started to push through to the surface. 'Oh, come now, I understand. Part of you feels ashamed for thinking about Tanya in this way, yet another part of you does not. And, you wonder, where is she now? What is she doing? Is she alone? Is she safe?'

'You leave her out of this! And you leave her alone!'

'Me? I have no intention of going anywhere near the lady. I cannot, however, say the same for the other men you have met. They are – how can I best put it? – unrestrained by the expectations of polite society.'

'Please.' There was now a hint of desperation in his voice. 'She has nothing to do with this.'

'This what, Mohammed? What is it she has nothing to do with?'

'I stayed in Donetsk because I wanted to complete my course,' Iqbal replied.

'You are protecting your girlfriend, which is gallant of you.' Iqbal's eyes widened. 'You see, I am not like the other men you spoke to before. I am a professional who is merely doing his job. As such, I know what you are thinking. I can read your mind.'

Iqbal stared at the floor. Vasilev fell silent. Was the student more than he claimed to be? How could a mere medical student, whose mind he knew he should be able to control, resist in such a manner? He took a deep breath and forced himself to sigh, as though he were growing bored by the conversation.

'So this is the issue with your story: I do not believe you. I think that you have been asked to remain here by British Intelligence.'

'That's not true. I came here to become a surgeon, not a spy.'

'You are very clever. Very clever indeed, but I know you are lying. I have proof. Your passport was found on the body of a dead Ukrainian soldier.'

'What?'

'Can you explain this?'

'No.' Iqbal's face now displayed fear. 'My passport was in my apartment.'

Vasilev spoke again, interrupting his train of thought. 'It looked like a new passport.'

'My passport *was* new; I got it to come here.'

'Issued by British Intelligence?'

'No . . . the UK passport agency.'

'Why was it found on the body of a dead Ukrainian soldier?' It hadn't been; Vasilev had made up the story.

'How do I know? I've been kept cooped up here!'

Vasilev bobbed his head; glad he'd made the student angry. He would keep pushing and perhaps Iqbal would slip up. He would use words for now; he didn't want to get physical just yet. He decided to tell another lie and assess the response. 'There was a second passport too with your photograph on it but using a different name. I think they were bringing you a new passport to enable you to assume a new identity.'

Iqbal didn't reply.

'Why don't you admit your guilt? Admit that you are a British spy?'

'How many times do I have to tell you I'm not?'

'Until I believe you.' Vasilev took a new cigarette from his pack and his Zippo lighter from his jacket pocket. 'You keep talking to me until I believe you.'

Izvarine border checkpoint, Russia–Ukraine border

Racine was impatient. The convoy had yet to set off. Weller stood by her side like a stray puppy. No she changed her assessment

– compared to the burly soldiers around him, he was more like the runt of a litter. A thin smile parted her lips.

'It's a beautiful sight, isn't it?' Weller said.

'It is,' Racine replied, although she didn't understand what he meant.

'I mean,' he continued, 'to see all the hard work and frankly love that has gone into this aid convoy is . . . well, it's something.'

'It is something,' Racine said, now trying to keep a straight face in light of Weller's blind stupidity.

They both stood watching the Russian soldiers making final preparations to move the convoy. Racine knew she would not have a better time to subtly question Weller about what the DNR were doing to stop Ukrainian saboteurs from infiltrating Donetsk. It could, after all, help her escape the place herself.

She began to talk, to ask careful questions, and she didn't have to wait long before Weller started to boast about how he had seen suspected spies and foreign mercenaries interrogated. According to him, there were several secret interrogation centres around the city, which neither the Ukrainian government forces nor the OSCE knew about. 'How can the OSCE ask for an exchange of prisoners if they don't know these special prisoners exist?' he quipped.

'Who interrogates these special prisoners?' Racine asked as she nodded at two Russian soldiers who passed, heading for a truck further up the column.

'Experts from Russia. It used to be the DNR – you know . . . our guys on the ground.' Weller used the phrase 'our guys' a lot when he spoke about the members of the DNR, which Racine felt was strange both for a journalist and a British national. 'They were, er, not the best at asking questions, so some specialists were brought in; you know . . . retired FSB and GRU types.'

'Have you been to any of these interrogation centres?'

Weller looked around the car park before he replied. 'I'm not meant to talk about this, but yes I have. I went to one place where they were questioning a DGSE sleeper.'

Racine tried not to react at the mention of her employer. She frowned and pretended not to understand the term. 'DGSE sleeper?'

'You know, a deep-cover agent for the French intelligence service – someone who had been in Donetsk for ages pretending to be someone else.'

She let her eyebrows theatrically shoot skywards. 'How did they know he was a DGSE agent?'

'One of the reasons specialists were brought in was because they couldn't prove it, even though he spoke French. He was a lawyer working at the prosecutor's office. Anyway, the new specialist "Raduga" let him go, just to see where he went. Where do you suppose he ran to when they let him go?'

'Home?'

'Exactly; he hightailed it to Kyiv and then jumped on a plane to Paris!'

'So, the man was French?'

'No.' Weller frowned. 'He was a Ukrainian. He was spying for the French. That proved it.'

'I see.' Racine knew Weller's reasoning was flawed, but pretended to approve nonetheless.

'And who do you think they brought in when they failed to spot a French spy? A French spy catcher!'

Racine felt her pulse quicken. She consciously reached out her hand and touched Weller's arm, a move she knew would ensure his confidence. 'A French, spy catcher?'

'Yeah, can you believe it? Raduga was a former DGSE agent who was really a Russian sleeper!' Weller's eyes bulged even more than normal, and his smile was so wide it seemed to split his face in two. 'How ironic yeah? I mean, it's all a bit Tom Clancy around here!'

'Wow,' Racine said, theatrically. 'I would love to go to one of those centres and report on the very important work done there.'

She touched his arm again. 'We could go together. It would make great copy for me and great TV for you if we managed to film a foreign spy!'

'I like the way you think, Olena! Let's do it! Look—' Weller moved closer to her '—it doesn't make much sense both of us driving to the same place. Why don't you leave your car here and ride with me? We could have some fun!'

Racine understood from the expression on his face that Weller's idea of fun would involve nudity. 'That is a nice idea, but I feel safer driving myself, having my own space.' She squeezed his arm. 'But we *are* going to the same place.'

Weller tried to shrug it off by stroking the roof of his car. 'Yeah, you're right. Besides, there wouldn't be much room for your stuff, my stuff, and my cameraman.'

'Where is he, your cameraman?' She'd yet to see his work colleague.

'Oh,' Weller replied, 'he's probably chatting to his old mates. He's ex-Russian army, you know; a real tough guy and pretty handy with a gun as well as a camera.'

'That is good.' Racine now understood: Weller's cameraman was also his babysitter.

'It is. I feel very safe.'

*

Two hours later Racine was driving directly behind Weller. A large man, presumably Weller's cameraman, sat in the front passenger seat. The car – a UK-registered, British racing green MG ZT – was Weller's pride and joy. Racine hadn't asked him why; yet Weller had explained to her how he'd driven the old sports saloon across Europe on a publicity run. The aid convoys were another publicity tool. Russian officials claiming that each truck contained essential supplies for the civilian population of the Donbas region, whereas the real contents were mainly weapons and ammunition for the

Russian army and its proxies. Of course the few trucks that were opened to have their contents filmed for the press did contain blankets, food, and water.

The attack had lost the convoy two hours and seven of the sixty white-painted Kamaz trucks. Whoever had supplied the attackers with their intelligence had done a great job as it was those exact seven trucks that had contained the majority of the RPGs and ordnance for the heavy weapons. The burnt-out carcasses of the vehicles had been left where they sat or simply pushed to one side by several armoured personnel carriers. Racine did not know how many Russian soldiers had died in the attack and no one else was discussing casualties.

After refuelling in the eastern outskirts of Lugansk, Racine continued to follow Weller's car and four uneventful hours later – eight after they had set off – the convoy came to a halt at a DNR checkpoint in the late afternoon sunshine.

Weller climbed out of his car and tapped on Racine's window. She turned off the engine and joined him on the grass verge. 'Here we are, the heart of the Donbas . . . Donetsk.'

They were on a slight rise overlooking the city's eastern suburbs. This side of the city had been hit by far fewer shells than the west and, if it had not been for the presence of all the white-painted trucks stretching out in front of her, the scene would have been almost idyllic.

Weller gestured towards the city with his right hand. 'Beautiful, isn't it?'

Racine had to agree. With the autumnal trees blurring the hard edges of the Soviet architecture, the industrial city looked almost inviting . . . almost. 'It is, but I am scared.'

Weller put his left hand on her shoulder. 'Of what?'

'Being shot.'

Weller laughed. 'It's as safe as houses, especially now that our guys are running things. Have you never been to Donetsk before?'

'No.' To the best of her knowledge Olena Gaeva had never

been to the Donbas. 'But friends have told me I should. So, what happens now?'

Weller pointed down the road at the men in combat fatigues talking to one of the truck drivers. 'The local DNR chief needs to sign a paper before the convoy will carry on to its final destination to distribute the aid. Some of it will go further into the city and the rest will go to a distribution centre.'

'Where is Strelkov?'

'He'll have driven straight on to the presidential office. Don't worry; he'll call you to arrange your interview time. He did the same with me. He always knows where you are. It's reassuring.'

'Yes, it is.' This worked much better for Racine; it would save time. 'When can we go to one of the secret interrogation centres that you told me about?'

Weller beamed. 'Tomorrow morning. I had my camera guy call ahead. He mentioned me and they immediately agreed.'

'That is good.'

'Darren, we must go,' a gruff voice commanded slowly from behind in Russian-accented English.

Weller moved away nervously and thrust his hands into his pockets. Racine turned to see a huge, flat-faced man glaring at them. 'Vadim, this is Olena.'

The cameraman switched to Russian. '*Priyatno poznakomit'sya.*' Nice to meet you.

'Likewise,' Racine replied, noticing how the man's eyes wandered over her figure.

Weller suddenly asked, 'Where are you staying in Donetsk?'

'The newspaper has made a reservation for me at a hotel.'

'Which one?' Racine gave Weller the details. 'Not too far from ours. So why don't you get back into your car and follow us in mine? We'll go via your hotel.'

'Thank you,' Racine agreed.

Vadim glowered at Racine and returned to the MG. He clambered into the front passenger seat and waited for Weller to start the engine. Racine shivered. It was exceptionally unusual for anyone to unnerve her, but this man had. There was something about him, a feral aura that leaked out from behind his eyes. One thing was for certain, she would never turn her back on him.

Mariupol, Ukraine

An SBU driver met Snow and Blazhevich at the airfield and took them to a warehouse commandeered as a forward operating base. The single-storey breeze-block building sat in an unused industrial complex on the outskirts of the port city of Mariupol. Just a hundred kilometres south of the area controlled by the DNR militants who had taken over Donetsk, the warehouse was guarded by both security cameras on the outside and a rotation of armed guards inside. As standard operating procedure, the car drove directly into the building. Blazhevich waited for the large double doors to shut before he and Snow clambered out of the car.

'I'm never letting you book the hotel again,' Snow said, deadpan.

'Ha, ha,' Blazhevich replied. His phone chirped. He answered the call and listened as their driver exited the building through a smaller side door, leaving them alone. Snow studied the interior of the warehouse. It was empty except for an area in one corner containing several army cots and another section that had been cordoned off with prefabricated walls to create an office. Snow heard Blazhevich ask a couple of questions, listen to the answers, and then end the call. 'That was Kyiv. They've found the base the SVR bomb maker was operating from. It's an apartment near Lisova metro station. Apparently it's going to take a couple of days to go through everything inside. Already they've discovered what looks like a contact list and enough material to make two more incendiary devices.'

'What about the bomber?'

'She's being held at SBU headquarters. I'll interview her when I get back tonight.'

'Good.' Snow thought she was a victim, no doubt, of the conflict, even though she had been made a party to it. 'Any idea how they knew about the film crew?'

'They were a German news team; the reporter apparently had been interviewed last week on Our News. We don't know if he has any significant ties with the Kremlin.' Blazhevich gestured to the back of the space. 'OK, someone is expecting us.' Blazhevich led Snow to the office in the corner. He rapped on the flimsy wooden door and, without waiting for a reply, entered. A wiry middle-aged woman with light brown wavy hair stood by a map table. 'Yulia.' Blazhevich, was jovial. 'How's things?'

The woman looked up, her blue eyes fixing on Snow. 'Getting worse.'

'This is the man I told you about.'

Snow took a step forward and extended his hand to the woman who was a foot shorter than he was. 'Good afternoon.'

'Is it?'

'You'll have to forgive Yulia; she was never one for social niceties.'

Yulia flashed Blazhevich a curt smile. 'Better?'

Blazhevich shook his head. 'OK, tell my friend here what's happening.'

'I left Donetsk using the same route you will follow to make entry. You will use the highway but from here onwards you will be travelling parallel to my route, on foot via the woods. It is the only way you will be able to enter DNR territory.' Yulia tapped the map with her index finger. It was large-scale and showed Donetsk and the surrounding area. 'There is a new camp here. I am afraid that we have as yet no intel on it.' She placed her finger on a different part of the map. 'It continues to be busy here, and Russian troops have been seen conducting house-to-house searches. What they were looking for we do not know. In short, the insertion route is still viable, but you must travel at night.'

'How's the rendezvous point?' Snow asked, eyeing the map.

'It was deserted yesterday; obviously I cannot say what will be there tomorrow.'

'Tell me more about the main roads in and out?'

Yulia grimaced. 'They are blockaded by checkpoints. Traffic passes both ways; everything moves at their discretion. If they deem you do not have the correct permits or they do not like your face, you are stranded or ordered to pay a fine, or taken away. I use them each weekend. In my opinion you will not be able to exfil by road.'

Snow thought as much. Getting Mohammed Iqbal out of Donetsk would prove as difficult as getting to him. 'Who is meeting me?'

Yulia folded her arms. 'I am.'

Blazhevich now spoke, 'Yulia is one of our most reliable and highly trusted agents.'

'I personally,' Yulia said, 'am against being used in such a manner for your operation; however, I have my orders from upon high.'

Snow sympathised; he knew it wasn't personal. Potentially compromising her cover was a serious concern. 'I understand, but the life of an innocent man is at risk.'

'As is the life of a Ukrainian patriot.' Yulia's blue eyes suddenly looked cold. 'Mine.' She pointed to a black sports bag on the floor. 'The equipment you requested is in there.'

'Thank you.' Snow took the bag.

'You will be driven to the insertion point tonight. I suggest you grab whatever sleep you can before you leave; there should be a spare cot around somewhere.'

'Thanks, Yulia,' Blazhevich said, and he and Snow left the room.

Once outside, Blazhevich continued, 'Yulia has always been intense. She is an excellent operative but is used to running the show. Donetsk is her hometown, so she sees this as highly personal.'

'I understand,' Snow said. 'If anyone invaded Worthing, I'd take it personally too.'

DNR checkpoint, Donetsk

Yulia Nikolaevna reminded herself that the anxiety she felt as she approached the checkpoint on the road to Donetsk was healthy. Her hands were moist on the wheel of her eleven-year-old Nissan Qashqai as Kalashnikov-clutching DNR militants ahead searched cars returning from areas outside the control of their 'republic'. Yulia was on her way home for the weekend after teaching all week in a makeshift classroom for a faculty of the Donetsk National University, which had officially relocated to Mariupol. At first, her weekly commute had raised suspicion and resentment from the men on the DNR checkpoint as they actively detained drivers, interrogating them in case they were Ukrainian spies. As time wore on and she had been deemed to be neither a spy nor a smuggler, the act of crossing the checkpoint had become less frightening and more tedious.

The truth, however, was that Yulia Nikolaevna was very much a spy and, as such, had been reporting back to Kyiv on developments in and around Donetsk each week. On the weekends she would return to the apartment she shared with her elderly mother in the city and run errands for her and her equally old neighbours, all the while keeping her eyes and ears wide open. She had seen more Russian soldiers arriving in the city from Russia's Far East to bolster the ranks of the DNR in addition to tanks and artillery pieces deployed to new areas. She took photographs with a digital camera and uploaded them to the SBU in Kyiv via a satellite handset, which she kept hidden in a box on the roof of a downtown apartment building. Not the same one she lived in, but the same building housing several of her mother's friends.

Whenever she travelled back into Ukrainian-held territory, she never ever carried the camera or anything else that, if discovered, may incriminate her. She had an eidetic memory and on arrival at the room rented by the university would type her observations onto a laptop computer. In the front passenger seat of the Nissan, Yulia was accompanied, as always, by her colleague, Borys

Honchar. In his mid-seventies, Honchar was the oldest serving member of the university by a decade. He had been a renowned economist during Soviet times, winning many awards and medals. He snoozed for most of the trip, only waking to complain when the militants brought the car to a halt. As a cover it was all but perfect.

'What? Are we there already?' Honchar sat bolt upright as the Nissan stopped behind a line of cars.

'No, Borys Konstantinovich—' Yulia used the economist's patronymic name as a mark of respect '—we have arrived at the checkpoint.'

'Idiots.' Honchar looked out of the car with irritation. 'Their state will never work; it is doomed to failure!'

'I agree.' Yulia had heard the rant many times before but found that it lasted for less time if she agreed.

'Just look!' He waved his hand at the scene ahead. 'The fact that they are now more concerned with confiscating tobacco and alcohol rather than searching for "Ukrainian saboteurs" is proof enough. They are bankrupt! They have neither the economic tools nor the resources required to run a beer bar, let alone a country!'

Yulia adopted a neutral expression on her face as the car was beckoned forward by a militant.

Honchar crossed his arms. 'The final insult, now we must switch to Russian. Come, Yulia, let us leave our Ukrainian brains behind us!'

Yulia tried hard not to laugh. Honchar was the only person to bring a smile to her face since the entire conflict had started. A militant held up his palm for the car to stop. He tapped on her window with his knuckles. It was the usual routine. She opened the boot; he examined it. She and Honchar got out of the car while the cabin was searched; then they were allowed to drive into Donetsk. Honchar fell asleep again until once more Yulia brought the car to a halt, this time outside his apartment building.

'Home sweet home.' Honchar stretched and reached for the

door handle as Yulia opened up the back. The elderly academic retrieved his battered suitcase, shut the boot and gave it a gentle tap with his hand – the signal that she could go. Yulia drove off to return at six a.m. on Monday morning.

Now alone, Yulia focused on her instructions. On Saturday morning she was to drive to an address on the outskirts of town and meet the same British agent she had met in Mariupol. She was to take him to another address in Donetsk. It sounded simple enough, and the task in itself was, but there was the ever-present danger of compromise. And she hated to think what would happen to her and her mother if she was captured by the Russians or the DNR. She took a deep, calming breath. There was no use in worrying about what may or may not go wrong. She had learnt that after surviving the previous year's shelling – she now feared nothing.

Ramada Hotel, Donetsk

After parking the Golf, Racine ditched Weller – declining his offer of a drink in the bar – and headed for the hotel lobby. On the glass door outside, a strange sign caught her eye. It was white and bore the Ramada logo on the top, an infographic of a mother with two children on one side, and an image of a Kalashnikov crossed through with a red 'prohibited' sign on the other. Underneath the composition, a sentence written in Russian and followed by bad English stated:

There are kids on the premises. Entrance with guns is strictly prohibited.

Racine had never seen a sign like it before, even in Lebanon or Syria.

She pushed the glass door and entered the lobby. The room was an explosion of red walls, leather sofas, and large impressionist paintings. It looked like a modern take on a French chateau. A blond man, dressed in a uniform that matched the red walls exactly, stood expectantly behind the check-in desk. Taking up half of the available seats and ignoring the polite notice on the door, a group of DNR militants sat with their Kalashnikovs clearly on display resting against their thighs. Immediately, each and every man stared at her. Whether they were offering 'security' services to the hotel, were residents, or were waiting for a commander, Racine did not know. She immediately assessed the threat and didn't like her conclusion. She was unarmed and if they wanted to detain her for any reason, it would be all but impossible to escape. She had to control the situation.

She took a deep breath, kept her gaze fixed in front of her, and walked purposefully to the desk. A room for three nights had been reserved for Olena Gaeva, she informed the man in red. The man confirmed the reservation and in turn informed Racine that due to the 'current situation' the hotel accepted cash only in advance. Racine duly paid in US dollars. As in other war zones and disputed areas, business always carried on and hard currency was king. Different palms now had to be greased as new people took power – no doubt the hotel's parent company referred to these as 'facilitating payments' and not bribes – there was after all, still a clientele willing to travel to Donetsk and the hotel continued to serve them.

Racine was given a room on the third floor and, ignoring the bellboy, carried her own bag to the lift. She felt the lustful eyes of the militants on her and, holding her head high, refused to make eye contact. Act like prey and that is what she would become. Only the closing lift doors ended their leers. Once in her room she locked the door, and with no door wedge available, she placed the desk chair in front of it under the handle, further strengthening it before moving to the window. She had a commanding view of the city, cut in two by the tree-lined Kalmius River. In the distance, black smoke rose from the most recent round of shelling, standing out against the orange streaks of sunset.

There was a deliberate knock at the door. Racine rapidly

searched the room for a weapon, her eyes landed on a corkscrew that she grabbed up and took with her to the peephole. Peering through, she saw a man dressed in a hotel uniform carrying a covered plate. He knocked again, four rapid knocks. Racine moved the chair, stood to one side of the door, and swiftly heaved it inwards.

The man remained motionless and waited for Racine to appear before he spoke. 'I have a gift from Baptiste.'

Racine relaxed; the man was the contact prearranged by her handler. 'Come in.'

He entered, and she shut the door behind him. He placed the covered plate on the desk next to the television. He put his finger to his lips to indicate that they should not speak; Racine nodded. The man got on his hands and knees and felt under the bed. After a few seconds he retrieved a small package, which he handed to Racine. She put down the corkscrew and cautiously opened the package to reveal a Glock 26 pistol, two spare magazines, and a custom suppressor. Racine attached the suppressor and checked the pistol then placed it on the unit by the television. Her contact moved into the bathroom and returned half a minute later with a plastic-wrapped envelope. She took the envelope and explored its contents. It was a new passport, a Ukrainian one in the name of Olena Onika; it was the correct documentation for whichever way she wanted to exfil the occupied city. The man snapped a quick salute and moved towards the door.

'Wait. What's under the plate?'

'A club sandwich,' the man said, 'aren't you hungry?'

'As a horse.'

Racine closed the door, replaced the chair against it, and voraciously ate the sandwich and accompanying fries as she looked out of the window at the fast-approaching Ukrainian night. The sandwich hadn't come with a drink, so she looked in the minibar. It was empty except for a couple of bottles of Georgian *Borjomi* mineral water. She sighed and sat on the bed. Apparently the corkscrew had been for show or from a time before the conflict when guests actually used the hotel for leisure. She knew that anywhere bar France, even a small bottle of pastis was too much to hope for, but cognac or wine? Just one mouthful of wine would have been nice. How was a drinking girl expected to work?

There was nothing else she could do this evening and the exhaustion of the travel over the last few days had caught up with her. She had to be operating at one hundred per cent if she was going to complete the mission. Ten minutes later she took a quick shower and then checked the view from the window again. An unusually heavy rain had started to fall. She placed her jeans, jacket, top and boots next to the bed and slipped into new underwear and a vest then climbed into bed. Racine fell asleep comforted by the sound of the raindrops on the window.

TEN

Fourteen Years Ago

Nice, France

Sophie removed her nose from the windowpane, then using the sleeve of her sweatshirt, wiped away the smudge. The man on the TV had got it wrong again. It was anything but the perfect day for a picnic. Sophie sighed as she studied the dark clouds. Like her they were miserable. Her father was away on business, which meant she was at home alone with her mother. She itched to go out for a run but knew her mother would turn a shade of cardinal red if she tried to. Her mother was of the school of thought who insisted damp weather created coughs, colds, fever and influenza. No daughter of hers was going running in the rain and risking contracting pleurisy! So instead of heading down the hill to the coast and jogging along the sea road, Sophie was sitting in her bedroom listening to Katy Perry singing about a boy changing his mind.

Racine sighed heavily and closed her eyes. She was tempted to call her friend Jocelyn and see if she wanted to come over but she knew that would make her mother go into 'super-baker' mode and create even more cakes and pies to stuff them all with.

Sophie opened her eyes and saw something that made her smile. Driving along the winding road that led to the bottom of her street was a red convertible sports car. She knew of only one person who drove a car like that. Quickly Sophie slipped out of her baggy Adidas sweatshirt and put on her faded Levi's jacket over her vest top. The doorbell rang. She shot out of her room and hit the stairs.

As always, her mother was like lightning and reached the door first.

'Hello, Madeline,' she heard the visitor say, 'I've come to take Sophie out.'

'You can't materialise like this, from nowhere, and expect to have my daughter.'

'Why not? I'm her aunt.'

Before her mother had the chance to reply, Sophie reached the bottom of the stairs. 'Celine!'

Celine Durand was fifteen years older than Sophie and had always felt like an older sister to her. Her large, dark eyes inspected Sophie from head to toe. 'You look well.'

'Well?' Sophie's mother folded her arms across her considerable bust. 'She won't eat, constantly leaves the house to go running at odd hours, and the rest of the time she ignores me!'

Sophie ignored her mother. 'Celine, I've been running like Dad showed me. Look, this is your old jacket. The one that was tight on me!'

Celine gave her approval. 'It's a perfect fit.'

'It's wet outside. Come in, Celine. Sit with us and have some cake.'

'Another time, Madeline. We're going out.' Celine's eyes narrowed slightly as she replied. 'Sophie, get your shoes on.'

'But when will you be back?'

'We'll call you,' Sophie said as she quickly pecked her mother on the cheek, out of habit, and left the house. She darted through the rain to Celine's MX5 and dropped into the passenger seat.

'Let's go, sis!' Celine said as she pulled out of the driveway and back onto the road.

'Where are we going?'

'Just driving. Where do you want to go?'

'Anywhere but here.'

'So how have you been?' Celine asked as they headed towards the coast road.

'Fine.'

'Just fine?'

'Yes.'

'You can talk to me you know. I'm not your mother.'

'I know.' Sophie paused and listened to the sound of the rain hitting the Mazda's soft top. 'She's been driving me mad with her baking!'

'That's because she misses your dad.'

'No. It's because she wants me to be fat again.'

'C'mon I'm sure that's not true, but I do think she wants to control you. Having you in the kitchen with her is one way she can keep her eyes on you.'

'Was Grand-mère the same?'

'Not at all. My mother wanted us out of the house. It was your mum who always tried to stay in. But even at the weekends, your grand-mère insisted we get up and get out – no lie-in for us. It was like living on a farm, I imagine.'

'I feel like I live in a zoo.'

Celine smirked. 'When I was little we used to pretend Madeline was my mum; it was our favourite game. Your mum used to be fun, you know, but she's always been bossy. Back then she was just like you, a rebel.'

'I'm not a rebel. I just don't like being told what to do.'

Celine concentrated on the road. The rain had intensified and now hammered against the little car, attacking the windscreen and threatening to knife its way through the roof. They stopped at a set of traffic lights and Celine pressed a button on the CD player. Immediately Roxette's 'Spending my Time' blasted out of the speakers.

'You and your golden oldies!' Sophie shouted above the ballad.

They pulled away from the lights and headed ever nearer to the sea.

Sophie turned the music down a notch and asked, 'Where have you been this time?'

'All over. Morocco last week for a day and then Saudi Arabia.'

'Your job's very exciting!'

'I'm just a flying waitress.'

'I wish I could do it.'

'You don't want to do my job. You'll do much greater things.'

Sophie shrugged. The idea of getting paid to jet around the world for Air France struck her as much more exotic and fun than being a lawyer like her dad.

Celine moved her right hand and felt inside the pocket of her stretch jeans. She pulled out her phone. *'Oui?'*

Sophie couldn't hear the words of the conversation, but knew from the tone it was a man. A smile spread across her face as she saw that Celine had started to blush. Her aunt ended the call and put the phone in her lap.

'Who was that?'

'Someone.'

'That was your boyfriend, wasn't it?' Sophie drew out the last word in accusatory manner.

Celine looked at Sophie, her face creased into a grin. 'Yes.'

Sophie nodded like a wise mother. 'Well, I hope he's good at sex?'

Celine burst out laughing, causing the car to swerve on the wet asphalt. 'He is!'

'You can't hide anything from me! So, what does Mr Sexy do? Is he an Arab sheikh?'

'He works with me.'

'Is he a pilot?'

'No.'

'What's his name?'

'You can ask him yourself. He's just invited both of us to lunch.'

'Today?'

'Yes. If you're nice, he may even order you a bottle of Orangina!'

'I'd prefer wine.'

'Ha ha!'

Sophie smiled. She was both happy and annoyed at the same moment. She didn't want to share Celine, but she also wanted to know who the mystery man was and being invited to meet him made her feel more grown up.

'He said I should bring my little sister with me. Pretend to be my sister, OK?'

'Of course, but I'm not that little.'

'I know, you're fifteen.'

'I'll be sixteen soon.'

'Exactly. In fact I'm worried he'll take one look at you and dump me.'

'Celine, that'll never happen. You're the most beautiful woman I know.'

'Ah thanks, sis.' Celine squeezed her knee.

The rain suddenly stopped as though they'd crossed through a waterfall and the sun appeared. As soon as it was safe to do so, Celine pulled the MX5 over, dropped the top and then, with the Roxette CD turned up to maximum they set off for their lunch date.

A quarter of an hour later Celine parked in a space a few kilometres up the coast and overlooking the sea. She tidied her hair then fixed her make-up – let Sophie borrow her lipstick – and then they walked across the road to the restaurant, which was perched on the edge of the cliffs. It was still early for lunch, and only one table was taken. But it was the best. A man sat with his back to the view. He had watched them approach. He got to his feet and waved. Sophie took him in. He had neat dark hair, and sunglasses with mirrored lenses partly obscured his face. He was wearing dark blue jeans, and a pink polo shirt under a blue blazer. He seemed a little older than Celine, which Sophie found odd, but also romantic.

'Celine!' The man bounded towards them then took Celine's face in his hands. He planted a full kiss on her lips. Sophie didn't know where to look.

'This is my sister, Sophie,' Celine said once their lips had pulled apart.

Celine's boyfriend took a step back and made an overt display of removing his sunglasses to regard the two women. 'You look like twins? Is this magic? Am I seeing double or have I been rendered mad by your beauty?'

'Hello,' Sophie replied, not knowing what to say to the handsome man who was more than double her age.

He now took Sophie's hand and kissed it. His lips felt soft on her skin. 'Mademoiselle.'

Sophie tried not to blush, and now looking into his eyes she could understand why Celine liked him. He reminded her of Alain Delon, the actor her mother fantasised over in the prehistoric films she watched. Sophie continued to stare, and so did Celine's boyfriend. 'I'm Sophie, but who are you?'

'Celine didn't tell you? My name is Sasha, Sasha Vasilev.'

ELEVEN

Present Day

Ramada Hotel, Donetsk
Racine's eyes were open. A rustling sound reached her ears. She lay still in the darkness and listened to an electronic 'beep', followed by her door opening, and the handle hitting the chair with a *thud*. Racine cursed; this was a complication she didn't need. Racine reached under her pillow for the handgun. Her hand groped around in the dark. She checked the floor in case it had fallen off, but it wasn't there. She cursed again. In the gloom she frantically swept the room as the door opened wider, but the chair now caught on the carpet. She could hear laboured breathing. The door opened further, the chair toppled over, and two men barged into the room.

And then she saw her Glock where she had left it, in front of the television.

Racine had milliseconds to react. She'd messed up and she knew it. If she'd not been so damn tired the Glock would have been under her pillow and then in her hand and her intruders would have a serious problem. Racine spun off the bed and onto

117

her feet. The men were fully in the room now. One moved directly for her bed while the other shut the door.

'Hey, bitch!' the nearest hissed softly in Russian. 'We need some company.'

Racine hadn't bothered to draw the curtains and in the moonlight she half-recognised the men as part of the DNR group from the foyer. Something metallic, a blade, glinted in the nearest militant's hand.

'Please . . . don't hurt me!' she said in Russian, letting her voice wobble with forced fear.

'Hurt you, bitch? Oh, it won't hurt if you don't let it! Now lie down!' The militant took a step forward as his right hand, the one holding the knife, jabbed in the direction of the bed.

'Please, no . . .' Racine made to move backwards then reversed her momentum and sprang forward. She stepped around the outside of the man's leading arm, grabbed his wrist with her right hand and slammed her left elbow into his unsuspecting face.

'Wha . . .' was all the militant managed to say before Racine twisted the knife out of his grasp.

He stumbled back, in shock, his left hand rising to his damaged face. His eyes looked at his empty right hand in disbelief.

There was a second glint and Racine saw a weapon rise in the hand of the other militant, who was standing in front of the door to her room.

Instinctively she hurled the knife in his direction. It wasn't a throwing knife and she wasn't a knife fighter, so it missed his head but it did make him flinch and that bought her some time. Racine threw her weight at the nearest militant, slamming him into the carpeted hotel floor and winding him. And then she was up and her hands were grabbing for the Glock.

Without issuing any warning, Racine double tapped the militant by the door, the retort from the suppressed Glock sounding like a pair of heavy books being dropped on a wooden floor. He crumpled backwards, his own handgun falling. Racine spun back now and levelled the Glock at the first militant, the one who'd called her a bitch, the one who was now whimpering at her feet. At point-blank range, she shot him in the head.

Racine quickly confirmed that both men were dead before using the spyglass in the door to check the hallway. It was empty, and the air was still; the hotel was asleep. She looked at her watch. It was shortly after three a.m.

Racine picked up the dirty-looking Russian-made Makarov pistol from the floor then searched both bodies. Each had wallets filled with $100 bills and a few smaller Ukrainian and Russian banknotes. She placed the pistol, cash, and knife on the table.

Racine sat on the edge of the bed. She'd been lucky and she knew it. Next time she went to sleep she'd do it fully clothed whilst cuddling her Glock. She started to shake, an effect of the adrenalin leaving her system. Fight or flight, except she'd had no intention of running. She steadied her breathing while she tried to decide on her next course of action. She had just killed two men, her first in Donetsk but definitely not her last. The ease with which she had dispatched them shocked her. No, that wasn't quite right. What shocked Racine even after eight years in the service was the fact that killing the two men had been a reflex action, a decision taken at a subconscious level and without considering another option . . . Another option she wished she had now was cognac, but she had to make do with taking a gulp of *Borjomi*. She threw the empty bottle in the bin and then saw a key card that wasn't hers lying on the carpet. An idea struck her.

She got dressed in black jeans and left the room. She walked the entire length of the hall until she was by the emergency exit and directly underneath the sole CCTV camera. She now chanced a casual glance up and saw that the wire connecting the unit had been cut. She let a breath of relief escape her lips. Whether this was a recent precaution or not she didn't care. Turning back, Racine made directly for the room across the hall from her own. Putting her ear up against the door opposite, she listened. A

119

heavy snoring wafted from within so she tried the room next to it. Silence. Racine gently inserted the key card into the slot and the sensor flashed green. As she had expected, the militant's card was a skeleton key. She moved inside the space, confirmed it was empty, and returned to her own room.

She knew she was strong, and could have probably hefted the smaller of the two corpses in a fireman's carry over her shoulder but didn't want to waste her time, energy and get her clothes covered in gore, so she pulled the duvet from her bed, and then rolled the body nearest the door onto it. After checking that the hallway was still empty, she dragged the body from her room to the vacant one. She removed the clean duvet from the bed and hauled the body off her bloody duvet and onto the bed. She then took her duvet back to her room and repeated the process. Once both dead men were on the double bed, she covered them with the duvet – bloody side down. She glanced at the two would-be rapists as they lay in a grotesque mocking clinch, and she felt satisfied.

She shook her head and questioned herself, as she had done many times before. Without doubt her father would approve of such actions but what would her mother say? She imagined her mother would fuss over the bloodstains. Her mother had always fussed, had been the most house-proud person she had ever known; until she had walked out on them when Racine had needed her mother the most. Racine took a breath, she was shaking but with anger at her mother, at her past, and at herself. Something caught in her throat as she glanced at the two corpses. In the silence, Racine accepted that the only thing she was really scared of was herself.

She checked there was no blood trail, took the fresh duvet, locked the door and returned to her own room. It was time to move but she had to stay in the hotel until the morning. Any sooner would raise suspicion and any later her handiwork would be discovered, the dead men in one room and the blood splatter in the other. She was on her own. Even the guy who had given her the Glock would be well on his way out of the theatre. Racine sanitised her room of her belongings, pocketed the Makarov, cash, and knife, opened the door, and tried another room diagonally across the hall in the opposite direction. Her luck held – it was empty.

After locking the door, she once again placed the chair in front of it before she examined the fridge. Water again! She climbed onto the bed fully dressed. She lay gazing at the cracks on the plastered ceiling above her as she thought through what had happened. Had her cover been blown or were the militants only after her because she was a woman staying alone? As there had been just two of them, she had to assume the latter. Racine now felt even more fatigued than earlier and without realising it, she fell asleep with her Glock still in her hand, thinking she was glad she'd had a chance to test it and annoyed that she'd had nothing to drink.

TWELVE

Kuibyshivs'kyi District, Donetsk

Aidan Snow watched the approach road from the first-floor window as the mid-morning sun cast sharp shadows across the empty street. On the edge of the forest to the north of Donetsk, the rundown dacha was in a cluster of houses that barely warranted a name. The hamlet itself had been abandoned after several rogue shells hit sometime earlier in the year. Many such places now dotted the landscape, some completely abandoned like the one he was in, others populated by the elderly and those too stubborn to move out.

Dressed in black Nomex coveralls, armed with an AK-74SU, and wearing a pair of NVGs, he'd made his way into the dacha in the dead of night. The coveralls, AK, and kit were now safely stored back in the black sports bag and Snow was outfitted in civilian clothes – a leather jacket and jeans. Unless he raided the bag, he had nothing but an untraceable Glock 17 handgun and his training for protection.

Although the operation was sanctioned by the SIS and the Foreign Secretary, due to the delicacy of the location, Snow had no backup. If caught, he couldn't call for an extraction team. It had been a decision that had not been taken lightly, but the SIS knew Russia had deployed its latest electronic listening devices to eastern Ukraine and was not willing to take the chance that Snow's presence could be detected and recorded as proof NATO countries were active in the conflict. It was old-school espionage, reminiscent of Cold War operations.

Snow was to get as close as he could to the location where Mohammed Iqbal was believed to be held, use whatever means necessary to gain entry, and, if located, secure Iqbal's release – a simple but by no means easy task. He was not going to risk an approach in daylight, so he had at least twelve hours to kill before he went in suited up and wearing the NVGs. Once Iqbal was secure, he would retrace his route, leaving Donetsk the same way he had entered.

A noise cut through his thoughts in the sleepy stillness of the early morning. A silver Nissan Qashqai deliberately turned into the rough, dirt road and came to a halt on the grass verge in front of the next house. Yulia looked unremarkable as she got out and casually leant against the roof, holding her mobile phone as though searching for a signal. Snow waited a beat then made his way downstairs. He pushed open the front door, and gently moved towards her.

'We need to go,' Yulia stated flatly, before getting back into the car and starting the engine. As soon as Snow was seated, they moved off.

'How is it out there?' Snow motioned up the road.

'Have you been to the city since this all started?'

Snow shook his head. 'No.'

'It's . . .' Yulia heaved a sigh '. . . different. Dangerous. The DNR control the police or have removed them. There are Russian soldiers, no longer pretending to be anything else, stationed to the south. The banks are closed, the ATMs don't work, and there are increasing shortages of basic foodstuffs. Even those few, misguided locals who once welcomed the DNR have now started to protest. It's a powder keg waiting to explode. However, life goes on.'

'And what about the OSCE?'

Yulia shook her head and there was venom in her voice when she spoke. 'They are paper tigers, and the Russians are not going to be put off by a few paper cuts.'

Snow agreed with the analogy. The Organization for Security and Co-operation in Europe (OSCE) was in Ukraine to observe and report on all parties adherence to the Minsk II ceasefire agreement. This included monitoring the position, use, and damage caused by heavy weapons, and facilitating prisoner exchanges. However, as an unarmed, civilian mission, there was little the OSCE could do when confronted by Russians toting Kalashnikovs and driving tanks. They had made no mention of Mohammed Iqbal in any of their reports or press conferences.

'Are they visible in the city?'

'They have patrols that go out and look for new infractions but mostly they hang around their hotel.'

'Where are they staying?'

'At the Hotel Park Inn. It's owned by Radisson.'

'Business as usual, eh?'

'Don't think me rude but I don't want to know anything more about you or your mission.'

'I understand.'

'Good. Because when I hear a detail, I cannot forget it.' She briefly explained her eidetic memory to Snow before saying, 'By car, the address you need is not that far from here; we shouldn't have any problems at all.'

'The Shadows know to attack tonight, after dark?'

'They do.'

'Thank you.'

Yulia cast a sideways glance at her passenger. 'Don't thank me. I am not doing this for you. I'm doing this for my country.'

'*Slava Ukrayina!*' Long live Ukraine! Snow said.

'*Geroi Slava!*' Long live the heroes! Yulia completed the patriotic phrase.

Snow smiled; Yulia was remarkable.

Ramada Hotel, Donetsk

The sound of someone banging on a door and calling 'Olena' woke Racine with a start. Grabbing the Glock, she moved to the spyhole. Through it in the corridor she could see a ponytail. The head turned and the fish-eye effect of the glass made the massive, wide eyes monstrous. Darren Weller knocked on the door of the room opposite and called out her name again.

Racine couldn't let him see her appear from a different room, so she waited for him to give up and leave. Weller produced a key card and held it to the lock . . . She couldn't let him see the blood! Racine put the Glock on the floor and quickly exited her new room before Weller was completely inside the old one. She called his name.

'Oh!' Weller was startled; he turned. 'Sorry. I called your room but there was no reply, so I thought I'd come up and check on you.'

'I got up early.'

'Ah, I see,' Weller mumbled sheepishly as he surreptitiously pocketed the key. He then tapped his stomach with his hand. 'I should have gone to the gym really, y'know, to keep up my abs of steel, but we need to hit the road before the military traffic starts to move about. Are you ready to leave?'

'I need five minutes.'

'I can wait inside if you like?' Weller raised his eyebrow.

'I will meet you in the lobby.'

'OK.' Weller walked away.

Racine waited until the lift started to descend with the Englishman inside before she returned to the room she'd slept in and collected her overnight bag. She brushed her teeth, washed her face, then tied her hair back and put on the minimum amount of make-up that would be expected of a Muscovite reporter. She slipped into her leather jacket and hid the Glock in a specially designed inner pocket. Rather than ride the lift down to the ground floor and present herself in a neat, metal box, she took the stairs. Hand in her jacket, poised on the Glock, readying herself for a possible firefight, she opened the door into the lobby. It was deserted except for Weller who was casually leaning against the front desk and chatting to the same staff member who had checked her in the night before. Racine continued to scan the lobby for any signs that she was walking into a trap.

Weller turned and called to her in English. 'All set?'

'Yes.'

'You look nice.'

'Thank you.'

'Great; let's go.'

Racine followed Weller out of the hotel and towards his car. He asked, 'Why didn't you leave your luggage?'

'I like to keep it on me.' Racine hefted it onto her shoulder.

'Makes sense.'

Racine noticed the car was empty. 'Where's your cameraman?'

'Ah, he's gone on ahead to get things set up. You know, lights et cetera. He's like a one-man production team. If he wasn't so ugly, he'd even be doing the interviews!' Weller chuckled and opened the passenger door. 'Milady.'

'Thank you.' Racine got inside and sat with her bag on her lap. She could feel the baby Glock digging into her side, the suppressor negating the sidearm's mini-design.

'*Poyechali!*' Let's go! Weller declared in Russian as he started the MG and drove away from the hotel.

Racine looked back at the hotel, knowing that she could never return. 'How far to this place?'

'It's right across the other side of the city. I'd say about half an hour, give or take. Depends if any of the roads are closed and what damage was done last night.'

'Damage?'

'The Ukrainians started shelling again. They hit a couple of residential buildings. My sources tell me that there are civilian casualties.' He stared out of the window.

Racine said nothing. From the intel she'd seen of previous

126

incidents, the men of the DNR had specifically chosen to launch their own shelling from positions hidden in between suburban apartment blocks.

'Nice car.' Racine smiled for effect.

'Thank you.' He grinned back. 'I've always loved MGs. My granddad used to work at the Rover factory and promised one day he'd buy me one, just like his boss had.' Weller stroked the steering wheel. 'His boss had a Rover SD1. Lovely-looking car; a bit like a Ferrari Daytona only larger and way cheaper. This MG ZT is the true successor to the SD1. It was one of the last off the Rover production line when MG Rover was closed for good.'

Racine wasn't listening; she was watching a line of stationary traffic ahead. 'Darren, is there a problem?'

'Nah,' Weller mumbled, 'DNR roadblock probably . . . nothing to worry about.' Weller crossed onto the other side of the road, switched on his hazard warning lights, and cruised past the line of cars. As he reached the roadblock, he put his hand out of the window and waved. Racine tensed. This was not the way to approach armed men in a war zone. Either Weller was completely insane or worse still he was leading her into a trap.

'*Zdravstvuyte.*' Weller greeted the men. 'Press.' The men waved the car on without a second look, more interested in searching an SUV that was at the head of the line. Weller beamed at Racine. 'Why so worried? I told you, people know me here. They recognise good journalism when they see it . . . and they also recognise the car.'

'Impressive. You must be doing a good job,' she replied with another smile, letting herself relax a little.

'Thank you, I am.'

'How much farther?'

'Another ten minutes, straight up this road.'

Weller continued to talk as they approached the target. He was happy to discuss his previous ex-pat life in Kyiv and the reasons he'd started to work for his Kremlin-funded employer. Racine oohed at his 'daring exploits' and laughed at his jokes; in fact the more she did so the more information he willingly and unwittingly gave her. He finally asked, 'Have you got a boyfriend, Olena?'

Racine suppressed her urge to slap him. 'No, I do not have a boyfriend. Moscow can be a lonely city.'

'Ah, ha ha.' Weller took a deep breath before speaking again. 'I was thinking that perhaps when we both get back to Moscow, I could take you out sometime?'

'If we both get to Moscow, I will take you out,' Racine stated with a smile that concealed the true meaning of her reply.

'Y . . . yeah, that would be great.' A broad smile creased Weller's face.

Minutes later Weller brought the MG to a halt. To their right and set fifty feet back from the road, several tall, nondescript apartment blocks clawed at the sky. In front stood two smaller commercial buildings; one housed a sorry-looking fruit and vegetable shop – a *gastronom* – with a bank, and the other was office space with a commercial garage taking up the ground floor. A large metal up-and-over door faced the road.

'Is this it?' Racine knew it was because the street sign on the nearest building tallied with the geolocation of the VKontakte images she'd seen in her briefing back in Paris.

'Yep. Our guys commandeered the garage from an Odessa-based company, and that's where they carry out the interrogations. I'll park us round the back; you can never be too careful.' As Racine subtly surveyed the exterior of the target building, Weller manoeuvred the MG onto a narrow path and backed into a space. He switched off the engine. 'You can put your bag in the boot.'

'Boot?' Racine knew what the word meant, but Olena Gaeva probably wouldn't, so she pretended to be confused.

'Trunk. Now let's go; they're expecting us.'

After stowing her bag, Weller led Racine to the customer door. He pressed a bell and was almost instantly beckoned inside. The door was shut behind them and harsh strip lighting made them squint. Racine made herself appear relaxed and impressed as Weller shook hands with an unshaven man in combat fatigues. He led them along a corridor past a reception desk with a nude calendar pinned above it and turned right. There was a flight of stairs immediately on his right. He walked past the stairs and along the corridor, then knocked on a door at the end. Without waiting for a reply, he entered the room. A tall, powerfully built man with a black, bushy beard stood as they appeared.

'Good morning. I am Artur but most call me Boroda. Please sit.'

'Thank you for allowing us to be in your facility.' Weller had switched to passable, if oddly accented Russian.

'It is a pleasure to have ON here to record our work,' Boroda replied without warmth.

Weller smiled, oblivious to the harsh tone. He retrieved a Dictaphone from his pocket and asked, 'So, Artur, can you tell me a little bit more about yourself and what exactly you do here?'

'Of course. Once I was FSB Spetsnaz; this is no secret. I became bored sitting at home eating borscht, so I volunteered my services. Now here I am, doing what I was trained to do.'

'What were you trained to do?' Racine asked, making sure she flashed her best smile.

'To interrogate enemies of the state.' Boroda's eyes remained fixed on Racine before he addressed Weller. 'Did you not want to get all these details on camera?'

'Of course. Has Vadim finished setting up?'

'Yes.' Boroda stood. 'If you would be so kind as to follow me.'

He led them out of the room, along the corridor and through a door on the right into what had originally been a large vehicle workshop. The room had been repurposed. It was furnished with a metal table and four metal chairs sitting in the exact centre. At one end the steel roll-up door was closed and at the other, Racine could just make out a door in the shadows. In each corner of the room a large spotlight had been set up to bathe the middle in flat, white light. Vadim stood at the far end, fiddling with the controls on a tripod-mounted television camera. Racine realised this was the same room Vasilev had been photographed in with Iqbal. Her pulse started to rise.

'Both of you, sit,' Boroda was curt, 'I shall return.'

Racine remained standing. She felt a chill. Something was wrong. She slowly moved her hand inside her jacket towards her Glock. Weller, meanwhile, started talking to Vadim. Racine assessed her options. The nearest unguarded exit was through the roll-up door or the smaller exit next to it, and if needed she'd sprint for that. As ever she was going to rely upon the element of surprise and her silenced Glock if she decided to abort the mission. The door abruptly opened and a pair of armed men entered, dressed in black fatigues and accompanying Igor Strelkov. The GRU colonel stalked to one of the chairs and sat. 'Ms Gaeva, please join me. I am ready for our interview now.'

'Of course.' Racine smiled to conceal her surprise and took a seat. Had Weller arranged for her to see Strelkov?

'I see you are confused, Ms Gaeva. Do not worry, everything is about to become clear. I pride myself in getting to know everyone I deal with, be they military or civilian, on a personal level. Now, your name I had come across; you I had not. So, I decided to reread your reports and ask around about you.'

Racine fought the urge to let her gaze move towards Strelkov's commandos. They were between her and the door she had come in by, but the one behind her was still unguarded. 'It is quite an honour that you enjoy my work.'

'Ah, but I do not, Ms Gaeva.' He raised his right hand and his men advanced, AKs now trained on her.

'What's happening?' Weller's voice was suddenly shaky and high-pitched.

Strelkov looked at the TV journalist and switched to English. 'Mr Weller, you are about to get an exclusive. I suggest you and Vadim start recording now.'

'Right.' Weller fell silent and stood next to Vadim who had, as ordered, commenced his filming.

'There are two Kalashnikov assault rifles pointed at you, Ms Gaeva, yet you do not look panicked?'

'I've been around weapons before.' It was the cameras she was more concerned about. Racine realised too late her voice was too steady for a reporter.

'I have read all your recent articles, in addition to some of those you wrote when you worked for a smaller publication. Indeed this other publication had you cover the opening of a new business centre here in Donetsk.'

Racine knew Strelkov was awaiting her explanation, but she said nothing; somehow the DGSE had messed up. It was better for her to let the GRU colonel speak.

'Did Mr Weller tell you his cameraman used to be in the Russian army? Well, that was not quite the case; Vadim was Spetsnaz, but he actually served under me in the GRU. Why am I telling you this? Well, Vadim has met Olena Gaeva before; Vadim knows Olena Gaeva very well – if you understand my meaning. He does not know you. You are not Olena Gaeva.'

Her cover was blown. Her training told her to rebuke Strelkov's accusations, to stick with her legend in the hope that it was a trick or a test. Racine's arms were folded, her right hand an inch away from the Glock. If she was quick enough she could possibly draw the handgun from its concealed-carry position before the Russians opened fire; however, it would be suicide and she didn't want to die today. She decided, for now, to stick with her legend. 'I do not understand. What are you saying?'

'Get to your feet. My men will now search you.'

Racine complied. One of the commandos placed his AK on the floor and stepped towards her. Racine felt herself tense, her mind calculating angles of attack and defence. She took a deep breath . . . There was a sudden banging at the door. Eyes darted towards the sound. Boroda swiftly entered, an angry look on his face. Just as he opened his mouth to speak, an explosion rocked the street outside. The steel roll-up door wobbled, as though shaken by an irate giant. Those in the room with her either dropped to the floor or took cover. Automatic gunfire quickly sounded, and a line of holes appeared in the shutters.

This was her chance.

Racine spun and drew her Glock.

The commandos were fast, and well trained.

A burst of 7.62 shells tore at the concrete floor where, less than a second earlier, her feet had been. She threw herself backwards, crashing into the camera. Ears all but deafened, Racine rolled into the shadows, desperately hoping to keep avoiding the rounds until she managed to get to the exit. Her hope was short-lived. Something grabbed her shoulders and lifted her off her feet. Vadim had one huge paw on her pistol hand and the other on the back of her neck. As she struggled, another set of hands grabbed her and the Glock was ripped away. A fist hit her in the stomach, and she was thrown to the floor.

'Secure her!' she heard Strelkov yell from what sounded like a long way off.

Vadim's huge hand grabbed her throat, and Racine scrabbled for air. Her feet thrashed around helplessly in the dust. The corners of her vision dimmed. Everything went black.

THIRTEEN

Chervonohvardiis'kyi District, Donetsk

'We are under attack!' Boroda shouted.

Strelkov followed him out of the room and back into the corridor. 'I can hear that. How many?'

'Ten . . . perhaps more.'

As they neared the front of the building, the rate of gunfire intensified. Strelkov opened his mobile phone to call for reinforcements and found that there was no signal. 'How many men do we have?'

'Five.'

'Five?' Strelkov was incredulous. 'That is all you have to guard this place?'

'It is a secret facility . . . We were not expecting to be attacked.'

Strelkov knew there was nothing to be gained by assigning blame. He had fewer men but he had the advantage of cover and three floors to choose from. 'I take it our men are on the top floor?'

'Those who were inside, yes.'

'Then that is where I shall go.' Strelkov made for the staircase as another explosion rocked the building and caused plaster to fall from the ceiling. One commando raced ahead of Strelkov while Boroda stayed behind him and covered the rear. On reaching the top floor, Strelkov entered the room at a crouch below the window line and drew his sidearm. Three DNR men fired their Kalashnikovs from the various windows at the street below. Strelkov chanced a look through the nearest window and saw the bodies of two DNR men. One had fallen on the pavement and the other in the road. Across the street an SUV lay on its side. He addressed the DNR man next to him. 'What happened?'

'That BMW and that minivan parked there. Men got out and shot our two guys. I hit the Beemer with an RPG. It was fortunate there were no civilians around.'

'One civilian death is a tragedy; a thousand is a statistic,' Strelkov paraphrased Stalin.

Strelkov took another look at the street. A moment later, a round snapped overhead, and another caused a piece of concrete to fly up and off the wall, barely missing him. He sat back down and checked his cell phone . . . Still no message. Was the local tower out or had his signal been jammed?

*

Aidan Snow had been to Donetsk ten years earlier, a time before SIS. Then it had also been autumn; or, as his American friends insisted on calling it, 'fall'. The leaves on the towering trees lining the boulevards of central Donetsk had rusted a myriad of reds, yellows, and browns. Snow thought he recognised the road they were on now as one such boulevard; the type Soviet planners loved, wide enough for two lines of traffic each way, or a single line of tanks. A pavement met tall trees before giving way to shops and apartment buildings. The traffic was light, but the road certainly wasn't empty as the first shoppers of the day were venturing out. The locals, he remembered, were less friendly than Kyivites but their lack of pleasantry had been compensated by the cost of the beer – in some cases, it had been half the price of Kyiv. Snow missed those carefree ex-pat days. Suddenly a distant explosion broke his reverie.

'*Bozhe miy!*' *Oh my God!* Yulia exclaimed in Ukrainian. 'I must pull over. I cannot risk going any further.'

According to his understanding of Donetsk, he was less than a block away from the target building where Iqbal was believed to be held. Snow opened the car door. 'I'll get out here. I don't know what's happening up ahead.'

'If that's The Shadows, they are a whole twelve hours earlier than agreed!' Yulia said.

Snow shut the door and watched as Yulia drove away without saying another word. He walked in the direction of the blast, bag in his left hand. After several steps, gunfire erupted. He jogged to the nearest store where he saw two other people had taken refuge in the porch.

'What's happening?' Snow asked.

The old woman spat her words out. 'Idiots with too many guns and too much testosterone!'

'I saw nothing,' the second woman barked defensively. 'I'm just trying to buy some food!'

Snow stepped back out from the porch and looked up the street. He could hear a full-blown firefight, but he couldn't see it. He skirted the front of the store and then the next. As he drew closer, the retort of the weapons became louder. In front of him a large, free-standing billboard still advertised a rock concert that had taken place before the start of the conflict. Snow moved at a crouch towards its thick metal legs and as he did so, the glass storefront behind him shattered. Snow went prostrate on the pavement, daring only to look up several seconds later. On the other side of the road, forty yards ahead, he saw men firing from the third-floor windows of a commercial building.

The target address.

The location where Iqbal had been tagged.

Gunmen dressed in civilian clothing, crouched behind parked cars and amongst the trees, took shots at the building. They manoeuvred and returned fire with practised military precision.

Snow stayed still; if he moved, he risked being caught in the crossfire. One of the assailants held up his fist and the men around him instantly ceased firing.

Snow's plan, like the building he was watching, was now holed. He lay, at the side of the road and attempted to figure out what to do next, how to get into the target address, and how to rescue Iqbal.

*

'They're leaving!' a DNR militant exclaimed.

Strelkov lifted his head above the windowsill and saw a group of men getting into a civilian minibus, one continuing to provide cover with a Kalashnikov.

'Hit it with an RPG!' Strelkov ordered.

'We don't have any!'

'What?'

'I used our last on the BMW.'

Strelkov grimaced. He moved back to the door and took the stairs down. He saw Boroda and another man guarding the front door. 'They've gone.'

'*Blat*,' Boroda cursed in Russian. 'Divide and conquer?'

'Perhaps. How would they know about this place?'

'Sir, there are still half a million residents living in Donetsk, a million eyes, any of which could be turned against us.'

'Check outside, confirm that we are secure,' Strelkov ordered the soldier, before addressing Boroda. 'What do you make of the woman?'

'She's strong and definitely well trained, but I'll break her. Come back tonight and she'll be singing like a canary.'

'Who is she with? The Ukrainians?'

'That would be my assumption, from the way she speaks Russian, and who else would want to infiltrate us?'

'What about Weller?' Strelkov asked.

A thin smile appeared on Boroda's lips. 'He is a useful idiot.'

'He vouched for the woman. He was responsible for bringing her to this facility.'

'You think that Weller knows something?'

'Anything is possible. All is fair in love and war, and I see he likes her,' Strelkov scoffed.

'Very well, I shall question him too. And if we have made a mistake, we shall apologise and issue him with a medal.'

'I'm leaving now for the town hall; let me know if you encounter any problems.'

'I've never met a problem I couldn't kill, sir.'

*

Snow got to his feet and watched the attacking group exfil as they sped past him on the wrong side of the road. They had to be The Shadows. It was too much of a coincidence for it to be otherwise. Snow had worked with many guerrilla groups and unofficial units during his career, and as a rule it was their unreliability that always messed things up. Once first contact was made with the enemy plans imploded. And in this case first contact had been made too soon. Snow was angry but knew that holding on to this would not in any way aid the mission.

He moved back to the storefronts and – again skirting the edge of the buildings – edged towards the scene of the firefight. He saw the smoking hulk of a BMW X5, its passenger door open to reveal several human shapes inside. Even from here he could tell they were dead. Across the road lay two bodies, unmoving.

Snow reached the end of the block, moved a few steps down a side street, and stopped behind a large dumpster. He was directly opposite the building that had borne the brunt of the attack, the target address. A pair of men dressed in black tactical assault gear burst out of the structure, each taking a different arc with their assault rifles. After they had signalled that the area was clear, a third figure stepped out. He wore standard Russian camouflage fatigues, had immaculately combed dark hair, and a small moustache; Snow quickly identified Igor Strelkov from his SIS dossier. A black Mercedes G Wagon appeared from behind the building, creating its own path as it bounced over the verge. From the way it churned the grass, Snow could tell it was armour-plated. Strelkov hopped in and it drove away just before several men emerged from the building dressed in mismatched fatigues. They checked the bodies of their fallen comrades before standing on the street and lighting up cigarettes.

Snow shook his head; the situation was surreal. He was in the centre of a European city observing the result of a firefight, an assault that had served no purpose. The attackers had lost several men and gunned down just two of the enemy, yet made no attempt to storm the building. Something about it disturbed him; what had been the point of attacking in daylight? Why had they changed the agreed plans? Snow kept an eye on the target in case whoever was inside moved Iqbal – if Iqbal was still inside.

As Snow continued to watch the building, he saw three white SUVs approach and it dawned on him what he'd missed. This had to be the reason for the attack happening now. The group's sole purpose was to draw attention to the address. Once the OSCE arrived to report on the firefight, they would demand access to the building – the building in which the DNR was illegally holding prisoners.

The three white Toyota Land Cruisers with 'OSCE' stencilled on both bonnets and doors drew to a halt directly outside the building. Had they appeared so quickly by chance or by design? Snow thought he knew the answer; the attack was planned and they had been called in advance. As the civilian monitors alighted from their official vehicles, the men of the DNR stopped smoking. With outraged faces the DNR men confronted the monitors and gestured towards the two corpses and the remains of the BMW.

An idea struck Snow. It was bold and it was dangerous, but

it might work. Snow put his bag in the dumpster – hoping it wouldn't vanish – and walked back onto the street. He carried on past the next store and crossed the road, angling towards the OSCE vehicles. A few curious locals, who decided that the arrival of the OSCE overrode their own fear of men with guns, had started to form a spectator group on the pavement. Snow stood behind them and watched the proceedings.

The main OSCE monitor was a lanky blond man. He spoke English in a loud voice with Dutch overtones; a beat behind, his translator expressed the requests in Russian. Snow counted nine OSCE personnel in total, which seemed like overkill, until he remembered that they were unarmed. As the lead monitor continued to argue via his translator with the man representing the DNR, Snow turned his attention to the three Toyota Land Cruisers. A narrow trail of smoke escaped from the last in line, the one nearest Snow. The driver was standing next to the vehicle and enjoying a cigarette. Snow scanned the area; all the attention was still on the monitor versus DNR showdown, the local residents were transfixed – happy to watch the big men with guns being berated by a bigger man wearing a white tabard.

Snow stepped off the kerb in the direction of the Land Cruiser. The driver's door was open, which meant that the central locking mechanism had not been engaged. Snow casually looked into the empty boot. He then checked the back seat and spotted several white tabards with OSCE stencilled on them. He glanced to his left; the driver was still looking across the road and exhaling cigarette smoke. In a fast, fluid motion, Snow opened the rear door, reached in, and grabbed a tabard. He left the door ajar so as not to make a noise and swiftly walked away from the vehicle. Snow looped around the target building and came back onto the street on the other side of the crowd. An old Audi saloon arrived and four more militants got out to bolster their number on the street.

Great, Snow thought, *the odds are getting tougher.* He hung back and waited. And then it happened . . . his chance. The Dutchman and three of his men were led into the building followed by two of the militants, while the new arrivals pushed back the onlookers. Snow watched and waited for the remaining OSCE monitors to start making notes before he slipped on the tabard and marched confidently towards the door.

Inside was a reception desk. A few motor-part supplier posters still hung on the walls above it, as well as an out-of-date Pirelli Calendar displaying a woman half wearing a red bikini. The militant sitting at the desk looked up, his brow furrowed. Snow spoke in English, 'Err . . . which way did they go?'

The militant lifted his right hand and pointed to his left. 'Office.'

'Thank you.' Snow hurried past the desk. The corridor turned to reveal a flight of stairs on the right and three doors. The door at the far end of the corridor was ajar and Snow could hear the Dutchman. Snow had three choices – one of the two remaining closed doors, or the stairs. He took the stairs up, walking lightly on his toes. The next floor was divided into two rooms, both empty save for discarded papers littering the carpet. He went up again and this time the floor was open plan and completely empty. He took a breath and ascended once more. As he crested the top of the last stair, he heard someone speak. He continued to walk, fingers mentally crossed that whoever was up there respected the OSCE vest enough not to shoot him. The room was a copy of the floor below except this one had empty shell casings spread across the carpet and a discarded RPG launch tube. If he were a real OSCE monitor, Snow would have started to take notes, but he was more preoccupied by the militant in a black T-shirt and camouflage pants leaning out of the window talking on a mobile phone.

As Snow's foot hit the top step, the militant turned; perhaps it was Snow's reflection in the glass that gave him away or the sound of his boot disturbing a spent shell casing – whatever alerted him also made him reach for his Kalashnikov, which had been left leaning against the wall. Snow may have been wearing an

OSCE tabard, but he wasn't going to let a spooked militant, hyped up from battle, aim a Kalashnikov at him. Snow burst forward, sprinting four steps before lunging. The startled militant dropped his phone as he tried to reach the rifle. Snow's right fist hit the man's nose, flattening the cartilage, while his left pulled the rifle out of his reach. Stunned, the militant grabbed his face with both hands. Snow now reversed the AK and brought the heavy, wooden stock down on the side of the man's head. The militant's eyes rolled back and he hit the carpeted floor with a subdued thud.

Snow rested against the window frame, caught his breath, and aimed the Kalashnikov at the entrance to the room. He waited a minute in silence; nothing indicated that the struggle had been overheard. Then the sound of a heavy diesel engine drifted up from the road. An unnerving thought appeared in his head. Snow looked out and his fears were confirmed. A green Kamaz truck was approaching, its rear cargo area open to expose two lines of little green men – Russian soldiers sitting on bench seats.

Snow ducked out of sight, surveyed the room again and saw nothing useful. He'd searched three floors and not found Iqbal. There was only one way to go. Regretfully, Snow discarded the AK and checked his Glock before thrusting it back in its pancake holster and walking gently down the stairs.

*

The last rays of the setting sun sparkled on the water below as they walked across the suspension bridge. The warmth of the day would soon be replaced by the chill of a Parisian night in late September. Most other day trippers had departed the park, leaving Racine and Baptiste to stroll in secluded silence. They reached the middle of the bridge and Racine spoke, breaking the stillness. 'We have to end this.'

Baptiste seemed confused. 'End this?'

'Us, we, this thing we have together. It's not right.'

Baptiste stopped walking, turned and stared at her. 'This is right. It feels right – you and me, here, now, just walking, like a normal couple.'

'But we're not a normal couple, Baptiste! We're a pair of DGSE officers, and you're my boss. We can't have this type of relationship. We cannot be with each other.'

'I can't help what my heart wants.'

'I can.'

'Racine, I love you, I always have. This is right, here, and now – just you and me. This is right.'

'But it's not just you and me. Don't you understand? The world outside the gates of this park won't accept it.'

'Do you love me?'

Racine didn't reply.

'Do you love me?'

Racine shook her head. 'No.'

Baptiste took a step back as though he'd been punched in the gut.

Racine continued. 'We need to go. Drop me off at a metro station.'

Baptiste swayed, as though he was falling, and grabbed the railing for support. 'Is there someone else? Is that it?'

'No.' Racine felt her heart harden.

'It's Noah, isn't it? I've seen the way you look at each other.'

'There is no one else. I can't love anyone.'

Baptiste stabbed his right index finger into his chest. 'But I love you.'

'I can't love anyone,' Racine repeated.

Baptiste came nearer. She felt his hands on her shoulders and then he raised them to her face and held her cheeks, but the hands were rough, clumsy. Then he squeezed and she tried to pull them away, but she couldn't move . . .

*

Racine's eyes opened lazily. They were unfocused but as her vision sharpened, she realised she was staring into Vadim's large, flat

142

face. He was crouching in front of her and his rough right hand was holding her cheek, whilst his left was inside her bra. He was grinning. Racine tried to move but found she was pinned – her back against a wall and her legs folded sideways beneath her.

'It is true, you are not Olena Gaeva. Your breasts are much larger, and firmer. I will very much enjoy screwing you, after Boroda has finished with his questions.' Both his hands now focused on her breasts.

Racine's arms were bound behind her back, her ankles were hobbled, and heavy tape glued her mouth shut. She had only one option, and it wouldn't be pleasant. Eyes wild with anger, she used her considerable core strength and jerked forward. Her forehead slammed against Vadim's nose. There was an audible crack. Sparks flared before her eyes, but Vadim was more hurt than she was. He let go of her breasts and fell backwards, blood pouring from his nose.

'Blat! Suka!'

Vadim felt his face. His eyes became wide at the sight of his hands, painted red with his own blood. He staggered to his feet, then he came at her. Breathing heavily through his open mouth, he grabbed her by the throat, raising her from the floor, attempting to choke the life out of her, but Racine jerked again – like a sit-up this time. She bent at the waist and pulled her arms forward under her backside whilst at the same time lifting her feet. Vadim's bloody hands lost their grip on Racine's neck and she dropped. Overbalancing, Vadim followed her. Falling forward, his head struck the wall behind her with a thud.

Hitting the floor, heavily, Racine grunted but managed to turn onto her side and complete her manoeuvre. Now her hands were in front of her, and she saw that they were held by nothing more than cable ties. Standing, she raised her arms above her head and then brought them down and out as fast as she could, towards her stomach as though trying to pull them through her body. There was a moment of pain as the plastic dug deeper into her wrists.

She swore under her breath, took a deep breath, and repeated the process. This time the ties gave up; they snapped and her wrists hit her stomach. She now tore the tape from her mouth and took several, hungry gulps of air. Vadim was still resting against the wall, like a dazed beast, his forehead and knees taking his weight. Racine desperately hopped to the other side of the room before she dropped to the floor once more, and frantically freed her feet. She heard Vadim start to move, and then realised that the door, her only way out of the room, was directly behind him.

Vadim slipped down onto his hands and knees, the rough unpainted bricks grazing his forehead as he did so. He shook his head and faced her, growling as blood dripped from his head and his shattered nose. He rose to his haunches, his face a monstrous mask. He slipped his left hand into his pocket and produced an object. It was a dark leather case – a sheath. From this he drew a knife. Racine noted the blade was matte black. 'I'm not waiting for Boroda. I'm going to kill you now.'

Racine inhaled deeply. Someone was going to die for sure, and it wasn't going to be her. Not today, not ever. She relaxed her body and took a mental inventory. Her forehead throbbed like hell, there was a dull ache in her throat, she felt woozy and her back was sore, but apart from that she was uninjured, and extremely angry.

Vadim slowly rose to his feet. He was a huge man in both height and physique, immensely strong and by the look in his eye, unaccustomed to losing. He was in essence a bully, but a military-trained one. And Racine knew exactly how to beat a bully.

He slowly backed away and turned the key in the door to lock it. He advanced, his massive meaty hands up. The fingers of his left hand were splayed whilst his right jabbed and slashed at the air in front of him with the knife, using his reach to force Racine into the corner. He crossed the small room in three strides. On the third step he planted his entire weight on his left knee and drew back his right arm. He was faster than she expected. He swung his knife hand at Racine's neck, the kind of blow that would slit her throat and kill if it connected. She ducked and shot out her booted foot at his left leg. It missed his knee and connected harmlessly with his thigh, eliciting nothing more than a grunt. The back of his hand now swiped at her, striking her shoulder like a hammer, batting her away.

Racine stumbled and Vadim's own, long leg lashed out. The kick connected with her solar plexus, jerked her up and off her feet as though she had been electrocuted. She crashed to the floor, winded. He fell upon her, pinning her legs, huge fist poised to pummel her face. Using every ounce of strength left in her core, Racine sat up, and suicidally ignoring the blade brought her head forward. Vadim had read the move – another headbutt – and raised his huge fists in front of his face to grab, and to stab her . . . but then Racine used her arms instead. She slammed both hands, open-palmed, against his ears in a bat-strike. Vadim's eyes went wide as he felt the disorientating pressure on his eardrums. He shuffled back, unsure if he was injured or not, swishing his knife wildly as he retreated. Racine used the time to get to her feet. She took a long, deep breath and felt the muscular pain as the air filled her bruised chest.

Vadim rolled his head and shoulders and squared off against her, knife in hand, face a bloody mess and eyes overflowing with hatred. He charged, seemingly losing control. This time it took just two long, powerful strides, to bring him within striking range. Again, he planted his entire weight on his left knee and drew back his right arm for the killing blow. This time, however, Racine did not miss. She delivered a kick to the side of his left knee. There was a satisfying click. Vadim's right leg was already moving forward and the torque on his left knee made it collapse. Following the trajectory of his fast-swinging right fist, Vadim lost his balance and fell, turning in the air and landing flat on his back. The wind shot out of his lungs, his fists slammed into the floor and the knife flew from his hand. His legs were still aloft, and he presented an open target. Racine darted around and kicked him hard in the groin. He automatically raised his head and torso to fold up into the pain, making his head an easy target. Racine kicked it.

Vadim went limp. Racine caught her breath and looked down at the bastard. He deserved to be dead and she didn't care if he was. There was a banging on the door, but she ignored it as she kicked him again, and again.

*

Back on the ground floor, Snow saw the office door was cracked open; the Dutchman was still in full flow, insisting he had the authority of all signatory member countries of the OSCE – including Russia – to investigate and report on the situation. Snow looked at the door on his right and noted that it had the kind of lock used on store cupboards. He sniffed at the doorjamb and smelled a pungent cocktail of cleaning products. Stifling a cough, he backed away and stood by the last closed door. Snow took a deep breath, fixed a quizzical expression on his face and entered the room.

Snow squinted, his eyes dazzled by the lighting in the room. In the very centre a vivid pool of white bathed a table and four chairs. One man sat at the table, facing away from him. He had shoulder-length hair tied back in a ponytail and was fiddling with a video camera. He was not Mohammed Iqbal. Past the table, in the gloom, Snow made out a second man. He had a thick beard and wore a uniform. He was banging on the door in a part of the room that had been bricked off. The bearded man was the first to see Snow. He stepped away from the door.

'This is not your business. You must go now,' he ordered in Russian.

Snow feigned incomprehension and spoke in English. 'Ah. Hello, I'm from the OSCE.'

The uniformed man frowned and when he spoke again had switched to English. 'You are OSCE?'

'Yes.' Snow picked a random name from his past, 'Piers Samson, OSCE monitor. And you are?'

'You can call me Boroda, and I am escorting you out of this building.' Boroda kept eye contact with Snow as he moved to block his view and attempt to usher him back out of the room.

'Hang on,' a voice exclaimed. 'We've met before!'

Snow switched his gaze; the other man at the table had turned his head. The ponytail belonged to Darren Weller. 'I think you're mistaken.'

Weller was now on his feet and pointing. 'Oh, no, no you don't. I know this man! His name is Aidan – Aidan Snow! He is not an OSCE monitor!'

'Whoa!' Snow held up his palms. 'My name is Piers Samson and I'm with the—' Snow shot his right palm out and hit Boroda on the jaw. The Russian stumbled. Snow stepped forward and delivered a quick elbow strike to the side of Boroda's head. The Russian fell and his sidearm came loose from its open holster and skittered away. Boroda, eyes wide, made a grab for it but Snow stamped down on his wrist and he grunted in pain. Snow drew his Glock and aimed it at Boroda's face. 'Where is Mohammed Iqbal?'

Boroda said nothing.

'Bloody hell, Aidan!' Weller blurted out.

Snow glared at the other Englishman. 'You couldn't keep quiet, could you?'

*

Racine stepped away from Vadim and put her hands on her thighs to regain her breath. A lethal cocktail of blind fury and training had served her, but she still had to serve her country, and in order to do this she had to locate and liquidate Sasha Vasilev. However, first she had to escape. She searched Vadim's

147

pockets and found a roll of American dollars. Stuffing them in her jacket, she retrieved the knife and its sheath from where it had come to rest. It was a completely different weapon from the one she'd taken from the militant in her hotel room, which was now in her bag in Darren's car. She briefly inspected the matte black knife. There was a serial number on the spine and in Cyrillic on the blade near the handle there was a stylised 'K' and the brand name 'Korshun'. It was Spetsnaz-issue. Racine shuddered. She concealed them in her jacket pocket.

Words penetrated from the other side of the door – she heard someone speaking English. A voice she hadn't heard before, a native speaker. Racine moved nearer to the door and, though muffled, heard the words 'OSCE Monitor'. If there was a monitor from the OSCE in the next room she could simply step out through the door and leave with them, demanding safe passage. But she needed to search the place for her target. Her mission was falling apart. Racine pulled the key carefully from the lock. The mechanism was new, oiled, and it slid out soundlessly. She peered through the hole. She could make out little except the edge of a circle of light and what could potentially be the leg of one of the floodlights set up for Darren's interview. So, was she really next door to the interview room? She had to use the door regardless. She reinserted the key and slowly turned the lock. It opened with the smallest of clicks, the sound dulled by the oil. She waited and listened for any reaction. On the other side the conversation continued, and the voices now seemed raised. Racine took a large breath let it out and then, as relaxed as she could be, slipped back into the room.

The man who had been talking had his back to her. He was wearing an OSCE tabard and was speaking in English, but he had a handgun pointed at Boroda, who lay on the floor. So if he wasn't a monitor who or what was he? And why was he using English to address Boroda? Past these two Weller still sat in the chair she had last seen him in. She couldn't see his face but the way he sat so rigidly upright implied that he was scared. There was no sign of Strelkov or any of his other men.

Racine's options were extremely limited. Either she announced her presence or she didn't, and either the 'monitor' shot her or he didn't. She couldn't appear as a threat, so what – would she play the defenceless woman held captive? The fact that Weller was unharmed gave her hope that perhaps this was someone who would let her, a non-combatant, pass. All these thoughts spun through her mind in milliseconds, whilst in front of her the conversation continued.

'I'm going to ask you again, where is Mohammed Iqbal?' the monitor demanded.

Boroda didn't reply, so the monitor kicked him. 'He was moved last night to the second facility.'

The monitor looked up at Weller. 'You know about this?'

Weller held up his palms. 'Hey, this is nothing to do with me!'

'*Like hell it isn't,*' Racine wanted to shout but instead, in her accent-less English, not the English of Olena Gaeva, but still sounding rather pathetic, she said, 'Help me! Please, I've been kidnapped!' She stepped out of the shadows with her hands held up showing empty palms. 'You're with the OSCE – please get me out of here!'

The Glock swung from Boroda to Racine and the monitor turned and took a step away to enable him to cover them both. He frowned. 'You're with Darren?'

'She most certainly is not!' Weller said, emphatically. 'She's a spy, an enemy!'

The man cocked his head to one side. 'Any enemy of Darren's is a friend of mine.'

'Yeah, she is an enemy!' Weller spat. 'She's not who she says she is, and neither are you, Aidan Snow!'

'And you pretend to be a journalist, Darren.' The man Weller had called Aidan Snow asked, 'What's your name?'

'Claire, Claire Kenmuir.' As she was speaking in English there was no point in using a fake Slavic name.

Snow frowned. 'My grandmother's name was Claire, but she had a *French* surname – Flagel.'

Racine tried not to react. Did Snow know who she was?

'Now that we are all having a civilised chat, may I at least sit in a chair?' Boroda asked, from the floor.

'Go ahead,' Snow said. 'But kick your pistol away.'

Boroda got to his feet and then made a show of booting his Makarov. It skated over the worn concrete, finishing up nearer to Racine than Snow. There was a moment of tension, of danger, as both of them eyed it and then eyed each other.

Racine spoke first. 'Are you alone?'

'Yes,' Snow said. 'Are you?'

'Yes.'

'How did you appear in Donetsk?'

'She came in with me, in a legitimate aid convoy! She pretended to be a Russian journalist. And then she broke my camera!' Weller's outrage at being duped had overcome his fear of being shot.

Snow kept his eyes on Racine. 'I don't think you need rescuing.'

Racine lowered her arms. 'It looks like you might.'

A narrow smile appeared on Snow's face. He kept his Glock pointed at her. Racine could see the cogs turning. 'Can I trust you?'

'Why? Do you have issues?' Racine returned the smile. Mirroring body language and facial expressions often helped when talking to men, she found.

'No, you bloody can't trust her!' Weller snapped, with petulance. 'And I bet she's not really called Claire either!'

'Darren, shut up,' Racine ordered.

She looked back to Snow. 'You can shoot him, if you like?'

'I'm tempted.' Snow's Glock pointed at Weller, who cowered, before it returned to Boroda. 'Where is the second facility?'

'Why should I tell you?'

'Because you enjoy having two working kneecaps.'

Boroda's eyes fluttered before he sighed and rattled off an address.

Snow asked Racine, 'Is that a real place?'

Racine rubbed her wrists. 'How would I know?'

There were noises outside the interior door – shouted commands and the sound of feet scuffling the concrete.

'Time to bug out,' Snow said.

'We can't use that door,' Racine replied.

'We?'

'I'm not staying here.'

'I see.'

'We'll go out the back. That's where Darren's parked his car,' she continued.

'I am afraid you will find the back door is padlocked,' Boroda stated. 'My men are coming for you. Better you drop your weapon now, Aidan Snow, and I'll make sure they are lenient with you both.'

'Lucky for us you dropped the key.' Racine kept her eyes fixed on Snow as she slowly moved towards the Makarov and collected it from the floor. 'I'll shoot out the lock.'

'OK,' Snow replied, looking tense.

Racine strode towards the door fitted to the left of the large, up-and-over garage doors. 'You keep watch on the other door whilst I shoot.'

'If you put a round in my back, I won't be happy,' Snow said.

Racine ignored him. 'As soon as I pull this trigger there's going to be a lot of angry, armed men rushing in here. And then what? Have you got a plan, or are you really on your own?'

'It's just me.' Snow now addressed the bearded man. 'You and Darren are going to be our shield. You'll walk in front of us, and if anyone asks, I *am* with the OSCE and you have handed your prisoner over to me. Understood?'

Boroda scoffed. 'I understand.'

Snow moved into position but kept a wary eye on Racine.

She held the Makarov in a two-handed grip, stood at an obtuse angle to the door, took a quick aim and fired. The retort was deafening in the unfurnished room, bouncing off the concrete floor and reverberating against the steel roll-up door. She took a step forward and kicked open the door, letting her momentum carry her out of the building and onto the street. She carved arcs left and right with the Makarov. 'Move!'

Boroda was next out, followed closely by Weller. Shouts now sounded from behind. The inner door flew open, and Boroda's men poured into the room to investigate the noise, AKs up and ready.

Boroda shoulder-barged Racine, knocking her to the ground, and shouted in Russian, 'Stop them!'

Racine hit hard, her whole body jarring and the Makarov coming loose. Boroda grabbed her lapels with his left hand and hit her across the face with the back of his right. Stars exploded before her eyes for the second time that afternoon and she tasted blood. A moment later Snow slammed the butt of his pistol into the side of Boroda's head. As the Russian relinquished his grip on Racine, wild rounds from the men inside zipped past her.

Weller was frozen, looking on at the trio. Snow grabbed him by the scruff of the neck. 'Where's your car?'

'It's the green one!' Racine answered before the panicking journalist could. 'You get him to the car; I'll slow them down!' Using the Makarov, Racine fired a pair of 9mm rounds back through the door, causing the militants to take cover.

Weller's car was the only green civilian vehicle in sight, and they reached it seconds later. 'Key!' Snow demanded.

Weller fumbled in his pocket and, hand shaking, gave Snow a key ring. On it was a picture of the flamboyant Russian pop star Philipp Kirkorov. Snow blipped the central locking system and got into the driver's seat. He placed the Glock under his left thigh.

In a few quick strides, Racine reached the car. She opened the rear door. Weller made no attempt to get in. 'Get in or get shot!' Weller didn't move. Racine swung a fist, which connected with Weller's stomach, doubling him up. She kicked him inside the MG before taking the front passenger seat next to Snow.

The DNR militants had now realised fully what was happening and their aim had become more accurate. Rounds hit the tarmac inches to the side of the car. By the time they'd readjusted, the MG was squealing out of the parking space.

'Take a left here!' Racine instructed.

'You said you weren't a local?'

'I've probably got a better sense of direction than you.'

Snow turned the wheel hard. The MG leant to one side, but it made the corner. He floored the accelerator and the sports saloon powered away from the garage as the OSCE men and Russian troops at the front of the building looked on, bewildered. However, neither the troops nor the DNR made any attempt to follow them.

'Bloody hell! Bloody hell!' Weller was shaking hard. 'What have you done? What have you done?'

Racine looked back at the journalist via the rear-view mirror.

'You've made everyone think I'm a spy. My career is over!'

Racine sighed. 'What a shame.'

'Quel dommage,' Snow said, repeating the same phrase, but in French.

Racine cast him a side glance. He definitely knew who she was.

Snow continued, addressing Weller. 'I've just rescued you from a DNR interrogation centre, you ungrateful git!'

'And what are you, the sodding SAS or something? And as for you!' Weller aimed his words at Racine. 'You . . . you hit me!'

'How are your "abs of steel"?'

'Up yours!'

Snow let out a chuckle. 'Did he give you his "abs of steel" routine too?'

'Yep.'

'I worked hard for these,' Weller said, indignantly.

They lapsed into silence as the car continued up the road.

Racine's head throbbed from the headbutts and Boroda's slap. She felt woozy, but she had no time to rest. She knew her limit and she hadn't reached it yet. Her identity as Olena Gaeva had been compromised, but there was no proof that her mission had. If she was lucky her target would be blissfully unaware that he was on her hit list. Her mission had undoubtedly just become a lot harder yet was still a go.

But who exactly was Snow, the man who was now driving them away from a firefight? More importantly why was he in militant-controlled Donetsk? The obvious answer was that he was there for Iqbal. His Home Counties accent confirmed he was British, so that would make sense. Had Jacob briefed his opposite number at SIS about her and the mission? Impossible. Finding and eliminating Vasilev had been Jacob's raison d'être for the entire time she had known him, and it had been hers also. So what then? Was there a leak or worse another mole? Snow didn't seem stupid, and from what Darren had said about her and the fact that he was insinuating she was French, meant he probably guessed she was there for Vasilev. Staring forward out of the grubby windscreen she realised she could change none of this and it didn't matter just as long as Snow didn't get in her way; and if he did the Makarov in her lap remained pointed at him.

'I know who you are,' Snow said. 'There have been whispers.'

'It's rude to whisper.'

'Why were you there?'

Racine now saw no sense in not telling him. 'I was looking for someone. He was meant to be at the garage with Mohammed Iqbal.'

'You know about Iqbal?'

'I saw a photograph of Iqbal with "the someone" I was looking for.'

'Who is your target?' Snow used the word pointedly.

Even though Weller was listening she decided to take the gamble and tell the Englishman. He might perhaps have more intel on his whereabouts. 'Sasha Vasilev.'

Snow said, 'I see.'

Racine said, 'Look, we need to talk but . . .'

'*Pas devant l'enfant.*'

Racine involuntarily cast Snow a look. He needed to stop being so damn obvious. 'Yes.'

'Hey, I did French at school too! You both need to stop the car and get out.' Weller's voice had broken, exactly like an upset child's. 'I don't care where you go. Just leave and I won't say another word, I promise.'

'I was going to drive you all the way back to Kyiv and turn you over to the SBU!' Snow retorted.

'What? No . . . no, please, they'll lock me up!'

'Exactly. You're banned from Ukraine and wanted for aiding and abetting terrorists, yet here you are in Donetsk!'

'This is the Donetsk People's Republic!' Weller protested. 'It's a sovereign state!'

'It's cloud cuckoo land, and you are one of the biggest cuckoos in it!'

Racine saw a DNR checkpoint ahead in the distance. 'Pull over.'

Snow drew the car over to the kerb. 'I don't think there's a way around it. Any ideas?'

'Darren can get us through,' Racine said. 'He did it this morning. Remember, he's loved by the terrorists!'

'They are not terrorists!' Weller crossed his arms. 'And, I refuse!'

Racine turned in her seat and pushed the Makarov deep into Weller's chest. 'You either get us through that checkpoint, or this goes through you. Got it?'

'OK.' Weller's face turned ashen.

'We'll switch places.' Racine climbed into the back seat. She noticed Snow pretending not to look at her backside. 'Get in the front, Darren.'

Weller obediently dipped his head, opened the door, and then swung back in through the front passenger door.

Racine whispered in Snow's ear. 'Now I have a gun pointed at your spine. It's your turn to tell me who you are, Aidan Snow.'

Snow locked eyes with her in the rear-view mirror. 'SIS.'

'I knew it!' Weller said.

'You know everything, Darren,' Racine said. 'Who is your controller?'

Snow paused and in the mirror his eyes darted right, towards Weller.

'Who is your controller?'

'His initials are JP,' Snow said, not wanting to give up the name in front of the ON journalist.

Racine searched her memory. She knew Jacob had links with all the western intelligence agencies. JP in that case would be Jack Patchem, head of the Russian Desk. She lowered her Makarov. 'I think, Snow, you'd better take off the OSCE vest now.'

'I'd forgotten I was wearing it.' Snow wriggled out of the tabard and stuffed it into the door pocket. 'Look, I need to find Iqbal and you need the person interrogating him.'

'So, stop wasting our time and start driving.'

Snow said nothing. He checked the mirror and moved back into the thin flow of traffic before coming to a halt at the end of the queue behind an ancient Ford Sierra.

'Go past them.' Weller was unable to contain his pride. 'I always do. Put the flashers on; they'll see it's me.'

'Will they?'

'They did this morning,' Racine confirmed.

Snow pulled out wide into the central reservation where the grit tugged at the MG's tyres. Racine held the Makarov low and out of sight and placed her mouth by Weller's greasy ear. 'If this doesn't work, you'll be the first to die.'

Weller let out a low moan and his entire torso became rigid, as though he were about to ride a roller coaster. As the car drew level with the front of the line, an overweight man in a brown Saab started to shout at them. A militant bent down and gazed into the car.

'Press,' Weller said, tightly.

The militant studied each of them in turn, grunted, and stepped back. Snow accelerated away gently.

'Do you know where you are going?' Racine asked.

'No. Do you?'

'Only generally.'

Snow shook his head. 'We should have brought Boroda.'

Racine put her hand on Weller's shoulder. 'I bet you know, don't you, Darren? You know where all these places are.'

Weller remained silent and stared out of the window.

'Is that true, Daz? You know where the other site is?'

'Why should I tell you? You're both instruments for the Kyiv Nazi junta!'

Snow started to laugh. 'Do you really believe the crap you peddle? After all you've seen?'

'You don't know what I've seen!'

'That's true, but I know what you've filmed. Look, you weren't the only failed journalist hanging around Kyiv. I never liked you as an ex-pat. I tolerated you – we all did. This is different . . . this is deadly serious. I've been sent by the same people who issued you with your passport to rescue a fellow British citizen, an innocent man who is being held and tortured because of the colour of his skin. So who are the real Nazis here? If you have any humanity left in your greasy little head, you are going to tell me exactly where this place is.'

'And if that fails—' Racine nudged him with her Makarov '—I'm going to shoot you in odd places until you do tell us.'

'Yes.' Weller exhaled sharply. 'I know where it is! Keep going the direction you are until we leave the city centre. It's in a village a few miles further on, towards the Ukrainian lines.'

'Directly in the line of Ukrainian fire,' Snow stated.

'Yes. What else did you expect from terrorists?' Weller said sarcastically.

FOURTEEN

Kalinins'kyi District, Donetsk

Strelkov took the call in his G Wagon; the further he'd moved away from the attack site, the stronger his cell signal had become. He was incredulous as he processed the news from the local commander who had called in from the Ramada Hotel. 'Are you telling me that she shot two of your men last night and you have only just now realised it?'

'Yes, Igor Ivanovich.' The militant's voice was unsteady as he addressed the de facto head of the military forces of the Donetsk People's Republic.

Strelkov could still not believe what he was hearing. 'She killed two of your men, dragged the bodies into another room, and went back to sleep afterwards?'

'It would appear so.'

'What business did your two men have with Ms Gaeva?'

There was a pause on the line. 'They . . . err . . . wanted to check her papers.'

'In her room, in the middle of the night?'

'Yes, Igor Ivanovich.'

'Let me remind you that this is one of the few functioning hotels in this city of any real worth. We cannot, and must not, have any of the guests intimidated. Your men may have been the dregs of society before we took power, but there is no room whatsoever for crooks and rapists now! Do I make myself clear?'

'Yes, Igor Ivanovich.'

'I'm glad she shot them; if they had lived, I would have ordered their cocks chopped off.' The woman posing as Olena Gaeva was more important, and dangerous, than even he had thought. By now he had no doubt she was a trained intelligence operative. But had she been sent for him or Vasilev? He'd inform the interrogator of his suspicions. Either way he had to find out who she was working for and what her mission was. Strelkov ended the call and immediately tapped in Boroda's number. The phone rang to voicemail. Puzzled, Strelkov called again.

'Igor Ivanovich—' Boroda sounded out of breath '—the woman and Weller have been taken from us.'

Strelkov's left hand balled into a fist, his knuckles turning white. 'Explain.'

The G Wagon carried on through the city streets as Boroda gave a quick situation report. 'Are you telling me that the British were attempting to rescue Iqbal?'

'Yes, the man was definitely British. Weller knew him.'

'Weller was involved?'

'He has to have been. First he brought in that woman, and he personally knew the British agent who rescued him. It is too much of a coincidence.'

'I agree. I do not believe in coincidence. And you gave him the location of the second facility?'

'Yes, because that would bring him directly to you, sir. They will all be walking into a trap.'

A sneer spread across Strelkov's lips. Finally, someone was thinking like a real member of the GRU. 'You have done well, Boroda. It is your men who have failed.'

'No, it is I who must shoulder the blame.'

'Meet me at the town hall. We shall go to the second site together.'

Strelkov ended the call. This was an interesting if very unexpected turn of events and something that he could use to his advantage. He reached into his large jacket pocket and retrieved the Glock 26 he had taken from the woman. He examined the custom-made suppressor. Whoever she was he approved of her taste in weapons.

Petrovsky District, Donetsk

The traffic lessened and the buildings became more bomb-damaged the farther away they travelled from the city centre and the closer they drew to their new target address. Their unusual car, the UK-registered British racing green MG ZT, acted as a beacon announcing their presence to the DNR. Racine looked to her right; they were nearing a residential apartment block. The ground floor, as was the case with many of these buildings, housed several shops. Partly obscured by trees, a row of cars were parked in front of the structures. It was the best place she had seen yet to ditch the MG and grab a new ride. As if reading her mind, Snow slowed the sports saloon and turned off the main drag. He made eye contact with Racine; she nodded.

'What are you doing?' Weller asked.

Neither operative replied.

'This is not the address!'

Racine noted that one of the stores was a beauty salon. 'True, but I'm pretty sure they'd be happy to give you a wash and blow dry or redo your nails.'

'So that's it, is it? I've become a figure of fun?'

'It's not a recent thing,' Snow added.

Snow took a parking space on the very end of the row under the protective branches of a large evergreen tree. Racine exited the MG and assessed the selection of cars. A plan had formed in her head, and the only vehicle that would make that plan work was of course the only vehicle that had someone sitting inside it.

'Stay here with him.'

Without waiting for a reply, Racine moved to the back of the MG, opened the boot, and unzipped her bag. She retrieved her Ukrainian passport and a beanie hat then shut the boot. Casually turning, she painfully put on the hat to cover her swollen forehead then sauntered across the empty spaces towards the silver Mitsubishi Shogun and gently tapped on the window. The man behind the wheel jerked awake and wound down the window. Racine stuffed the Makarov in his face. 'I need your car.'

The man didn't react. Racine swung the door open. The man remained immobile.

'Give me your car. Now.' Racine punched the man in the throat with her left hand. His eyes bulged and he brought his hands up to his neck. Racine took hold of his jacket and heaved him out of his seat. The man stumbled to the pavement, making a gurgling sound. Racine climbed into the Shogun as he collapsed onto his hands and knees. 'Stay down, or I'll shoot you too.'

She shut the door, started the 4X4 and reversed out into the access road before swinging around the corner and parking just out of sight at the side of the building on the grass. She jogged the ten steps back to the MG.

'Get out,' she ordered Weller.

Weller climbed out, hands on his head like an Edvard Munch painting and moaned. 'What have you done?'

'Nothing she's not done before,' Snow said, shutting his door.

'Now explain to me exactly where this place is, or I'll do the same to you,' Racine stated.

Weller stuttered with fear, 'I . . . I don't know exactly.'

'What?'

'I don't know!' Weller screwed up his face. 'I lied! You scared me! You're a homicidal maniac!'

'*Merde!* We don't have time for this.' Racine took a step forward and punched Weller in the stomach. His gut felt surprisingly solid, the act of punching him surprisingly satisfying.

'Where are they holding Mohammed Iqbal?' Snow said.

'It's a village a couple of miles down that road . . .' Weller gasped. 'Please! That's all I know.'

Racine was an assassin but not a cold-blooded killer. She had principles, and Weller, although an annoying imbecile, was a non-combatant. 'Get out of here, Darren.'

Through the pain there was relief on Weller's face. 'What?'

'She told you to sod off,' Snow stated.

'If I hear any reports about today's events that mention him or me, I'll find you. Understand?'

'Yes.'

Snow leant into the MG and retrieved his OSCE tabard before locking Weller's car and taking his keys. 'Darren, you need to get out of Donetsk, before you get yourself killed.'

Racine climbed back into the 4X4 and started the engine. Once Snow had got into the passenger seat, she rejoined the main road. In the mirror she saw Weller leaning forward vomiting into the gutter. 'We shouldn't have let him go; he's a lose end.'

'He's a bell end,' Snow replied.

Racine let her mouth form a smile.

'You've got blood on your face,' Snow stated.

'Thanks.' Racine pulled down the sun visor, removed her hat and checked her face in the mirror. She spat on her hand and wiped Vadim's blood from her cheek. She then prodded her forehead. It was raised and it hurt but it was not yet too discoloured.

'What happened?'

'A large Russian decided to attack my head with his nose, twice.'

'That was unwise.'

'It was.' Now that Weller was not around, Racine had a question she wanted to ask the Englishman; she needed to know if there was a security leak. 'You said earlier you knew who I was, so who am I?'

'I think you are a DGSE agent with the codename "Racine", and you report to "Maurice Jacob".

Racine decided to deflect and answer his question with one of her own. 'And who are you?'

'You know my name is Aidan Snow, and I work for the SIS. I've been briefed about possible foreign assets operating in the area.'

'How did SIS learn about my mission?'

'We knew sooner or later the French would want to get their hands on Sasha Vasilev. We were correct; he is, after all, at the top of your most wanted list. I honestly don't know how we learnt about your specific unit, which officially doesn't exist.'

Racine frowned, the existence of *The Department* was highly classified, supposedly a state secret. 'I work alone.'

'So do I.'

'Don't get in my way.'

Snow laughed. 'Am I that clumsy?'

Racine cast him a side glance. No, she thought he was anything but clumsy. However he was extremely tall and now that she thought about it bore a passing resemblance to Gerard Butler. Fanciable, if that was your type, she imagined, but definitely memorable. She didn't know why but she wanted to talk. 'You met Weller in Kyiv?'

'I did,' Snow said. 'I was there to teach English.'

'That was your cover for SIS?'

'No, it was my job.'

'You were a teacher? So, what were you before that? Military obviously. I'm guessing SAS?'

'What is this, twenty questions?'

Racine didn't reply.

'What about you?'

'What about me?' Racine said as she slowed to negotiate a pothole.

'How long have you been with the DGSE?'

'Who says I am?'

Snow frowned. 'I see. I open up to you and you, what, you refuse to do the same?'

'Why would I?'

'Oh, I don't know, to gain my trust, to bond with me?'

Racine frowned. 'This isn't speed dating.'

Snow chuckled. 'Ever tried it?'

'It's too slow. Isn't Aidan an Irish name?'

'It is.'

'So?'

'So what?'

'So why does an English spy have an Irish name?'

'Why does a French spy have the codename of a seventeenth-century playwright?'

'Racine is my surname.' She glanced at Snow. 'Happy?'

'Ecstatic.'

'I'm not telling you my first name.' Racine was angry with herself for giving too much away, but Snow was right; if they were to reach both of their mission objectives, and at the moment it looked as if their targets were together, they did indeed need to trust each other.

'My name is the result of my dad's sense of humour. I was conceived at The British Embassy in "Aden",' Snow said.

Racine looked at him but made no reply.

Snow probed again. 'Your Home Counties accent is faultless.'

'It should be. My father paid a lot of money for me to finish school there.'

'That's odd for a Frenchman, to send his daughter to England.'

'We're an odd family.'

'Odd is good.'

There was a brief silence before Snow spoke again. His tone had changed and he said, as way of a statement rather than a question, 'France has sanctioned you to assassinate Vasilev.'

'I'm not here to collect a fine on his library books.' She looked at him. 'Does that offend your British sensibilities, your sense of fair play?'

'No. I know what he did to your agency. I understand that bringing him back to stand trial is not an option.'

'My turn. Why are the British so eager to rescue Iqbal? Who is he?'

'He's a British student who found himself in the wrong place at the wrong time.'

'Is there ever a right time?' Racine had had enough chat. 'So, what's your plan?'

'My plan was for The Shadows to hit that garage tonight so I could go in with them and get Iqbal.'

Racine frowned. 'They're the ones who attacked the garage? They did it for you?'

'Yes and yes.'

'So why did they attack in daylight?'

'I don't know but look on the bright side – it saved you.'

'Hm. When we get to this new place, do you have a plan in mind?'

'They know we're on our way – why else would that Russian give up the address so easily?'

'Perhaps he gave us the wrong address completely?'

'I don't think so.'

'No, neither do I,' Racine agreed. Weller had seemed to know of the place and was too scared to lie about it. 'We need a new plan.'

FIFTEEN

Thirteen Years Ago

Nice, France

It was the end of the summer term, the end of the school year and the end of her time at that school. And Sophie was relieved that her troubles were all behind her. Her father had used his full persuasive powers to stop the police from pressing charges against his daughter. He had asked them what would have happened to her if she had not defended herself? Why had the gendarme roughly grabbed her and not identified himself first? Her mother, however, had not been swayed. She had become ashen at the news of the fight, as she called it. Drawing on a wave of pent-up emotion she had screamed and shouted at her husband, demanding what kind of a man turns his daughter into a hooligan? What type of a man corrupts an innocent girl? What kind of a man is happy that his sweet little girl has been taught to attack the police? So, it went on with her mother screaming herself hoarse and her father silently accepting what he had done.

It had been a traumatic time because after this event came the worst news of all. Celine had died, and Sophie had found herself looking at a headstone with the name Celine Durand carved into it and an inscription. She tried to read it but the tears in her eyes prevented her from doing so. Her father was by her side and her mother was in front of them stroking the top of the stone. She opened her mouth to speak to her mother, to try to comfort her, but the words would not come.

Sophie took a deep breath. That had been two months ago, and school was now over for the summer. Sophie knew that she could spend more time with her mother, to try to understand her and make her proud of her again. Sophie of course was still grieving for Celine, but she desperately missed her mother.

The school was a large, square steel and concrete 1970s building. In the local area it stuck out like a sore thumb, built to educate, not for any architectural merit. Sophie, however, was oblivious to all of this as she strode out of the main gates and saw her father waiting for her in his BMW.

He told her he'd finished work early for the day and wanted to take her out for a treat. They drove to the nearest McDonald's, much to her confusion and delight, him telling her that it was fine to eat what you wanted, once in a while. They took their food to go, he parked the car and they sat together on a bench overlooking the harbour. Sophie sensed something was wrong. Her father hadn't touched his cheeseburger. He sighed and said, 'Your mother has left us.'

'I'm sorry, Dad,' Sophie replied.

'It's not your fault.' He put his arm around her and squeezed.

'It is.'

'No, Sophie, your mother has been ill for a long time and I've been too busy and too angry to see it. She refused to talk to me about it, even when I found out she had been taking pills for depression. She was grieving, unhappy, but it wasn't your fault. It's a chemical imbalance. No one knows what causes it. Sometimes people just need to be alone, and sometimes people are just depressed and sometimes, however hard we try to love people, we are just not meant to be together.'

'Are you upset?' Sophie asked, looking at the boats bobbing below in the gentle swell.

'How could I ever be upset or sad, when I have the best girl in the world for a daughter?'

'I love you, Dad,' Sophie said, her eyes wet.

'I love you too, more than anything in the world.'

They sat in silence for a moment, watching the birds hover on the warm air currents and the boats bob on the sea below.

'I miss Celine." Sophie said.

"So do I, she was feral like you."

"I'm not wild!'

Her father chuckled, 'How would you like to go on holiday?'

'Yes! When?'

'Tomorrow?'

'Tomorrow?'

'Just the two of us. It'll be fun.'

'I'd love to! Where are we going?'

'Hm, what about London? You speak English, don't you?'

'You know I do.'

'Good that's settled then. We'll go to London and say hello to the Queen.'

SIXTEEN

Present Day

Near Oleksandrivka, Donetsk region
The G Wagon slowed to turn off the highway and onto the much smaller lane leading to the facility. At the security barrier, a bored militant ambled towards them. His de rigueur Kalashnikov was held in his left hand. He placed it on the ground as he manoeuvred the barrier up.

The Mercedes continued and negotiated the gravel road, which soon became a mud track leading into the middle of the six-house village that accommodated the interrogation facility. A white Kamaz truck, part of the last humanitarian convoy, stood to one side. As tall as the single-storey dachas, it looked like a gigantic beast in the small clearing. Boroda and Strelkov got out and made directly for the building that housed Vasilev's office. They found Sasha Vasilev sitting contentedly, smoking and reading papers.

Strelkov feared no man but Vasilev unnerved him; he got the feeling there was something sinister behind his eyes. He asked with forced authority, 'Where is Iqbal?'

'In his cell; unless he has escaped.' Vasilev stubbed out his cigarette on the edge of the battered desk and threw it on the floor. His jaw clenched. 'He's mine. Why do you want him?'

'The British have sent a team. It is inbound now.'

'The British?' Vasilev frowned. 'So they do want Iqbal? Are we not protected here? Politically they would not dare engage us. We are in DNR territory; that would be an act of war.'

'It is a small, deniable team.'

'How small.'

'We know of two operators.'

'Two?' Vasilev's face became a leer.

'One is a woman,' Boroda stated. 'She is not British.'

Vasilev's leer warped into a smile and he inclined his head. 'There was a time when only Mossad deployed female operators to undertake "wet work".'

Strelkov shook his head slowly. 'Mossad are not coming. Think about it, Sasha, Israel would not seek to damage their relationship with the Kremlin. It cannot be them. This woman must be someone else. I believe she's Ukrainian; that is the only explanation that makes sense. She was sent to infiltrate us and got caught up with the British mission.'

'Perhaps.'

'We shall lie in wait for the pair of them. It would be a coup to catch either one but both together? That would be a truly international incident.'

'It would. Take Iqbal and put him in your vehicle,' Vasilev ordered Boroda. The Russian looked at Strelkov, who bobbed his head in consent.

As Boroda left the room, Strelkov addressed Vasilev. 'You should go too; it would be unfortunate if they attacked and you were to get shot.'

'I appreciate your concern.' Vasilev collected the papers from the desk and made for the door.

Strelkov paused for a beat before he followed. He gazed around the hamlet and counted six DNR militants. He knew others would be inside. More than enough to capture the man and woman who were on their way, but overwhelming force was needed if his hasty plan was going to work. They had to be lured into the open where they would have no option but to surrender. And then things would become highly political.

A leaf from a canopy high above landed at his feet; the colouring fascinated him, starting at one end with a red of almost a burgundy and ending at the other with a golden auburn. Nature truly was beautiful. He bent down to pick it up and then what sounded like a giant wasp buzzed his ear. The glass exploded behind him and Strelkov flattened himself into the earth. His eyes searched for the source of the silenced round, as the dirt by his cheek suddenly kicked up. 'Incoming!' he yelled.

There was a roar and an RPG tore through the clearing and hit the truck. The warhead exploded and a second later, a larger explosion lifted the rear of the Kamaz up in the air before it slammed back down against the earth. Another RPG sailed over-head and hit one of the houses, collapsing a wall.

*

Iqbal was jerked awake by the thunderous detonations outside his new cell.

Either his jailers were celebrating or the place was being attacked. Or perhaps he was being rescued?

Iqbal dragged himself to his feet and moved to the door. It was impossible to see through, but he could feel vibrations and smell burning as a whole succession of gunshots sounded. Images of the hostage rescue teams from action movies, blowing open doors, made him step back and away. It would be just his luck to get blown up by someone on his own side. Iqbal moved to the opposite side of the room. There were shouts from outside, some in languages he couldn't identify, and then the shock wave from a huge explosion shattered the glass in the window high up on the wall above him. There was a whooshing sound followed by a second explosion.

The door burst open and two men crashed into the room. Iqbal recognised them as two of his guards. They hauled him from the room. Outside the sun was high in an azure sky. Rounds snapped by them as he was dragged bodily across the compound, his feet seeming to catch every sharp object making him cry out. The air cracked as a round missed Iqbal's ear by millimetres. A yell pierced the air next to him. Stunned, Iqbal looked around; one of the militants was on the ground, holding his leg and moaning.

'Run! Run!' the guard urged.

A strong hand towed him. More rounds zipped past. Iqbal started to move on legs made weary by incarceration and interrogation. Four steps . . . five steps . . . He glanced back; the guard was flat on his back. He took another step. He felt suddenly weightless as he was thrown sideways by a blast-wave. Iqbal landed hard and tasted blood in his mouth. The world around him dimmed. The shouts and gunfire felt suddenly distant, as though he was hearing them from underwater. Thick hands grabbed him, hauling him up. Dazed, he didn't notice who had hold of him or where they were going.

*

Strelkov rolled sideways and scurried down the side of the dacha. He drew his sidearm, an MP-443 Grach and studied the tree line. The attackers – he was absolutely certain that there were more than one – had used the dachas opposite as cover. The RPGs had been well aimed, both hitting their targets and incinerating the facilities' supplies. Strelkov was pinned down. Two silenced rounds had been directed . . . *targeted* at him. Was he the target of this assault now? Had he been followed, or somehow tracked? He pushed the idea to the back of his mind – he had always been a target for the Ukrainians. His head delivered to Kyiv would be a huge prize. This had to be the British working with The Shadows.

The men of the DNR were firing back, preventing the attackers from entering the village. He was reassured to see that at least a few of them moved like real soldiers rather than the drunken or drug-riddled thugs he'd encountered before. There was a noise behind him. He spun onto his back and brought the Grach up in front of his chest as a man flew at him out of the undergrowth. Strelkov didn't hesitate; he fired twice, the rounds ripping apart the man's chest. The body fell six feet short of him.

Strelkov got to his feet as a pair of men appeared. The nearest sent a ribbon of rounds in his direction. Strelkov shot him in the face as the rounds tore into the brick wall to his left. He fired again at the third man, who slumped backwards, his rounds tearing into the wall. They were coming from all sides; he had to retreat. He sought out the G Wagon and loped around the edge of the clearing towards it. Then something exploded from the trees and hit him in the waist and knocked him to the ground. Strelkov was winded. He was pushed onto his back and a blade flashed in his peripheral vision. Instinctively, he bucked and jerked to his left. The blade passed his eyes so close he felt the air part.

Strelkov clubbed his attacker's head with his pistol, and twisted his shoulder. Off balance, the assailant slid. Strelkov sought out the knife hand, grabbed the wrist, twisted it back, and plunged the blade into the man who was holding it. The aggressor jerked and Strelkov saw his face. A horror registered in the man's dark brown eyes and blood seeped from his lips as Strelkov pushed the blade deeper.

Strelkov turned away from the attacker and nodded at Boroda as he came tearing back towards him from the direction of their armour-plated G Wagon. Strelkov knew that unless the attacking force were using specialist rounds, they would not be able to hit Iqbal or Vasilev. On the count of three, with Boroda providing suppressive covering fire, both Russians surged back to the safety of the Mercedes.

SEVENTEEN

Donetsk region
A pale blue autumnal sky hung above the tall trees lining the road to Donetsk. All was still.

Racine lay on the cold, forest floor twenty feet back from the edge of the highway. The damp from the earth below had started to seep through her jeans and her leather jacket had ridden up, causing her back to become covered with goose pimples, but Racine had been trained to ignore the cold, to ignore both physical and mental discomfort. Through the gaps in the trees, she watched the road to the west, as it snaked towards the small Ukrainian-controlled town of Marinka while Aidan Snow, who lay ten feet to her left, covered the road as it headed east to the militant stronghold of Donetsk. Once a busy artery, the road was now home only to military vehicle and trucks carrying essential food supplies.

It would be only a matter of time before Racine's abandoned Mitsubishi Shogun drew the attention of a passing DNR patrol. They had the location of the interrogation centre, but to just walk in would be madness, especially when they assumed the militants were expecting them. They needed intel and cover and driving in as members of a DNR patrol would hopefully provide them with both. She was, however, very aware that their plan was thinner than a Paris Fashion Week model.

Again, the words and face of Baptiste swam back into her mind. Were the odds that stacked against her? Was it expected that she wasn't coming back? Was Jacob just using her to settle an old score? She knew the answer to all three was yes, but the score was not merely a personal one. It was the honour of her country she had to settle. It was time both Russia and Vasilev realised the cost of their actions against her, France, and the DGSE.

Snow spoke quietly. 'Are you sure you want to do this?'

'Yes, 007.'

'If I was Bond, I'd have brought a picnic and a bottle of champagne.'

'Right now, I'd settle for a swig of cognac.'

'How very French.'

'Or a pastis.'

Snow pulled a face.

The plan she had outlined to him was, in essence, simple but relied on her being used as bait. It also relied on luck. 'Something's coming.'

Racine kept her eyes on the road as a white car appeared from around a bend. The car slowed and she recognised it as a white, boxy, Soviet-era Lada 1600. It was one of the world's worst cars yet still functioning some thirty years after the Soviet Union had ceased to do so. The Lada stopped and two men lugged themselves out. Racine studied the pair, no more than thirty feet away from her position. They wore rough, forest-pattern camouflage fatigues, had heavy stubble, and carried AKs. More importantly, to distinguish them from both the Ukrainian army and the volunteer Ukrainian battalions so near to the frontline, they each had a white band affixed to the left arm of their field jackets.

Racine eased herself up to a standing position, brushed down her black jeans, and left cover.

The two men were so engrossed with trying to open the Mitsubishi that they did not see her until she had left the cover of the trees and almost reached them. The first looked at her and then the second. The men made no attempt to raise their weapons or to challenge her. To them, she was just a woman. Racine's Makarov was in her jacket's internal holster, ready if she needed to use it, but she wanted to keep things quiet; and for such instances she would use a different weapon.

A grin cracked the nearest man's unkempt face in two. 'What are you doing here?'

'My mother lives in the next village,' Racine replied quickly, in Russian, making the fear in her voice more pronounced. 'I have come to see if she is OK.'

'That is fortunate for you—' the grin became a leer '—as that is exactly where we are going. You must understand this is a dangerous place. We are here to protect it from the Ukrainian government forces. It is not a good idea for a beautiful woman in an expensive car to be seen on her own.'

'Thank you, I will be fine – it is not far.'

'Open the back. We need to see that you are not smuggling anything into our territory,' the second man commanded.

'OK.' Racine made a show of moving hesitantly around the two gunmen, who did not make any effort to let her pass. She felt their hungry gaze on her as she leant forward and pulled the large release lever on the Shogun's tailgate.

Transferring his Kalashnikov to his left hand, the second militant slapped the side of the Mitsubishi with his left. 'This is good transport.'

The first man now took a step sideways and peered at the dirt-covered number plate. 'Where did you get it from?'

'It doesn't matter where she got it from, she's giving it to us.' The first militant laughed. His bloodshot eyes now met with hers as he edged nearer to her. 'We are commandeering this vehicle for the militia of the Donetsk People's Republic.'

'You can't. How am I going to get to see my mother? How am I going to get home?' Racine said.

The militant tutted. 'We will take you to see your mother, and then you can both join the other prisoners in the village.'

'Prisoners?' Good, they were getting somewhere. 'What prisoners?'

'It is a very serious situation. The villagers were collaborating with the Ukrainians, helping their army spy on us.' He made a show of shrugging to illustrate his indifference. 'We are holding them until they tell us what they know.'

'If you're a good girl, I'm sure we could arrange something.' The nearest militant took a lunging step forward, attempting to grab her.

She'd had enough.

Racine's speed and strength took both men completely by surprise. She pivoted sideways, moving around the militant's reach. Her left elbow delivered a sharp, vicious strike to the side of his head, rocking it directly into the path of the blade she held in her right hand. It buried deep in his head behind his ear. He dropped, lights out, dead.

The second militant, mouth agape and eyes wide, had his hands up in the air as though he was trying to hold back some giant weight. As he stumbled backwards his mouth moved, but no discernible words came out. Racine advanced, he fell flat on his back and Racine struck him heavily in the groin with her boot. He rolled sideways, doubling up, holding his crotch. Tears started to roll down his face.

'We need one of them alive,' Snow said, in his Moscow-accented Russian as he appeared at her side.

Racine realised she had perhaps gone too far, but she was impatient. 'Do we?'

The militant, now in a foetal position stared up at the pair. 'Please you do . . . you do need me alive! Please don't hurt me!'

'Hurt you?' Racine crouched down and placed her blade against his filthy cheek; he flinched as it made contact. 'I've already hurt you. Unless you tell us exactly what we need to know, I'll kill you.'

'Anything! Anything!'

Racine nicked his cheek with the blade and he started to shake.

'First question,' Snow said, taking over, to her annoyance, 'where is Mohammed Iqbal?'

'Who?' The man's face contorted as he tried to understand the name.

Racine cut his face again. 'The British student.'

'He's a Paki!' the militant sobbed.

'Ah . . . so you know who he is? Where is he?' Snow asked, continuing to use Russian.

'We have him in the village.'

'With the other prisoners?'

'No. We lied. There is only him. He is being questioned by Raduga.'

'We have the right place then,' Snow said to Racine.

'I'm sorry!' The militant's eyes were wide with fear and blood flowed from the two cuts to his cheek.

'You are going to drive us to the village, and you are going to show us where Mohammed Iqbal is being held,' Snow stated.

'B . . . but they'll kill me if I take you there!'

Racine grabbed the man's throat with her left hand. 'I'll gut you like a pig if you don't!'

'OK . . . OK . . .' the militant stuttered.

'Roll over, lie on your stomach, and put your hands behind your head,' Racine ordered. As Snow watched the road, Racine frisked their captive and found an old Nokia handset in his pocket. 'You use this to communicate with your base?'

'No . . . to call my mother.'

She studied the phone; it was an antiquated, battered 8210. Small but with long battery life. It was a model now used by drug dealers or anyone who was concerned about surveillance. The lack of Bluetooth and Wi-Fi meant that, unlike modern smartphones, it could not be hacked to become a GPS monitoring device, merely crudely triangulated by way of monitoring cell towers. Racine put the mobile phone in her jeans pocket. 'Maybe I'll let you call her later.'

Racine now moved away and wiped the black blade clean on the dead man's jacket sleeve; she wondered how many victims Vadim's knife had claimed since being issued to him. She searched the corpse and found a second, identical cell phone. She handed it to Snow. 'We've got to get the body out of here.'

Snow nodded. 'We'll throw him in the boot of the Lada. After that, you get in the back of the Shogun and keep down. Laughing boy here will drive and I'll ride shotgun.'

Racine glared at Snow. 'What makes you think you're in charge?'

'Old age?'

Racine didn't reply.

Snow made the remaining militant haul his dead comrade into the boot whilst Racine conducted a quick search of the Lada and found nothing of use. They left the car by the side of the road; anyone desperate enough to steal it was welcome to it. After stowing their kit – which now included the militants' newish-looking Russian AK-74SUs – Racine climbed into the back of the Shogun and hunkered down below the window line. Snow sat in the front passenger seat, his Glock in his left hand pressed against the militant's stomach. 'Drive.'

The Mitsubishi hove itself back onto the road and, jerkily at first, the militant drove them towards Donetsk.

'Tell me about the village,' Racine ordered.

'What do you mean?' The militant raised a shaky left hand and wiped the blood from his cheek.

She spoke slowly, precisely, to ensure he understood. 'How many of your men are there?'

'Ten.'

'From the DNR?'

'Yes.'

'How many Russians?'

'Just one, Raduga the Russian intelligence officer.'

'Russian Intelligence,' Racine repeated.

'That's an oxymoron,' Snow stated flatly.

'So eleven men in total?' Racine continued.

'Yes.'

'Any defences?'

'What?'

'Is the road to the village guarded?' Snow said.

'One man at a barrier.'

'And ten more in the village?'

'Yes.'

'How many buildings are there in the village?'

'I don't know. It's a village in the woods.'

'OK.' Snow glanced in the rear-view mirror; Racine was out of sight. 'You ready?'

'I'm a woman, I'm always ready,' Racine replied.

'The turn is up ahead,' the militant announced.

'Listen to me.' Snow's words were low and his voice calm as he explained their plan. 'One wrong move and she'll shoot you in the back of your head. Do you understand?'

His mouth moved but nothing came out.

'The gentleman asked you a question,' Racine said.

The militant swallowed and croaked, 'Yes.'

'Now,' Snow continued. 'I am a member of the GRU from Moscow. I have come to inspect the prisoners. This is my official vehicle and I have ordered you to drive me. Understood?'

'Yes.'

'The lady behind you is a new prisoner.'

'OK.'

Racine wasn't happy. Her instinct was to lead but there were times when she was forced to use her gender as a weapon. She was again going to play a role she hated: 'the frightened female'.

She checked that her blade was hidden under her jacket and mentally prepared herself.

The Mitsubishi moved off the highway and onto a narrow road. Less than a minute later, they came across the improvised security barrier. A white-painted pole, which looked like it had been removed from a car park. It was pointed skyward.

'That's not normal . . . the barrier is always down,' the militant noted.

'Stop the car.' Snow cracked open his window and sniffed.

A familiar scent filled the interior of the 4X4.

Racine sat up and leant forward. 'There's been a firefight.'

'What?' The militant didn't comprehend.

'If it's a trap they'll have already seen us,' Racine said.

'There's no point in getting out and losing what mobility and cover we have. Just make sure you're ready to use that AK.'

'Always,' Racine replied.

'OK. Carry on, keep driving, like you normally would do.'

The militant wiped a bead of sweat from his forehead and they started to move again. The Shogun rocked as it traversed the gravel road that soon became a mud track. Snow shifted lower in his seat, to reduce his profile. The militant swung the wheel to the left and they entered the village. Instinctively, he slammed his foot on the brake as he registered the scene before him. Now, unobscured by the tall, dark trees, smoke rose from two of the small houses and the other four looked as though they had been peppered by gunfire. A white-painted Kamaz truck sat on its front two wheels, the rear two torn away. Several bodies lay on the ground. The militant looked at Snow and then back at the village.

The windscreen suddenly crazed. A retort sounding like a giant wasp registered in Racine's ears – time froze and so did she.

She instantly recognised the buzz.

It belonged to a rifle round.

There was barely time to blink, and definitely no chance to react.

This was the end.

The head of the militant snapped back. The round had been fired at him. It entered the man's skull, pierced his brain and exited spraying blood, gore and bone over Racine's shoulder and face before becoming embedded in the headrest.

With the militant jammed in the driving seat they couldn't move the Shogun. Regaining their senses, Racine and Snow both grabbed their door handles and threw themselves out and onto the ground. She landed heavily on her shoulder, winding herself, but Kalashnikov in hand, she pushed into the undergrowth bordering the turning. She didn't see where Snow ended up. She lay still and waited. There were no more shots; the only sound was the wind rustling the tops of the trees above her. It was an ambush, of that she was sure, but it didn't make sense. Why would the DNR, or the Russians, shoot one of their own men?

Footsteps approached, slowly and with hardly any noise, but unmistakable on the dirt track. She raised her head ever so slightly and could see directly under the Mitsubishi. A pair of boots stopped by the driver's door and another halted several feet away from her. She held her breath and then the undergrowth exploded as rounds pierced the greenery.

'Come out slowly or the next bullet will go in your head.' The words were in Russian but the accent was from somewhere else.

Racine didn't move. The order was not being aimed at her, nor was the barrel of a Kalashnikov, which she could now see through the foliage.

'Do you really want to die in the dirt like a beast of the field?'

'OK,' Snow said.

'Get up,' the voice demanded.

She now saw Snow deliberately drag himself forward and out of cover, then stand face to face with the gunman. In the sunlight filtering through the tree cover, Racine noted the man's civilian clothing.

Snow spoke in English. 'You're not a member of the DNR.'

The gunman's thick eyebrows arched on hearing the words; he replied in American-accented English, 'No, I'm not.'

Racine inhaled deeply then burst up and out of the foliage, Kalashnikov trained directly at the man's head. It was a reckless move, but it was the only one to make if she wanted to control the developing situation. 'Drop your weapon or I drop you.'

'Stop!' the gunman exclaimed. 'My men will kill you.'

'And you'll be dead,' Racine stated coldly.

The gunman carefully placed his rifle on the ground. 'So, you are the agents from Paris and London?'

Racine blinked. 'What do you know about that?'

'Everything. I am the man who has been talking to the DGSE in Moscow for you, and with the SBU for you. We are The Shadows.'

'Prove it,' Racine said.

'Please stop pointing that at me.'

'Tell your men to lower their weapons.' Racine was icy calm.

'You heard her – do it!' the gunman called out in English.

Ahead and past the vehicle, Racine saw a handful of men step out of the trees surrounding the dachas. They held a mixture of weapons, but they were pointed at the ground. 'Now prove to me you are The Shadows. Who was your contact at DGSE?'

'Jean Larcher.'

Racine lowered her AK.

'He's the Moscow station chief?' Snow asked.

'He's the cultural attaché.'

'Where is Mohammed Iqbal?' Snow asked.

'There was one prisoner. When we attacked, the Russians hurried him away.'

'Where is Sasha Vasilev?' Racine asked.

'Raduga also escaped. We were targeting Igor Strelkov, and it was he who took them to safety.'

'Strelkov was here?' Snow was surprised.

'Yes. We followed him to this place.'

'Followed?' Snow looked closer at the men and recognised

a couple. When he spoke his tone was bitter. 'Your attack on the garage was too early. You were meant to hit the place after nightfall.'

'The opportunity to hit Strelkov, once his presence was confirmed, could not be ignored. You must understand he is our "enemy number one".'

'We were there,' Racine confirmed, 'during the attack.'

'I am sorry for what has happened. What more can I say?' Ignoring Racine, the gunman slowly raised his hand towards Snow. 'My name is Victor Boyko. I am retired Ukrainian Special Forces and the leader of The Shadows.'

Snow sighed and shook the Ukrainian's hand. 'You don't look retired to me.'

Racine was curious. 'How did you follow Strelkov?'

'There is a tracker on his Mercedes and his cell phone is being monitored.'

'I see.' It was clear to Racine that the group was being aided by several foreign intelligence agencies. 'Do you know where Strelkov has taken Iqbal and Vasilev?' she asked.

'Yes. He's back in the city centre, near the Circus.' Boyko gave him the address.

'Then that is where we need to go.'

'I am sorry about the man in the Shogun. Was he one of yours?'

'No. He was DNR and I didn't like him much,' Racine stated.

Boyko looked them in the eye, one at a time. 'Take out Vasilev, rescue your British student, but leave Strelkov to us. Understood?'

'Agreed.'

There was a sudden shout from one of The Shadows. 'Drone!'

The group looked skyward. Without cloud cover, the drone was visible against the blue sky. Less able than its US counterpart, the Russian UAV flew lower and slower and, although unarmed, it carried a powerful digital camera to track and relay targets.

'They use it to spot for their Grad rockets. You must move, now!' Boyko ordered.

Without any argument, Racine and Snow jogged back to the Shogun. Snow arrived a fraction ahead of Racine so dragged the dead man unceremoniously out of the driver's seat and took his place at the wheel. He put the SUV into reverse as he heard a distant whistle. After Snow floored the accelerator pedal, the Shogun's wheels took a split second to grip the dirt and then it jerked backwards. The silver paintwork scraped against branches and he spun the steering wheel.

The first shell fired from stand-off distance, but guided by the drone, hit the clearing a matter of feet from where the 4X4 had been parked. In the rear-view mirror, Snow saw flames and black clouds rising from the trees. Good luck and bad timing had saved them again. A thought struck him; he pressed the button to slide open the sunroof. 'Is it following us?'

Racine looked up, squinting. 'I can't see it.'

'OK.' They had to believe it was, but there was no way they could ditch the Mitsubishi before they got back into the city suburbs.

*

'How many?' Strelkov asked the drone pilot. He gripped his phone and looked out of the apartment window at Leninskyi Avenue below. Behind him Iqbal was tied to a chair. Vasilev lounged opposite him and smoked a cigarette.

'Approximately nine men. There is also a vehicle leaving the scene. Shall I pursue?' The reply came via the speakerphone.

'Do not engage the vehicle,' Vasilev ordered.

Strelkov repeated the command. 'That is a negative on the vehicle. Keep the feed on the terrorists. I want them destroyed.' Strelkov ended the call.

'Your foreign team are in the vehicle, in my opinion,' Vasilev replied.

'It would appear so, but I need air support, a helicopter, to follow it.' Strelkov sighed. 'Yet manned airframes are beyond the level of support Russia is prepared to provide.'

'The DNR has no air force.'

'But it apparently has armour,' Strelkov said, his temper and frustration apparent.

'This foreign team will come here. Of that, I am sure,' Vasilev said.

Strelkov frowned. 'Is there something you know that I do not?'

Vasilev folded his arms and nodded. 'The Shadows have found you twice today, so what does that tell you?'

'I'm a target?'

'And?'

Strelkov's eyes widened momentarily as he looked at his phone. 'It's bugged?'

'Either that, or your Mercedes, or both.'

Strelkov glared at the British student who sat tied to a wooden chair. He switched to English. 'Why is it, Mr Iqbal, that so many people are willing to risk their lives for yours?'

Iqbal seemed dazed. 'I don't know.'

'Who are you, Mr Iqbal?'

'I'm no one.'

'Everyone is someone. Although some are far more important than others,' Strelkov stated.

'It is not who *he* is but who his *father* is,' Vasilev said, also now using English. 'Is that not true, Mohammed?'

'My father is just a doctor.'

Vasilev pulled his chair closer and faced Iqbal. 'He is a close, personal friend of the British Foreign Secretary?'

'They were friends as kids and lived in the same street,' Iqbal said. 'That's all I know.'

'Your father's friend, the Foreign Secretary, is going to pay for sending men against me; I can assure you of that.' Strelkov sneered at the dishevelled Brit.

'Men have been sent for you? I don't understand.'

'We shall make a film—' Strelkov faced the street once more '—and in that video you shall confess to what you have done.'

'What have I done? I came here to study!'

'I will give you a list of your offences to read. You will also condemn the British for sending in their Special Forces against the peace-loving people of Donetsk.'

'I thought I wasn't a hostage?'

'You are not,' Vasilev confirmed, a thin smile on his lips.

'Then why make a hostage video? Why make me read out a false statement? Isn't that what terrorists do?'

Strelkov turned, the anger he felt clear on his face. 'It will not be a hostage video! It will be a prisoner interview with ON.'

'A prisoner of what? Of war? Let me see the Red Cross, Amnesty International or the OSCE. If I'm a prisoner, charge me with something. If not, let me go. Otherwise, I am a hostage and you are terrorists!'

Strelkov stalked across the room, reached out, grabbed Iqbal's throat, and squeezed. 'You need to be thankful that currently I have need of you; otherwise, I would throw your body into the gutter to rot.' He let go and Iqbal fought for air. 'Do I make myself clear?'

Iqbal tried to nod.

Vasilev gestured towards the door. He got up and Strelkov followed him out the room.

'What is it?' Strelkov barked, in the hallway.

'I am close to getting Iqbal to talk. You must not interfere by using your own bullish methods of interrogation.'

'You dare to tell me how to speak to a prisoner? After all that has happened?'

'That is the reason I am here. Why the Russian President ordered me here. I still need to understand why this man is so important to the British. This is now more than propaganda for the DNR. Iqbal may yet provide us with some real intelligence.' Vasilev's tone was level.

'On the British?'

'Perhaps. Yet, I believe we can use him to get ourselves an even bigger prize. The room is wired for sound and vision, and the footage is securely stored on my servers. I suggest we leave Iqbal here as bait. If this "rescue team" appears we will have them on camera and will be able to both identify them and listen to every word they say to Iqbal.'

'Then what?'

'You leave a few men here – expendable, for show, but don't tell them or it will seem too easy – and have a large rapid-reaction force on standby. Close by. This will prevent the foreign team from leaving. We will then have three high-value hostages. However, you are the military mind here; I am merely the interrogator.'

'Very well, Sasha, very well.' Strelkov's words were conciliatory, although his own tone was not. He was in charge of the military of the DNR, but both men reported directly to the Kremlin. It was not a command structure he believed to be workable. 'I will stage two trucks out of sight.'

'That is a wise move.'

Strelkov's anger started to rise, but he merely nodded.

EIGHTEEN

Petrovsky District, Donetsk

'No sign of our mutual friend,' Racine stated as they passed Weller's MG.

Snow felt in his pocket; he still had the car keys. 'I wonder where he's gone.'

Racine cleaned the last of the blood and grime from her face with a wet wipe, found in the glove box, 'Perhaps he took my advice and went to the beauty salon.'

'Perhaps.' Snow noticed something ahead. 'Bugger.'

'Bugger.' Racine rolled her eyes; it had been one of the first British swearwords she'd been taught.

'Up ahead, ten o'clock. That's the man you stole our ride from.'

'I see him . . . and the Russian troops he's with.'

'Hang on, they haven't made us yet.' Snow slewed the Mitsubishi to the right, shot down a side street, and turned left behind an apartment block.

'This means we'll have to ditch our ride sooner rather than later.'

'Agreed,' Snow said.

Snow continued to drive along the smaller road that ran parallel to the one watched by the Russians.

Racine noticed people standing at a bus stop. 'Have you seen any cars?'

Snow scanned the street. 'No.'

'Exactly. They seem a bit thin on the ground here, and the Russians are watching the road.'

'So?'

'What's that over there?'

'A bus stop.'

'We hide in plain sight . . . we get on a bus. Stop the car.'

'That's . . . crazy.' Snow slowed the Shogun and parked next to a playground. 'We'll have to leave the longs.'

'Longs?'

'AKs.'

Racine reluctantly agreed; even with their collapsible stocks, there was no way to conceal the assault rifles under their jackets.

Racine got out of the car and Snow casually followed suit. She took his hand; it wasn't as rough as she expected. They walked side by side up the street for a while, until they found a row of bus stops. The absurdity of studying a bus timetable in a de facto war zone was not lost on her, but nevertheless she looked for one that went in the direction they wanted. Eventually they found the correct stop. Racine checked the old timetable secured behind a cloudy, plastic panel. Before the conflict a bus route had gone into the city centre and near the Circus, and she hoped it still did.

Around her, residents were attempting to get on with their daily routines. She had to admire the spirit of the Donetsk locals and their refusal to allow the conflict to dictate their everyday lives. She'd started off ambivalent to the crisis – it was just another foreign conflict to her – but now she'd started to despise the Kremlin for the chaos and carnage it had caused. The people of the East deserved better. If taking out Vasilev also helped the Ukrainian people, it was an added benefit.

Racine linked arms with Snow and pushed these thoughts aside; they were just another couple waiting for a bus. Snow was quiet, watchful, but to the untrained he gave off an air of brooding indifference. He was taller than Baptiste, his muscles thicker. She imagined briefly what he'd look like with his shirt off. She whispered in Russian in Snow's ear. 'Do you think any of The Shadows made it out?'

Snow nodded as though she had passed on a pearl of wisdom to him. His reply too, was soft. 'The Russians were firing those shells blind; that drone didn't give them much accuracy.'

Two women ahead of them started to complain in vexed tones about the bus service. Racine counted eleven of them in total waiting for the bus into central Donetsk. In any disputed territory there were always those who sided with the occupying forces, and the DNR must have maintained some essential services to keep the little local support they had. How many of those awaiting the bus's arrival believed in the DNR, she didn't know, but guessed they'd be in the minority.

The dirty, yellow bus came to a halt and the passengers surged towards the open door. The first, a heavy woman wearing an equally heavy woollen coat, moaned at the driver that he was late. The driver, in return, relayed a story about a road closed due to a stray shell. As they climbed aboard, Racine noticed a single bullet hole marked the bus's front panel and its indicator light was missing. She handed the driver the fare and asked about the route.

Outside, the street was quiet save for a solitary old man, arms laden with heavy shopping bags, gingerly navigating the broken pavement. They took seats halfway up the bus.

Snow asked quietly, 'How far?'

'It's a way yet. We have to go right into the centre and out the other side a bit.'

'And get past our Russian friends.'

They didn't talk for a while as even though both of them could pass for Russian, their conversation would be listened to intently by the other passengers and then probably, she imagined, dissected later at numerous dinner tables by the 'babushka network'.

The bus slowed as it turned away from the residential street and onto the larger through road. The traffic was heavier than earlier in the day but nothing like it must have been pre-crisis. Half an hour later, as the bus drove further into the city centre, the visual signs of war damage lessened to be replaced once more by the surreal tableau of life interrupted. More people were on the streets, a 'Press' kiosk sold Russian printed newspapers, and some shops were open. The only sign of change was the juxtaposing of a tank, with Russian markings crudely obscured by dull, green paint, standing watch on a street corner next to a bakery. A line of shoppers snaked past it onto the pavement, ever hopeful of getting a loaf of freshly baked bread.

'If we grabbed that tank,' Racine said softly into Snow's ear, 'we could steam in, snatch our targets, and steam out.'

'You can drive a tank?' he whispered back.

'Of course, can't you?'

Before Snow could reply, the bus abruptly stopped. Without warning, an armoured personnel carrier roared across the inter-section. The driver cursed.

'There it is,' Racine stated.

The address was on Leninskyi Avenue, a wide road where both trams and trolleybuses had run alongside four lanes of traffic – although now, only the buses continued to work. The target building was four storeys tall. Unremarkable except for the fact that it was across from the large 'Kosmos Circus' building which before the conflict had kept its Soviet-style entertainment shows going nightly. A group of battered German saloon cars were parked haphazardly outside the target address, half blocking the pavement. It was standard parking procedure for Ukrainian Mafiosi who presumed themselves to be above the law – even more so now that they wore uniforms and carried assault rifles.

The specific address was on the third floor, on the end nearest the Circus. A small road separated the building from another, smaller block, which housed a grocer's shop and café on its ground floor. An Italian-style dry cleaners took up the ground floor of the building to the other side. On the side of the building a crude ladder of iron rungs led to the roof. As the bus sluggishly moved past, a group of four uniformed men left the café and entered the address. At that distance, Racine couldn't tell if they were Russian military, or DNR.

'If we'd been earlier, the place would have been empty,' Snow noted.

Racine was more philosophical. 'We now know there are probably a minimum of six guns inside.'

The bus continued on to the next stop not much farther up the road. Racine and Snow followed an elderly couple off the bus; they all waited for a break in the traffic and then crossed the street. The pensioners headed for a large pharmacy while the intelligence operatives turned left and leisurely walked back towards the target address. Two minutes later, they had passed the target and were sitting at a table at the back of the café, discreetly watching the communal front door. Snow sat with his back against the wall. Racine excused herself, on the pretext of finding the bathroom, and returned a short while later.

To keep up the appearance of being a couple, she placed her arms around Snow's neck and whispered into his ear. 'There's an exit at the back that leads to the road behind and there's a playground surrounded by more apartments and trees.' Snow smiled. Racine sat next to him, also not wanting to have her back to the door. She held his hand. 'Have you ordered?'

'Yes.'

'Good. What?'

'I got you a black coffee. You don't look like a milk girl.'

'Girl? What am I, twelve?'

'On a scale of one to ten.'

Racine shook her head slowly. 'Your hands are cold.'

They said nothing more until their order arrived. The other customers too were quiet. Racine spooned three sugars into her black coffee – it would taste awful, but she needed the fuel and didn't want to chance the unappealing-looking food. Snow bit into a jam tartlet. In silence they continued to watch the building, knowing they couldn't stay static for long. Their command of Russian and their accents were good enough to mark them out as being from Russia, but this still made them strangers in a town whose population had significantly decreased since the creation of the DNR. The longer they remained in the café the more they would stand out.

Their fellow customers looked to be immune to the upheaval; however, Racine knew appearances were often very misleading. The couple had 9mm handguns concealed in inside pockets – Racine had a Makarov and the knife whilst Snow carried his Glock. Racine was envious – she missed her silenced Glock. She reached for her coffee and her hand froze mid-air as she saw movement from the target address. A soldier in full battle dress stepped out onto the third-floor balcony, took a cursory glance at the road below, and disappeared inside.

'That changes things,' she announced as she snuggled into Snow's large shoulder.

She was still trying to reassess their approach when four men – the same ones they had seen enter the building ten minutes earlier – exited and climbed into two separate dark-blue BMWs. She noted they were DNR. 'That's some of them gone.'

'We need a new plan.'

'We need intel.' Racine stood.

Snow pointed at the remaining pastry. She shook her head. In her peripheral vision, Racine noticed the café owner was watching them. She put her hand on Snow's cheek, drew his head down and kissed him on the lips. She felt his lips resist ever so slightly before he put his hand on the back of her head and started kissing her back. The kiss lasted longer than she had anticipated, but she reasoned it was good for their cover. It wasn't the worst kiss she had ever had.

The pair left the café.

Immediately to their left and outside the Circus building there was a string of closed kiosks. While Snow watched the target, Racine walked farther on to where several pensioners had set up impromptu stalls. At the nearest an elderly man sat on a wooden chair alongside a board pinned with a variety of cigarettes. Partially hidden from the target building by the kiosks, he wore several layers of clothes and a fur hat; he would have looked at home in the Arctic Circle. At the next stall sat an equally ancient woman with a trolley of assorted women's clothes.

The man was already staring at her, so she asked him, 'What's happening across the road?'

'What do you mean?' He looked up, with watery eyes.

'That building on the end; I saw a Russian soldier on the balcony.'

The elderly man peered at the building before he answered. 'It's been taken over by the Russians; well, two of the apartments have. The owners moved away when the DNR appeared. The rest of us stayed.'

'You live there?'

'On the third floor; the Russians are now my neighbours. They aren't bad; some of them are Buryats, from Siberia. They look like Mongolians. They've shared their food with me, we've had a few drinks, and I told them about my time in the Red Army. The DNR are nothing but the old bandits wearing new clothes.'

'I see.'

The elderly man carried on, clearly glad of someone new to complain to. 'Since all this started, I've had hardly any money or food. The Kyiv government has stopped paying my pension. The DNR claim they are looking into paying me. But so far? I get a bit of bread if I'm lucky.' He looked up at her hopefully and then continued. 'I have old colleagues who live in Crimea, and they now receive triple my pension. Why Russia doesn't take the Donbas, I do not know.'

Racine focused on the intel she needed, ignoring the politics. 'Are the DNR and the Russians inside there now?'

'Yes.' He frowned. 'They brought someone in earlier. They keep prisoners there. Can you imagine? My building turned into a makeshift military prison.'

Racine started to shake and then put her hand to her eyes and pretended to cry.

The pensioner squinted and bluntly addressed Snow, who had appeared by Racine's side, putting his hand on her shoulder. 'What's wrong with her?'

Snow took his cue, 'They have her husband, my brother-in-law. He's not from here. We've been trying to find where he is but the DNR keep moving him about. If only we could speak to the Russians about him, they may let him go. He's a medical student, and he's done nothing wrong.'

'What does he look like?'

'His family is from Pakistan,' Racine whimpered, through her fake tears.

'The man they took inside had dark skin, even darker than the Buryats. I wish I could help you more, but I have to stay here, and sell my stock; otherwise I won't be able to eat.'

Racine removed several one-hundred-dollar bills from her pocket. 'These are yours if you can get us inside the building. Then we can talk to them.'

The old man's eyes were suddenly wide. 'How much money is that?'

'Three hundred American dollars.'

'Put your money away, before someone steals it! That is more than two months' pension!'

'Please help us.' Racine slowly put the notes back in her pocket.

'If this is some kind of a trick, it's a wicked one.'

'No trick,' Snow said. 'Please help us.'

The old man licked his lips. 'What would I need to do?'

*

Iqbal tried moving his arms again and found just how tight they were tied behind his back. His shoulders ached from the stress position. He had been left alone for what seemed like hours. Where was his watch? And his trainers? Had they been left at the last place? No one seemed to care.

Iqbal looked at his feet; they were a mess. His blue socks, which he'd been wearing for over a month, had turned black and clung to his feet in bloody tatters. He doubted he'd be able to walk and hoped his cuts weren't infected. The most annoying part of all was he absolutely stank. As a medical student and a Muslim, he'd been used to washing several times a day and changing his clothes almost as often – even if it meant washing his clothes in the bathtub of his outdated Donetsk apartment. It was the indignity of the situation that angered him; there was no need for it. At least this place was furnished. The realisation that the attack on the last place he was held at was probably a rescue attempt had filled him with hope and a new energy, but that had been ripped away when he'd been taken away by Strelkov.

Now, although his surroundings looked better, his outlook was bleak. It seemed to him he was now more of a hostage than a prisoner and they wanted to turn him into a performing monkey. That wasn't just it though. He was being used as bait to lure in those sent to save him. Iqbal felt helpless, and there was nothing he could do to change it. He remembered seeing a documentary on the British Tornado pilots shot down and captured by Iraqi forces during the first Gulf War. He'd watched it with his parents years after the events and could still hear his mother's words. 'Poor boys! What must their mothers feel, seeing them bruised and held like that?' He was determined he wasn't going to put his parents – his mother most of all – through that type of pain.

Iqbal hoped Strelkov was right – that the SAS or someone had been sent in to rescue him. But why would anyone take such a risk for a Muslim student from Birmingham, regardless of who his real father was? He was just some dumb kid who'd ignored everyone's advice to leave Donetsk because he loved a local girl. He felt confused and very alone. In the silence, Vasilev's questions about his relationship with Tanya repeated in his head. Did he love Tanya? Had he ever? Did she love him? Had she ever? Did they have her too? Was she safe? Was she dead? His chest started to pound. He felt as though a black hole was swallowing him up.

He shook his head. He had to try to remain positive; otherwise, these bastards would win. That was it . . . if he was forced to make a video, he would appear on it with a wide smile and act as happily as he could. Who cared about propaganda? He cared about his parents and his family – that was all.

Empowered by his revelation, he decided he wanted to be untied. 'Hello!' he called. He waited . . . There was no answer, so he called again. When there was again no answer, Iqbal tried shouting. 'Hello!'

The door opened forcefully and a DNR militant entered. 'What is it you want?' he demanded in Russian.

'Toilet, please, toilet.'

'Shit yourself.' The man shut the door.

*

The pensioner was called Yuri and had, in a previous life, after his compulsory military service, worked on the Soviet railways, travelling far and wide. 'Even to Tallinn,' he happily told them both. Racine and Snow helped him pack up his makeshift stall and together the three of them crossed the road near the Circus. They drew level with the apartment building and without any issues, Yuri walked up the steps to the open front door. Racine and Snow followed. Racine noticed huge cracks in the building's walls and the balconies looked rusty. As Yuri reached the top of the steps, the door of a ground-floor apartment opened, and a Russian soldier greeted him in the hallway. He had a smooth, round, flat face and coal-black hair spilling out from his cap. 'You finished early for the day?'

'That's right. I have guests; my sister's son and his girlfriend.'

The young soldier eyed Snow with suspicion; his expression changed when he saw Racine smiling at him, and he started to blush.

'I need to see some identification documents.'

'Come on, you know me,' Yuri said. 'You know me so well I even let you beat me at cards.'

'You let me?' The soldier blinked before he smiled. 'No, old man, I am the better player!'

'Come by tonight. I'll have something for us to drink and then we can really see who the better player is.'

The soldier looked past the trio onto the street before he nodded and beckoned them into the apartment building. Without another word, he went back inside his flat. Yuri pressed the button for the lift and the three of them rode up to his floor.

Yuri's apartment – like most of its age – had two front doors, an inner and an outer. The outer was wooden with a spyglass and the inner door was steel covered in padding and quilted faux leather. Yuri shut both doors and held out his hand. 'My money.'

'Of course.' Racine put her hand in her pocket, retrieved the bills, and held them out.

Yuri licked his lips as he took them. He nodded, then removed his boots, hat and coat. 'Come into the kitchen.' Yuri led them down the hall, past a bedroom and around the corner. 'Sit.' He pointed at a thin bench seat, upholstered in burgundy leatherette. 'Now tell me again what is happening here?'

The old man filled his kettle with water from a bottle before setting it on the gas stove whilst Racine elaborated what Snow had explained on the street but in greater detail; the cover story seemed to appeal to Yuri's sense of moral justice, as much as the dollars had appealed to his wallet.

'Where are you really from?' Yuri asked as the kettle started to whistle behind him.

'Moscow,' Racine stated, her accent backing up her claim. 'But I live here now.'

'Hmm,' Yuri grunted. 'That is what it sounds like but . . . ah, it is not important. I am not a traitor, neither to Ukraine nor Russia; let me make that clear. I just want my pension paid on time and for the city to go back to the way it used to be. I don't really care who is in charge as long as that happens.' He rose and removed the kettle. 'You want tea? I have no coffee – it costs too much.'

'No, thank you,' Racine replied.

'Is the apartment next door the same as this one?' Snow asked.

'What do you mean?'

'The layout . . . the floor plan; is it the same?'

'It is the exact reverse.'

'That means the living room is next to your living room?'

'Correct. The two balconies are awfully close. A design flaw, if you ask me. I found the neighbour's teenage son on my balcony once; he was after my pickled cucumber.'

Racine remained stone-faced. Snow, attempting not to snigger, said, 'Never mess with a man's cucumber.'

'Exactly. They have gone now, fled. And my cucumbers have long since been eaten.' Yuri pointed to a collection of empty jars on the windowsill. 'I used to pickle the cucumbers and tomatoes from my allotment.'

'How many Russians are in the apartment?' Racine asked.

Yuri let a large breath puff out his cheeks. 'There are – I believe – always several guards and then there are the men who do the questioning.'

'You've seen them?' Racine asked quickly.

'Yes. They look like officers and are older, but not ancient like me.'

'Have you seen them today?' Snow now asked.

'As I told you earlier, I saw your medical student relative being taken inside. One of the interrogators was with him.' Yuri took a tin containing tea from the cupboard and spooned loose leaves into a china cup.

'Thank you. You've been very helpful.' Racine smiled.

'I am not senile.' Yuri studied them. 'Whatever you are about to do, I don't want to see it. If the Russians ask me about you, I will have to tell them everything I know. Everything you have told me. I will say you threatened me. Held me hostage. Do you understand?'

'We do,' Racine replied.

'Thank you for the money. Now I have to eat something and then I shall sit here and listen to the rubbish Russia is broadcasting on our radio.'

Taking this as their cue to leave, they walked back to the hallway.

A radio switched on in the kitchen, a commercial Russian station, followed by the sounds of food being prepared.

'Do you think Iqbal is still next door?' Snow asked.

'If he's not, we have a problem,' Racine said. 'A kitchen, bathroom, bedroom and a living room. The living room has a balcony, so he'll be in the bedroom.'

'Which is bang in the middle of the flat.'

'We need to breach from two sides.'

'Balcony and front door,' Snow said.

'I'll take the balcony.' Racine wanted to be first in. 'Look at the size of you. I'll go; I'm less likely to be seen.'

'No. You take the door – they'll be less likely to shoot you.'

'No. I'll take the balcony. You'll probably fall off.'

'OK.'

Racine noted an odd look in Snow's eyes. 'What?'

'This may be a gamble too far. It could be a trap. You know that right?'

Her inner voice warned her that it was, but her outer voice betrayed no emotion when she replied. 'We don't have a choice. Are you scared? Do you need another kiss?'

'I need Iqbal alive.'

'And you think I can't take care of myself?'

'That's not what I meant.'

Racine shook her head. 'I'll see you next door.'

She silently headed into the living room. She opened the balcony doors and stayed low, studying the neighbouring balcony. It was empty. She gauged the distance – less than two metres. If she balanced on the railing, she'd be able to jump across. Making sure the Makarov was secure inside her jacket, and now committed, Racine stood. The cool autumnal air hit her face. She casually looked out at the street below. A bus pulled in at a stop, several unremarkable-looking cars passed, pedestrians hurried on the pavement and in the distance a pair of military trucks turned right onto a parallel street.

No one looked up.

No one paid her any attention.

She climbed onto the railing as near to the wall as she could; it creaked and wobbled but held. She bent her knees, took a deep calming breath, swung her arms and then launched herself forward as though she were attempting the standing long jump. It felt like she was floating as the railings of the target balcony grew nearer, but then she noticed the handrail was wet, as if the whole balcony had been recently washed. The soles of her boots clipped the slick, paint-covered iron and she jerked forward. Racine tumbled face first towards the damp concrete. She lowered her right shoulder, took the impact but mitigated this by rolling and coming to a halt against the railings on the far side of the balcony.

She was winded and momentarily immobile. As she recovered the door to the living room opened. The sound of a television wafted out and was immediately followed by a figure holding a Kalashnikov. He was an athletic-looking man in military-issue fatigues, a Russian soldier not a member of the DNR. Not seeing her at first, he pointed his AK one way, and then the other. He spotted her and paused. Confused, he hesitated; his mind attempting to understand what he was seeing.

Racine kicked out viciously at his shin. The Russian grunted and hopped, off balance. Now Racine sprang to her feet and grabbed the Kalashnikov with both hands. They pirouetted, and the Russian still on one foot slammed backwards into the handrail. It creaked loudly in protest, and Racine drove the Russian harder into it. He was strong and determined. Racine now threw herself against him, her momentum rather than her weight making the railings groan again, and then something snapped. The pair froze as a section of the railing plummeted to the ground three floors below. The Russian teetered on the edge, eyes wide. Racine let go of the AK and kicked him hard, in the chest. The burly Buryat fell backwards off the balcony, mouth open but not making a sound. Racine stepped away from the edge, panting. So much for sneaking in and out unnoticed.

She withdrew her Makarov from her jacket, took a final deep, calming breath then spun around the open door and into the room. Eyes and pistol tracing arcs, she dissected the room, searching for threats. It was empty save for the distinctively Soviet-era furnishings and a modern television. Her eyes glanced at the screen and noted what seemed to be Sylvester Stallone brandishing a large machine gun. She continued on as cinematic explosions sounded. Directly ahead the double doors leading to the hall were open, and then the doorbell rang.

Positioned on the opposite side of the flat to the kitchen, the sound of *Rambo III* blaring from the television had masked her scuffle on the balcony. She stepped out into the hall, and turned left with the reassurance of nothing but a wall behind her. Up ahead a large Russian soldier was already at the door and pulling it open. His head snapped sideways when he noticed her and then he jerked backwards as a single shot sounded. The tall figure of Aidan Snow pushed past the falling man and into her line of sight. His Glock angled her way, but when he saw her, he nodded and shut the door.

The assault had turned noisy. Speed rather than stealth was required.

Racine pointed at the door to the room on her left and then at herself. Snow acknowledged her instruction as they both heard sudden shouts and movement from the kitchen. The SIS operative now focused his Glock up the hall.

Racine's left hand reached for the doorhandle of the room to her left when a round, fired blind, ripped through the wood and tugged at her jacket. She jerked back and away to the side, flattening herself against the wall. A second round erupted, this one lower. Footfall sounded now from the direction of the kitchen and Racine saw a Russian soldier dart around the corner, with a short-stock Kalashnikov up and ready to engage them. Snow sent a pair of rounds into the man's head. Finger on trigger, the soldier was propelled backwards through the bathroom door and sprayed the hall with white-hot rounds. He came to rest sprawled over the toilet bowl.

Racine checked her jacket and noticed a hole through the fabric. The bullet had missed her, but the expensive leather was ruined. She cursed under her breath; she'd get another one made up and charge her employer for it. More importantly, however, she felt her side and confirmed that it was only her clothes that were holed. The stench of gunpowder stung Racine's throat and an eerie silence now fell upon the flat. It was too quiet, and their assault so far had felt too easy. She noticed that Snow seemed worried too. More sounds came from the kitchen, a hurried conversation. Did that mean there were two more men there, or only one using a phone? Either way they were not her primary threat – whoever had taken pot shots at her through the door was.

That was where Vasilev would be.

Snow had his Glock trained up the hall, ready to take on anyone who was still in the kitchen. He glanced back at her, as she pointed at the door, then herself and then him. He nodded and, moving quieter than she would have expected, he positioned himself up against the wall on the far side of the door.

She locked eyes with him and mouthed: 'Three . . . two . . . one . . .' before she kicked in the door.

They bomb-burst inside, each carving out different arcs with their pistols, searching for hostiles. She moved left and low and he went right. Their weapons abruptly stopped moving as they found two figures, a soldier and a hostage. The soldier was standing behind the hostage, using him as a shield. The hostage looked dirty and afraid.

Neither was Vasilev.

The soldier had one hand around the hostage's neck and his other on a Makarov held an inch away from the man's skull.

'Drop your weapon or I'll kill him!' he shouted, in Russian.

Without hesitation Racine fired. The soldier's head was instantaneously replaced by a crimson cloud.

'Ahhhh! Please nooo!' the hostage shouted, in an odd accent Racine took to be regional British.

'Is that your man?' Racine asked.

Snow let out a deep breath. 'It's him.'

'Of course I'm him,' Iqbal said. 'Don't shoot me!'

'How many Russians are in the flat?' Racine asked.

Iqbal squinted. 'There were two guarding me. I don't know how many others there are.'

'Stay here,' Racine ordered and turned on her heels back to the door.

'Wait! Don't leave me,' Iqbal visibly started to panic and raised his still-bound wrists.

'We've come to take you home. We'll be back,' Snow said.

Iqbal nodded.

Moving as quickly but as lightly as she could, Racine passed Snow, taking the lead. She didn't want him obscuring her view.

Racine swung back out into the hall, and changed her stance, making herself smaller. She hoped Snow knew she was taking 'low' and leaving him to take 'high'. They tactically moved down the hallway then rounded the corner, Snow sideways on to watch their six, the sound of their footfall inaudible. Racine held up her fist. They stopped; she cocked her head to listen. The door to the kitchen was half closed, and through the opening they could hear a voice now speaking in a hurried, but quiet tone. They knew from the layout of the apartment next door that the kitchen was L-shaped so the seating area would be immediately to the side of the door.

Moving with speed and precision, Racine entered the kitchen. She saw one man.

Not Sasha Vasilev.

The soldier was standing with his back to the sink. His left hand held a mobile phone, and he was talking into it. On the small kitchen table, a Kalashnikov lay just out of reach. In his right hand he held a Makarov, which was a mistake, but he was barely out of his teens, and his reaction saved his life. As soon as he saw Racine he recoiled. Both phone and pistol fell from his grasp and thudded on the linoleum floor as his hands shot above his head and he jabbered, 'No . . . Pl . . . please!'

'Don't move,' Racine snarled, in Russian.

'We need to leave,' Snow stated, 'and quickly.'

'Go. Take his AK.'

Snow took the rifle and left the kitchen.

Racine addressed the cowering, young soldier. 'Where is Sasha Vasilev?'

The soldier's mouth moved but the words it formed were silent.

Racine darted forward and pistol whipped him about the head. The soldier crashed to the floor. Racine bent down, grabbed him by the hair and manhandled him to the table. She had no time to be polite. 'They're all dead. If you want to live, answer my question.'

'Y . . . yes,' the youth stammered, blood dripping from a cut on his temple.

'Who were you calling?'

'Str . . . Stre . . . Strelkov.'

'To tell him we were here?'

The soldier said nothing, but his eyes betrayed the truth and he started to shake.

'Did you tell him we were here?'

'He . . . he wanted me to confirm your arrival.'

Racine realised Strelkov knew they were coming; they'd been lured into a trap. 'How many men?'

'Two . . . two trucks. Fifty Russian troops.'

'How far out?'

'Three minutes away.'

She'd seen two trucks from the balcony. Racine felt a roaring in her ears. They were out of time. 'Where is Vasilev?'

'Vasilev?'

'Raduga, the interrogator.'

'He went home.'

Racine shuddered. Had he escaped, fled back to Russia? 'Home? Where?'

'A penthouse apartment on Pushkin Boulevard.'

'Do you know the exact address?'

'Yes, I've been there.'

'Tell me.'

He told her.

*

'You're British? You're the SAS?' Iqbal asked.

'Not all of it,' Snow replied as he placed the Kalashnikov on the floor and worked on undoing the bonds around Iqbal's wrists.

'Relax. You're being rescued.'

'Is that true? This isn't some kind of a trick?' Iqbal's eyes became moist and he had to sniff back his tears.

'It's true,' Snow confirmed. 'I'm going to take you home, Mohammed.'

'My name's Mo . . . to my friends,' Iqbal said as he pushed himself to his feet, grimacing.

'My name is Aidan.' Snow noticed the state of Iqbal's feet. 'Can you walk?'

'Course I can bloody walk if it means getting out of this place. Just got a few cuts and bruises. Nothing a pint couldn't put right.'

Snow inspected Iqbal's feet. 'What size do you take?'

'Eleven . . . 44 European.'

Snow checked the feet of the dead soldier. 'It's your lucky day.' He heaved the man's boots off and made a face at the smell. 'Perhaps not.'

'Dead man's boots,' Iqbal noted, flatly.

'I wouldn't take his socks. Here.'

'Ta.' Iqbal took the military boots. He closed his eyes and winced as he gingerly slipped his first foot in.

'Your feet need to be looked at, but we've got to get you out of here first.' Snow eyed Iqbal up and down as he put on the second boot. His clothes were filthy, and there was fresh blood splatter on his face.

'Ready.' Iqbal stood. Tears welled in his eyes.

'It'll get better, trust me. The more you walk, the less it will hurt . . . but then your feet will fall off.' Snow smirked.

'Great.'

There was an angry banging on the front door. 'We've got company. Mo, listen to me, I need you to get behind that interior wall and stay down until I say otherwise, got it?'

'Wait, I think I heard Raduga talking about sending more soldiers, about them waiting for you to arrive first.'

'You think?'

'My Russian's rubbish.'

'OK.'

Snow met Racine in the hall. She had an AK to the back of the young soldier. 'Unwanted visitors.'

'It was a trap. There's a Russian force of fifty, two minutes out.'

'Racine, get out the way you came in. You don't need to be here.'

'What about you and Iqbal?'

'We'll manage. We'll have to. Now move!'

Racine said nothing. There was no time and no other option. She left the soldier with Snow and carried on into the living room.

'Speak to the men in the hallway. Say "everything is fine",' Snow now ordered the man.

'F . . . fine?'

'Yes, fine,' Snow said, prodding him again.

'Everything is f . . . fine,' the young soldier stuttered, his voice faltering.

The banging at the front door became more insistent. A brusque voice commanded, 'Open the door. That is an order!'

Snow chanced a glance through the peephole. In the hallway, Russian soldiers had taken up tactical positions; crouching in cover, keeping their rifles trained on the door. Was this the reinforcements or yet more men? An older man, an officer, stood at the front brandishing a pistol; his fist became comically large as he brought it towards the door and banged. Snow backed away; this was not going to be easy at all. The troops hadn't opened fire yet but they would.

'Speak,' Snow ordered. 'Be louder.'

'Everything is fine,' the soldier said, again.

'Open the door . . . immediately!' the officer barked.

There was no other way out. Snow moved to the side. 'I'm going to open the door, and then you will walk out.'

The soldier swallowed and said nothing.

'Tell him you are going to open the door and come out.'

'I'm going to open the door and come out.' The soldier's voice was croaky.

'Louder,' hissed Snow, 'say it louder.'

The soldier repeated the sentence, his voice louder but still strained.

'Now!' Snow ordered.

The soldier took hold of the handle and then jerkily pushed the door open. Unseen by him, Snow had dropped to the floor to the side of the door, with the AK in front of him. Snow imagined the collective Russian trigger fingers taking second pressure. It opened farther, the young soldier stepped out, and Snow opened fire. Just off the floor, angling up, the rounds tore at the shins of the officer and the centre masses of those farther away. AK on full automatic, Snow sprayed the landing, hoping to overwhelm and subdue the opposition by using aggression as a force multiplier. Several soldiers had escaped his fusillade but as he watched them readying to attack, they spun away, taken out by precise shots coming from what he could only reason was the doorway of the next flat, the old man's place.

'Clear!' Racine yelled and then burst into his field of fire, weapon up.

Six Russians lay either dead or incapacitated. The young soldier huddled in the corner with his hands over his head. Racine booted him to the floor. 'Face on the floor, hands on your head.'

Snow got to his feet, a smile had unconsciously formed on his face. Racine was quite an operator. He tactically advanced into the hall and kicked away the rifle of an injured soldier. To his left, the officer lay on his back, both lower legs turned to a pulpy mess. Tears of pain ran down his face. His left hand was in his pocket, Snow's eyes grew wide as the Russian withdrew it. Time seemed to slow as Snow stared at what it contained.

'Grenade!' Snow shouted as he swung the Kalashnikov and drilled the officer's chest with a burst of rounds. The Russian fell limp, the grenade rolled, and Snow dove to the floor in the opposite direction. When Snow opened his eyes eight seconds later, he knew it hadn't been armed. The olive-green, egg-shaped RGD-5 grenade had a delay fuse of approximately four seconds. Snow got to his haunches and double-checked the grenade before he pocketed it. He looked at Racine; she seemed calm, almost icy. 'Thank you,' he said.

'Thank you, I couldn't shoot my way through them all.'

Snow went back inside for Iqbal. He found him crouching on the balcony, peering over the edge.

'We have to go.' He placed his hand on the young Brit's shoulder.

'There's a whole group of people down there.' Iqbal pointed through the balcony doors.

Snow glanced at the street below; a circle of gawking locals stood around the body of a soldier. The most worrying development, however, was the two Russian army trucks now disgorging troops outside. 'Come on.'

They exited the apartment; Iqbal put his hand to his mouth at the sight of the carnage.

Racine had turned over one of the Russians, removed the dead man's military jacket, and thrust it at Iqbal. 'You need to wear this.'

Iqbal was numb. 'Why?'

'Camouflage,' Racine said.

'The Russians are on the street, we need to hustle.' Snow switched out his AK's magazine for one taken from the nearest Russian.

'*Merde!*' Racine swapped her own magazine. 'We need to exfil.'

Snow agreed. 'Those troops will breach this place any minute.'

He moved to the end of the landing and looked out of a window that had a clear view of the rear of the block and the other buildings beyond. 'On me, we'll go out the back. It's clear for now but you can bet it won't stay that way.'

Snow advanced down the stairs, the AK tracking his line of sight. Iqbal was second and Racine was tail-end Charlie. As they reached the bottom of the first-floor steps, Snow held up his fist to indicate that they should stop. Racine pulled Iqbal backwards against the wall, three steps above.

Snow crept forward until he had eyes on the ground-floor flat used by the Russians. The door was open. Had the occupants been included in the assault team upstairs? There was only one way to find out, yet he couldn't waste time checking. He stood by the door with his AK trained inside, and was about to beckon Iqbal and Racine past when movement in another direction caught his eye. AK and eyes moving as one, he turned to face the exterior first-floor window. It was an architectural feature designed to illuminate the stairwell and provide views of the communal playground below. What Snow saw through the discoloured pane, however, was a line of Russian troops advancing across the space. Strelkov's soldiers had arrived.

They were trapped.

'We've got company. Russian troops coming from the rear.'

'*Putain!*' Racine swore, the whispered curse floating on the landing.

'Wh . . . what are we going to do?' Iqbal's voice was strained.

Snow pointed to the door of the apartment. 'We go in there; we hide. It may buy us some time, and they'll think we're upstairs.'

'Upstairs,' Racine said. 'I'll go upstairs. You two get in there.'

Snow frowned. There was no time for questions or debate.

＊

Racine raced back up the stairs, knowing that there was danger below but none above. She reached the floor with the dead Russians, grabbed two more magazines for her Kalashnikov, then carried on up the stairs to the top floor. The landing was empty and the doors to the remaining flats were shut, their residents either absent or cowering behind settees. She was sorry she'd given them nightmares.

In the corner of the space, a green-painted steel mesh door now blocked her path to the last few steps and a smaller wooden door that led to the roof. The padlock seemed more solid than the frame it was attached to. She slammed the butt of her AK down against it and was rewarded not with the lock breaking but with the frame twisting. Using the famously indestructible Russian rifle as a lever she pulled the frame some more until the space between it and the wall was big enough for her to squeeze through.

The wooden door gave her less trouble; a well-placed stomp of her right foot was all it took to splinter the wood.

She stepped out onto the roof. A breeze not detectable at ground level whipped around her, carrying the shouted instructions of military men below.

Shouldering her Kalashnikov, and moving at a crouch, her boots crunching on loose gravel and debris, she edged to the front of the building to see soldiers readying themselves to stream inside. She ignored these and moved to the back. Immediately behind the building was a narrow street with cars parked on one side, dumpsters on the other, and then a grassy area that passed for a playground surrounded by tall trees. It was a classic layout that was found in most cities and the towns of the former Soviet Union, and it reminded her of the older Paris *banlieues*. Past the trees the buildings in the next street were smaller, older two- and single-storey houses and industrial units and it was here that she saw the Russians. She counted twenty, perhaps more. They were approaching weapons up, in a tactical formation, scanning the area ahead – but not looking up . . .

Racine had a plan. She had one Kalashnikov, but she also had ninety rounds. She checked the selector switch was on 'semi-automatic', so she could fire single shots, dropped to her haunches and rested the AK on the protective railings at the edge of the roof. The wind was less on this side and the Russians were now advancing to within range of her rifle. On the ranges she'd trained on the most popular foreign weapons including several versions of the rifle now in her hands, so knew its capabilities, and her own. Hitting the men at this range and elevation, however, was not going to be a duck shoot.

She slowed her breathing, looked down the iron sights and squeezed the trigger. Her first round zipped past the lead Russian and hit the concrete path to his right. There was a slight pause before any of the men reacted. They moved backwards bumping and concertinaing into each other, weapons sweeping erratically.

Racine realised; they may be Russian army, but they were not specialist commandos. She fired two more single rounds in quick succession. The second man in line spun on the spot as a round hit his left shoulder and he lost his weapon. Now the troops started to take action, dropping to their knees or adopting other firing stances but none opened fire, as Racine's position remained undetected.

Racine switched the selector to 'burst' and aimed towards the middle of the pack of men and fired two brief bursts. Three soldiers this time were hit. She chanced a third burst as her vision now flashed with return fire. Racine retreated from the edge until she couldn't be seen and moved as quickly as she could parallel to her first position along the edge of the roof.

When she popped up again her angle was different, because she was further away, but that was her plan. With a new magazine, she fired again in rapid, staccato bursts until the magazine emptied, her shots missing but again getting the Russians' attention. She stepped back, moved further away, switched her magazine for a new one and now in a third firing position, half-emptied the third magazine in the direction of the Russians in a single burst.

The Russians were advancing. They were following her progression along the roof and moving away from the end of the building – the corner where Iqbal and Snow were hiding. Racine only hoped she'd done enough to create a big enough diversion because now she had to escape and continue her own mission.

Running, stumbling and crunching along the centre of the roof unseen, she reached the door she had come out of. She looked inside and saw no one but on a lower floor could hear the sound of boots on the steps and curt commands. She continued on to the far edge of the roof and the curved steel railings that protruded from it. Racine glanced over the edge of the building, the side that faced nothing but its smaller neighbour. The four-metre-wide space between the two buildings was empty. For a crazy moment she contemplated jumping from one roof to the next but instantly dismissed the idea, this wasn't some Hollywood action film. Holding her Kalashnikov now with her left hand, she turned around and swung her legs one at a time over the edge and just hoped that the rusty rungs would hold her weight until she was low enough to jump to safety.

*

Although only a metre from the ground, the flat had an enclosed balcony on the back wall of the building. With the top of his head just appearing over the line of the windowsill, Snow watched the Russians manoeuvre and fire, clearly aiming at someone shooting at them from the roof and being led away from his position. He'd started to like Racine more and more.

Snow moved back into the empty flat, which stank of soldiers – sweat and greasy food – to find Iqbal washing his face and hands in the kitchen sink. 'We need to go.'

Iqbal looked up, water dripping from his nose and eyebrows. 'How?'

'Through the balcony at the back; it's clear for now.'

They headed for the rear of the flat, as outside the front door the sounds of troops in boots continued past and up the stairs. It wouldn't be long before the Russians started to search the place flat by flat. With luck, they'd reach their own lodgings last.

The pair crouched as they entered the balcony, Snow checking their escape route again.

Still clear.

After undoing the latch on the two connecting central windows he pushed them wide then, holding his Kalashnikov to his chest, stepped up and dropped out. Hitting the ground, he immediately bent his knees and then twisted to face the backs of the retreating Russians. They were some distance away at the opposite corner of the building now, but they were still well within weapons' range and if they looked back he'd have no chance.

Snow silently but urgently beckoned Iqbal to join him. After hesitating for only a second or so he landed on the ground next to Snow. 'Get to the next building; try the back door.'

Iqbal nodded and said nothing but also didn't move.

Snow pointed to the door barely twenty metres away. 'Go!'

Now Iqbal loped away, favouring his right leg.

Snow started to back away from his position and was now in the gap between the two buildings. There was a noise to his right and he saw a figure approaching him. Their eyes met and she joined him.

'Nice of you to drop in,' Snow said.

*

'We need to move.' Racine was impatient. She could feel her mission slipping away from her and babysitting Iqbal wasn't going to help. Outwardly she remained calm but inside she chastised herself for failing, for being foolhardy and rushing into an assault without an ounce of planning or absolute proof that her target was there. This was not, however, the time to doubt herself or her skills, and she wasn't alone. She was glad still to have Snow by her side. He was a professional just like her, perhaps even as good. She wouldn't break away from him just yet.

There was a shout and then another. The Russians had turned back.

Racine dropped to one knee and opened fire with her AK, providing the other two with covering fire.

'Moving!' Snow raced for the rear of the next building.

Racine's rounds made the Russians duck back behind the far edge of the building, but then her AK clicked empty on her last magazine. She dropped the assault rifle and sprinted after Snow and Iqbal. Iqbal had already gone through the back door, but Snow was now on a knee with his AK covering her and aimed at the retreating troops. She reached the rear door, still shuddering from having slammed shut, opened it and plunged into the interior gloom as Snow opened up with his Kalashnikov.

Racine heard footsteps at the front of the building and the creak of a door opening. She bounded up the steps, from the rear exit and into the hallway. She saw two figures. The first was Iqbal, who was cowering by the front door; the second was an old woman who was fiddling with her keys and attempting to get in through the door to her flat. She had a huge bundle of clothes on a trolley behind her. Racine recognised her as the woman who'd been selling clothes outside, next to Yuri. Racine reached into her pocket, found a couple of $100 bills and thrust them into the woman's hand.

'I need a coat.'

'Th . . . this is too much,' the woman stammered.

'I'm worth it.' Racine took the first thing she saw, which was a heavy-looking woollen greatcoat. Military chic, she imagined. It was oversized and she slipped it on over her existing leather jacket. 'Thank you.'

She now focused on Iqbal. He was peering out of the front door at the street. Racine knew she had to act. They had no time to wait for Snow, and besides the Russians were looking for a group. She made a decision.

'Mohammed, take my hand. You are I are a couple.'

'W . . . what?'

She grabbed his hand. 'Don't let go,' and then she slowly pushed open the front door.

Looking one way and then the other, she scanned Leninskyi Avenue. Back in the direction she had come from, the two military trucks stood blocking the street in front of the building Iqbal had been held in. In the other direction, however, past the apartment block, a bus had stopped on the road. It was headed the wrong way but it was their only chance of getting away unseen. A huddle of locals were busily boarding the bus and trying to escape the ensuing firefight.

Racine knew it was movement that drew the attention of the human eye, and she also knew she had to move. Fighting every instinct that told her to stay hidden or sprint away, she walked out of the front door, holding hands with Iqbal, and took the steps down at a casual walking pace. He was visibly limping, and she just hoped no one picked up on it. The pair headed for the bus. She could hear shouted instructions behind from a voice she recognised, and she could all but feel eyes looking in her direction. Ahead now she saw a further door of the building swing open and Aidan Snow nonchalantly take the steps down. An elderly woman was on his arm. Despite herself Racine smiled; Snow looked like a doting son. He got to the bus before her and helped the babushka on board. Racine and Iqbal managed to join the bus queue just as the last two passengers were about to board.

Racine paid the driver. He eyed Iqbal suspiciously but made no comment and they moved up the aisle. On the street she now saw soldiers frog-marching residents, including Yuri, away from the building Iqbal had been kept in and yet more soldiers outside. Inside the bus, the back bench seat was empty save for a solitary passenger – Snow – who had deposited the old lady near the front. Snow stood and let Iqbal squeeze into the corner. Racine scooted onto the end of the seat, facing down the aisle.

No sooner had the bus moved off than it started to slow again, its route blocked by the two trucks. Through the shared seat, Racine could feel Iqbal shaking; she noticed Snow put left his hand on the younger man's leg and squeeze. Meanwhile, his right held his Glock in his lap, hidden from sight.

The driver performed an abrupt, emergency stop. A woman near the front of the bus cried out as a group of soldiers, brandishing assault rifles, blocked their progress. They fanned out across both sides. Another passenger crossed herself with her right hand.

Snow pushed Iqbal down below the level of the windows.

The other passengers were either silent or whispering to each other. All well aware that civilian buses had been caught up in the crossfire before or simply been targeted. Experience had told them to keep their heads down and give the men with guns no reason to view them as a problem. Racine huddled against Snow – taking on the role of a cowering girlfriend – but below seat-level, both their handguns were good to go. If she had to fight her way out of the bus, she was going to be the first to open fire.

Outside, the door to the target address was open and armed militants were standing on the pavement. She saw the owner of the café, the same man who had taken her order, being questioned by a soldier who appeared to be in charge. The café owner pointed at the direction of the bus stop they had used earlier before gesticulating towards the balcony above.

Snow was watching too. 'Not good,' he uttered quietly in Russian.

Racine made no reply.

The bus stayed ominously still, its engine idling. A black Mercedes G Wagon containing four men appeared and parked in front of the bus, blocking the lane. Two of the occupants got out and joined the huddle on the street, while the other two stood guard over their vehicle. Both Racine and Snow recognised two of the newcomers. One had an immaculate moustache and dark head of hair, and the other a thick beard.

'Strelkov,' Racine muttered. 'and Boroda.'

'What an unpleasant surprise,' Snow said.

'If they spot us, the game's up,' Racine added.

'What's happening?' Iqbal asked, his voice low.

'Sit tight, but if I tell you to move, you move.' Snow looked at Racine. 'How shall we play this?'

'Hard and fast.'

There was a rumbling noise and a Russian armoured personnel carrier lumbered into view. It stopped on the opposite side of the road and disgorged more Russian troops wearing combat fatigues without their identifying insignia. They fanned out to further prevent the traffic from negotiating the impromptu roadblock. The few cars that were on the road had already stopped, the nervousness of their drivers clearly visible. Racine swivelled in her seat and tried the catch on the large window behind her. Her fingers came away brown with rust where it had oxidised shut. Iqbal coughed and a passenger farther ahead on the bus turned to look back. As he did so, Iqbal coughed again. The man stood up slowly, confusion on his face. Racine could read his mind, *'Why is he trying to hide?'* Racine felt her pulse start to quicken; she realised that their options were narrowing as the seconds ticked by. The man continued to stare, and then darted for the exit, hands held aloft.

'*Merde!* Time to go,' Racine exclaimed, loud enough for the other passengers to hear. 'We're going out of the back. Put your fingers in your ears,' she said to Snow and Iqbal as she turned, raised her Makarov, and fired a round through the rear window. In the confined space, the retort was thunderous as the window exploded and boomed through the length of the bus. In Russian she yelled, 'Everyone out! Now!'

There were screams as terrified passengers started to move, but not fast enough.

'Out!' Snow caught on, raised his Glock and pumped a round into the roof halfway down the bus as an incentive.

Racine vaulted up and out of the shattered rear window, her new coat protecting her from the worst of the jagged glass. She landed in a crouch, weapon up, and sent three controlled shots around the bus into the Russians who were already moving tactically towards the vehicle. The soldiers scattered, taking up defensive firing positions as one of their number was struck down. Now the passengers from the bus ran, arms raised, onto the road, blocking the Russians' line of sight. She was sending civilians into a possible crossfire and hated herself for it, but there was no other way to make their escape, she just hoped the soldiers retained enough humanity not to shoot.

Above the screams, as though in a fog, she heard Snow shout, 'Mo! GO!'

Moments later Iqbal landed in a heap beside her. She hoped to God – or whoever was listening – he hadn't broken anything. Shots now rang out from the front of the bus and she saw Snow explode into the street and sprint full pelt down the outside of it. They had only a matter of seconds before their human shield thinned and incoming rounds attempted to tear them apart. As if to underline this she heard the zip of the first round. The real firefight had begun.

Without time for words, or explanation she slipped out of the heavy coat, hauled Iqbal up by the collar and half-dragged him away from the bus. Every step took them further from death. In front of her, from the way they had come traffic stopped – frozen; some drivers had abandoned their cars while others sat open-mouthed at the unfolding scene. The nearest vehicle to her was a dull-red Audi 80. The driver raised his hands upon seeing Racine. She motioned for him to get out and when he shook his head, she sent a round into his side mirror. She motioned again and this time the man scurried out.

Racine dove into the driver's seat as Iqbal scrambled into the back. She put the car into first, floored the accelerator, and aimed in Snow's direction as he tore towards them. Nearing the SIS man, she hauled on the handbrake and performed a tyre-squealing turn, bringing the vehicle to a halt in the opposite direction. Snow leapt into the passenger seat and before he had chance to close the door, Racine sent the elderly German sports saloon screeching along the wrong side of the road.

'Are you hit?' Snow shouted at Iqbal in the back seat.

'I think I've skinned my knee.' Iqbal's voice was shaky. 'Apart from that, no.'

'Good.' Snow met Racine's eyes in the rear-view mirror. 'And now?'

Racine changed gear and pushed the Audi harder. 'We get out of here.'

NINETEEN

Leninskyi Avenue, Donetsk

Strelkov stared at the disappearing car for a long moment as the men around him continued to fire their assault rifles. He screwed his eyes shut before taking a deep breath and shouting, 'Cease fire!' The Russians stopped immediately; the few DNR militants who had appeared followed suit several seconds later.

Strelkov was incredulous. The man and woman had not only overcome the men left in the apartment, but also torn through the ten-man team in the flat below, and evaded his reinforcements.

Strelkov turned to the nearest militant. The man was unshaven and reeked of alcohol. Strelkov had no doubt the fool would drink himself to death within a few months. 'Call your units, set up roadblocks. Get these civilians out of here, treat any that are wounded.'

The militant saluted. 'Yes, sir.'

Strelkov inclined his head, turned and headed back to his G Wagon. 'Take me to Vasilev's apartment.'

'Yes, sir.' Boroda started the engine. 'Permission to speak, sir.'

'You may.'

'I do not understand. Why is this Iqbal so important? He is just a student.'

'And a king is just a man with important parents.' Strelkov stared out of the window at the empty stores.

'Sir, surely we should use our men to chase the escaped prisoner and not the DNR?'

'No, Boroda.' Strelkov shook his head. 'We should not. We will distance ourselves from the man. The DNR must take responsibility for him, not us, and we have given them the weaponry to do so.'

'These fools cannot be trusted to do anything.'

'That is why I am trusting them with this. The winds are changing, Boroda; you and I may soon be needed elsewhere.' Strelkov had become increasingly unhappy with the men of the DNR, especially when he thought back to his previous assignment. 'In the Crimea, our approach worked. Why was that? It was because of the Russian soldiers under my control. The locals were merely backup dancers. Here, the DNR act like they are prima ballerinas!'

*

Behind them, no one gave chase and the rounds now fell short; in front of them, a building resembling a glittering cake box appeared and the road wound to the left where Leninskyi Avenue became Golden Ring Avenue. On one side, the city dropped away to reveal a lake known as Miskyi Pond and beyond that, Shcherbakov Park. In peacetime, it was the scenic heart of Donetsk where families, couples, and the elderly strolled. Now, however, the area was empty.

'Do you know where you're going?' Snow asked Racine.

'Sort of,' she replied in her almost accentless English. 'I've got a pretty good memory for maps.'

'Here.' Iqbal leant forward. 'That bloke was in such a hurry to lend you his car that he dropped his phone, and he didn't have a passcode!'

'Great. See if you can open it and find a map app.'

Snow took the Samsung. 'Tell me Vasilev's address?'

Racine recited it from memory. A minute later, a Russian female voice provided them with turn-by-turn directions.

'Can I ask a question?' Iqbal leant against the back of Racine's seat.

'Shoot,' Racine said, without irony.

'Why are you after Vasilev?' Iqbal said, earnestly.

Racine eyed the student in the rear-view mirror. 'He's a murdering traitor.'

'Nasty.'

There was an explosion in the road ahead and Racine slammed on the brakes. Iqbal slipped off his seat and Snow steadied himself against the dashboard. 'Incoming!'

Through a cloud of white smoke, they could make out the unmistakable shape of a Russian BMP-2 – a light armoured vehicle, faster than a tank and suited to urban warfare. It could shred them with either its 30mm auto cannon, coaxial 7.62mm PKT machine gun, or – if the crew really wanted to make a point – vaporise them with its ATGM launcher firing AT-5 Spandrel missiles.

'What's the GPS say about this?' Iqbal gingerly climbed back onto the seat.

'If he can't see us, he can't shoot us!' Racine tugged the steering wheel to the right and the worn Audi's suspension all but buckled as they slewed into another street.

'Hey, I know where I am!' Iqbal pointed. 'This is University Boulevard, but it's a one-way street!'

'We're only going one way!' Racine replied. It would work for them; the BMP-2 would get snarled up – even if it went over the civilian vehicles.

They grazed an elderly Lada with the outdated Audi. Immediately on their left was a branch of a Raiffeisen Aval Bank, which had been re-appropriated by the DNR. Racine mounted the pavement to move past several angry motorists before bouncing back down on the road. The heavy retort of the BMP-2's 30mm auto cannon sounded behind them, a chunk of building fell onto the road, and their rear windscreen imploded.

Racine shot a glance in the rear-view mirror. The BMP-2 had also mounted the pavement but was now trapped where the walkway narrowed; stuck in between the solid exterior wall of a building and a cement truck. The armoured vehicle tried to move forward and tore down a blue and white awning proudly advertising an insurance company.

'I hope he's fully covered!' Snow said.

There was a loud thud, and the Audi shook. Racine tugged at the wheel; the saloon had become sluggish. 'Time to bail out.'

Snow turned and spoke to his fellow countryman. 'You are going to open the door and run. Take the first turning you find and wait for me there. Understood?'

'Understood.'

'Head down, hand on the door handle. Ready?' Iqbal nodded vigorously. 'GO!'

Iqbal fell out onto the pavement as Snow fired a pair of rounds back at the Russian armoured vehicle. The rounds wouldn't penetrate the armour, but they might disturb the gunner's aim.

Racine was out of the car and running up the street, every sense firing as she sought out possible threats among the civilians cowering in doorways and behind cars. She felt as though she were running through jelly but understood it was just an effect of the adrenalin on her muscles. At the first corner she turned left, immediately passed a second empty bank, and found herself in a small residential street. Iqbal skidded around the corner, clutching his chest. Racine reached back, seized him by the arm and together they ran towards an unfinished house on the other side of the street. She pushed him down the steep, sloping entrance ramp of the underground garage before dropping prone in the gloom, against the rear wall. Looking back up at the street above with her weapon raised, she was a hard target to spot and a harder target to hit.

She heard the impact of 30mm rounds and imagined the chaos it was causing. Whoever the gunner inside the turret was, he cared little for civilian casualties. A window in the building on the corner exploded and a fraction of a second later Snow appeared, arms and legs pumping. Racine popped her head up and beckoned him over. Snow careened down the ramp and landed heavily at the bottom, his cheek bloody. 'Are we all OK?'

Iqbal, face red, bobbed his head.

'We can't stay here,' Racine stated.

'And we can't make a run for it either,' Snow replied.

Racine looked around. There was a temporary door in the wall behind them, a cheap one-piece item secured with a padlock. 'Kick it – your feet are bigger than mine.'

'I'm glad I have my uses.' Snow arched his back and then drove his booted right foot forward as though attempting to move it through the door. The wood cracked but the door didn't budge. He tried again. This time the wood splintered and the door opened. 'Ladies first.'

Racine hustled Iqbal inside and Snow then shut the door as best he could behind the three of them.

The interior of the garage was a featureless concrete box with a solitary door halfway along on the right. Weapon at the ready, Racine moved towards the door. She doubted the building was occupied but she wasn't clairvoyant. Through the door was a concrete corridor with two rooms without doors on either side. She motioned to the left with her left hand, as though chopping the air. Snow got the message and passed her to check the first room on the left. A couple of seconds later he emerged and then darted into the room opposite. Once he had established this was also empty he repeated the process with the last two rooms. They now moved to a set of concrete stairs leading to the ground floor.

'On me,' Racine said, now taking the lead. The first three steps she took facing forward, before twisting around and carrying on sideways, her Makarov extended above her head. She paused. The air seemed still, stale, and the scent of paint assaulted her nostrils. She darted up the last two stairs, all but vaulting into the void that was the ground floor. The room was large, dusty and empty apart from a stack of used paint pots in one corner. On the left-hand side, where windows had been designed to face the street, thick plastic sheeting had been affixed and billowed inwards holding off the worst of the outside world. The room was dry. It was a decent job. At the same end, an attempt to lay parquet flooring had started and then stopped – another example of life interrupted in Donetsk, she imagined.

Racine remained motionless and listened. There were no creaks from the floor above, no rustling, no scratching of minute concrete particles on boots and no hushed commands. She crossed the room and exited into the hallway. Directly to her right a double-height front door stood proud, plastic still coating a square decorative window. To her left a set of stairs led up to the top floor and beyond these was a double-width open-plan room – a kitchen she imagined. She could see it was empty and she heard no sounds of occupancy. Directly opposite her was a room that she presumed mirrored the one she had just left, but without access to the garage. Did civilians like their houses to be symmetrical? She'd never designed a house, so how would she know? Although Baptiste had once attempted to get her to do so on Minecraft. She frowned. Why was she now of all times unfocused? It made no sense and then she sensed Snow in the room behind her. Racine ushered him forward and pointed ahead. She remained in the hall whilst he cleared the last room.

Snow reappeared and they started to climb the second set of stairs. Again the room she entered was empty. Air billowed in through a hole in one of the plastic sheets and bird droppings decorated the floor, a finished, expensive-looking parquet floor.

Once more she and Snow checked the entire space before finally accepting that they had the place to themselves.

Snow called down to Iqbal, 'Come on up.'

Racine moved to the window and peered out. The street was no longer empty. Civilian traffic now crawled along, directed by men in mismatched fatigues holding rifles. She furrowed her brow. Were they directing traffic away from the road they had just inadvertently blocked or was it some lackadaisical way of searching for them? Whatever, the more civilians on the street the easier it would be for her to slip away, but first the militants and their Russian friends had to move on.

'I don't like it.'

'It's not The Ritz,' Snow replied.

'It's not even a Travelodge,' Iqbal added.

Racine sighed. 'Outside. Look. Amateurs.'

Snow joined her at the window.

'What now?' Iqbal asked.

'We can't leave yet. Rest up,' Snow said.

Iqbal sat down against the wall and folded his arms. Racine continued to observe. From her vantage point she could see where the pavement met the start of the sloping entrance to the underground garage but not the door they had gone through. 'They can choose to search this place at any time, and we've not got the firepower to stop them. We need to barricade the garage door, to at least give us a warning and a bit more time. We'll use the paint pots.'

*

They'd been static in the empty house for almost an hour. The lack of movement had made Racine's adrenalin levels drop and her body ache as she started to realise the full extent of her injuries. She slowly transferred her weight from one foot to the other and rolled her shoulders, to stop her fatigued muscles from tightening. Nothing, however, soothed her throbbing head.

So far, no more than a glance had been cast in their direction by the DNR forces on the street outside. She and Snow had kept watch whilst Iqbal rested. He lay on his side against the wall, having given in to exhaustion. Racine thought he looked like a postcard Parisian beggar and was tempted to ask Snow why he was worth rescuing. It was, she imagined, the first time he'd been able to sleep for a long while in relative safety. He had his own personal security detail, de facto parents, keeping overwatch. Two lines of a poem once learnt and not forgotten found their way into her fatigued thoughts. The words resonated with her. It was a poem about parents and how they mess you up. She quietly recited them aloud.

'Larkin,' Snow said, leaning against the wall next to her.

'You studied Larkin?' Her eyebrows arched.

Snow nodded. 'Yes but I can't remember much.'

'Perhaps we just remember the parts that mean more to us?'

'So did your parents mess you up?' Snow asked.

'Of course.' She looked up at the Englishman. She'd never really spoken about it to anyone, but somehow now wanted to. 'My mum force-fed me bread, tarts and cakes until I was as big as a ball, and then my dad trained me until I lost it all.'

'Trained?'

'He was ex-army – like you.'

'I can't imagine you as a fat kid?'

'Neither could he.' Racine half-smiled at the memories of her and her dad out running and then sparring together at a time when it had just been the two of them, a time after her mother had walked out on them. A time after Celine was dead. She blinked. 'What about you?'

'I've never been fat, except between my ears.'

'That's not what I meant.'

'My parents were . . . are quite nice actually. My dad was a diplomat and my mum enjoyed being a diplomat's wife. I was an embassy brat.'

'Where?' She'd decided she wasn't going to talk about herself anymore.

'Here and there.'

'C'mon, I doubt your formative years are classified.'

'Moscow mainly but also East Germany and Poland.'

'Hence the language ability?'

'I used to give my embassy driver the slip and take the metro home. I'd sit and eavesdrop on the Muscovites.'

'When was this before The Revolution?'

'One of them.' Snow shook his head and smirked. 'And you?'

'I've just got an ear for it.'

'Only the one?'

'Is everything a joke with you?'

'Twelve times out of ten.'

Racine's eyes narrowed. 'You said I was a "twelve" earlier.'

'I did. And I meant it.'

Iqbal snored and then muttered something in a thick, sleep-addled voice. Racine asked, 'So who are his parents?'

'They're his mum and dad,' Snow replied.

Racine sighed and looked out of the hole in the plastic at the street. 'Is there a Mrs Snow?'

'Apart from my mother? No.'

'Was there ever?'

'No.'

'It's the job, isn't it?' Racine asked.

Snow sighed. 'And you?'

'No partner and no children either, just in case you wondered.'

'Why would I?'

'Because I'm a woman.'

'Sexist.'

Racine opened her mouth to reply but then a sound from outside stopped her. On the street below a tracked military vehicle of a design she didn't recognise slowly negotiated the uphill turn before moving away from their location. Behind it a group of men walked with weapons held in the ready position. 'Looks like they're moving their circle outwards.'

'As long as they think we're ahead of them we'll be OK.'

Racine looked back at Snow. 'There is no we. We need to split up. I'm going on alone.'

'We'll always have Donetsk.'

Iqbal snorted and woke up. 'Wh . . . what?'

'Good morning,' Snow said.

Iqbal peered at the pair before suddenly realising where he was. 'Did I snore?'

'Like a train,' Snow said.

'More like a warthog,' Racine added.

'Cheers.'

Racine asked Snow, 'How far to Vasilev's?'

Snow felt for the Samsung he'd stuffed in the pocket of his jeans before leaving the car. He'd removed the battery to prevent it from being tracked but now powered it back up. The screen was cracked, but it still worked. 'About a click east of here.'

Racine held out her hand and Snow gave her the phone. She checked the route on the screen then handed it back. 'Have you still got that grenade?'

'Why? Are you planning on blowing Vasilev up?'

'A "girl" needs options.'

Snow felt in his jacket pocket. 'Here, I know it's an unusual gift for a first date.'

'Thanks. I love it.'

'I'm glad because I don't have the receipt.'

'Really? How can you two act so normal?' Iqbal asked. 'We've been chased by and shot at by a bloody tank.' Iqbal started to mumble to himself, as though he had just remembered what he'd been through. 'A tank, I've been shot at by a bloody Russian tank.' Iqbal shook his head and continued to mutter. Snow sat next to him.

Racine looked through the hole in the plastic. Outside, the street was now still. There was no more military traffic, but she could hear distant male voices shouting. If Vasilev was at home then it was logical to infer that he had finished his duty for the day. If he was going to leave his flat again for food or entertainment she did not know. She had a window but had no idea how large it was. She turned her head. Snow was talking quietly to Iqbal, probably using Jedi mind tricks or whatever it was that the SAS and SIS had taught him. Her father was a huge fan of *Star Wars* and passed this on to her. Her mother had allowed her to have a 'boy's toy' – a Princess Leia doll – however, she'd always rooted for Boba Fett. Without doubt, Snow was a Jedi. And a handsome one at that.

She sighed. Mission mode. She worked alone, always had, and always would. Being with Snow had been convenient, but that was all she could ever allow it to be. The Russians and the DNR were looking for a group of three – not a lone woman and a pair of men. Although she wished Snow and Iqbal well, their successful escape was of no importance to her country. From now on it was her against the enemy, her against the Russians. 'Time to say goodbye.'

'*Bonne chance,*' Snow said.

Racine checked the street again. '*Merci.*'

Snow took a step towards her. 'Look, if I'm ever in Paris . . .'

'If you're ever in Paris, watch out for the dog shit.' Racine winked and abruptly walked downstairs.

Golden Ring Avenue, Donetsk

Racine pocketed her Makarov and continued along the street until she took a left and cut back down to Golden Ring Avenue. What little traffic there was had become backed up because of a road-block created by a green Kamaz military truck. In the distance, she saw the BMP-2 that had shelled them earlier reversing jerkily back onto the avenue and two taxi drivers standing by their cars gesticulating at the scene.

'Take me to Pushkin Boulevard?' she asked the two men.

'What currency?' asked the first driver.

'Twenty dollars US.' Racine was in no mood to haggle.

'Done.' The second driver opened his car door.

As they drove away, the driver regarded Racine in his rear-view mirror. 'Did you need me to perhaps wait for you, or take you anywhere else? I can do that. Walking or stopping cars is just not safe anymore.'

Racine thought for a second; a car would be useful. 'I will pay you one hundred dollars if you wait outside the address for me and then take me to another.'

The driver grinned. 'You bet.'

Military vehicles blocked the road ahead. Racine instinctively felt for her Makarov pistol, still secure inside her jacket.

'Don't they understand that people have a living to make? That we have lives to get on with? No matter, we're turning here.' The taxi took a right, passing an empty sports shoe store on the corner. 'I used to get my kids' trainers there . . . now look at it.'

'Are we far?' Racine asked.

'This is Pushkin Boulevard. Which number do you need?'

Racine was about to answer when she spotted a black Mercedes G Wagon parked half on the pavement ahead outside Vasilev's address. It had to belong to Strelkov. 'Pull in over there and wait.'

'What about my money?'

Racine reached into her jeans pocket and withdrew a fifty-dollar bill. 'Here, half now.'

'Thank you.'

The taxi passed the Mercedes and came to a halt at the next building that, before the conflict, had housed a phone store for the Turkish provider 'Life'; now all that remained was the blood-red signage. Parked nose into the kerb, the taxi was one of many anonymous vehicles. 'Life,' the taxi driver grunted. 'What life do we have here now?'

'I may be a while. Please wait for me.'

233

'You're the only fare I've had today; of course I'll wait.'

Racine exited the taxi and angled herself towards the corner of Vasilev's building and the side street. Unlike many of the dodgy, Khrushchev-era Soviet buildings on the city outskirts, the architecture here was grand – almost Parisian – and the ground floors of the buildings in the area were faced with huge, irregular-cut granite slabs. Very decorative, also easy to climb; the balconies of the first-floor flats were no more than twelve feet off the ground. Reaching the side of the building, Racine was in a blind spot and unable to be seen by the G Wagon. She peered around the corner of the wall and saw that, although the Mercedes was facing away from her, its side mirrors had been angled to provide views of the street behind and the pavement. She wasn't going to get past without being seen.

Racine cast a glance around. The side street was empty; all the traffic was on Pushkin Boulevard. She walked back into the road then ran at the wall. Using her training in *parkour* she launched herself up the side of the building with two powerful strides, twisted to her right, grabbed the railing, and vaulted onto the balcony.

Shoulders protesting, she flattened herself against the wall to the side of the balcony door and counted to ten as she caught her breath, thankful that this balcony was bone-dry. It would have done little for her self-esteem to fall arse over tit a second time. She listened. There were no shouts from below, or within. She edged left and peered through the glass. The living room was empty, yet she could hear a television. Racine tried the handle; it moved, and she pushed the rickety door open. Once inside, she closed it, drew her Makarov, and edged forward through the room. She placed her feet carefully; her rubber soled boots made hardly any noise on the parquet floor, and the television drowned out her footfall. She glanced at the TV; it was showing a Russian military parade and a brass band was playing.

Once out of the living room she warily entered a hallway,

unable to hear if anyone was approaching. On the right and in the corner, she saw the front door; to her immediate right, another door led to what she could see was a bedroom. It meant that anyone in the apartment was probably behind her in the kitchen or the bathroom. She strode to the front door and slid back the bolt; as she did so, a toilet flushed. Racine turned the handle and was through the door before the owner returned from the bathroom. Directly in front of her was a lift shaft, hidden behind a cage. Looking up, she saw that the lift was at the top floor, outside Vasilev's penthouse apartment.

Racine took the stairs. The walls – as in most former Soviet buildings – had a two-tone paint job, green at the bottom and cream from the waist up; in her opinion, neither colour worked. She took the steps two at a time until she reached the fifth floor where she started to move as quietly as possible. Creeping around the final step, she was confronted by two front doors facing each other. The lower floors had four apartments each; here it was reduced to two, giving her a fifty-fifty chance of choosing the right one. However, one of the doors had two Russian soldiers posted outside.

*

'Strelkov.' Vasilev's voice was low and the tone even as he sat on the huge imported Italian leather settee. 'You should have left more men to guard Iqbal. Now we have lost him!'

'I should have? It was your plan, Sasha. Where were you when he was taken?'

Vasilev pointed up at Strelkov with his finger. 'That is different. I am an intelligence officer not a combatant.'

Strelkov laughed out loud. 'You are whatever we need you to be!'

'So tell me, Strelkov, what is that?'

Strelkov didn't reply. Vasilev let out a sudden laugh then

gestured with his arms, expansively; an action that immensely annoyed Strelkov. 'It matters not. What could Iqbal know? He was only a poor student in the wrong place at the wrong time.'

'Really? You now believe this, or is this because your techniques failed on him?'

Vasilev slowly got to his feet, eyes locked on Strelkov's. 'My techniques never fail. I do not fail. I am the best, which is why our president sanctioned my services.'

Strelkov's rising anger had triumphed over his feeling of intimidation. 'Yet you got nothing out of him? He must know something. Twice today we were attacked. He was then rescued by professionals. What government does that for just one man?'

Vasilev didn't reply. His eyes were cold.

Strelkov's upper lip twitched. 'I was never in agreement with our president's plan to put you on display, but I as a patriot had no choice but to comply.'

'No choice? A true patriot would never have contemplated questioning the Russian President's orders. Don't you get it, Strelkov? The president personally welcomed me back into our beloved country. The passport he presented to me is a symbol of Russian sovereignty. It is a statement to those who would oppose us – it proclaims that Russia will, can and shall protect each and every one of its Russian speakers regardless of wherever they find themselves. By posting my photograph online, we are not taunting the west, we are showing them they shall not win the war against our nation, our sovereignty and our very existence.'

'You are a true patriot,' Strelkov said, thinly.

Vasilev's gaze drifted towards the clouds floating outside. 'I was torn away from the breast of Mother Russia and forced to become French. My parents gave me no choice, no consultation. Why was this? Because they were corrupted by capitalism and greed. They planted me in that cesspit Paris, expecting me to forget my culture, my language, and my identity. But I had a

236

conscience and a plan. I knew that by working within the system, within the DGSE, I could bring about change.'

'Very noble.'

Vasilev's eyes focused again on Strelkov. 'Never question me again, or I'll break you.'

A smile spread across Strelkov's lips. 'You and whose army? The DNR?'

Vasilev laughed. 'You are a funny man, Igor. Real Russian humour was something I missed in Paris. The French were too contented, too kind.'

'Yet that did not stop you from betraying them?'

'How can one betray something one is not part of? My passport and ID papers may have said "French" but the blood in my veins was and always shall be Russian. I am a Russian patriot like you, Igor. Mine was a long game. Once I was in Paris and I saw the contempt the west had for us Russians I knew I had to be the one to teach them a lesson. Do I feel remorse for those in Paris I killed? No. Do I feel regret for those French agents I exposed overseas? No.' Vasilev's eyes burned with pride as he continued to glare at Strelkov.

A thin smile appeared on Strelkov's face. 'I have never murdered a woman I loved.'

'What do you know of that?'

Strelkov smirked. 'I know everything about you. You did not choose the timing of your return to Russia. You were forced to flee because your lover was about to expose you.'

Vasilev sighed. 'That is true. She was a foreign intelligence officer. One woman was worth nothing compared to the success of my mission. By the same token, the loss of Iqbal does not compromise our operation today. I am sorry, Igor, I really am for perhaps taking it too slowly with him. Maybe this was a time when brutal methods would have worked? In my heart of hearts, however, I do not believe that he knew anything. I mean who would trust him with anything? Right?'

Strelkov remained silent for a beat before he spoke. 'Nevertheless, the fact remains that Iqbal was rescued by a foreign team and you sit here in your apartment seemingly oblivious to the fact that if the British can snatch Iqbal then the French can snatch you?'

'Let the French come for me.' Vasilev held his head high. 'Do not worry for my safety. I am ready for them; besides to send in troops here, that is an act of war.'

It was now obvious to Strelkov that Vasilev was either not thinking correctly or perhaps had some kind of plan he was not divulging. 'I am the soldier; you are the spy. Do I really need to spell this out to you? This was a black operation, a deniable mission and as such there can be no official reprisal or sanction from the British if we liquidate their team.'

'Their mission is complete. They have Mohammed Iqbal.'

'They have not yet left our territory; of this I am certain. Iqbal is in no fit state to leave on foot. They must use the roads, and the DNR have all roads in and out of the city sealed. Regardless of this, however, we must get ahead of the situation . . . I shall update the VKontakte page and issue a statement that we let Mohammed Iqbal go because we were satisfied he was merely an innocent medical student.'

'The DNR will lose credibility.'

'It will gain respect and display its humanity. Admitting one's mistakes builds respect, and that is what the Donetsk People's Republic needs.'

Vasilev shook his head slowly and collected a half-empty bottle of vodka from the sideboard. He filled two shot glasses and handed one to Strelkov. 'Do you really believe in all of this, Igor?'

Strelkov took his drink. 'The Donetsk People's Republic? No, not all. The concept of Novorossiya – a new larger, grander Russia that encompasses all of our stolen territories including the Ukrainian lands? Absolutely. We Russians are the greatest race on earth, Sasha – on that we do agree. I will not rest until we are united.'

'Then you will be very tired.' Vasilev raised his glass in salute. 'To Novorossiya!'

Strelkov threw the vodka down his throat. 'I will leave you now. Iqbal is gone but tomorrow there may well be new prisoners for you to interrogate.'

TWENTY

Eight Years Ago

Central Paris

It was mid-afternoon and the café was empty, as it had been on her first time there with her boss – Maurice Jacob. They sat at the same table, with two glasses and a bottle of red wine between them as the owner, Francois, busied himself polishing glasses behind the bar. Jazz music wafted quietly from an unseen radio.

Jacob held up his glass. 'This is to you, Racine, the newest member of *The Department*.'

Racine was still getting used to not being called by her first name, but it was the way Jacob operated. 'Thank you.'

Both intelligence operatives drank. Jacob closed his eyes for a moment and listened to the music, his head swaying slightly. When he opened his eyes, Racine noticed that they seemed misty.

'There is something I need to tell you.'

She said nothing, as an uneasy feeling started to wash over her. She sipped her wine.

'You are not the first member of your family I have had the privilege to work with.'

Racine's mind quickly processed the statement. Her father had been a Legionnaire.

Jacob spoke again before she could, as if reading her thoughts. 'It was not your father, although I'm sure his skills would have been useful to us.'

Racine's eyes narrowed as fragments of information and newly remembered memories started to join and form a truth she had never expected to see. 'Celine?'

'Yes.'

The words flew from her mouth, the question desperate to find an answer. 'Do you know who murdered my aunt?'

'Yes.'

'Who killed Celine?'

Jacob raised his glass. There was a tremor in his hand, as he drank the contents. Putting the empty glass down he met her gaze. 'His name is Sasha Vasilev, and he was a traitor.'

'But, he was her boyfriend . . .' She shivered, as though a sudden icy draught had crept into the room. She saw him standing at the restaurant, like a film star, the first time she had met him, and she saw the love Celine had for him.

'I'm sorry. I couldn't tell you before, not until you were officially part of the service.'

Racine felt the room start to sway. Her head shook, as though subconsciously she was trying to deny it. Her words poured out, like a fountain. 'Celine's death pushed my mother over the edge. It made her go mad, it made her run away, it made her leave me. Celine was a sister to me; I didn't think I could go on. The police said there was nothing they could do, no leads, no suspects . . .' She fixed him with cold eyes. 'You knew who had done that to her, and you said and did nothing?'

Jacob refilled his glass before he replied. 'Legally I was not able to say a single word. Celine Durand was an outstanding intelligence officer. She had a magnificent brain, remembered a myriad of details and was a great mission planner. But her greatest asset was her possession of a sixth sense for picking up on anything that was out of the ordinary or didn't feel right. One could call it a threat radar. It saved several operations. Tragically that is why she died. She realised what Vasilev was doing, and he murdered her. She was about to expose him for the creature he really was.'

'But you let him go. France let him go!' Racine's voice was loud, accusative.

'He escaped. The Russians got him out. Immediately afterwards, a number of our agents and operatives overseas went silent. His actions, his betrayal of the Republic of France, sentenced them all to death. He was my protégé and recruiting him, training him, and affording him the opportunity to betray us was my mistake. I was guilty of it all. There is nothing I can do to change the past. There is everything we can do together to change the future. This is why I want you in my department. I want you to find him and kill him.'

'I will.' There was no millisecond of pause or doubt. It was unthinkable that she would not agree. 'Where is he now?'

'We do not know.'

Racine emptied her glass and let her boss refill it.

'I am sorry.' Jacob reached down for his attaché case. From it he pulled out a document folder. He placed it on the table between them. 'There are two files in there. One is on Vasilev. The other is a summary of the pathologist's report on Celine.'

Racine took the folder, and her hand shook. A pair of A4 pages stapled together – photocopies of an official document – made up the top document. The notes on her aunt. Her mouth became dry, and a sudden lump appeared in her throat. Racine took her glass, knocked back its entire contents and then started to read.

The body of Celine Durand had been discovered at the Paris apartment of fellow DGSE officer Sasha Vasilev. It was believed, the author noted, that at her time of death Durand had been in a relationship with Vasilev. She had suffered cuts and contusions on both her arms, which the pathologist recorded as defensive injuries. Blood loss had been determined as the cause of her death brought on by a severing of the carotid artery. A jagged wound that ran the width of her neck had all but decapitated her. The murder weapon was deemed to be a serrated kitchen knife found by her side. Further away from the body, but also on the floor in the hallway, was a broken vodka bottle. It was smeared with both the tissue and blood of Sasha Vasilev. The pathologist surmised this had been used either to attack or to defend against Vasilev.

Racine looked up at Jacob. He met her eyes and nodded slowly.

'Six of our colleagues are dead because of him.'

TWENTY-ONE

Present Day

Central Donetsk

Hidden in her spot on the floor below, Racine heard the penthouse door open. She remained still and waited for the lift doors to open and close. It descended, at an arthritic pace, towards the ground floor. Racine looked down the lift shaft and caught a glimpse of Strelkov and two soldiers exiting through the cage at the bottom. Did this mean Vasilev was at home, and if it did, was he alone? Did the man know he was in danger or did he presume that Iqbal had been the sole target? Racine assessed her options. The safest course of action would be to wait until he exited the apartment, but that could be hours, and that he would expect, if he expected anything. In the meantime, the dragnet would draw ever tighter as the DNR and the Russians searched for her, Snow and Iqbal.

She had no choice.

She could risk waiting no longer.

She had to act.

And then the door to her target's flat opened.

Racine moved back away from the railings and into cover.

Below her the lift began to rise. It stopped, on her target's floor. The doors opened, a passenger – she couldn't see who – stepped inside and then it descended once again. Racine waited until it reached the ground floor then peered down. She saw the top of a man's head, and then part of his face. Her target. He crossed the foyer towards the door to the street beyond. Racine raced down a flight of stairs until she was level with a window that faced the street. She looked out. Sasha Vasilev was crossing the road and heading towards a shop of some sort. An unexpected anger abruptly engulfed Racine as the absurd normality of the scene struck her. Her target was sauntering away without a care, relaxing after a usual day at the office.

Racine's eyes twitched and her vision became blurred as she remembered the full pathologist's report. It had shocked, saddened and disgusted her, but it had driven her ever since. And her boss had used it as a perfect, if perniciously blunt recruitment tool.

As a teenager she had mourned the loss of Celine and as an adult she dreamt darkly of confronting her killer and executing him. The scene had played over in her head, on a loop as she slept, the build-up, details and dialogue rewritten innumerable times. But she knew there would be no grandstanding. She would not tower over him giving an account of his crimes and letting him beg for his life or plead for forgiveness. When the time came, she intended to act in a clinical, decisive manner. Sasha Vasilev would immediately cease to exist, and Celine Durand's legacy would live on.

Racine blinked, her eyes unexpectedly moist. A hard determination now replaced any softer emotion she may have felt. There was a noise from above – the door of an apartment opening and then the shuffling of feet. She readied herself for action, but then she heard the door close again and there was silence. Had it been perhaps one neighbour checking on another? The lift was not called and there was no further footfall. As she listened other sounds now drifted into her ears – the movements and words of the many residents carrying on in the war zone.

Outside her target reappeared. She tracked Vasilev as he retraced his route. He was carrying a gaudy-looking plastic bag. Vasilev disappeared from Racine's field of view and she moved back to her original hide. The lift started to ascend. She waited until it was one floor below her before she moved upwards with it. Hidden by the side of the lift and standing several steps below the level of the floor, she waited as the doors opened and her target exited. He headed directly to his door. He transported his bag into his left hand and using his right reached into his pocket. Pulling out a set of keys, he set about clumsily unlocking the door.

Ramped up on adrenalin and rage, Racine sprang forward, crossing the space to Vasilev's door in rapid strides. She slammed the sole of her right boot squarely into the middle of his back, transferring her weight through it and forcing Vasilev to crash past the door and into his entrance hall. Vasilev landed on his face and slid forward on the polished parquet floor as his shopping bag shot sideways, smashing a mirror on the side wall. Racine drew her Makarov with her right hand, grabbed the side of the door with her left and swung it shut.

This was it.

The time to pull the trigger.

Time to end Vasilev's life.

Time to complete her mission.

Yet this was the first time she was killing as much for herself as she was for France. She felt her pulse rise as she gazed at her aunt's killer, the man who had murdered Celine, as he started to groan and regain his senses. The liquid contents of his bag began to trickle towards him, following the edges of the wooden tiles like the first waves of a tide reclaiming the shore.

Racine's finger was on the trigger.

Her finger felt the pressure.

Vasilev started to push himself up from the floor. His back was towards her.

Racine said, in French, 'Hello, Sasha.'

Vasilev twisted around. Racine's finger tightened on the trigger, but she let him stand. They were the same height. Their eyes met. Bewilderment momentarily flashed across a face Racine had not seen for fourteen years.

There was a tremor on Vasilev's lips before he spoke. 'Celine?'

'No.'

In her mind the past and the present collided. She was both with Celine meeting Vasilev for the first time and now alone and grown, meeting him again. She was the teenager, whose life he had irrevocably damaged and she was the woman wreaking revenge.

'I am Sophie Racine!'

A noise. A metallic rasp.

A weapon.

A shrill, sharp sound, rubber slipping wood.

The bottom of a tactical boot moving . . .

Racine threw herself to the floor as a barking, burst of rounds from a Kalashnikov slammed high into the door behind her. Prone, gun outstretched, on the floor, in the entrance hall Racine was an easy target. To her right there was a wall, to her left Vasilev and the shattered mirror, and behind her the door. No cover, nothing at all, and nowhere to go. Immediately in front of her, large wood and glass ornate double doors marked the entrance of the living space. They were open and from inside she could see four men in military fatigues had now taken up positions. Two were at the rear of the space, standing, part-obscured by structural pillars; two others were nearer and crouched behind heavy-looking pieces of wooden furniture.

Racine's Makarov roared twice, the sound echoing off the wooden floor and all but bare walls. Her shots hit the nearest crouching gunman in the shoulder, making him spin backwards and his rifle clatter to the floor. The three others didn't return fire. Their rifles were trained on her, three assault weapons at near point-blank range.

Racine sensed movement to her left . . . Vasilev. His boot collided with the side of her head. The impact lifted her up and sideways. She slid into the wall, her Makarov spinning from her hands and her vision greying out at the edges.

'Pick her up!' Vasilev ordered.

Two pairs of tactical gloved hands grabbed her under the arms and hauled her to her feet. Her knife, liberated from Vadim, fell from her jacket pocket onto the floor.

'That was very impressive,' Vasilev said, in French with an amused tone in his words.

'Shall we search her?' a gruff voice asked, in Russian.

'What else will she be carrying – ballet tickets? Take her into the living room,' Vasilev snapped back.

Racine's head dropped as the two gunmen dragged her – her open jacket flapping – through the doors and into the next room. Her vision started to clear as she scanned the space. Against the far corner next to the balcony doors was the largest and longest L-shaped leather settee she had ever seen. The two gunmen pushed her onto it whilst a third kept his Kalashnikov trained at her head. The gunmen moved away. Two of them now had their AKs aimed at her, whilst through an arch the third attended to the fourth's shoulder in the open-plan kitchen. The injured man moaned and cursed her in guttural Russian.

Vasilev sat on the other side of the L, his back to the balcony. Sunlight streamed in around him. He was cast into semi-shade in contre-jour effect. 'I hoped we would meet again. I did so much enjoy the time we spent together, before I had to leave France. You accepted me like an uncle.'

Racine didn't reply. There was a rushing in her ears. Every part of her wanted to leap at him, destroy him. Her hands were by her sides, palms flat against the seat, ready to spring up.

Vasilev leant forward slightly and studied her face. 'Looking at you, I feel like I am a time traveller. You have not merely inherited her looks but in addition her tenacity.' He paused, then leant back lazily against the plush leather. 'I loved Celine. Is that what you expected me to say? It is the truth. I was in love with your aunt – Celine Durand. I always will be. Which is why it tore me apart when I was forced to leave her.'

'You murdered her.' Racine struggled to control her raging emotions.

'Three months ago, my Tunisian operation was thwarted by a lone female operative. Imagine my surprise, and I shall be honest, my joy, when the only member of the team to escape sent me a photograph he had taken of this "Wonder Woman". It was you, little Sophie Racine all grown up.'

Racine made no move to reply. Something told her if she listened to Vasilev's diatribe she may learn something, and he had already told her there had been a fourth man.

'How could this be, that the French had such a woman working for them in a unit that I knew nothing about? I was once the expert on all matters DGSE, but that was over fourteen years ago and, as I am sure you are aware, intelligence is so time-sensitive.'

Something started to connect in Racine's mind. A small frown appeared on her brow.

'That!' Vasilev pointed at her, a quick smile flashing on his face. 'That is the same "tell" Celine had. You've made the connection, haven't you?'

Racine managed to bite back her reply.

'I knew you would come for me. I engineered it. Even that pompous Strelkov knew nothing about it.'

Despite herself she said, 'How?'

'Ah.' A grin appeared on Vasilev's face. 'Think about it, Sophie, a Jewish lawyer, no less, from Donetsk appears at the offices of the mighty DGSE stating he has been interrogated by one of France's most wanted men – me. Yet this walk-in happens a day after the DNR post a photograph of me on their official VKontakte page?

Implausible but compelling and verifiable, and I calculated it all. Both events were real; both events happened. I was concerned you might not make it to me, but I had no other choice. Your journey had to be real, and here you are.'

'I am not a traitor,' Racine stated.

'I knew you would understand. Imagine what an advantage Russian intelligence will have by gaining the very latest intel on the inner workings of the DGSE, especially their hitherto unknown clandestine operation team – 'The Department'. Imagine how the Russian President will reward me. You see, there were rumours about a female assassin carrying out daring, impossible, deadly missions – but the thinking in Moscow was this must be Mossad. How wrong we all were. Tell me, Racine, does Maurice Jacob still drink at that awful, dingy little café by the Seine? How is his drinking problem now? Does he still carry around that awful hip flask?'

'I am not a traitor,' Racine repeated, raising her right hand to point at Vasilev, an act that made the twin Kalashnikovs twitch, before she let it drop into her lap.

'There are many methods to elicit your secrets without your consent. Some physical, others pharmaceutical, although these can also – I must warn you – exact a toll.'

Vasilev paused again. An expression crossed his face that was hard to read. Racine remained silent. It was now clear that he had no intention of killing her immediately, but this did not give her any hope.

There was a banging at the front door. The barrels of both rifles jerked towards it. Vasilev's head turned. 'Let them in!'

Racine's right hand speedily snaked inside her jacket, into her concealed pocket. Her fingers grabbed the grenade.

The two gunmen moved.

'Not you!' Vasilev roared. 'Fools. You, in the kitchen, answer that.'

Racine sprang to her feet. She removed the pin and began to

count down from five, the longest five seconds of her life. The gunman from the kitchen came through the arch and froze, the two gunmen in front of her started to swing their aim back to her and Vasilev, head turning, eyes widening, started to shout.

She tossed the grenade at him. His hands shot up in a reflex action to stop it from hitting his face. Panicked, the soldiers began to shoot and rounds tore into the floor. Racine leapt over the back of the settee, took two steps and threw herself through the glass and wood of the balcony doors. She hit the concrete and spun to one side, forcing her back against the exterior wall. The grenade detonated. Eyes closed, she felt the shock wave through the wall.

Racine rose to her feet, using the wall for support. She took long, deep breaths. The ringing in her ears began to die away. She pushed off and threw herself back through the cloud of dust and smoke that was drifting from the shattered doors, expecting at any moment to be greeted by a hail of gunfire.

Immediately inside the white walls had been blackened. Vasilev lay face up, behind the shredded settee, as though he had been blown over the back. He had managed to divert the grenade as the parquet floor was smouldering from where it had exploded. This, however, was directly between the two gunmen. They were unquestionably dead, and Vasilev was motionless. Blood seeped from the side of his mouth and the back of his head. However, there was movement and noise from the two men in the kitchen.

One was on his hands and knees and the other was slumped sideways against the kitchen island. Racine scooped up the nearest Kalashnikov and fired a burst into them both, before advancing into the kitchen to deliver more rounds to the chest of each.

Before she could return to Vasilev, another explosion shook the flat. The door – someone had made entry. She swapped out the magazine on the AK and moved back into the lounge at a crouch. Her eyes flicked to Vasilev – he still had not moved – then to the entrance hall. Three armed men were advancing over the battered door and into the flat. The further in they got, the better their angles would become. Switching to full auto, Racine unloaded the magazine at the trio before moving forward. She dropped her rifle and grabbed the remaining rifle from the second dead gunman. She scampered into cover behind a wooden cabinet. Erratic return fire barked back at her, but she jinked left and opened up on the other side.

One of the three was down, the second was holding his leg, whilst the third was aiming his rifle with one hand, desperately attempting to pull his injured teammate to safety with the other. Racine shot them both in the head.

In the tinnitus silence of the flat she coughed. Gunpowder clawed at her throat, but nothing stirred. She advanced to the door and stepped out onto the landing. There was no one in sight, but it wouldn't take long for more Russians to arrive. The door of the other penthouse was open. She couldn't ignore it. With nothing to lose she moved over the threshold. The layout was the same as Vasilev's own flat but this one had military cots littering the main room instead of expensive furniture. She realised then that the men who had been with Vasilev had been billeted there. She shook her head – she'd even heard them get into position earlier.

Moving further into the second flat, weapon up, she found an ammunition store. There were several AKs and a bag of grenades. She took two grenades, one for each pocket. Flickering lights coming from another room now caught her eye. She entered and came face to face with a room of monitors and hard drives. The screens were on and displaying a video feed. Her eyes narrowed as she recognised it as the flat where Iqbal had been held. The rooms were empty but she could make out strike marks from the rounds fired. She had not come to collect intel but to terminate Vasilev yet she now had to destroy this evidence of her presence in Donetsk. Pulling the pin on a grenade, she placed it on the floor directly between two servers and sprinted out of the flat.

She on the landing when an explosion shook the apartment building for the third time that day.

Back in Vasilev's flat now she saw the Makarov she had dropped earlier lying in the hallway and not far from it her knife. She collected both, left the AK and made once again for her target.

Vasilev was propped up against the wall, next to the shattered balcony doors. His voice was ragged. 'Very . . . very impressive.'

'I am.'

Her eyes met his.

She fired twice.

The Makarov roared. Two 9mm rounds struck Vasilev in the chest, jerking him back into the wall. He slid sideways, his gaze still on hers. Irregular breaths escaped his lips and then his eyes rolled up and he became still.

She stood, immobile like a statue, like a monument to revenge, unable to remove her eyes from Vasilev's corpse. The Makarov felt suddenly heavy in her leaden hands. She realised there was no blood at all seeping from his chest wounds. It was as though she had missed, or the rounds hadn't penetrated his chest. He was wearing a ballistic vest.

Vasilev's eyes snapped open. Racine pulled the trigger, placing a bullet an inch above and precisely between them.

TWENTY-TWO

Voroshylovs'kyi District, Donetsk

As far as Snow could tell, the DNR had not sent any men after them up the hill on foot – but that did not mean that they were not being watched. Farther along the road and to the right, a fourteen-storey Soviet monstrosity of an apartment block had overlooked their hiding place, and anyone who had happened to stare down from their balcony would have been able to see Snow and Iqbal lurking. No one had come and after waiting for a further five minutes, the pair had broken cover and started to amble along the street.

'Where are we going now?' Iqbal asked.

'We're going to get a lift from the people who should have helped you in the first place.'

'The A-Team?'

'No, the OSCE.' Snow smirked. He was glad Iqbal had managed to keep his sense of humour. 'You do like your Eighties TV.'

'Of course, man. Daytime satellite TV, a student's best friend. Back home, that is.'

'Have you ever been to the Hotel Park Inn?'

'The Radisson?'

'Yes.'

'Then yes, I have. My dad's got one of their reward cards. When he and Mum came to visit me, they stayed there.'

'That's where the OSCE is based.'

'Great, it's not far up the road from here.'

'OK, we need to get moving.' He walked casually with Iqbal limping at his side. Iqbal was probably one of the only ethnic Pakistanis left in Donetsk. They needed to get off the streets but the risk of being spotted stealing another car or hailing the wrong taxi was too great. An engine growled behind them, loud for a civilian vehicle. Snow spun. An armoured all-terrain 4X4 GAZ Tiger was negotiating the corner. Snow grabbed Iqbal by the arm and hurried him off the pavement. Walking with a normal gait but as quickly as he could, Snow took them down the side of an apartment building and around the corner. Half a minute later the Tiger passed on the road, the turret gunner leaning against his 7.62mm PKP Pecheneg machine gun. Someone had literally brought out the big guns to find them.

Snow noticed that Iqbal had started to shake again. 'Come on, Mo. We gotta go.'

'Ladies first.' Iqbal tried to calm his nerves.

They cautiously got back onto the pavement. Snow continuously scanned the road ahead and its passing motorists and pedestrians for potential risks. In his pocket, he had his right hand clasped around his Glock. The road ahead ended in a T-junction. They turned right to take them farther away from the traffic and their pursuers.

They crossed the road and walked uphill. Huge trees lined the narrow street and their bright autumnal leaves offered some concealment from the other side. At the top, they turned left at the T-junction. Snow noted the name of the street: *Red Army Boulevard*. Unlike Kyiv's impressive street of the same name, this one was narrow, had residential buildings on one side, and sheets of corrugated iron sealing off wasteland on the other. A large sign next to an abandoned bank read: '*Office furniture for rent'*. The surrealism of urban warfare never ceased to amaze him. He imagined that the business had already ceased trading. Turning the next corner, they walked into the back of the Tiger. Snow grabbed Iqbal's arm and hustled him back the way they had come, using the only cover available – a low brick wall.

'Did they see us?' Iqbal's eyes were wide.

Snow looked around; they weren't visible from the road. They stayed put, waiting for the Tiger to move on before Snow led the pair back onto the road.

They continued on their route for another six minutes before Iqbal pointed. 'That's the Radisson.'

Bordered by giant evergreens, it was a squat utilitarian building that would not have been out of place in any Scandinavian country. The vehicles outside, however, were out of place. Snow counted six white OSCE Land Cruisers and several civilian SUVs with DNR flags attached to their bodywork.

Had Strelkov predicted their destination? Were the militants waiting for them? Snow took a deep breath and turned to Iqbal. 'Now listen . . .' Snow reached inside his jacket and withdrew the creased OSCE tabard '. . . we are going to walk in there, past any militants or Russians, and we are not going to stop for anyone.'

Iqbal looked unconvinced. 'OK . . .'

Snow handed Iqbal the tabard. 'Put this on.'

'Me?'

'Yes, you. The DNR have never shot an OSCE member and I don't see why today is going to be any different. Now follow my lead.'

Snow stepped out of trees and walked, head held high, directly towards the hotel reception. Iqbal was at his side, attempting to walk equally as proud and ignoring the pain in his feet. They took the ramp up; each step made them more visible to those inside. A militant in combat fatigues sat on a railing by the double doors, a cigarette hanging from his lips. It fell from his open mouth as he saw Iqbal approaching. Snow locked eyes with the man and spoke in his best plummy British accent: 'Good afternoon.'

The militant gave a nod, his mouth still open, and they passed him. Inside, the reception area was white and minimalist except for the mustard-yellow reception desk and the dark brown wall immediately behind it. Both had stylised images of miners on them, painted in what looked like real mustard to Snow. The hotel employee on duty was young and wore an immaculate purple waistcoat over his white dress shirt.

'Hello there, I need your help.' Snow continued speaking English. 'We have arrived today and were meant to be met by a colleague. I'm terribly sorry, but I've forgotten his name.'

The receptionist wrinkled his brow. He finally asked, in lightly accented English, 'Is he a guest at this hotel, sir?'

'Yes, he is. Perhaps you know him? He's even taller than me, has blond hair, and is Dutch.'

'Oh, I see. That is Mr Freek Benscoter.'

'Freek?' Iqbal repeated the name, incredulously.

Snow addressed the receptionist again. 'Could you possibly call his room and ask him to come to reception?'

'Of course, sir.' He looked down at his computer, found the room number, and tapped it into his phone. Snow followed his fingers. Benscoter was in room 361. He put the handset to his ear and when the person at the other end picked up, he relayed the message quietly. He replaced the handset and gave Snow a professional smile. 'If you'd like to take a seat, Mr Benscoter will be down in a moment.'

'Thank you.' Snow scanned the foyer again. The DNR militant from outside had since entered and was standing next to another man by a side door. They were both talking and staring at the reception desk. 'Come on, we'll move to the lifts.'

The two militants followed Snow and Iqbal with their eyes. Snow watched a light on the lift indicate that it was descending.

The doors pinged and a giant stepped out. Snow breathed a sigh of relief; it was the same monitor he had seen at the garage.

Benscoter stopped when he saw Iqbal in the OSCE tabard. 'Who are you?'

'We need your help,' Snow stated.

'You are English?'

'Yes.' Snow looked back at the two DNR men; one was now on a mobile phone while the other still stared at them. 'This man was held illegally, against the terms of the Minsk II agreement, by the DNR. He is also a British citizen. I rescued him today.'

'Rescued? Who are you?'

'I'm working on behalf of the British Foreign Office.'

'I see, and what is it you want me to do?'

'I need the OSCE to drive us out of Donetsk and back to the Ukrainian lines.'

'We are here to observe. We do not take sides.'

'You facilitate the release and handover of prisoners? This man was illegally held by the DNR.'

There were noises behind and the two militants started to walk towards them.

Benscoter looked over their heads at the men in uniform. 'I see your point. You understand that I am not the boss. You must persuade Gordon Ward; he's in charge and, like you, he is British.'

'Show me your papers,' the militant who'd been smoking grunted to Iqbal.

'Everything is in order,' Snow said. 'We have every right to be here.'

The second militant glowered at Snow and took a step forward. 'No Eeenglish.'

'You must go. This is official OSCE business!' Benscoter's voice boomed.

'*Suka,*' *Bitch,* the second militant hissed and both DNR members moved away.

'Please,' Snow implored. 'This is serious. We need your help.'

258

Benscoter held the gaze of the retreating militants. 'I see it's not safe for you to wait for Gordon here. Follow me.' Benscoter pressed the open button and they followed him inside the lift. Once the doors had closed, he cast his eyes over Iqbal. 'How long did they hold you for?'

'What's today's date?' Iqbal asked. Benscoter told him. 'Two months.'

'Where were you held?'

'A couple of places – I don't know where.'

'Why were you in Donetsk?'

'I was studying at the medical university.'

The Dutchman shook his head. 'This whole thing is a farce. I was in the Dutch army and I've served as a UN peacekeeper, but what good we are doing here I do not know.' The lift stopped and the doors pinged open. Benscoter continued to talk as he showed them into his room. 'At least we *are* here and reporting on what we see.'

Snow walked to the window and looked out on the scene below. From the room's limited vantage point, nothing seemed to have changed since they had entered the hotel. 'Where is Ward?'

'I am expecting him back at any time. He's normally out and about, talking to the locals. He likes to think of himself as a man of the people – "hearts and minds" he calls it.'

'I see.' Snow knew what 'hearts and minds' was; the SAS had invented the doctrine.

'Listen—' Benscoter pointed at Iqbal '—you look and smell like shit. Please use my shower. I'm afraid that I don't have any clothes that will fit you though. I'm going back downstairs to wait for Gordon. It is better if your request comes from me.'

'Thank you.'

Benscoter glanced at Snow. 'Thank you for letting me do something of help for once.'

After the Dutchman had left, Snow turned to Iqbal. 'You heard the man, strip.'

'But I hardly know you.'

'Mo, get in the shower.'

'I don't suppose we could call room service? I'm starving, man. A club sandwich would hit the spot. Make that a chicken club. I've been dreaming about fried chicken.'

'Wash. Soon we'll be eating chicken in Kyiv.'

Snow found the unit under the television. It contained a small fridge, barely cold and stocked with two bottles of Georgian mineral water and a can of Fanta. Snow drank one of the waters leaving the other and the Fanta for Iqbal, and moved to the window. He opened it and cold autumnal air wafted in; the temperature had dropped.

Snow looked around the room and his eyes fell on the television; it had no doubt stopped playing BBC World or CNN. Mo started to sing in the shower just as there was a noise at the door. Snow drew his Glock as the door opened and a large figure entered.

The Dutchman stared bug-eyed at him, instinctively raising his hands. 'It's me.'

'Sorry.' Snow put the Glock away.

The Dutchman closed the door. 'I received a phone call, and Gordon is five minutes out.'

'Did you talk about us or our situation?'

'Of course.'

Snow closed his eyes. 'The Russians are monitoring the mobile network. I don't know how good they are, but somewhere there is now a record of you talking about us, which will eventually be flagged and acted upon.'

Benscoter's mouth fell open.

'Here's what I need you to do. Meet Ward at the front of the hotel and have him go to the goods entrance. Mo and I will meet you there.'

'He hasn't agreed yet to take you.'

'Make him agree; be persuasive.'

'I'll see you downstairs.' Benscoter exited the room.

Snow felt in his jeans pocket for one of the two small Nokias he and Racine had taken earlier in the day. He couldn't risk using it but some of the numbers stored on it could possibly assist the SBU. He'd pass it on to Blazhevich if, when – he reprimanded himself – they made it out. 'Mo.' Snow knocked on the bathroom door. 'We need to go.' Snow checked the window; he couldn't see any more DNR or Russians than before, but that did not mean they weren't there.

Mo exited the bathroom with a towel held around his waist. 'That's better.'

Snow noted the dark purple bruises on the Brit's arms, legs, and torso. 'You need to get dressed; our ride is on the way.'

'Right.' Mo vanished back into the bathroom. In the world outside the window Snow saw a white SUV appear through the trees and enter the approach road.

'Ready.' Iqbal hobbled over to the bed and sat. He was dressed in his dirty clothes. He held the OSCE tabard up. 'Shall I?'

'Yes.'

Iqbal slipped the tabard back on over his jacket, and then reached for his boot.

'You'll never get those boots back on with the state your feet are in. Wait a sec.' Snow took the pillow case from the bed, ripped it along the seam, and then tore it in two. He crouched in front of Iqbal. 'I need to bind your feet. This'll hurt, but it's the only way.'

'Go for it.'

Snow took the thin cotton strip and wound it tightly around Iqbal's right foot.

'Did you learn how to do this in the SAS?' Iqbal winced. 'Look, I'm not daft. I get it that you are some type of super-spy. What about that Racine?'

'Super-spy?' Snow smirked.

'What is Racine?' Iqbal repeated. 'Is she CIA?'

'Why do you say that?'

'She's too fit to be British.'

Snow smirked. 'She's not CIA.'

'What then?' Iqbal persisted. 'French? You mentioned Paris.'

'Hot,' Snow stated, with a straight face.

Iqbal burst out laughing, and then started to cough.

Snow handed Iqbal the can of Fanta. 'Drink that. You need the sugar.'

Iqbal emptied the can speedily and then said, 'Dog shit.'

Snow frowned. 'What?'

'I went to Paris once. She's right – the streets are covered with dog shit. I blame those women with little dogs in big handbags.'

Snow tried not to laugh. He noticed a plastic hotel laundry bag by the side of the bed. 'See if there is a half decent pair of socks in there you can borrow.'

Iqbal put the bottle down, leant forward, and picked up the bag. He pulled out a pair of grubby grey socks. 'These'll have to do.'

'I hope our Dutch friend hasn't got athlete's foot.'

'Don't even joke.' Iqbal feigned disgust. 'Look . . . I know it's your job, but thanks. Really . . . thanks for rescuing me.'

'It's what I do. We're not out of the woods yet though.'

Iqbal shook his head. 'All those people dead, Russians and DNR, just to get me out.'

'Mo, it was their choice to hold you against your will. They knew the consequences. And after all—' Snow put a hand on his shoulder '—you're a very important person.'

'Yeah.' Iqbal snorted. 'Do you know the real reason why they sent you to get me?'

'Because you are a UK national held illegally by terrorists.'

'But who did your boss get the order from, the Foreign Secretary?'

Snow replied, 'I can't comment.'

'Robert Holmcroft is my father. My birth father.'

'The Foreign Secretary is your father?' Snow was shocked.

'Yep. That's the big secret. My mum and dad and Robert used

262

to live on the same street and knock about together as teenagers. My mum and dad were promised in an arranged marriage, and when Robert got Mum pregnant, she pretended it was Dad. The date was near enough to their wedding that no one twigged. Robert Holmcroft went back to finish his last year at university, became posh, and joined the Foreign & Commonwealth Office. A couple of years later he used his connections to make sure my dad was offered an ex-pat medical job in Qatar. That meant we were happily out of his way for a few years. I found out who I was when I was eighteen. That was some birthday present I can tell you.' Iqbal drained the remainder of the water. 'I know what you're thinking – skin colour, right? Robert is a white bloke, yeah, but Mum's genes were dominant. This whole thing is a secret, but I'm telling you because . . . oh, I don't know why I'm telling you.' Iqbal shook his head.

It made no difference to Snow who Iqbal was. 'Did you tell Strelkov or Vasilev about this?'

'No, they hadn't a clue.'

'Mo, you are one cool customer.'

'Tanya used to call me "cool" . . .' Iqbal stopped mid-sentence.

'Tanya was your girlfriend?'

Iqbal bobbed his head. 'Before I was taken.'

'I'm sorry.' Snow got to his feet and checked the hallway through the spyhole. There was nothing he could do about Tanya. He wasn't going to search Donetsk for her.

'Bugger,' Iqbal grunted in pain as he laced up his boots.

'Right, let's go.' Snow took the lead with Iqbal hobbling behind. They turned left out of the door and walked past the lift to the stairs. When they entered the stairwell, Snow paused and looked at a plan affixed to the wall showing the emergency exit. He traced the path with his finger. As the hotel was on a slight hill, the goods exit was a floor lower than the reception. As they reached the reception floor, raised Russian voices wafted in. Snow pushed on until they reached the bottom where the floor was littered with cigarette butts and the walls were unpainted plaster. Snow pushed open the fire door and saw a door to the kitchens on his immediate right; on the left was the exit to the loading area.

'Stay close,' he whispered before he chanced a glance into the kitchen. Apart from two men in chef's whites, it was empty.

Approaching the back door, he heard subdued voices. Snow took a deep breath and opened the door. Sunlight streamed through the gap and he squinted. In front of him was a white vehicle with OSCE stencilling on the side; next to it, were Benscoter and a second man. The man was thin and, over a grey three-quarter length coat, wore the distinctive blue OSCE vest of a senior member of personnel. Snow remained still for a moment to scan for possible threats before he spoke. 'Gentlemen.'

The man with Benscoter jerked and turned to see who was there. 'I'm Gordon Ward, Chief Monitor. You are the men that Freek told me about?'

'Yes,' Snow confirmed, 'and we need you to get us out of Donetsk.'

'While I do sympathise with your predicament, as I told Freek, I'm afraid that ferrying you across the lines is really out of our scope.'

'Your scope is to facilitate the release and repatriation of prisoners.'

'That is quite so; however, did you know that there are currently in excess of two hundred and forty-five military prisoners alone held by the Donetsk People's Republic? We are working hard with both sides to negotiate their release and the many more civilians they have incarcerated. I cannot, and will not, jeopardise the integrity of the OSCE for the sake of two men.'

'Gordon, we as the OSCE have a moral duty to help here,' Benscoter reasoned.

'We are neutral observers.'

'The Russians know we've made contact with you. If you don't help us you will have chosen a side . . . theirs,' Snow warned.

'And if we help you, following your logic, we will have chosen a side too.'

'No. You will not. You will have fulfilled your mandate.' Snow heard diesel engines growing louder. 'As an officer of the Secret Intelligence Service, I am officially asking on behalf of Her Majesty's Government for your assistance.' Snow fixed his eyes on Ward's. 'Please immediately drive us out of Donetsk and to the Ukrainian lines at Marinka.'

Ward bristled. 'What identification do either of you have?'

'How many other Brits have you bumped into on the streets of Donetsk recently?' Snow was exasperated; the man in front of him was a jobsworth who would have been much better suited to working as a parking attendant.

'Look, much as I would like to help—'

Snow took a step forward, his nose almost touching that of the older man. 'You either help us or, God help me, I'll find out where you live and when you finally return to the UK, I'll pay you an unsocial visit. Do you understand me?'

'Are you threatening me?'

'One hundred per cent.'

Ward was silent.

Iqbal broke the stare-off. 'Listen, fellas, I'd walk home if I was able to.'

'Gordon, I'll drive them myself.' Benscoter held out his hand for the keys.

'Very well.' Ward reached into his pocket, retrieved a set of keys and handed them to the tall Dutchman.

Benscoter blipped the locks on the Land Cruiser. 'Get in.'

Snow helped Iqbal into the back and followed him in. Snow instructed Iqbal to sit low in his seat. Benscoter drove smoothly away from the hotel, with his boss riding shotgun, and joined the road that led through the park. Snow saw no new DNR vehicles or personnel. It was too soon to relax, but he had started to feel better about their chances of escaping Donetsk.

TWENTY-THREE

Kalinins'kyi District, Donetsk

A crowd had gathered outside the apartment building and DNR militants had started to arrive, not quite sure of what to do. Knowing as they did who lived in the top floor, they formed a loose cordon and waited for their Russian masters to arrive. Racine had slipped through the front doors with a group of worried residents. Her taxi driver had been edgy but also eager to see what had been happening in the apartment building, so he had waited for her. He now ended his phone call and popped his handset back into his pocket. 'That was my brother, Slava. It's not good news. All the checkpoints out of Donetsk are locked down. Every car is being examined and every passenger is being searched. I'm afraid you chose an extremely bad day to leave the city.'

Racine had anticipated as much, and having it confirmed made her choice of route easier. If security at every checkpoint was increased, the most heavily guarded would need the least; in theory, her theory, it would become the weakest link. 'Which of the checkpoints normally has the most men guarding it?'

'That would be on the H15 before Marinka. It's the busiest road leading to the Ukrainian army lines. There is always at least one armoured vehicle there and lots of men.'

'Can you take me there, please?'

The driver threw up his hands in exasperation. 'Lady, didn't you hear? All roads are now blockaded by the DNR. You wouldn't be able to get through.'

Racine noticed a Mercedes G Wagon had turned into the street and was heading directly for the front of Vasilev's building. 'I'll give you another two hundred dollars if you take me.'

The driver turned in his seat. 'Why do you want to escape so badly?'

Racine looked down at her lap and let the tears stream from her eyes. If money wouldn't work, emotional blackmail might. 'My husband took our daughter, Masha, to Kyiv. I was to follow with my mother, but she fell ill and . . .' Racine put her head in her hands.

The driver let out a sigh. 'It's OK. There, there, my little one.' The driver's tone changed. He leant over and stroked her head.

'It was my mother's heart. The noise of the shelling and the worry. It just stopped and it wouldn't start again.' Racine started to sob. The tears and the pain were real enough, even if the reason for them was not.

'I'll take you there, but I'll have to drop you before the checkpoint.'

Racine blinked and took his hand. 'Thank you, thank you.'

The taxi driver's face softened. 'How old is Masha?'

'Five.'

'Ah, that is the best age, when they are so innocent yet think they are worldly wise. I have two daughters, Oxsana and Natasha. They are teenagers now.' He turned in his seat and started the engine.

'I'll still pay you the extra two hundred dollars.'

The driver glanced at Racine in the rear-view mirror. 'Just give me one hundred. I would do this for free but, as you must understand, here we all need the money.'

The taxi rejoined the flow of traffic and Racine wiped her eyes. She saw her mother, and she saw her aunt – Celine. She saw her laughing and pretending to be her sister. Racine's chest heaved and the sobs continued. Too numb to cry as a child, it was the first time she had properly cried since Celine's death. She hated herself for it but knew that it had to come, her grief could be held back no longer. She was crying for her dead aunt and for the loss of her mother, the woman who had left her weeks after her own sister's death. She now vowed to track down her mother, and explain what she had done, that the nightmare was finally over.

She thought about her father now – her brave, proud father who had looked after her ever since and who she knew would give anything and do anything for her. She had to get back home to him. She had to explain it all, even if it broke every law in the land, and if it did her father the lawyer could represent her. She wiped her eyes again and feeling an odd, unfamiliar sense of insecurity pulled her beanie hat down further over her ears and aching forehead.

The tears had stopped. She now focused her attention on the world outside the taxi. She started to recognise the route she had taken less than two hours before with Aidan Snow. She imagined he and Iqbal had made it out; given his level of training, yes, she was sure he would have. Racine focused on her own escape now and cut away from all other thoughts or concerns. The traffic on the roads was very light and by the time they neared the H15, there was nothing at all passing them in the opposite direction.

The driver turned into an empty service station that in happier times had stalls outside selling seasonal products, including water-melons. 'That's it; this is as far as I can take you without being questioned. Are you sure you want me to leave you here, in the middle of nowhere?'

'Yes, thank you.' Racine handed the driver two one-hundred-dollar bills.

'We agreed on one.'

'I insist. I have a feeling there won't be many fares for a while.' Racine opened the door and climbed out.

'God be with you.' The driver crossed his head and chest.

Racine shut the door. The only god she needed with her right now was Ares. She quickly moved into the cover of the shadows given by the cinder-block building. She watched the taxi swing across the highway and head back in the direction of Donetsk. The road was silent – no traffic passed in either direction. Racine felt a chill, as if humanity had vanished. This close to the checkpoint, the highway was naked and lined only by waist-high hedgerows. She had no idea if the trees had been removed or if they had never existed. Racine pushed through the hedge at the back of the parking area and made her way slowly parallel to the road towards the checkpoint half a mile ahead. She would have much preferred to have moved at night, but the longer she took to make good her escape the harder it would become.

The soil in the field was dry underfoot, slowing her progress and making it almost impossible to run. She would have to get back on the highway sooner or later and hoped that when she did, she'd be able to use the elements of stealth and surprise to pass the militants manning the checkpoint.

She checked her Makarov: a single clip less the rounds she'd used on Vasilev. No good in a firefight, no good at all, but at least it was small enough to conceal. She startled as the first mortar shells of the evening landed in the distance to the north. Hunkering down, she waited. There was no return fire from the checkpoint or anywhere nearby, and the evening became still once again. A wind started to blow and brought with it voices from farther up the highway. At this distance, the words were unintelligible, lost on the breeze, but the meaning was not. Short, sharp, staccato instructions given by men.

She'd once heard a linguist describe French as reminiscent of doves cooing. If that was the case she'd add that Russian sounded like dogs barking. Racine came level with the last car in line at the checkpoint, still some hundred yards from the barrier itself. She proceeded at a slower, more deliberate pace, each step held with it the risk of discovery, the risk of setting off a flare tied to a trip wire or stumbling into an IED left by either side.

On the opposite side of the highway, she saw a green, soft-sided Kamaz truck. Several young Russians stood outside it talking amongst themselves. She drew her Makarov. If spotted, a fraction of a second would be all the advantage she would have. She pushed on, unseen.

The sun was still in the sky, but cold shadows fell across the fields, just as the cold shadows of death covered Eastern Ukraine. Racine moved closer to the hedgerows to take full advantage of what little darkness there was. Twenty yards ahead the foliage abruptly stopped and empty fields met the highway on either side, stretching into the distance against a big, brooding, sky. The road carried on ahead in a straight line, which fell and rose with the undulating countryside, causing natural areas of dead ground. On her side of the road, a makeshift guard hut stood angled across the grass verge; on the other side, a BMP-2 sat with its barrel pointed at the Ukrainian lines in the distance, invisible behind the trees.

Racine stood immobile by the last piece of cover. She could hear the intense male voices much more distinctly, and the higher-pitched, less forceful replies of women. Racine got to her haunches and gently burrowed into the hedge. Dry, stubborn twigs pricked at her and scarred her already battered leather jacket. Once on the other side, she saw men in military fatigues on the highway itself with assault rifles slung on their shoulders searching the waiting vehicles. She prayed they didn't have dogs.

The car at the head of the line was a shabby, silver Ford Granada – a refugee from the 1980s. Its boot and all four doors were open, and its two elderly occupants were arguing with the militants. Racine considered her position. There was no way she could creep into a vehicle and cross the checkpoint without being detected. She spotted a drainage ditch butted up to the highway but disregarded it as too exposed and too shallow. What she needed was a diversion.

A white Toyota Land Cruiser trundled past the line of cars and stopped in the middle of the road. The DNR men searching the queuing civilian vehicles switched their focus and advanced on it. Racine wriggled backward into the hedge, emerging again on the side furthest from the road. She ran at a crouch to where the hedge ended. She crept around the edge and watched. Like bees to honey, the white Toyota was soon engulfed with a ring of DNR militants.

'The checkpoint is closed, I tell you,' one of them said, his forced English loud in the quiet evening air.

'And I tell you . . . you do not have any legal authority to impede the passage of an OSCE vehicle carrying out its monitoring mission,' a voice, tinged with a guttural accent, boomed in reply.

More militants joined the discussion with looks of amusement on their faces. One moved to stand directly in front of the Land Cruiser and, using internationally recognised hand signals, told the driver to turn off the engine. The driver initially ignored the instructions and amusement started to turn to exasperation. The English speaker with the deep voice got out of the vehicle. He was a giant, obviously from Northern Europe, perhaps Scandinavian or Dutch. Towering over the assembled militants, his OSCE tabard glowed under rays of evening sunlight. His voice thundered as he read them the riot act. All eyes were on the confrontation. This was her chance.

Racine took a deep, calming breath and moved forward. Her Makarov was in her right hand and her arms and legs were loose. Daring not to turn her head, she fixed her eyes on the barrier ahead and the makeshift guard hut. Suddenly, voices raised and she imagined fingers tightening on triggers, yet she continued to move and she saw a militant step out of the guard hut. His hand, which held a green apple, had frozen en route to his mouth. He stared dumbfounded at Racine. Makarov extended in front of her, she broke into a sprint. Racine covered the last few feet to the guard hut before the militant could spit the bite out of his mouth and voice a warning. He dropped the remainder of the apple and raised his fists but was too slow. Racine shoulder barged him to the ground. His arms flailed out and his head struck the tarmac with a nauseating crack. He started to choke on the apple still in his mouth. Racine rolled left and came to a halt behind the guard hut, weapon up. She counted to five before breaking cover and looking back at the checkpoint. The OSCE monitor was now gesturing angrily, as was the nearest militant.

Racine put her handgun on the ground and reached for the choking militant. She grabbed him by the shoulders and dragged him out of sight. His face was red and his eyes had started to bulge. He looked no more than eighteen. Racine cursed and gave in to her humanity, the little voice inside her head that was telling her he didn't need to die today. She heaved the choking youth into an upright position, grabbed him around the chest, and squeezed. Fruit and phlegm rocketed out of the militant's mouth and he started to cough. He doubled over and then, in a move that surprised Racine, grabbed her Makarov. He twisted his shoulders and swung his arm to bring the barrel to bear on her.

Racine ducked left, grabbed his chin with her left hand and the back of his head with her right, and jerked her hands in opposite directions. The militant's neck snapped and he slumped sideways. Racine fell backwards, and let the grass engulf her. She exhaled noisily; she was angry, not at the fact she'd killed him, but that she had almost paid the price for showing a moment of weakness, a moment of normal human emotion. Racine collected her Makarov and pushed herself away from the corpse.

Shouts began to emanate from the checkpoint. Rising to a crouch, her breathing now controlled, she peered around the low, concrete block wall of the guard hut. The OSCE monitor climbed back into the Land Cruiser and sat at the wheel while the militants stood directly in the vehicle's path, Kalashnikovs across their bodies. Their commander was several paces away talking animatedly on a cell phone and waving his arm at the vehicle.

As Racine continued to watch the scene unfold, she saw a flash of someone in the rear of the Toyota. Not quite able to believe her eyes, she stared. Mohammed Iqbal. Her focus instantly switched to the commander. He was pushing his cell phone into his chest pocket with his left hand while his right was drawing his sidearm.

Racine's mission was to terminate Vasilev, which she had done. She had passed the checkpoint and was clear to exfil and yet Iqbal was not. His rescue had not been part of her operation. With her mission accomplished, she should leave now, but she knew what she had to do, not as a weapon of France but as a tool of justice. Racine raised her Makarov and shot the commander twice in the back. The retorts in the still, evening air served as a shock wave to the militants who dived in every direction possible, scrambling for cover.

Racine ducked behind the guard hut, felt in her pocket for the second grenade she'd taken from the flat, and pulled the pin. She hurled it across the road and into the field just past the BMP-2. As it exploded, drawing attention away from her position, she ran into the guard hut. Inside she saw a Kalashnikov and, more importantly, an RPG. She dropped the Makarov. A smile creased her face. Without hesitation she raised the RPG to her shoulder, stepped out of the cover of the hut, took a long second to aim and pulled the trigger.

The grenade left the launcher at one hundred metres a second and slammed into the BMP-2. The blast knocked Racine from her feet and hurled the launch tube away over her shoulder. Racine lay motionless for a blissful second before she hauled herself up to her haunches. Out of the blast range, the Land Cruiser was undamaged and the Dutch monitor sitting inside open-mouthed. And then Aidan Snow materialised next to him in the front passenger seat. He scanned the scene and then he saw her.

The DNR men swung their rifles wildly. One spotted Racine and shouted a warning. Racine fell to her knees as a line of rounds flew over her head. She scurried backwards and grabbed the

Kalashnikov from the guard hut. Still reclining, she fired a burst of 7.62mm lead into the men of the DNR. The AK had been left on fully automatic and the thirty-round magazine emptied almost immediately. Racine let go of the Russian assault rifle, picked up her Makarov, scrabbled to her feet and sprinted away from the checkpoint. She heard gunfire and shouts but nothing more.

With any luck, the grenade and then the RPG round would fool the DNR into believing that they were being targeted by several attackers, perhaps The Shadows. Racine counted on the militants making sure they were safe before they pursued her. She also hoped that the OSCE Land Cruiser had got through the checkpoint. She glanced back but was already in the dead ground provided by a dip in the road. If she kept on running, she'd soon be out of small arms range but not of any motorised militants.

Slowing her pace to one she knew she could keep up for miles if needed, she kept moving and prayed that the first vehicle to catch up with her would be one to offer her a ride, and not the DNR. She continued to run, concentrating only on the road ahead and covering the maximum amount of ground with each stride. The guttural grunt of an engine reached her ears and then changed into a whine. She cast a glance over her shoulder as a car appeared. It was the Ford Granada. Racine slowed and waved her arms.

The driver came to a jerky halt, his window open. 'Get in, quick!'

Racine discarded her Makarov, fell onto the back seat and then the old Ford moved off. 'Thank you.'

'Don't thank us,' the driver replied. 'It was you we need to thank.'

'You are fearless, my dear,' the elderly woman sitting in the passenger seat gushed.

A white blur appeared in her peripheral vision. Racine turned her head as the OSCE Land Cruiser drew level and then sped past.

'I'm not fearless,' Racine said. 'I'm female.'

TWENTY-FOUR

Unknown location, Donetsk

Powerful hands pushed Weller into the chair and roughly removed his hood. Bright fluorescent lights hit his pupils like needles. He winced, the livid bruises around his face contracting as he screwed his eyes shut. Gradually he opened them and as they focused, an image swam into view in front of him. It was a man with an immaculate moustache, and a short back and sides.

'I hope you feel as bad as you look—' Strelkov was speaking English '—but you are alive, unlike my colleague Sasha Vasilev.'

Weller opened his mouth to speak but it was so dry that it could make no sound.

'Vasilev was murdered in his Donetsk apartment. We do not know who the assassin was, but I am sure you do.'

Weller shook his head, his mouth opening and closing like a gasping fish.

Strelkov produced a glass of water, leant forward and held it to Weller's split lips. He drank greedily and started to cough.

'Take your time.'

The water was tepid and tasted oddly metallic, but Weller managed to speak. 'I don't know who killed Vasilev . . .' he paused to cough '. . . and I didn't know he was dead. You must believe me.'

'Why?'

'Because it's the truth.'

Strelkov scoffed. 'That would be a first, a journalist who tells the truth.'

'Please. Don't hurt me again and I'll tell you all I know.'

'You will tell me all you know however I treat you, but it was not I who beat you. It was my men. They know exactly where to hit a man to make him talk, or to make him die. I would rather prefer that you did not die.'

Weller felt a sense of relief. He was going to make it. After being abandoned by Snow and the woman he had taken his advice and gone into the beauty salon, but he had not had his nails manicured. He'd paid the bemused assistant to first wash and then cut his hair. His trademark ponytail had been turned into an altogether more updated style, which made him look almost unrecognisable, but recognised he was. He was picked up by a DNR patrol on the eastern outskirts of Donetsk as he attempted to leave the city in the direction of the Russian border. A day later, after being beaten unconscious, he had woken in a small, dark room that smelled vaguely of fish. And then he'd been hooded and placed before Strelkov.

'You know the answers to a couple of very important questions. You can answer these for me. Will you do that and save yourself an awful lot of pain?'

'Yes. Yes, I want to answer all your questions!'

'Very well. Who assassinated Sasha Vasilev?'

'What?'

Strelkov repeated the question. 'Who assassinated Sasha Vasilev?'

'I don't know! I don't know!' Weller pleaded.

'Admit the truth. You are a foreign agent.'

'What, me? No . . . no . . . that's just . . .'

Strelkov checked his watch. It took a few minutes, depending upon the subject's weight and susceptibility, for the drugs he had administered in the glass of water to take effect. Weller was rail-thin and as far as Strelkov was aware had not received any training in resistance to interrogation techniques. Or perhaps, Strelkov mused, he had? Was Weller really a sleeper for SIS? Had the pathetic persona been an act, a legend created by British intelligence?

He noticed Weller's mouth relax a hint and his eyes close ever so slightly. The drug invented during the times of the KGB and used on political prisoners had been refined, tested and perfected. The exact cocktail of the drug he had was highly classified; in fact he knew of only two others officially sanctioned to use it. It was a drug of last resort, because of the extremely high likelihood of permanent side effects. For this very reason Strelkov had not entrusted Vasilev to use it. And, Strelkov reasoned the man had after all been a traitor. Strelkov gazed at the useful idiot. Once he had retrieved the intel, he cared not a jot if the man's mind was no more. 'Tell me about the man who rescued you. What was his name?'

'Aidan Snow,' Weller answered without hesitation and then continued to speak, faster than before. 'I knew him when I was in Kyiv. I used to see him around in the bars and at "The Hash".'

'What is "The Hash"?'

'It's a drinking club with a running problem.'

Strelkov frowned, the drug made for the occasional misplacement of words, so he ignored this and asked. 'What was Aidan Snow's occupation in Kyiv?'

'He was a teacher at an international school.'

'A teacher?'

'Yes.'

'Four years ago, you knew him as a teacher?'

'Yes.'

'Yet two days ago he materialised in Donetsk as what, James Bond?'

'Yes.'

Strelkov paused. 'What is your real name?'

Again he spoke without hesitation. 'Darren Weller.'

'How long have you been working for SIS?'

'Wh . . . who?'

'MI6.'

'I . . . I'm not a spy. I'm a journalist, you know I'm a journal . . .' Weller's head started to slump and a smile spread across his face, which was at odds with the tone of his voice. The drug was increasing its hold.

'Did you know Aidan Snow was coming to Donetsk?'

'No.'

'When was the last time you saw Aidan Snow?

'Two days ago.'

Strelkov exhaled his frustration. 'With the exception of two days ago, when was the last time you saw Aidan Snow?'

Weller struggled to raise his head, the drugs making him unusually exact, like a child. 'Three years and ten months ago.'

'Where was this?'

'In Kyiv, on the Maidan. He was drinking beer.'

Strelkov inclined his head, 'Maidan' was short for 'Maidan Nezalezhnosti' – Kyiv's Independence Square. 'What else do you know about Aidan Snow?'

'I think . . . he used to be in the Army.'

'You think?'

'A friend told me.'

'And who was this friend?'

'Arnaud Hurst, a teacher. He worked with Snow.'

'In the army?'

'No, at the school in Kyiv.'

Strelkov knew Weller would only be able to function for so long before the synthetic serum rendered him incapable of speech and then made him sleep, perhaps never to awaken the same. 'Do you work for MI6, Darren?'

'No.' Weller shook his head, emphatically. 'I am a patriot of Russia and Novorossiya!'

Strelkov examined Weller's face. It was chemically relaxed. He let a thin smile form on his lips, finally assured that the useful idiot was just that and not anything more clandestine. 'Darren, I believe you.'

'Thank you . . . Igor.' Darren's smile was large.

No one called him 'Igor', but he let it pass – after all, they were now friends having a chat. 'Darren, as one friend to another, who was the woman with you?'

'She was gorgeous!'

'But, who was she?'

'I thought she was Olena Gaeva, but she wasn't.'

'So who was she?' Strelkov persisted.

'I don't know. Snow thought he knew who she was, but he didn't say her name.'

'Did she give her name?'

'No, but . . .' Weller opened his mouth wide, and his eyebrows seemed to shoot skywards, as if he had just remembered something of vital importance. 'She said she was in Donetsk to look for someone – her target. She said she had come for Sasha Vasilev!'

Strelkov leant forward, interested. They were finally getting somewhere. 'The woman was sent to assassinate Sasha Vasilev?'

'I don't know, she just said Sasha Vasilev was her target.'

'Darren, think, search your memory.' The serum was already doing this but if he could make the Englishman focus it may aid the process. 'Do you know anything else about this woman?'

'No.'

Strelkov became angry. 'Think!'

'I . . . I . . .'

Strelkov took a breath, brought his breathing under control. 'When this woman spoke, did she have an accent?'

'I'm not sure about when she spoke in Russian, but . . .'

'English, Darren. When she spoke in English, did she have an accent?'

'When she was pretending to be Olena she sounded like a Muscovite.'

'And when she wasn't, did her voice change?'

'It was just no accent . . .' Weller's head lolled to one side, but then his head snapped up again. 'Snow spoke to her in French.'

'In French?'

'Yes . . . in . . . Fren . . . ch . . .'

Strelkov's jaw tightened. French, of course, that made sense. Vasilev's former masters had decided to dispatch him. Weller looked to be asleep, but it was too soon; perhaps the dose had been incorrect? 'Darren,' Strelkov shouted, 'Darren! Listen to me.'

Weller's head jerked up. 'Yes?'

'Was the woman French?'

'The sexy wom . . . woman.'

'Darren, was she French?' But his head was lolling. 'Are you loyal to the people of the Donetsk People's Republic?'

'Yes.'

'And do you want to be a good journalist?'

'Yes.'

'Very well. You must rest now. Tomorrow, you will file a full report to camera. It will be on how the Western intelligence services have attacked the Donetsk People's Republic and those noble volunteers who have travelled here to give their assistance to its development.' If the man was mentally still able to, Strelkov mused. He was angry that the footage of Snow and the woman Vasilev boasted of gathering, had in fact been destroyed by the woman. He let out a sigh; there was nothing he could do about that. It was a glass of spilt milk.

*

Strelkov left Weller and walked up a flight of stairs past an armed DNR guard, who gave him a passable attempt at a salute. He nodded in return as he entered the ground floor of what had before the conflict been the Donetsk town hall, but now had become the 'Palace of the President of the People's Republic of Donetsk'. The president was not in. It was mid-morning and too early for the drunken puppet to be out of his crowded bed. Strelkov found another set of stairs and took them to the very top of the government building.

He pushed open the door to the roof and stepped outside. He was an outdoors man at heart and when on leave was rarely inside. Even in temperatures of twenty below he much preferred to be hunting or ice fishing at his dacha than wasting his time in bars, restaurants and shops. There was real beauty in Mother Russia, the wild Russia of a landscape unchanged for millennia. This, however, was not the case in Donetsk. Even the roof where he stood now was littered with bottles and old cigarette ends from where DNR members had stood watch during times of heightened tension. When the winter snows arrived at least they would hide the ugliness around him. Strelkov was a realist; he understood and accepted that without the motherland's umbilical cord of men, weapons and supplies, the pseudo state of The Donetsk People's Republic would die. He was bitter – what could have been a truly great Slavic nation was, due to the ineptitude and indifference of its people, already starting to fail. He hated failing. It was time for him and his men to move on, but before he did it was his duty to report to his superior in Moscow.

Strelkov retrieved his phone and speed-dialled a Moscow number. It was answered on the third ring, the encryption software at both ends shook hands and then his director answered.

'Well?' Regardless of the encryption, neither man used the other's name on their official calls.

'I have reason to believe that Sasha Vasilev was assassinated by the French.'

'The French?' The man's rage was little tempered by the distance between them, 'Is this the type of result I can expect from you? Not only do you allow a man, a valuable asset, who was assured safe haven by our president to be murdered in front of you, but now you tell me that a western power was behind the hit?'

'That is correct.'

'And how did you come to the conclusion?'

Strelkov explained. His own anger at the situation had now turned cold, but he was not resigned, he had a plan. 'Regretfully what is done is done, and I cannot change this but I have an idea of how this situation can be used in a positive manner which, I may say, will benefit our cause more than Vasilev's skills ever could.'

There was a pause, punctuated by electronic static before the director spoke. 'Well, I am listening.'

Strelkov started to talk and when he had finished, he could tell by the tone of his voice that the director in Moscow had a thin smile on his often-sullen face.

'Very well, I shall advise the president of this.'

The call ended, Strelkov put away his phone and gazed into the distance where he saw smoke rise. The shelling had started again.

*

Distant shelling had distracted the Ukrainian soldiers at the checkpoint marking the start of Ukrainian government-controlled territory. A young soldier had peered into the old couple's car. Recognising them he'd only asked to see Racine's passport. She felt in her jacket and handed over her Ukrainian passport in the name of Olena Onika. After a cursory glance and then a quick search of the boot, they were allowed to continue on their way with the rest of the civilians escaping the conflict. The extraction plan, although modified, had worked. Racine had managed to enter Ukraine but she also had to leave it. At least, she mused, no one with guns would be attempting to stop her this time.

As the old car wafted and rocked on its soft suspension and the heaters blasted stuffy, warm air, Racine battled to stay awake. The fear and the adrenalin of the past two days had now been replaced by post-mission malaise, an acute lethargy. It had many names – soldiers called it battle fatigue – but she just knew that although very much alive, she felt like death.

*

Racine continued to travel with the elderly couple until they arrived at their final destination, the city of Poltava in central Ukraine. She'd offered to drive part of the way but Dima, the old man, would not hear of it. It was a matter of principle to him that he get his wife and their new lady friend to safety. He was a safe driver, slow but steady. Some eight and a half hours later, after traversing in the darkness, what resembled miles of dark undulating waters but in fact were Ukraine's flat, fertile fields, they arrived at a dacha belonging to Dima's relatives. The owner, his cousin, offered to put Racine up for the night but she politely refused and just asked to use their telephone. Calling a number at the French embassy in Kyiv, she gave an authorisation code and stated what her requirements were. Half an hour later Dima dropped her off at the railway station in time to board the overnight train to Kyiv.

It was just before four in the morning when Racine alighted at Kyiv's central railway station. She felt exposed, alone, vulnerable. It wasn't a city she had been to before and one she hadn't planned to visit. Bedraggled passengers pushed past her. She allowed herself to be carried along with them, a piece of flotsam on an encroaching tide.

The cafés and kiosks were shut for the night, not opening for another hour and a half, but the street was noisy. Grimy, yellow minibuses, called 'Marshrutka' waited for passengers, to ferry them to outlying regions. Several taxis stood hoping to get a fare in the lull after the nightclubs had closed and before rush-hour started.

Two taxi drivers accosted her, much to their annoyance she respectfully refused their services, and stepped purposefully from the kerb. Her directions were simple. She headed straight ahead and joined a street lined with three-storey ornate apartment blocks and not so ornate utilitarian office buildings. She carried on walking for five minutes, leaving the station behind her, and became the only living thing moving in a predawn road of ghosts. All senses alive, checking for tails or watchers, she turned left onto one of Kyiv's wide avenues. In full daylight it would be thronged with traffic but now it was still. She drew level with a large, steel and concrete box of a building she recognised as a department store. She took a step back into an alcove next to the entrance and vanished into the cold black shadows. Racine smiled thinly as she noticed Kyiv's own Soviet-era Circus across the street. In communist times there had been clowns everywhere.

Ten minutes later, with only the occasional rumble of a passing taxi breaking the nocturnal city silence a dark saloon car drew up to the kerb. A dumpy, middle-aged woman, dressed in an ill-fitting trouser suit, heaved herself out. She stood on the pavement and looked around. Checking her watch, she exhaled loudly.

Racine emerged from the shadows and addressed her in French. 'It's a bit early for a walk, Madame.'

The woman spun, surprised, and placed her hand on her chest. She pulled a face. 'You made me jump,' she chided, in Parisian-accented French.

Racine raised her eyebrows. She knew it had been short notice, but had the DGSE really sent an untrained agent to collect her? 'I'm sorry, Madame.'

'It's Mademoiselle. The only thing I'm married to is my country. Now don't mill about, get in.'

Racine didn't move. 'Who's the driver?'

'One of our local Ukrainian staff. Please get in.'

Still Racine stayed put.

'Jacob would not be happy with me if you missed your flight.'

Racine knew this to be true, and did as she was told, now assured by the woman's invocation of Jacob's name. Moments later the car, an older model Volkswagen Passat, sedately drew away from the kerb.

'There is a package for you in the seat pocket.' The woman glanced back over her shoulder. 'Check that it contains everything you need.'

Racine switched on the reading light, reached for the large, brown envelope and assessed its contents. It contained an Irish passport, using her photograph, issued in the name of Estelle Malcolm, five hundred euros in mixed-denomination notes, a handful of Ukrainian hryvnia and a business-class ticket for the Ukrainian International Airways ten a.m. flight to London's Gatwick airport. She pocketed the cash and ticket, then checked the passport for entrance stamps. 'Thank you. This looks fine.'

'Good.' The woman was happy. 'It will be about thirty minutes at this time of night to get to Boryspil.'

*

They arrived at the airport as dawn broke. The driver had not spoken at all and the woman only opened her mouth again to say, *'Bon chance.'* Boryspil International Airport was awake and open for business. It was too early for Racine to check in, so she used the hryvnia to buy a large café latte and a pastry at the coffee shop. She wasn't hungry but knew she needed to eat. An outsized fish tank formed part of the partition wall of the eatery and she took a table near this, hidden from onlookers but able to peer through the water at the concourse beyond. The tropical fish inside made faces at her.

Racine was one of the first to check in and after making full use of the business class lounge to clean up, the first to board the plane. The flight was just over three hours. She ate her business-class breakfast, served her by an impossibly fresh-faced blond steward with perfectly gelled hair, and then snoozed for the rest of the flight. At Gatwick she was the first off, whizzed through immigration. She joined the back of a group of British tourists returning home from an Orlando flight, and was ignored by the customs officers as she entered the green corridor. She changed terminals and at the EasyJet counter bought a ticket on a flight to Paris. Her Irish passport held up to the checks at both Gatwick and Charles de Gaulle.

Exhausted but her training keeping her vigilant, Racine caught a taxi to a location on the opposite side of Paris to where she needed to be and then took a meandering route utilising buses, two more taxis and finally the metro. Eventually arriving home she locked herself in her secure flat and set the alarm system. She desperately wanted to wash and get into bed but there was something she had to do first. Racine wearily moved to her bedroom chest of drawers, opened it and pulled out her secure work iPhone. After powering it on she sent a simple message to Baptiste and Jacob:

Mission was set up by Vasilev to abduct me. Must find out how?

Depositing the iPhone on her bedside table, she thought about switching her personal phone back on too but decided she didn't have the energy. She gingerly undressed, not wanting to see the physical toll the mission had taken on her body, and got into the shower. The water was the best she'd ever felt and its warmth started to relax her. Eventually she forced herself out of the shower. Minutes later, barely towel-dry, she collapsed into bed.

TWENTY-FIVE

Central Paris

Racine's dreams as always were vivid but now rather than events of her childhood it was images of the mission that assailed her slumber. She relived randomly selected parts, almost like a trailer for a Hollywood film – except she was the hero. The trailer continued, complete with villains dying and vehicles exploding. Finally she was at Sasha Vasilev's doorstep, her gun rising to take her first shot, to complete her mission, only this time when she squeezed the trigger nothing happened. Vasilev stepped forward, grabbed the gun, and forced the barrel into his mouth. And then his face changed to that of Aidan Snow.

Racine's eyes opened. A strange expression on her face. She frowned. Why was she dreaming of nonsense? And then before she could give her dream any further thought her stomach rumbled. She was hungry. She checked her bedside clock. She'd slept for twelve hours straight. Racine painfully padded to the kitchen, acutely aware of her many bruises. She needed caffeine – she was ideologically opposed to decaf – and started the coffee machine then used the microwave to defrost a couple of croissants, incomparable to those her mother used to make but tasty enough.

Ten minutes later, with a greasy smear on her lips and a

concoction of strong painkillers dissolving amongst her breakfast, she started to write up her after-action report. Apart from any intel that could be shared with the wider DGSE, the document had a readership of two – Baptiste and Jacob. It was classified, would not bear her name, but was a record nonetheless of the mission she had undertaken. Ninety minutes of manic typing, and a pot of coffee later, Racine sent an encrypted email to both men. She felt tears form in her eyes but rubbed them away before she stretched, showered, dressed and left her flat in search of something more substantial to eat.

That evening, red-eyed, Racine sat with a glass of wine in her hand and a plate of cheeses balanced on her lap as Alexa shuffled through the hits of Roxette. She felt exposed. Crying was an alien act to her. It had started in the taxi in Donetsk and she wished it would stop. It struck her as strange that tears were freely flowing for someone who had died almost a decade and a half before. The mission, her killing Sasha Vasilev, had brought with it closure but also grief and emptiness. Her mother was god knew where, her father was in Nice with his girlfriend and she was in her DGSE Paris flat, loveless, friendless, and bruised.

She remembered her personal phone was still off. What would another day mean to anyone? She'd switch it back on tomorrow, when she was ready to face the real world, and that was when she would talk to her father. She was used to the post-mission emotional and physical comedown, a conflict cold-turkey, which took several days to pass regardless of the mission outcome. This was different somehow, more personal. She finished her glass of wine, reached for the bottle and realised it was empty. Moving her cheese plate, she padded to the kitchen, uncorked her second bottle of Monoprix special-offer wine. If she finished that she'd switch to pastis or perhaps cognac, her father's favourite.

She returned to the settee, shouted at Alexa to stop and switched on Netflix. Her work phone rang, but she ignored it – she was officially off duty and would be so for a few days. It rang through to voicemail. And then a text message arrived. Giving up, she transferred her wine to the coffee table and looked at the message from Baptiste on her iPhone's screen.

All OK?

She sighed, knowing that if she didn't reply he'd think something was seriously wrong. So she called him back rather than sending a text. Racine had no intention of playing instant message ping-pong with her ex, even if he was also her supervisor.

Baptiste answered immediately, as though he'd been holding his handset. His voice was warm and soft. "Allo, you're alive then?'

'Yes, I am.'

There was a pause before he replied, 'Your voice is croaky. You sound upset. Are you sure nothing's the matter? I can come over if you need anything, if you need to talk?'

'No. I'm fine.' Embarrassed, Racine realised her tone was harsher than she had intended.

'OK. Look, are you watching TV?'

'Netflix.'

'Change the channel.'

'Why?'

'I've just got word: ON are about to go to a live interview with Darren Weller.'

'Riveting, thanks,' she replied before ending the call.

She swapped Netflix for the Russian ON channel and caught the end of a commercial for a Russian bank before the news programme continued. She took a large swig of wine, refilled her glass and settled down, nervously, for another type of light entertainment.

*

Racine watched the grey-suited 'Our News' anchorwoman, Sharron Machin stood in a semi-casual manner to the right of an immense plasma screen in the ON television broadcast newsroom. As she spoke directly to camera the display to her left was covered with a gigantic still from an earlier report by Darren Weller. It showed the Englishman standing in front a derelict train in a disused goods yard. His long hair tied back, he stared down the lens. Machin addressed her own camera. 'British journalist Darren Weller has been found alive and well in Donetsk after going missing whilst covering the conflict in the east. In a shocking revelation Weller was held illegally captive for two days by the members of the Security Service of Ukraine and agents of Britain's MI6. We now have the first chance to speak to Darren, who joins us live from central Donetsk.'

The word 'LIVE' whooshed across the screen. The plasma display became a split-screen, showing Weller sitting behind a desk on the left and rolling footage of his most recent reports on the right. The footage had been chosen to emphasise his status as a war correspondent. It included explosions in the near distance, swirls of smoke from smouldering buildings, Weller dressed in a DNR uniform carrying out weapons drills and a bombed-out bridge. In Donetsk, Weller sported a new shorter hairstyle, but what was most noticeable was the stubble and two-day-old bruising on his usually boyish face.

Machin, still standing next to the display spoke. 'Darren it's good to see that you are alive and well. ON lost contact with you earlier this week – we had no communication with you for two days. Tell us what happened?'

'Yes, thank you, Sharron.' Weller took a sip from a glass of water on the desk. He winced as his did so, overplaying the discomfort. 'I was travelling with my cameraman Vadim, to the site of the latest Ukrainian shelling. A group of Ukrainian soldiers had placed an illegal checkpoint across the road. We were stopped and ordered out of the car. When we informed them we were accredited jour-nalists, they just laughed. And then they attacked Vadim.'

'They attacked your cameraman?' Machin asked, with her trademark incredulity.

'That's right. The Ukrainians struck Vadim with the butts of their assault rifles and then when he was on the ground, they kept kicking him in the face and head. Their leader stated if I couldn't prove who I was, he couldn't guarantee that I was going to live.'

'And then what happened?'

'They left Vadim at the side of the road; I thought he was dead. I was blindfolded, handcuffed, and dragged away. I was terrified.'

The camera pulled back wide to show the studio, with Machin standing next to the giant screen. She put her finger to her ear. 'And we're just getting this. ON cameraman, Vadim Azarov, is now confirmed to be in hospital receiving treatment for his injuries. Good news, Darren, I'm sure you'd agree.'

'Very good news.'

'So then what happened?' It was clear to Racine that Machin wanted to move the narrative along and get to the really sensational part.

'Then Ukrainians took me away, I don't know where, and I was in a locked room without water or toilet facilities for two days. They kept questioning me. You can see the bruises on my face from their "questioning".'

'What were they asking you?'

'They accused me of being a Russian spy, a terrorist and working for terrorists. They informed me that I had a Russian passport and had entered Ukraine illegally. All of this was completely false. Each time I told them the truth, they punched me.'

'Who hit you?'

'There were three of them. One was an SBU specialist. The other two were MI6 agents.'

The camera cut to show a close-up of Machin's reaction. Her eyebrows had arched above the frames of her glasses. 'Let's just clarify this: agents of MI6 were illegally interrogating you in Donetsk?'

Now the camera cut again to a similar close-up of Weller. He wagged his head emphatically. 'One was definitely an MI6 spy

– the man. The woman I believe she was too, she had an English accent but she spoke in French to him.'

'She spoke in French?'

'Yes, they thought I couldn't understand it. They used it as a code. I'd met the man before in Kyiv, when he was undercover pretending to be a British teacher. I'd never seen the woman before.'

'You'd met one of them at an earlier date? Do you think you were specifically targeted by British intelligence?'

'There is no other explanation. I report on the real truth on the ground. The Kyiv junta and their allies don't like it.'

Racine rolled her eyes as she watched Machin feed Weller the next question, in a very obvious attempt to maximise the drama. 'Darren, do you know the name of the MI6 man?'

'Yes I do.'

'Can you tell me and our viewers this spy's name?'

'Yes I can, but not at this time. Once I'm safely back in Moscow and have spoken to the Russian authorities, there will be a full, official investigation and then a press conference.'

Machin nodded. 'Let's talk, if we can, a little about how these interrogators treated you.'

'They used what the Americans call "enhanced interrogation" techniques. They waterboarded me.' Weller's hand shook as he reached for a glass of water. There was silence for a few seconds whilst the studio cameras showed Machin's reaction, and then the shot returned to show both Weller and the woman in the studio. 'They kept telling me I was working for Russian terrorists. I kept telling them the Ukrainian army was not fighting Russians in Donetsk, but people from Donetsk. They wouldn't listen to me. The SBU took my computer and demanded my passwords.'

'As you would imagine, ON has reached out to the British Foreign Office and the SBU for a statement on their involvement in this incident. Neither have answered our questions. Darren, tell me about how you escaped.'

Weller cleared his throat before he spoke. 'There was shelling outside, the door to my room burst open, someone came in and removed my cuffs. I was too afraid to move. I just sat there until the shelling stopped. When I removed my hood, the Ukrainians had gone. I was in a village outside Donetsk. I must have walked about sixteen kilometres before I found someone who'd let me use their phone.'

'I also understand that the Ukrainians stole your car and equipment?'

'That's right, they drove my car away when they abducted me. Then today I've just discovered I've been cyber-hacked!' Weller shook his head in disbelief. 'They busted open my entire system and changed my passwords. All my accounts have been hacked, my Twitter account, my Facebook account, my VKontakte account, my email account, my YouTube account. They've deleted two thousand videos I uploaded. Videos that showed the truth on the ground for real people. I've been cyber-attacked and I'm fighting to get my life back.' Weller paused to calm down. 'They called me an enemy of Ukraine, but four years ago I was the only foreign journalist defending Ukraine, saying "come to Ukraine".'

The interview then became circular, reiterating the same points again. Racine watched until the segment finished before switching off her TV. She emptied her glass of wine and closed her eyes. If nothing before had persuaded her that ON purveyed fake news, Darren Weller's interview just had. She was amazed and amused at how easily the lies had flown from his mouth, but more than this, reading his face it seemed that Weller believed every word he was saying.

Her phone pinged to inform her she'd received another text message. It was again from Baptiste. *Who interrogated him? The DNR? The Russians?*

All of the above? she replied and wondered who in reality had actually attacked Weller? It made little difference to her. But

Vadim was alive, apparently. She should have kicked him harder, the bastard, she mused.

Another message arrived. *OK. We will discuss the implications of his interview. How they knew someone was coming for Vasilev. Goodnight.*

Racine didn't reply. She refilled her glass, raised it in mock salute at the blank screen and then finished her bottle.

TWENTY-SIX

DGSE Headquarters, Paris

A paper copy of Racine's after-action report lay on Jacob's desk. He stared at it for a long moment and crunched on his breath mint before addressing Baptiste. 'How exposed are we?'

'We are of course the prime suspect,' Baptiste stated. 'Vasilev was a traitor to France. He was assassinated hence it must automatically be the French who did it.'

'There is no evidence of our involvement?'

'With the exception of the British operative knowing that Racine works directly for you, none. There is no evidence to prove Racine pulled the trigger.'

'Good. This Aidan Snow is one of Jack Patchem's men. Of course SIS won't say anything.'

'Racine should not have let Weller go.'

'Do you imagine Aidan Snow would have been happy if Racine had killed one British national in front of him, whilst aiding him in the rescue of another?'

'It was not his choice. It was our mission,' Baptiste said.

'Would he then have offered to help her?'

'I concede, he was useful.'

'So what of Weller's assertions that he was abducted by "MI6"?'

Jacob asked. 'We know this is a fabrication but what purpose does it serve?'

'Propaganda masquerading as news?' Baptiste shrugged. 'Weller was beaten by someone and doesn't want his bruises to go to waste.'

'That makes sense,' Jacob allowed.

'I don't understand why Weller didn't mention the DGSE. He had every chance to do so?'

'Ah, that is political,' Jacob said. 'It would say nothing for Russia's ability to protect one of its own if it came to light that the DGSE assassinated Vasilev in Donetsk. That would make the Kremlin strongman look like a weakened fool. That is the reason why Weller is making the most of the SIS involvement and kidnap story. This is why he is going to hold his news conference.'

'What do you mean?'

'Why hold a news conference unless there is more news? We know he can't give Racine up, but he is giving up Snow.'

Jacob tapped the report. 'Aidan Snow was known to Weller, which was an unfortunate coincidence but what do the Russians actually have? The words of a stooge versus that of the British Foreign Office? Of course, the general public will believe the British did indeed kidnap Weller and interrogate him. But will they care, and what of it in the grand scale of things?' He paused and looked down at the report again. 'Can the Russians positively ID Snow? Do they have photographs, CCTV footage?'

'Vasilev told Racine there was footage, yet knowing how clumsy the DNR is, they would have surely posted it on social media. Racine states that she destroyed possible recording equipment at Vasilev's address.'

'So the question I really should have asked was, what can we expect from this ON news conference when it happens?'

'Nothing new,' Baptiste stated.

'Nothing news,' Jacob quipped.

Tverskaya Street, Moscow, Russia

Tverskaya was one of Darren Weller's favourite streets. He appreciated the scale of the huge baroque granite buildings on each side and the view of the Kremlin and Red Square at the bottom. Taking Tverskaya wasn't the quickest way to the ON offices, but it was the route he liked the best. He felt like he was in a spy film, outwitting the KGB, always one step ahead of them. He smirked. Now of course the KGB had changed their name to the FSB and his own government's intelligence service was his enemy. So what did that make him, a traitor outwitting MI6? No. He was no traitor, he was the voice of truth. So was he a defector? That was it. He was an economic defector who had forsaken the west to work in the cold east to uncover secrets. Whatever he was it made him feel good.

In fact Darren felt extremely good because he had just spent the night with a twenty-one-year-old ON news intern named Vera. He'd wowed her with the story of his heroics in Donetsk, but he left out any mention of having fallen for the tricks of Racine and Snow, who almost cost him his career. Still, no matter. He was to have the last laugh now. Weller was on his way to meet with colleagues at the ON offices to discuss the final details of the afternoon's news conference, which would make him a household name the world over. As a journalist this was his moment: he was going to shove two fingers up at Aidan Snow, the British government and all of those who didn't believe in him. How dare they disrespect him the way they had in Donetsk? It was annoying, he thought, that he wasn't eligible for a Pulitzer Prize. Surely his heroic reporting from the front line would have put him in the running for one?

As he bounded along the wide pavement, with the crisp mid-morning air reddening his cheeks, he wondered when the first snows of winter would fall. Some forecasts said this week; others not for a while yet. Moscow in fresh snow was special. The rough edges were removed, and it reminded him of childhood

Christmases. Yes, he loved Moscow and there was nowhere else he would rather be. He grinned and shook his head, and spoke aloud, 'I love you Moscow!' He ignored the odd looks from the passing pedestrians.

Traffic was heavy but moving freely now that Moscow's extended rush hour was over. He drew level with the swanky Ritz-Carlton Moscow. Several large men in long, dark coats were exiting the hotel and ushering a smaller man towards a Mercedes limousine, which stood trailing mist from its large exhaust pipes. Weller paused to let them pass as unseen to his immediate left a brown UPS van pulled up.

As he watched the scene in front of him, hoping to perhaps recognise a Russian celebrity, he felt a sharp pain in his neck. He blinked and raised his right hand to rub it, but it was grabbed by a gloved hand and twisted behind his back. Before Weller had time to resist or voice his distress, his legs buckled. His gaze dropped to the pavement and he felt himself being dragged towards the van. A moment later he landed heavily on his back and was afforded a view of the Moscow morning sky for a second before the UPS van's door was shut. Weller felt his eyes starting to close but just before they did a bearded male face appeared. A Chechen?

Central Paris, France

Racine felt comfortable in this part of the city. It had retained its last-century charm, there were no gaudy chain stores or overtly gauche boutiques and it was not thronged with tourists, especially at this time of year – too late for falling autumnal leaves and too early for Christmas. It had been a place she had often walked during her student years, a time before her eyes had been opened to the true nature of the modern world. Ironically it was also where the bistro was that Jacob had first taken her, and where she was today eventually heading.

Carrying out counter-surveillance measures was second nature to Racine, and she was good at it. She approached the promenade seemingly without a care in the world, before leaning against the guardrail to ostensibly gaze at the opposite side of the river Seine.

The art of counter-surveillance was not just looking for watchers but forcing them to show themselves. This meant exposing herself too. Racine breathed deeply and fought the urge to move. She retrieved her work iPhone from her coat pocket and touched the screen, mimicking the mindless actions of social media devotees. She grinned and then shook her head, as if she were an idiot reacting to a post – probably some pathetic meme about cats. She wasn't a fan.

And then there was movement. A couple casually walking hand in hand towards her. She stole a photograph of them before pretending again to be enchanted by what was on her screen. The couple were tall, white, in either their late forties or early fifties. Their brightly coloured down jackets glowed beacon-like on the overcast Parisian promenade. Racine assumed they had to be American. They closed to a distance of fifteen metres and then the woman abruptly stopped, turned her back on Racine and kissed the man. It lasted a while and then, carried on the wind, Racine caught a few of the words spoken between the lovers. She learnt his name was Clint and that the excited accent was indeed American, probably from one of the mid-west states, which went with their corn-fed appearance. The woman held up her own phone, leant against him, stuck her arm out and posed for a selfie. She struck several different stances, like a woman half her age, to make sure that the background showed both her and Paris off in the best light.

Racine felt uncomfortable. She wasn't a fan of outward shows of affection, probably she mused due to the way her parents had behaved. They undoubtedly loved each other but her father's military background made him somewhat remote. 'Like father, like daughter,' Jacob had said to her all those years ago, during her recruitment phase. They'd both killed for France, so at least her father and she had that in common. She realised she'd better call him, just to say she was still alive.

Racine started to walk away from the couple and crossed the road. Up ahead, she noticed an Asian man looking in the window of a shop. It was a place, Jacob had once told her, which sold the best ballet dresses in Paris. How he knew this fact she had never asked. As she drew nearer to the man his phone rang. He answered it and spoke animatedly. She didn't recognise the language, but from his intonation suspected it was Korean. He turned to face her, still talking, and at that moment Racine felt her internal threat radar 'ping'.

In her peripheral vision she saw a car swoosh around the corner. She slowed her breathing, changed course, altering the angle between herself and the man on the phone, and headed for an alleyway three doors along. The large, low-slung, BMW saloon came to a stop, Racine inhaled, and her body readied itself for action – fight or flight . . . and then an Asian woman stepped out of the car and hugged the man on the phone. He untangled himself and pointed at the window display of the ballet shop. Without breaking her stride Racine entered the alley.

Buttes-Chaumont Park, Paris

Baptiste left his Renault in the Saemes Robert Debré car park. It wasn't the nearest one to his destination, but it had twenty-four-hour CCTV and was a place from which he could walk a meandering route and carry out counter-surveillance techniques, certain of spotting anyone who chose to follow him. It wasn't that he thought he was being followed rather it was an act that had been drummed into him so much that it became routine. The streets were quieter than usual and although it wasn't raining, grey storm clouds scudded across the sky. He was glad he'd decided to go out for a walk sooner, rather than later. Later he would be at home with a pack or two of Pelforth Brune. He'd first tried it as a teen because he liked the brewery's Pelican mascot. Taking a walk or drinking a beer were his preferred methods for clearing his head, and now he really needed it cleared.

Racine's mission had been a setup. He'd been fed the intel on Vasilev specifically to draw Racine to him. *The Department*, eager for any leads, had believed themselves the hunters, but Baptiste had made Racine the hunted. Yet the intel had been real, genuine, verified. And that was the beauty of Vasilev's plan, as Baptiste understood it. Baptiste had placed the woman he loved in danger, mortal danger and knew that he could never forgive himself for that. The issue was, however, could she? If he ever had hopes before about them getting back together those dreams were now as dead as Vasilev. He sighed heavily. He was a fool. A fool in and out of love.

Satisfied that he wasn't being tailed he finally took one of the many entrances into the Buttes-Chaumont Park. The park was unlike any other in Paris. Inaugurated in 1867 by Napoleon III, it was built to disguise an old network of quarries. As such it had hills, streams, a waterfall, a lake with an island and its most impressive feature a sixty-five-metre suspension bridge over the lake. Given its proximity to central Paris in the 19th arrondissement it was favoured by locals who wanted to escape into countryside without leaving the city. It was a place Baptiste often went to unwind and to forget about his work.

The mission had been a success. Vasilev was dead, but far more importantly to him, Racine had returned. He saw the suspension bridge in the distance and remembered walking across it with her. Although he never told her this, that had been one of the happiest moments of his life. He'd known it was wrong to start a relationship with an officer junior to him, but their mutual attraction was too strong to ignore. The problem wasn't the difference in age or culture; it was their chosen profession. Neither could allow themselves to have a relationship that could be used as leverage against them. They were to use Jacob, a lifelong bachelor, as an example. So whatever they had, ended before it really was given a chance to start.

He slowed and then stopped, pretending to massage his left calf. He had the sudden sensation that he was being watched. He looked around. The park was all but deserted; in fact the only movement came from the rustling trees. Baptiste started to move again and took the winding path up the hill to the bridge. He stopped halfway across and leant against the guardrail. It was the same spot he had stood, when Racine had ended it with him. He had felt a piece of himself die that day, right there. He stared into the distance, not really noticing the view. He got the urge to hear her voice, even if it was cold.

Baptiste pulled out his iPhone and was puzzled to see that he didn't have a signal. He checked his settings, and all seemed normal, except for the fact that there was no signal whatsoever. He'd read a book once about visualisation; visualise your dreams and they will come true was the belief. He visualised himself calling Racine and telling her his true feelings. He visualised her telling him that she loved him back. Maybe she would forgive him, and they could leave France and have a different life together. He closed his eyes to fully visualise this. There was a freshness to the air; the wind started to build and he could smell the rain. Baptiste took in a deep breath and let it out. Yes, he was going to talk to Racine, he was adamant, and he'd tell her how he felt.

The sound of approaching footsteps reached his ears. They seemed so close. How had he not noticed them until now? He turned away from the railings.

A tall man was striding towards him, already a good distance across the bridge. There was a black bag in his left hand but his right hand was rising and it held something that made Baptiste's breath catch in his chest – a handgun. Baptiste was in danger – the man had crept up on him. He'd made an amateur mistake. He had done what Jacob had always told him not to do: he had let down his guard. The narrow bridge was the perfect kill box. It was too late to run, yet unarmed it was his only option. Baptiste turned and started to sprint away, his feet slapping loudly. But then in the eerily quiet park there was another sound, a suppressed gunshot.

The round struck Baptiste in the back, propelling him forwards. He thrust his hands out and slid across the bridge. An instant wave of cold washed over him, quickly rising from his lower back. He tasted blood in his mouth. His hands grabbed at and attempted to grip the cold, metal railings beside him, but he couldn't seem to make his fingers work properly. He managed to turn and his eyes looked back the way he had come. A pair of polished black shoes approached. They stopped beside him. Baptiste raised his head. The man was dressed in a long, dark overcoat, undone and flapping against his legs. Even though the sunlight was weak he wore a pair of sunglasses with bronze lenses. His face seemed somehow familiar to Baptiste. The man's right hand gripped a suppressed Ruger Mark IV .22 semi-automatic.

The assassin fired two more rounds. In the right circumstances, Baptiste knew the Ruger could be as quiet as someone snapping their fingers loudly.

Twin needles of ice stabbed him in the chest. He felt his eyes closing, but a hand grabbed him and heaved him back up against the railing. Summoning every ounce of his draining strength, Baptiste swung his fist at his attacker. The man ducked his head, and the punch missed his chin, landing weakly on his temple. As Baptiste's fist started to fall it brought with it the sunglasses. Baptiste stared at the face underneath. He saw the red birth mark above the attacker's left eye and time seemed to slow. The assassin smiled. Baptiste recognised him as the Ukrainian lawyer, Magidov.

'You,' Baptiste gasped.

'Me.' Magidov sneered.

Vision dimming, Baptiste furiously attempted to understand what was happening. What had gone wrong? Magidov's identity as a Jewish lawyer had been confirmed, hadn't it? But he was a Russian agent. The man was part of Vasilev's plan, and not just the intel he had delivered. It was back to luck and coincidence, but bad luck and fabricated coincidence.

Unable to fight anymore, Baptiste felt himself being lifted up and over the guardrail. Rushing air told him he was plummeting towards the dark water some sixty-five metres below.

*

The sign on the bistro door read *closed*, and it was to all but the two customers who sat at a table inside. Francois approached the table and deposited a bottle of red wine and a pair of wineglasses. 'In all the time Maurice has been coming in here, you are the only woman who has ever accompanied him.'

Racine asked, 'Is that true?'

'It is not.' Jacob cleared his throat. 'Thank you, Francois.'

'It is.' Francois winked at Racine, then withdrew to the bar, where he switched on a thick, wall-mounted television, the bistro's only visible concession to modernity, and continued to polish his glasses.

'Have you heard from Baptiste today?' Jacob asked.

'No. Why?'

'I had wanted him to be here, but I'd forgotten he had the day off, and of course he is not answering his phone. I could fire him for that.' Her boss's face crinkled as he grinned. 'Never mind, you and I shall drink for the three of us.' He poured the wine, then raised his glass. His eyes had become moist. 'I want to thank you for righting a wrong that I have caused, for destroying a monster that I created. In my long career there has never been another person whom I have appreciated nor valued more than you.'

'I'm sure there must be.'

'No, and this is not the wine talking. No one else is like you. Your career will eclipse mine.' They drank then lapsed into silence, neither Racine nor Jacob knowing quite what to say. Jacob eventually broke the uneasy quiet. 'Sasha Vasilev is dead, which is excellent. There is no evidence that it was us – excellent again – and, Racine, you are alive.'

'Excellent,' Racine said flatly, her face emotionless, and emptied her glass. 'I'm glad.'

Jacob shut his eyes as waves of relief and remorse in equal measure washed over him. He had set Racine up for this journey, trained her for it, but he knew that now it was finished she would not find the closure she needed. Yet he felt free, liberated from the cold shadow of Sasha Vasilev, but he knew that nothing would mitigate for the loss of life Vasilev had caused. The families of the agents he had given up, the agents who over the course of Vasilev's twelve-year tenure with the DGSE had been lost. There was nothing more Maurice Jacob could do to honour their names but continue the fight for France and her people. And his protégée – Racine – was the tool with which to do this. He regarded her sitting opposite him and knew that she had weathered a storm of emotion. He knew for him his journey was close to the end, but for her it had just started.

'A toast, to Celine Durand!' Jacob noticed a catch in his voice as he said her name.

'Celine.' Racine's own voice sounded suddenly reedy.

Jacob emptied his glass.

'Maurice, I think you may want to see this,' Francois called over from the bar.

Jacob craned his neck, peered at the screen, then clambered to his feet and joined Francois in order to get a better view. It was showing a live report from ON.

Our News anchor, Sharron Machin, stood at her well-rehearsed spot to the right of the gigantic plasma screen in the ON television broadcast newsroom. Darren Weller's face filled a large portion of the display to her left and was accompanied by the headline 'Kidnapped?' Machin addressed the camera. 'British journalist Darren Weller has been kidnapped on the streets of central Moscow hours before he was due to speak at a news conference regarding the involvement of the British Secret Intelligence Service in his illegal interrogation in Donetsk. We can now go live to ON's Anna Chepura who is at the scene of Weller's abduction.'

The word 'LIVE' whooshed across the screen, giving way to the feed from Moscow. The plasma display became a split-screen. It showed Chepura standing on a busy Moscow street on one side and a feed of Darren Weller's reports on the other. Chepura started to speak, her American-accented English seemingly out of place in the Russian capital. 'It was here on Tverskaya Street outside the iconic Ritz-Carlton Moscow, earlier today that ON journalist, Darren Weller was abducted in broad daylight. Eyewitnesses report seeing at eleven-twenty-five this morning a brown UPS delivery van stop here, just outside the hotel. Two men dressed as UPS employees got out of the van and then reportedly grabbed Darren Weller as he passed. And against his will, they proceeded to bundle him into the van, before pulling back out into traffic.'

'Anna, do we have any idea who these men were who kidnapped Darren?'

'None at this stage, but the Moscow politsiya have confirmed the van was reported stolen from the maintenance department of the UPS depot an hour before and has now been found abandoned, just a kilometre or so away from here.'

The footage of the studio was now replaced with that of a politsiya cordon around a brown, UPS van, parked haphazardly on the pavement under a granite-faced bridge. Two politsiya Ford Focus saloons blocked the underpass on the side nearest to the van, whilst a politsiya officer funnelled traffic through the remaining lane opposite.

'Thank you, Anna.' Machin in the studio wore a grim expression as the camera returned to her now sitting at a desk.

'Ha! They did it!' exclaimed Jacob and immediately drained his glass.

Francois eyed him warily. 'You want another bottle?'

'Of course.' Jacob toddled back to their table and sat heavily. 'We are celebrating!'

'You knew about this?' Racine asked.

'I did.'

'Are we responsible?'

'No.'

'Who is?'

'A-ha.' Jacob tapped his nose in a conspiratorial manner, then leant forward a little. When he spoke, his voice was a whisper. 'The British.'

Racine said nothing.

Francois deposited the second bottle, looked at his old friend then rolled his eyes at Racine before getting back to the TV.

Jacob continued talking now in his usual tone. 'Of course, it's interesting to see how ON, and by definition the Russian authorities, are spinning this.'

'How so?'

'I have it on good authority that the men chosen to undertake this for the British were ethnic Chechens. Yet no mention has been made of this, because of course it does not fit in with the Kremlin narrative that there is no longer a threat of terrorism from Chechnya.' He raised the bottle. 'More wine?'

Racine inclined her head and he poured. 'So where is Weller?'

'He's made his own prison bed and now he must lie in it.'

'I don't follow you.'

Jacob smirked. The lines in his face had seemed to lessen and there was a twinkle in his eye. 'I believe by openly broadcasting footage of himself in a conflict zone, with an illegal foreign militia, in which he wore a military uniform and fired an assault rifle – albeit at practice targets – Weller contravened the UK's strict anti-terrorism laws.' He paused to take a mouthful of wine and closed his eyes as though he was savouring the taste and the victory. 'Apparently Interpol will be issuing a "red notice" for him tomorrow. Of course, as an Interpol signatory country, if Weller were to suddenly appear in Ukraine, the Kyiv authorities would have no choice but to immediately arrest him and extradite him to the UK.'

Racine laughed. It was harsh treatment, but in her opinion, Weller deserved it and what was more he would now be unable to call out Aidan Snow at his news conference.

*

As late afternoon became early evening and the lights were switched on, Racine had stopped drinking and Jacob had not. Several potential customers were turned away from the bistro causing Francois to half-heartedly complain. But it was an unwritten rule that Jacob had the place for as long as he required it and today, he really had required it.

'I think we can say, we made up for the absence of Baptiste with our alcohol consumption,' Jacob said. 'And it was not plonk.'

Racine smirked. 'Plonk.'

'Yes, you see, I use that word you used, all those years ago when we first met, and I first brought you here. You were a surprise, an explosion. And you still are, Racine, like your famous namesake, renowned for your "elegance, purity, speed, and fury".'

Racine frowned. 'Thank you.'

'Ha, ha! Wikipedia, I stole that line from Wikipedia – look it up. But I dare say it is as befitting to you as it was to his prose.' Jacob reached for his glass raised it then peered into its bottom. 'Ah, it appears that either my glass is faulty, or we have finished another bottle.'

'We have.' It was their fourth and just under three of those had disappeared into Jacob. 'I think it's time we left.'

Jacob closed his eyes. 'I think I agree.'

'You need to call your car.'

'I do.' He slowly stood. 'And I shall do so on my way to the little boys' room.'

Racine watched him go, then stretched and yawned. It wasn't the wine that had tired her per se, but the combination of the wine and the company. She was fond of her boss in moderation; she realised what a momentous time it was for him. She sincerely hoped he had achieved closure on the issue of Sasha Vasilev. But had she? She had been sent to Donetsk to kill a man in cold blood. A man who had taken in her aunt and then taken her life. What did she now feel about that? Did she feel anything? She'd thought revenge would have been more satisfying than this.

The truth was she felt no different and nothing had changed. Celine was still dead. Her tears had run dry and the emptiness had expanded. She was an assassin for the French Republic but was she also a killer, a murderer? Was she any better than the wretches languishing in La Santé or any of the nation's prisons for taking a human life? Yes, she stated categorically to herself, she was. Vasilev had been evil. He had caused the deaths of good people, loyal people, noble people – fellow intelligence officers, and a woman she loved like no other. He'd answered for his crimes, and she had been the chosen instrument of French justice.

It wasn't the first time she had questioned herself, and it certainly wouldn't be the last. She remembered her father telling her: 'If you think too hard, you go mad'. She allowed herself a sad smile. She was mad all right. Racine realised she still hadn't called him and made the resolute decision that she would in the morning. But not too early; she couldn't be cordial with a hangover.

Racine raised her own glass and finished the sip that had been sitting collecting dust for the last ten minutes. She wanted to drink more, and would do so at home, with Netflix. She idly wondered if anything worth watching had been added and retrieved her iPhone, to check the app, but then remembered this was her work phone. Her finger hovered over the photos icon. She touched the screen.

The last image was of the American couple by the river, 'Clint' and whatever the woman's name was. It was not the clearest of photographs. She pinched to enlarge it. She frowned. There was something about it that did not seem right. The woman was holding his left hand and looking intently at his face, but Clint was looking intently at Racine, and the way his right hand was held by his side, fingers splayed like a cowboy, like a gunslinger, like someone who had a gun. She let out a breath through pursed lips. Perhaps she was being paranoid, but it still didn't mean that Clint wasn't out to get her. She selected the photograph and sent it to a DGSE email address with the subject line 'ID Request'. She then tapped out a text message to Baptiste:

You've missed all the fun! X

She frowned, not understanding why she'd added a kiss at the end.

'He's on his way.' Jacob announced as he ambled back to their table. His movements had become slower and his words were slurring. 'Any moment now. You know it amazes me how my driver is never far away . . . like a bird of prey . . . no . . . like a drone . . . circling high above . . . forever watching and awaiting his orders.'

'We all have our jobs to do.' Racine slipped her phone back into her pocket.

'True, Sophie, very true.'

Her name sounded alien on his lips. It was the first time she could remember him using it, but this was also the first time she had seen him this drunk.

'I insist that he delivers you to your door too. It's far easier than you taking your usual roundabout route home. He'll carry out the safety checks for us.'

Racine opened her mouth to refuse but changed her mind. She slipped into her coat and then felt her phone vibrate. She expected to see a cringeworthy text from Baptiste.

There was a knock at the door. Francois quickly went to see who it was. A man and a woman, a couple, were peering into the bistro and looking perplexed. 'We're closed, I'm sorry.' Francois cut him a curt smile and repeated the phrase in English, the most popular foreign language.

'We were just about to leave. Please do not let us stand in the way of your livelihood!' Jacob called out.

Francois turned to his old friend, mouthed '*merci*' and then unlocked the door.

In the shadows, Racine couldn't see their faces but noted they were tall and well dressed, wearing long, dark wool coats over suits. Businesspeople perhaps after a quick drink following a successful meeting or perhaps having an illicit affair in the city of love? As long as they had money, she doubted Francois minded either way.

Racine looked back at the screen of her iPhone. It was a reply to her 'ID Request'. She opened the email. Her snatched photograph had been a 74.2 per cent match to a known former East German Stasi operative named Otto Linus.

She looked up, and now saw that for the second time that day Otto Linus was looking directly at her. His right hand was held by his side, fingers splayed like a cowboy, like a gunslinger, like someone who had a gun. The woman from earlier was standing next to him, her right hand holding a black briefcase, and Francois was smiling and gesturing to one of his many empty tables.

'Racine.' Jacob was on his feet gently swaying. 'Are we going, or are we not?'

Linus's hand started to move.

The woman's hand started to move and so did Racine.

With her left arm she swung at Jacob, knocking him off his feet. Dropping to her knees, and using both hands, she flipped the table over onto its side, so that the heavy top acted as a shield.

Linus's hand was moving across his body to an underarm holster and it was costing him valuable time. The woman was raising the briefcase with her right hand, as her left came around to support the base.

Racine instinctively ducked a millisecond before a burst of 9mm rounds flew from the concealed sub-machine gun within the briefcase and ripped into the wooden panelling behind her. Racine drew her Glock 26 from its holster and immediately returned fire over the table. Her first round hit the woman in the forehead and her second in her chest as she was already falling backwards into oblivion.

Linus threw himself over the top of the bar as Racine tracked his progress with her Glock. In the second it would take him to recover, she moved. Running forwards, affording Linus no time to respond, she vaulted the bar top, firing blindly as she did. Glasses and bottles exploded and then she saw Linus, scrabbling on all fours. He dropped his right shoulder, rolled, and thrust his arms up. He and Racine fired at the same time, two, three, four rounds until Linus abruptly stopped. The two-handed grip on his handgun faltered and then his arms fell by either side of his dying body. Racine watched his eyes flicker for several seconds and then go still.

Racine pushed herself away from the dead German and using the bar for support hauled herself to her feet. Francois was standing stock-still in the exact same spot he had been, only now his skin was grey.

'We need to get out of here,' Jacob ordered as he gingerly pushed himself to his feet.

'Are you hit?' Racine checked him over.

'No. You?'

A trickle of blood ran into her mouth and she felt her face. 'Just a cut, flying glass.'

Jacob peered at the corpse behind the bar. 'I've seen this man before. He was looking in a shop window just before my meeting with Jack Patchem.'

Racine was about to reply when there was a sudden movement at the door. She spun, alert, weapon up. Jacob's DGSE driver entered and on seeing the carnage and Racine's weapon, raised his hands.

'Take us home,' Jacob ordered and headed for the door.

Racine stopped him and pushed past through the entrance and out onto the moonlit Parisian street. She couldn't see anyone else, but that didn't mean they were alone. She darted left and immediately ducked past the DGSE Citroën into the doorway of the next shop. She drew arcs with her sidearm left and right. The street was deserted. She studied the parked cars, none of the windows were cracked open or appeared to be misty. She took a deep breath to force more oxygen into her lungs then sprinted diagonally across the street to another shop entrance; it was an action she hoped would elicit a response from any backup team.

Eyes sweeping left to right, all senses on alert she saw and heard nothing – no footfall, no firing from hidden gunmen. She stared back up at the bistro and then watched down the street towards the river. On the larger road traffic trundled past, unaware of the firefight that had just happened. And then a car turned off, and its headlights threw the street into a high contrast of shadow and light. Racine fell to one knee, pressed herself into the wall of the building and took aim. The car was a large saloon, but it wasn't until it swept past a streetlight that she saw it was a dark Citroën. The next lamppost gave her the number plate; it tallied to that of Jacob's DGSE car. It was a clone. Jacob's driver had been too prompt for the attacker's plan.

Without hesitation Racine opened fire. Her first two rounds hit the windscreen, causing the shatterproof glass to craze and then the next two took out one of the front tyres. The car slewed sideways, mounted the kerb and struck a lamppost. Racine sprinted for the car, Glock held out in front, firing as she ran – taking the attack to the enemy. Airbags, having momentarily inflated, now lay limp across the dashboard and interior panels. The driver's side window was open. She fired through it at the man who sat stunned behind the wheel. Hands held up uselessly he jerked as each round hit him. He was the only occupant, and she recognised him. The Asian man who'd been peering in the ballet shop

313

window. She ceased firing and he slumped lifelessly sideways as the car slowly started to roll backwards down the hill.

Jacob's driver was in the bistro doorway, his own handgun in a two-handed grip. He nodded at Racine, deferring to her as she came to a crouch behind his car. 'Do we stay, or do we go?'

'We go. Get Jacob and the barman into the car – I'll cover you.' She changed her magazine.

'Right.' He turned to wave his boss through the door, but then Racine saw him raise his Glock a moment before a volley of semi-automatic rounds exploded through the front window of the bistro.

Racine went prone behind the Citroën. Her mind flashed back to earlier that day at the riverside. The American couple, the Asian couple, and their driver, who she had not seen leave the car. A team of five. She'd taken out three . . . The other two were inside the bistro . . . They'd somehow flanked her and entered from the back . . . There was a second burst of gunfire and then the bistro went quiet. Ears ringing, she almost missed the footsteps as they crunched on the broken glass. Someone was exiting the building. Knowing that she was about to make herself a very large target at a very short range, but also that she had no other choice, Racine sprung to her feet.

She came face to face with Francois. His eyes were wide, and the right arm of his white shirt was crimson. He stumbled forward, as though pushed. It was then Racine knew he was being used as a shield. He started to fall towards her, she dived right, away from him, away from the back of the Citroën.

Landing on her back, she was winded but unloaded half her magazine into the fourth team member, the small, Asian woman who was holding an HK MP5. The assassin convulsed as the fusillade hit her. Four down, but where was the other one? Still inside the bistro or outside acting as overwatch, and ready to kill her with a single well-placed high-velocity round?

'Is there anyone else inside?' she shouted, to get his attention and to compensate for her damaged sense of hearing.

Francois opened his mouth, said nothing and shook his head.

Not convinced, Racine knew she had no need to check the woman as half her head was missing, so she moved in to cover next to Francois. He was slumped against the car cradling his right arm.

He looked at her and something in his eyes made Racine stop dead.

'They killed Maurice,' he said.

TWENTY-SEVEN

Gare du Nord, Paris

Hat pulled down, scarf pulled up, the man responsible for shooting Baptiste boarded the last express train of the day from Paris's Gare du Nord to Amsterdam's central station. In just under three hours and twenty minutes the American assassin who had pretended to be Ukrainian would be two hundred and seventy miles away from Paris.

The carriage was not full. The American's seat was by the window and as the train glided out of the station the seat next to him and those across the aisle remained empty. The row in front was occupied by a pair of backpackers and their paraphernalia, but as their seats faced away from the American there was no chance for them to study his face. As the train slipped further and further away from the French capital, his chances of being challenged lessened. The American doubted the body would be found until daybreak, which gave him a minimum of ten hours before the authorities had any inkling a contract had been enacted. A crime committed.

Beneath his scarf, he smirked. The line between crime and contract was, in his case, a thin and bloody one. He was a professional undertaking a professional task but one that stipulated he break the law and commit the crime of murder. Since joining the commercial 'circuit' he found himself no longer shielded from this. His smirk turned into a yawn as he started to relax in the stuffy carriage.

The American gazed out of the window. His own ghostly reflection glared back at him like a spectre, the red birthmark seemingly winking at him. He had faced his inner demons many years ago. He'd come to an agreement with them, an understanding of their needs and how his work would fulfil these. Their hunger had grown as he had. First they nibbled on the pain he inflicted upon himself. A bruise here, a cut there. This, however, had been too little for their tastes, too bland for their palate. He graduated to breaking the bones of others, and with every snap a jolt of joy surged from within. Even this soon became insufficient for them and so the American had had to find something more to satiate their desires. Something that could not be surpassed. But how to offer this without raising the suspicions of those around him, of those who could stop him?

The choice had been his only one. He enlisted. He went to war. War fed the demons more than they had ever dared hope for. And then abruptly it ended. Yet they continued to demand death, a regular sacrifice in order to leave him sane. Else they would hound him, tell him, and compel him to kill. The death of the French intelligence officer would be sacrifice enough, he hoped, for a while. His reflection glowered, the port wine stain above his left eye a constant reminder to him of the blood the demons within demanded.

The American screwed his eyes shut, took a deep breath and when he opened them again it was his own face he saw reflected, without emotion. Becoming the professional he was once again, he scoped out his fellow passengers, not making eye contact but assessing their distorted reflections in the double-thick glass. The backpacking couple in the row in front, and a solitary woman seated two rows behind, were still the only other occupants. He imagined their lives served no purpose and that they would be ultimately forgotten. Each was caught in their own little, pathetic worlds, leaving Paris on a wintry November evening.

But not him. Not the American. He would be remembered for being at the top of his game and all those who had ever doubted him would be forced to deferentially apologise. Inner needs notwithstanding, he was motivated to stay in the business to prove himself, to prove that he was darn good at what he had been trained to do and could continue to operate even without the help of his supposed overlords, who hid in offices bearing seals on the doors. Undertaking the contract on the French intelligence team had hardly been testing for the American. He didn't need to demonstrate that he was an operator to be trusted with high-value targets, although what value the agent named Baptiste had, seemed minimal to him. It was a disappointment, in his mind, that he had not taken out those he viewed as the salient targets – Jacob the DGSE Director and his pet female assassin – but as the team leader he understood enough about leadership to distribute the jobs fairly.

Besides, he was the only one with the necessary skills to pose as Magidov, the Ukrainian lawyer he had left dead in a garage in Donetsk. He had completed his part of the contract and would now await payment, safe in the knowledge that the other four were doing the same in their boltholes. He would observe with interest in the morning how the French and international news networks reported on the attacks. The American liked shaping headlines, and it wouldn't be the first time it had happened.

DGSE headquarters, Paris, France

In the age of social media and smartphones it was virtually impossible to keep the news of the attack on the DGSE unit from the general public. Grillot had faced pointed questions from his boss, the director of the DGSE, and of course the Minister of Defence, Tristan Ignace, which had led to a heated debate. Eventually the minister had decided to stage a press conference emphasising the French government's outrage at the attack.

The sizeable conference room at DGSE headquarters in Paris had been chosen as the most appropriate venue, and the international reporters and journalists admitted had been carefully vetted not to exclude those with known links to the Russian government. Whilst Minister Ignace was not going to directly implicate Russia, at this stage, he wanted to deliver a blunt warning to them. An aide had informed the assembled members of the press that the minister was prepared to answer questions only after he had given a short statement.

Minister Ignace entered the conference room with a determined stride and stood at a lectern emblazoned with the seal of the French Republic. Ignace assessed the amassed reporters and briefly acknowledged a couple of them before he started to speak. 'At approximately 18:00 yesterday an armed group entered a bistro in central Paris where Maurice Jacob, a Deputy Director of the General Directorate for External Security, was enjoying an after-work meal.' Ignace paused for effect. There were murmurs around the room and several camera flashes. 'They opened fire on Deputy Director Jacob and his driver, Henri Labon. A firefight ensued as Labon engaged them with his service firearm. A highly trained intelligence officer, Labon was able to neutralise all four of the attackers; however, not before both he and Deputy Director Jacob were fatally wounded. The attackers, I do not use the word "gunmen", consisted of two men and two women, all of whom we have now identified as foreign nationals.

'Let me be clear, whilst the effects of this attack are undoubtedly terrifying, this was not an act of terrorism. The four members of the group were known contract killers. This was a paid-for assassination of a valued servant of both the Republic of France and her people.' Ignace now looked at one of his preferred journalists and nodded, the signal that the press was now free to ask their questions.

'Minister,' the reporter from France's major state television news programme addressed Ignace, 'do you know who was responsible for this assassination plot?'

Ignace nodded slowly. 'At this current time, it is too soon to categorically state who we believe the orchestrator to be, but let this be known: once our investigation is complete we will not keep any secrets from the people of the republic.'

The same reporter posed a follow-up question. 'Were there any survivors of the attack?'

'The owner of the bistro, Francois Fournier, who also received gunshot wounds, is the sole survivor of this outrageous attack.'

*

In Amsterdam the American drained his beer glass and placed it slowly on the bar. Outwardly his emotions were in check but inside his anger was rising. The barman, oblivious to his turmoil, gave the American the universal raised-eyebrow nod.

'I'll take another, thanks,' the American said, with forced joviality.

The bar was small, quiet and just out of the city centre. The American had chosen it specifically because if forced to leave in a hurry it had both a front and rear exit, which led into a maze of streets. It also had a large television, which currently was showing live footage of the French press conference, courtesy of BBC World. As he continued to watch, a chill hit him as he heard, in response to a pointed question by a reporter, the French minister give the full names of the rest of the kill team. Ignace truly was not holding back. The American was secure in the knowledge that on the French side only Baptiste knew his part in the mission, and of course Baptiste had been permanently silenced.

Still the team had gone in sterile so how had they been identified? Fingerprints, facial recognition software? He was certain he personally had left no trace when he had dealt with Baptiste, and the others had not known his name and believed him to be Canadian. A question niggled him: why had the minister not mentioned either the woman or Baptiste? Unless it strengthened the French narrative, or unless they had survived? But how could a professional team of four not have taken out the woman? Was she really that highly skilled or were they really that bad? He remembered watching her work in Tunis and a chill ran down his spine. If she was still alive, things would not be easy for him.

And what of Baptiste? He'd pumped three rounds into the man before hurling him from a bridge. He must be dead. Was it that his body had not been discovered, or as yet remained unidentified? The American ordered a whisky chaser and gulped it down, the burn he hoped suppressing his nerves. As he continued to watch, more journalists posed questions. Ignace was asked about the victims, the implications of the assassination and what France would do next. The conference ended and the live feed switched back to the presenters in the BBC studio, where a British security expert gave his thoughts. The American finished his beer, paid and left the bar.

It was twenty hours since the attack, and following rules set by the broker, he and the rest of the team were not to check in for another four. That was also the time when their fees would be sent to their specified bank accounts. The American did not trust digital technology and for this very purpose did not own a cell phone or any other electronic device. His favoured means of communication was via internet-based email draft folders. He and the broker had the password for an email account. He would log in, open the draft folder, compose a message and leave it there, unsent in the folder. The broker, via a virtual private network which masked his internet IP address, would then do the same. Once read, each draft was deleted. It was as slow and foolproof as possible. Unless the broker's keystrokes were being monitored, there was no evidence of the account's existence. However, in a world where mobile internet was now the norm, the American was denied the luxury of the anonymous internet café, and those who now chose to frequent such places did so for social reasons and were usually known to the owners.

The American stumbled out of the bar and headed directly for the nearest busy street. His gait was rolling and his expression whimsical, but it was all an act. He bumped into a man in a suit as he exited a chocolate shop and momentarily grabbed hold of his shoulder to apologise before he carried on around the corner. Once clear, the American straightened up and lengthened his stride pattern – putting distance and several more turns between him and the man. He entered a square, removed his right hand from his coat pocket and looked at the stolen iPhone it now held. He touched the screen and let himself relax slightly as he noted it was not passcode protected. Accessing the internet, he logged on to the email account supplied by the broker, opened the draft folder and composed a message.

Check in. Contract complete. Awaiting payment.

He had no idea how long it would take for the broker to reply but decided to keep hold of the iPhone for the next hour. If it was reported lost before then it would send its location to whoever was looking for it. Either way he'd leave it on the sidewalk.

Fifteen minutes and a mile later, the American found himself outside a hotel. He casually checked the iPhone and saw that another message had replaced his own.

No payment due. Contract not complete. Complete the contract. You have one month.

Shaking with inner rage, the American deleted the message, and signed out of the email account. He turned sharply, dropped the iPhone into the canal and then headed for Amsterdam Central Station.

EPILOGUE

Cercottes, North-Central France, one week later
Colonel Christophe Grillot removed his reading glasses and put them back into their case. The after-action report on the contact with the kill team lay on the desk in front of him. He knew most of it by heart; nevertheless it did not make Maurice Jacob's death any more believable.

Two DGSE officers had been lost. Deputy Director Maurice Jacob and his driver, Henri Lebon were slain at the bistro. Agent Jean Baptiste Moreau, however, had survived the attempt on his life. His would-be assassin had vanished without trace. Baptiste had been discovered by an amorous couple on the banks of the lake at Buttes-Chaumont Park. He'd sustained three small-calibre gunshot wounds, in addition to a list of other injuries to internal organs and bones, consistent with falling from a height of sixty-five metres onto concrete-like water. Baptiste had been placed in a medically induced coma, and the doctors were still unsure if he would ever be revived.

Neither Jacob nor Baptiste had any relatives to ask questions or cause potential problems and the driver had been an unmarried, only child. At least that was something, Grillot thought, then felt sickened by himself. A life taken was a life taken regardless of who it was. He'd lost people before, both on the battlefield and on intelligence operations, but this time it hit him hard.

He looked again at the photographs of the four members of the kill team who had been identified, and willed their images to talk to him, to tell him who their broker was. To tell him who the fifth assassin had been. Otto Linus and Teresa Jana were both former East German Stasi operatives who after the Berlin wall had come down worked on the circuit as a married couple. Hwan Jun Gim and Min Jeong Lee were former members of the North Korean State Security Department, who had allegedly defected for commercial reasons. Racine had eliminated them all.

The fifth member, the man they believed to be responsible for the attempted assassination of Baptiste, had vanished. All that remained of him were a few blurry images captured by CCTV cameras placed at the exit to the park. Facial and gait recognition software had set upon this in an attempt to back-trace the suspect's movements. As yet, this had not yielded any tangible result, neither had Minister Ignace's decision to go public with the killers' identities.

It occurred to Grillot that none of the team had been top-notch; they had been professional, dependable and yet disposable. It was almost as though they had been specifically chosen for the task so that they could be knowingly identified. Was that what was really behind the personnel choice? Was it another ploy by the broker's client, as if to say, '*You have identified the killers and look – they have no link to us?*' The more Grillot thought it through, the more this made sense. It was a tactic straight out of the Russian Hybrid-War playbook, plausible and sustainable deniability. But was their deniability sustainable? For the moment it seemed to him that it was. With the team's details having been splashed across innumerable newspapers and TV reports, he imagined their broker would be hiding under a well-insulated rock.

Although Grillot believed it was Russia who had ordered the operation, proving it was another matter and both his boss and Minister Ignace wanted that proof. None of the assassins had any direct link to the Russian authorities. Finding the broker responsible for offering the individual killers their contracts was the first issue; getting him or her to talk was the second. Finding any material link between the broker and their client was the third and finding a connection between the client and Russia, if indeed that was who had sanctioned the operation, was the fourth. But then what? Would France officially prosecute whoever was responsible for the assassinations? Of course they would not. And accusing Russia of a crime of any sort, Grillot knew, was like pissing into the wind; you may feel relieved at first but then you realise you are covered in piss.

However, it was not his ultimate decision what his country did. It was a cycle of violence without end. He felt deflated.

A knock at the door dragged Grillot back from his dark thoughts. 'Come in.'

Racine entered. He pointed to a chair. She sat. Since the attack, on his orders, she had been hidden in what Grillot viewed as one of the safest facilities in all of France – the Paratrooper Specialised Training Centre, Cercottes. The centre was where the DGSE trained and tested its clandestine operatives and as such any assault on it would be a suicide mission.

'How are you?' he asked.

'I'm fine. How is Baptiste?'

'No change.'

Racine looked down, took a deep breath then met his steely gaze. 'I want to put in a request to return to active service, sir.'

'Of course you do.'

'Sir?'

'A week is a long time in our business, it is true, but would you not be better off staying here for a while? Becoming an instructor to the new intake, passing on your skills?'

Racine frowned. 'Am I being punished?'

'No, you are not.'

'Am I being held accountable for what happened?'

'No.'

'But I am accountable. I didn't check all the entrances and exits. If I had done so, the woman would not have been able to get the drop on Henri and Jacob. She would not have been able to kill them.'

'It is not your fault. You must not torment yourself.'

'Sir, it's a simple fact, black and white. I made a mistake and I want to put that right.'

'By doing what exactly? Killing everyone responsible?'

'Yes.'

'I see – and where would you stop?'

'I wouldn't.'

'You'd even assassinate, say, the Russian President?'

'I would.'

'I believe you.' He exhaled slowly. 'I know you were close to Maurice Jacob, close to Jean Baptiste Moreau. You want justice for them but—'

'With respect, sir, that is not it.'

Grillot wet his lips. 'Tell me what is?'

'They tried to kill me. I want to kill them all, but I can't.' Her gaze hardened. 'I have to end the hold they have on me, this circle of violence. Either I do this by killing them all, every single last one of them including their superiors so there is no one left to come after me, or I end it by accepting that what they did cannot be changed. And I move on. Revenge cannot beat them. Revenge is what they are expecting. Revenge fuels them, it feeds them, and it recruits others who follow them.

If I act like them, I am them. If I am not driven by the past, I am not controlled by their actions. I cannot change the past because I no longer live there. But Deputy Director Jacob and I once did. That was our mistake. He ordered me to kill our past, and that is what killed him. If I am allowed to move on, I am free to act, to seek out danger. I will become the incarnation of danger itself. Colonel, the DGSE needs me to be dangerous.'

*

Le Fin

* * *

ACKNOWLEDGEMENTS

Writing is the best job in the world, and I am extremely grateful to those around me who have by turns inspired and supported my literary journey.

My biggest inspiration has been my wife Galia, for without her I would not have been able to carry on. I'd also be unable to write without my two sons Alexander and Jonathan, writing something that they one day will read and hopefully enjoy spurs me on.

I need to express my thanks to my editor at HQ, Finn Cotton, and my agents, Justin Nash and Kate Nash, for believing in my work and wanting to champion me and publish it.

I'd like to thank my friends both inside and outside of the book world for putting up with me being grumpy, hiding away and ranting about my new book, my next book, my next idea, and for being vocal supporters. This is a long list but includes: Neill J Furr, Liam Saville, Paul Page, Chris Salter, Steph Edger, Paul Grzegorek, Alan McDermott, Charlie Flowers, Jacky Gramosi Collins, Louise Mangos, Jamie Mason, Rachel Amphlett, Michael Jones and Karen Campbell.

Lastly, I must thank you, the reader; if it were not for you I'd simply be talking to myself!

If you loved *Traitors,* keep reading for an exclusive
extract from the first thriller in the Jack Tate series!

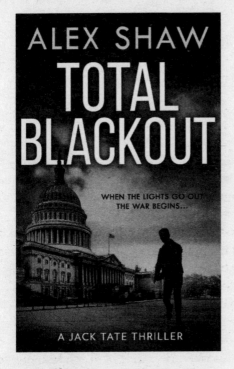

When the lights go out, the war begins …

PROLOGUE

Washington, DC

The co-conspirators stood on their balcony at The Hay-Adams. The White House was less than four hundred metres away. The balcony afforded them a grandstand view. Within minutes Maksim Oleniuk and Chen Yan, the founders of Blackline PMC, were going to launch the largest attack on the United States of America since the Japanese attack on Pearl Harbor, perhaps the biggest attack ever on the country. Maksim Oleniuk certainly hoped so. He looked down and smiled at the Chinese oligarch who had funded his dream of striking the US. It had been her finances – billions amassed from minerals and electronics, in partnership with his access and expertise as a former Russian Military Intelligence Officer, which had created this paradigm-shifting moment. Oleniuk found his partner highly attractive but understood she was the very last person in the world he should approach. He sipped his chilled champagne and wondered if she could read his mind.

'What are you thinking of?' Yan asked, surprising him, making his face colour in the gloom. Her American accent was flawless, perfected whilst she gained an MBA at the New York Institute of Technology. It put Oleniuk's Russo-British accent to shame.

'I am just thinking that never have parents given birth to such a powerful child.'

She inclined her head, a stoic expression on her face. 'Our child will live and die in the same instant, yet leave an eternal legacy.'

'Legacy,' Oleniuk repeated. It was something he had strived to create and the perfect word for the occasion.

They stood like expectant parents, the former GRU officer rocking from foot to foot and the Chinese billionaire stock-still, but both were nervous, excited and scared of what was to come.

The timing of the detonation had been mandated to utilise empty airspace, or airspace as empty as it ever could be over the continental United States. The location was hugely symbolic; the US seat of power deliberately selected, politically central rather than geographically so. Oleniuk's scientists had stated the risk of damage to the retina was small yet did exist if they were to stare directly at the epicentre of the detonation with the naked eye. For this reason, Oleniuk and Yan wore wrap-around sunglasses with specifically engineered lenses shielding their eyes. They gazed out over the balcony at the empty air a mile above the floodlit White House.

At exactly five a.m. there was a flash so quick that if the pair had not known exactly where to look it would have been missed, then a silent, purple detonation flowered. It bloomed like a monstrous, inverted Fourth of July firework. Its petals spread earthwards and then faded to be replaced by a mauve glow, creating a spectral false dawn.

Oleniuk felt the tingling sensation he had been warned to expect wash over him, as each individual hair on his body stood up on end. At that very moment, as if choreographed, every single light around the pair vanished. The White House lights disappeared, the floodlights on the lawn were no more and the stately residence of the President of the United States of America was plunged into darkness.

The glow started to fade; the night sky now taking on the

appearance of the bruised eye of a heavyweight boxer, before it gradually became black once more. The co-conspirators removed their protective eyewear. They had delivered a form of vengeance like no other the modern world had ever seen and, ignoring ancient, fanciful tales of vengeful gods, the single most powerful.

Oleniuk put his arm around Yan. 'We have done it.'

She did not reply; however, she did give him a sideways glance. Oleniuk quickly moved his arm. 'I am sorry. I was overcome with emotion in the moment. I do apologise.'

'It is understandable, given the circumstances.'

They continued to gaze at the capital city of the United States – dark, silent but not dead. The majority of the population were safely asleep and those who weren't would interpret the loss of power as a citywide outage, a total blackout.

ONE

Two days earlier

Camden, Maine, United States

The assassin was Russian, one of their best. He had to be to make the shot. His hide was in an elevated position on a hill, half a click away from the target. It was the closest he was prepared to go, given the timescale and his schedule. Three targets to hit in three consecutive days. A reckless order in the Russian Army and certainly an unheard-of contract on the private circuit. But he was the best, and he had accepted. And he was now on target number two.

The ever-changing eddies and the elevation made the shot challenging. It was a job for a two-man team, a shooter and a spotter, but the assassin had always preferred to work alone. The assassin was not acquainted with failure; this was something that simply did not enter his thought process. Preparing to fail started with a failure to prepare, and Ruslan Akulov never failed to prepare.

His target was on time. He tracked him in his crosshairs. The man exited the rear of the house through a pair of double-height patio doors, sipping his Pinot Gris, blissfully unaware of the Russian's presence. Retired senator Clifford Piper lived in a sprawling mansion overlooking the town of Camden, Maine. The deck, where he stood now and would soon fall upon, commanded panoramic views of the harbour, West Penobscot Bay, and the evergreen islands.

Akulov had seen mansions before, castle-like homes constructed for the rich and corrupt, which dotted the outskirts of Moscow like mushrooms, while the rest of the population lived in shacks or high-rise concrete boxes. Never before, however, had he encountered one in a setting as spectacular as this. He agreed the panorama was impressive, but the man was not. He knew all about Piper. He hated him. As a senator Piper had preached his own brand of American imperialism, damning all those who dared speak out against Uncle Sam. He was a hawk, voraciously attacking Venezuela, North Korea, Russia, and China. He threw his words like missiles from the safety of Washington, a coward who would not dare repeat his slurs in the face of the enemy.

But, had he been punished for the innumerable deaths his rhetoric had caused or the hatred his words had incited? No. The senator had been allowed to retire to his mansion, and his three-million-dollar view. Not bad for a dacha, or as the Americans called them "vacation properties". The Russian let a sneer form on his face. The property would be vacated soon enough. He had watched his target, and knew his routine well. Piper took a glass of wine at eleven o'clock each morning on his deck in order to appreciate his view. Akulov had also enjoyed the vista. The ocean – like him – was a contradiction. By turns calm and violent. Not that he was naturally a violent soul, but he employed violence in the defence of his country.

The target was a widower, his wife having perished along with twenty-eight other Americans a year before, in a terrorist attack in Jakarta. But for the Jakarta team this had been a failure. Bitter fate had intervened in his employer's plans, made the senator succumb to food poisoning and unable to leave his hotel

336

suite to join the bus tour. The bus his wife was on, the bus that had been boarded by gunmen who slaughtered every passenger. Grief-stricken, the senator had resigned and retired. The Jakarta team's failure ensured that Piper was added to the hit list given to Akulov, and Akulov did not fail.

The maid appeared. She stood by her master's side. She held his hand. Through open curtains, the Russian had observed the old man consoling himself by screwing her. It had not been at all arousing but Akulov had made himself watch, much like a wildlife photographer cataloguing the mating rituals of primates. Piper had grunted; the maid had not.

Mercifully at that precise moment the pair were only talking. At this distance, in the open, he could not hear the sounds escaping their lips, but he imagined they were the sickening words lovers pass to one and other. It wasn't his business. He didn't care what was or was not being said, what was or was not being promised. But what about the late wife? Would she have wanted her husband to become a monk or would she have approved of his new bedfellow? Piper looked contented, and had done so each day the assassin had observed him. Even now he continued to sip his wine, oblivious to the fact that a single .338 Lapua Magnum round from the Russian's suppressed rifle was seconds away from entering his chest and ripping out his heart.

Akulov adjusted the scope of his German sniper rifle. In ordinary times, Piper's death would be seen as a clear message to his country's leader, but these were about to become extraordinary times. The senator's death today would be ignored by tomorrow, and perhaps not be investigated until months after his death – if at all.

Akulov had not entertained the idea of killing the woman, even though strategically it made sense. She was the only other person in the house and leaving her alive would mean the alarm was raised that much faster, but he had no desire kill her. She was an innocent, a civilian and that went against his code. Besides, he mused, her relationship with Piper was sufferance enough. The maid stepped away and walked back into the house. Moments later her rotund shadow crossed a kitchen window.

Now Akulov steadied his breathing, watched the sway of the large trees dotting the property and the direction of the gulls as the grey-haired, potbellied Piper raised his wine glass to his mouth for the last time. Akulov made his final adjustments and calculations then gently squeezed the trigger. The .338 round rocketed towards the unwary enemy of Mother Russia, tore through his torso, punched out a fist-sized hole and kept going before it drilled itself into the timber-clad wall of the mansion.

*

Jack Tate didn't see the blue flashing lights in his rear-view mirror immediately; he was lost in the lyrics of Bruce Springsteen's "Born to Run". As the song drew to a close, he heard the sirens and then saw the police vehicle gaining ominously behind him. Tate swore; he couldn't believe that after all his years of training and active service, he'd made such a rookie mistake. He knew the drill; he pulled the Chevrolet Tahoe over on the shoulder, powered down the window, turned off the engine, and placed his hands in clear sight on the top of the steering wheel. As a police officer stepped out of the liveried Crown Victoria, the next song on Tate's radio started. He tried not to laugh – it was the Eagles' classic "Desperado".

The officer drew level with Tate's window but stayed several paces back, as procedure dictated. He asked him to switch off his music and then hand over his driver's licence and insurance documents. He spoke to Tate without checking them. 'Is this your vehicle, sir?'

'No.'

'Who does it belong to?'

'The rental company.'

'I see.'

'So what did I do wrong?'

The officer's brow furrowed and he took a moment to form his next question: 'You're British?'

'From London,' Tate replied, as the warm August air overcame the lingering cold of the Tahoe's climate control.

'You were ten miles an hour above the limit back there. We've had a lot of accidents on this stretch of road over the years. People see the view, get too excited and then . . . well, it's not a pretty sight.'

'I understand.'

The officer nodded. 'And what is your destination today?'

'Camden.'

'Business or pleasure?'

'Just a holiday.'

'Holiday?'

'Vacation.'

'On your own?'

Now it was Tate's turn to frown; these questions didn't seem to be usual for a traffic violation. 'Yes, on my own.'

The officer gestured with his left hand, the one holding Tate's documents, whilst his right slid towards his belt and rested on the butt of his firearm. 'This is a large vehicle for one person.'

'The rental company was out of stock. They gave me a free upgrade.'

'Stay in the vehicle, sir. I'll be back in a moment.'

Still holding Tate's documents, the officer backed away to his patrol car, where his colleague had been talking on the radio. Via his mirror Tate saw a brief exchange between the two before they approached the SUV, each angling for a different side of the Tahoe, weapons drawn. Tate frowned. Every instinct he had, every part of his training, told him to hightail it out of there, put the car into drive and pull away, wheels spinning, leaving the officers choking in the dust . . . but he was on holiday, not on deployment, and these were police officers not enemy combatants.

'Step out of the vehicle with your arms raised and place your hands on the vehicle!' the second officer barked.

Tate sighed. This wasn't what he needed, and unlike the cops back home, they were armed. He had no choice but to comply. This was where mistakes happened; this was where he was putting his life in the hands of men in uniform he didn't know, trusting them and trusting their training. It wasn't the first time he'd had more than one loaded weapon pointed at him. Tate slowly opened the door and shuffled around the side of the SUV as the roadside dust danced at his feet and the sun warmed his back. He kept his eyes firmly fixed front and centre, and watched the armed men approach via their reflection in his window.

'I'm going to search you now,' said the first officer. 'Are you carrying any drugs, needles, or concealed weapons?'

'No.'

Tate felt the officer pat him down before he said, 'Place your hands behind your back.'

Tate thought he knew what was coming next, but neither officer recited the Miranda to him or advised him of his rights. This he also found off. The nearest officer cuffed his wrists tightly, the left cuff pressing snugly against his metal watchstrap, forcing his Rolex further up his arm. Tate asked, 'Can you tell me what you think I've done?'

Neither officer spoke as they frogmarched him to the Crown Victoria. They opened the back, pushed him in, and shut the door. A moment later, the Crown Victoria's "Interceptor Pack" engine growled, and, with lights flashing, the driver navigated the flow of traffic heading towards Camden.

The officers were silent, tense. One kept his eyes on the road whilst the other repeatedly glanced back at Tate. The rear of the car was stuffy, and Tate tried to get himself comfortable, as the handcuffs dug into his wrists and ended up forcing him to lean sideways. He should have been worried, sitting cuffed in the back of a US police cruiser, but he wasn't. The emotion that he felt the most at that exact moment was annoyance. The cops had made a mistake. It was clear that this was about much more than speeding; that would have earnt him a ticket, a financial slap on the wrist – not steel cuffs. They'd picked on the wrong man. He'd enjoy telling them so, but there was no point in saying anything now. He'd not say a word until they'd arrived at the station, attempted to process him and realised their error. There would be an embarrassing "no hard feelings" conversation where the local law enforcement officers would try to persuade him that Maine was an exceptionally safe place to spend his vacation.

He allowed himself a bitter smile as he gazed out of the window at the sparkling sea below. This wasn't how he'd planned to arrive in Camden but at least the views did not disappoint.

After some scenic driving and negotiating the small roads, the police cruiser came to a halt outside a single-storey red-brick building. Cautiously, the two officers hustled him out of the car, through a column-adorned porch – which to Tate seemed like an architectural afterthought – and into the Camden PD station. An officer stood behind a processing desk at the front of the office. Posters were stuck on the walls: a mixture of tourist information, photographs depicting the local countryside and text-heavy notices. The desk officer glanced down at his desk then back up again and nodded at his colleagues. He looked worried and his voice sounded it too. 'Belongings?'

'In his vehicle,' one of the officers replied.

'I'll take his watch.'

The officer on Tate's left undid the strap and handed the watch to the desk officer. The man's eyebrows rose as he noted the brand before he placed it into a Ziploc-type plastic bag then put this under the counter. 'OK. Room one.'

Tate remained a compliant, silent witness to the unfolding events and let himself be pushed further into the station, past the desk and into the open-plan interior. The office door opened and a large figure stepped out, folded his arms and looked on as

Tate was led through a door on the right. Inside was a narrow corridor with three steel doors on one side. The nearest was open. The two officers locked him inside and left him alone.

The room was lit with a fluorescent bulb contained in a wire cage, which starkly illuminated a metal table in the centre space. The table was affixed to the concrete floor with steel pins, as were two chairs, one either side of the table – one facing the door and one facing away. 'Welcome to Camden,' Tate muttered to himself and shook his head. It was by no means the first time he'd been in a police interview room, but it was the first time he'd been in one as an innocent man.

Still cuffed, Tate sat at the table facing the door. In the British Army, he was used to planning operations and, for this, intelligence gathering was crucial, but here there was no intel to collect. He'd assessed the situation but could come up with no other explanation for his incarceration other than the fact that he'd been picked up in error. A case of mistaken identity. Someone who matched his description had done something, and something serious at that. So why hadn't he been read his rights? Why hadn't he been Mirandized? It still made no sense to Tate. He tried to get comfortable on the metal chair, managed to slouch a little and kick his legs out underneath. He closed his eyes and let his mind wander to the first time he'd been in a police cell. Even all these years later it still made him chuckle.

It had been on a family pilgrimage to North Wales to see his mother's cousin. He and his brother hated going. They'd stay for a week, several times a year. With parents who didn't approve of Game Boys, the brothers passed the long car journey playing "car cricket". His brother was always "in bat" first. The boys would stare out of the rear windows of the Volvo looking for pubs. Once they spotted one, they'd read the name or look at the gaudy sign hanging outside. For each "leg" that appeared in the pub name (physical or pictorial) the person in bat scored a "run" up to the maximum of six per pub. If the name did not contain any legs, the player in bat was "out", and the other player was now "in bat". Pubs such as "The Coach & Horses" and "The Highwayman" always scored a "six" as there were either horses in the name or on the sign. Some pub names caused arguments, some made them laugh, and some did both – "The Cock" had been one of these. Their father said he preferred "legless pubs"; their mother tutted.

In Wales they played with a local friend – Richie Williams. He lived across the road and according to their mother was a bad influence. The boys would kick a ball about or go exploring with Richie. On several occasions they'd been chased away from the fairway of the Prestatyn Golf Club. But this last trip had been different. His brother had not wanted to go out – he was sixteen and studying for his GCSEs – but fourteen-year-old Jack did. He'd sneaked out to meet Richie and that was where, according to his parents, his problems started.

Richie boasted that he knew where the Golf Club kept the fireworks ready for their Summer Ball. He dared Jack to break in and take a rocket. And Jack did. But Jack, who never backed down from a dare, didn't stop at just one rocket. Jack took four rockets and two display-size Catherine wheels. That night he shimmied onto the roof of the local Tesco's superstore and set up his own display. The CCTV cameras had alerted the local police to their activity but not before Richie and Jack had set off the fireworks.

As Jack sprinted across the car park he was illuminated, not by blossoming fireworks but by the full beams of a North Wales Police Range Rover. That night was the first time he had been put in a police cell and it was the last time he had seen Richie Williams. It was also the last time they ever went to Prestatyn. That event had been the beginning of the end of his relationship with his parents. They weren't his real parents; he'd been in long-term foster care with them. He didn't miss them, as much as missed their son, his brother. And that was the reason he was on a road trip in the US.

Tate's eyes snapped open as the door creaked. The desk officer entered. 'I've got to take your prints – Chief Donoghue's orders. Will there be an issue?'

'No issue at all.'

'British?'

'English.'

'Like the Queen.' The officer had a legal pad -sized black plastic case in his hand. He retrieved a card. It had a printed table on it, columns to receive the inky print of each digit. 'Hold up your hands.' Tate did so and the officer inked the tips of each finger with a spongy implement from his case. 'Now on the card, roll each fingertip slowly once, from left to right.'

Tate complied. Once satisfied with the prints, the officer abruptly stood and left the room. Tate stared at his dirtied fingers, thought about rubbing the ink off onto his jeans but couldn't be bothered. Instead he stood up and wiped them on the clean, whitewashed wall directly next to the door. It was like finger-painting, a childish but satisfying act of defiance. Tate sat again. He didn't know how long he'd be stuck in the room for. How long would it take the local authorities to realise their mistake? One of the army's many mottos had been "eat when you can and sleep when you can" because you never know when you'll get another chance. There was no food, so Tate closed his eyes and tried to sleep. Fleetingly the stolen fireworks again bloomed in his memory and then he woke with a start, his neck stiff and his head groggy.

'Get up and follow me.' It was the desk officer again.

The officer led Tate out of the cell, back into the open-plan squad room, along the full length of the space and through a door into the big office at the back. The large man he'd seen earlier was sitting at a desk. He nodded Tate into the empty chair opposite him.

'I'm Chief Donoghue of the Camden Police Department. Care to tell me, Mr Tate, the reason for your presence in Maine?'

Tate examined his inky fingertips. 'Vacation.'

'That's what you told my men. But I'd like to know the real reason.' Donoghue leaned back in his chair and laced his fingers in his lap. Tate noted that his bulk was muscle rather than fat. He had the look of an old soldier – a short, no-nonsense haircut and a stern brow. 'You see the thing is, Mr Tate, we think you may be just the person we have been looking for.'

Tate remained silent. In his experience, men in authority liked to hear the sound of their own voice, regardless of how much power they had. And this was Donoghue's desk, in Donoghue's town. He took in Donoghue's office. The same white walls as his holding cell but here the concrete floor was covered with grey carpeting. The wall directly behind displayed several framed certificates as though to confirm his legitimacy to all those sitting in Tate's seat. The desk itself was bare save for a laptop and a blue Maine PD coffee cup. There was a modern coffee station on a unit, and a coffee table with two comfy chairs.

'What job do you do back in the UK?' Donoghue asked.

'I'm a Human Resources consultant.'

'And the name of your employer is?'

'Fir Tree Consulting.'

'Branches everywhere? That's cute,' Donoghue said without humour. 'Can you verify that?'

'I've probably got a business card in my wallet somewhere. It's in my car, but I'm sure your men have already checked it.'

'You've got an attitude there, Mr Tate.'

'That's right, Chief Donoghue; we are both wasting our time here.'

'Do you have an issue with authority figures, Mr Tate?'

Tate shrugged. 'Not when I see one.'

The police chief's nostrils flared, but his tone remained neutral. 'You are doing what, exactly, during your vacation here?'

'Driving around, taking in the sights.'

'How long do you plan to be in the US for?'

'Like it says on my car rental agreement, a month.'

'That's a long vacation.'

'There's a lot to see.'

'Did you serve, Mr Tate?'

'You mean like a waiter?'

Donoghue pursed his lips. 'You know what I mean.'

Tate shrugged again. 'You've got my details and my prints. I imagine that you'll have a pretty good file on me soon enough.'

'Is that how you want to play this? Really?' Donoghue's eyes narrowed. 'Why are you being so unhelpful, Mr Tate?'

Tate sighed. 'Yes, I served.'

'Where?'

'Afghanistan.'

'Infantry?'

'Yes.'

'See much action?'

'More than I would have liked. What am I being charged with?'

'Nothing at the moment, apart from driving in excess of the speed limit.'

'So why haven't I been read my rights?'

'You may or you may not be aware that the *Amended PATRIOT Act* provides me with increased powers to hold and question "persons of interest" without charge. You, Mr Tate, are a person of interest.'

'I'm honoured you find me so interesting, but I still don't know what this is all about.'

'OK.' Donoghue pursed his lips again. 'At lunchtime today, a prominent local resident was murdered. It looks like a contract killing. A single shot was fired. I'm still awaiting confirmation on the type of round used, but it was pretty big – we believe some sort of sniper rifle.'

Tate's eyebrows rose. It *was* something serious. 'And you think I have something to do with this?'

'Something, or maybe nothing, or maybe everything. An SUV,

346

like the one you were driving, was seen leaving the area. A surveillance camera captured a suspect fitting your description.'

'Who was the murder victim?'

'A retired senator by the name of Clifford Piper; you ever heard of him?'

Tate shook his head. The only Piper that flashed in his mind was the wrestler – "Rowdy" Roddy Piper.

'His wife was killed last year in a terrorist attack. He retired afterwards.'

Tate vaguely remembered the headlines. 'I've never heard of him, and I wasn't there. My SUV has a tracker, and you can check that against your intel.'

'Intel?'

'Your reports.'

'Yep, see, I know what "intel" means. I'm just surprised that you'd use that term. I don't think you are who you say you are, Mr Tate.'

'So you are going to hold me until what, you decide that I didn't shoot a senator with a Barrett?'

'Who said anything about a Barrett, Mr Tate?'

Tate remained silent for a moment; he was tired and snappy. 'It's the most reliable 0.50 rifle, in my opinion, and it's what I'd use if I wanted to make sure of hitting a target with one round. One large round. There's a pretty good suppressor available for it too, and in a semi-urban environment you want to make as little noise as possible.'

'Ha,' Donoghue said with a knowing nod.

Tate was getting bored; he wanted to be on his way. 'You don't have the murder weapon – just a large hole and a deformed round. And the fact that you didn't mention anyone as having heard the shot leads me to believe that the shooter used a suppressor. A 0.50 calibre makes a hell of a bang without one.'

'What did you do in Afghanistan, Mr Tate?'

'I soldiered.'

'What exactly did you do in Afghanistan?'

'I can't tell you.'

'Oh, yes you can. Weren't you listening to me? The *Amended PATRIOT Act* gives me—'

Tate stood. 'Yes, I heard.'

Donoghue got to his feet with surprising speed. 'Where the hell do you think you are going? Sit down!'

The two men sized each other up, Donoghue incensed, Tate impassive. A loud knock on the office door, followed quickly by an officer entering the room broke the standoff.

'Chief, this is urgent.'

'On my way. Officer Kent, please escort Mr Tate back to his holding cell. He won't be any trouble, will you, Tate?'

'None at all,' Tate said flatly.

If you're an Alex Shaw fan, read the whole Aidan Snow action thriller series in order!

Book 1

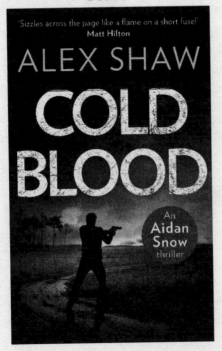

Aidan Snow thought he could escape his past.
But now it's back, with a vengeance…

Book 2

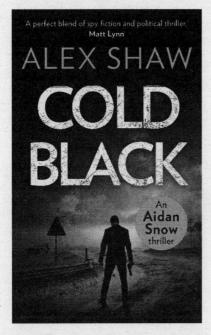

'A perfect blend of spy fiction and political thriller.'
Matt Lynn

ALEX SHAW

COLD
BLACK

An
Aidan
Snow
thriller

Aidan Snow is back with a mission that is bigger than ever.

Book 3

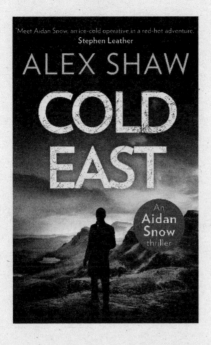

The clock is ticking. Will Aidan Snow be able to save the world, before it's too late?

Dear Reader,

We hope you enjoyed reading this book. If you did, we'd be so appreciative if you left a review. It really helps us and the author to bring more books like this to you.

Here at HQ Digital we are dedicated to publishing fiction that will keep you turning the pages into the early hours. Don't want to miss a thing? To find out more about our books, promotions, discover exclusive content and enter competitions you can keep in touch in the following ways:

JOIN OUR COMMUNITY:

Sign up to our new email newsletter:
http://smarturl.it/SignUpHQ

Read our new blog www.hqstories.co.uk

🐦 https://twitter.com/HQStories

📘 www.facebook.com/HQStories

BUDDING WRITER?

We're also looking for authors to join the HQ Digital family!
Find out more here:

https://www.hqstories.co.uk/want-to-write-for-us/

Thanks for reading, from the HQ Digital team

HQ

If you enjoyed *Traitors*, then why not try another gripping thriller from HQ Digital?

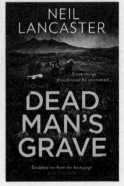